KASEY MICHAELS

A MIDSUMMER
NIGHT'S SIN

D0650836

HQN™

ISBN-13: 978-0-373-77610-8

A MIDSUMMER NIGHT'S SIN

Copyright © 2011 by Kathryn Seidick

This edition published by arrangement with Harlequin Books S.A.

For questions and comments about the quality of this book please contact us at Customer_eCare@Harlequin.ca.

www.Harlequin.com

Printed in U.S.A.

Dear Reader,

Did you ever meet someone who just made you feel good, glad to be around him, glad to be alive? Someone you just have to look at in order to smile, feel good about yourself and the world in general? Rare, wonderful people.

Robin Goodfellow Blackthorn, known affectionately as Puck, is one of those special people. Sweet, lovable, mischievous Puck.

I didn't know all that, of course, when he first invaded my subconscious, but once I "met" him— well, I was hooked. He made me smile, he made me laugh—he made me look around at life and see the good about everything. He reinforced my belief in happy never-endings.

What possible defenses could a young woman like Regina Hackett raise to avoid succumbing to Puck's charms? How can you look at a man who smiles into your eyes and asks, "Do you love life? I do. I love life!" and be able to just walk away?

Oh, how I love Puck. I hope you do, too!

And then please watch for *Much Ado About Rogues* to read about Black Jack Blackthorn, Puck's brother— and the definite flip side to his fun-loving sibling!

Happy reading!

Kasey Michaels

To the two astonishingly accomplished women
my sons married, Susan and Tammy, with love

A MIDSUMMER
NIGHT'S SIN

What revels are in hand? Is there no play,
To ease the anguish of a torturing hour?
William Shakespeare
A Midsummer Night's Dream

PROLOGUE

HE DIDN'T FOLLOW fashion, he made it. He had the air of the finest salons of postwar Paris about him, fairly reeked of suave sophistication. When he'd taken to growing his blond hair nearly to his shoulders, half of the young fashionables had rushed to do the same, a few going so far as to resort to hairpieces.

He rode a strawberry roan stallion with a white diamond-shaped blaze. Sales of strawberry roan stallions soared, as did the profits of one Jacques Dupuis, former jockey and a true artist with whitewash.

He could make a violin weep, turn a pianoforte naughty and played the flute because he thought it amusing. Unemployed music masters found themselves beleaguered with demands for lessons, and those who would term any music "a beautiful noise" hadn't yet had their ears abused by the efforts of dozens of tone-deaf young French fops.

He shunned the theater, and tickets sales plunged. He made a joke, and all of Paris laughed. Young ladies dreamed of him, young men fought to be seen with him. Hostesses showered him with invitations…to their parties, to their boudoirs.

They called him Puck, the name delighting them. He was so very unacceptable, yet welcomed everywhere.

He was *le beau bâtard Anglais,* the beautiful English bastard, the beloved pet of Paris Society, and completely, wholly delicious.

And now he had said his adieus to the openly distraught Paris and returned to the land of his birth, just in time for the new London Season.

Where he was known only as Robin Goodfellow Blackthorn.

Bastard.

PUCK POSED AT THE mantelpiece in the lavish drawing room of the even more lush mansion in Grosvenor Square, the very heart of fashionable Mayfair. He appeared nonchalant in his fine French clothes, his cravat a masterpiece, his tailor's appreciation for his client's fine physique evident in the exquisite cut of the broadcloth jacket and form-fitting trousers molded to his long, lean body.

He wore his most ingratiating smile with the ease of long practice and concealed the intelligence in his fascinating blue-green eyes. Everything depended on how he handled the events of the next few minutes, yet to the casual observer, he seemed affably stupid and as dangerous as a dandelion.

In truth he was on his guard, wary of these two gentlemen, whom he knew to be considerably more complex than just another pair of boring Englishmen, who might be able to trace their ancestry back to the Great

Flood but couldn't be trusted to otherwise know enough to come in out of the rain.

They'd been playing a game for the past quarter hour, speaking of this and that and the other thing, each pretending the other was anything but what they were. Who'd win this dance of wits and deception was anyone's guess, but Robin Goodfellow Blackthorn invariably preferred to wager on himself.

"I do admire the English countryside," Puck remarked, apropos of nothing that had been said thus far. "The area around Gateshead, for example, is quite laudatory. Why, I could wax on about the place for hours."

Handed that sort of encouragement, Baron Henry Sutton at last cut through the aimless, polite banter, which Puck had known the man had been itching to do since his arrival.

"You'd blackmail us?" The baron looked to his friend, one Richard Carstairs, and said, "And there it is, Dickie. The bastard's attempting to blackmail us."

"Oh, hardly, my lord, although I must remonstrate just a little, as I see no reason to bring the circumstances surrounding my birth into the thing," Puck protested, stepping away from the mantelpiece and further into the game. "I was merely reminiscing on my earlier brief acquaintance with Mr. Carstairs here, when we were both passing a lovely evening in Gateshead last year. Charming place, if a bit off the beaten track for a gentleman such as Mr. Carstairs. Jack, however, one might discover anywhere, mostly when one least expects to, and up to mischief, of course."

Dickie Carstairs, a fair-skinned, round-cheeked fellow, whose rather soft body hinted that his main love in life would most probably be a toss-up between his cook and his next meal, turned to the baron, his eyes gone wide. "Hear that? He brought up Jack. Nobody's supposed to know about Jack. His brother, for God's sake. Bound to be as wily. Told you we shouldn't have come here. *Summoned.* I don't much care for that."

The baron, clearly the sharper of the two, both in looks and in manner, turned to glare at Puck. "Your brother will hear of this."

Puck's smile only broadened. "Oh, yes, indeed, I'm convinced he will. Jack seems to hear about everything, one way or another. He's uncanny that way, don't you agree? We call him Black Jack, inside the family, that is. He's the most romantic of us. Give him my best, would you? And how is— What was the fellow's name? Ah, now I remember. Jonas. And how is Jonas? I would imagine the nasty man is toes-up in some unmarked grave somewhere far from London and a more civilized English justice, but then, I have a dramatic bent of mind sometimes."

"If you're hinting that we took him out and—"

"Dickie, that will be enough," the baron said silkily. "All right, gloves off, Mr. Blackthorn. Clearly you're aware that your brother and Mr. Carstairs and myself occasionally perform some small services for the Crown, as they become necessary."

Puck held up his hands. "Rather a *disposal* service, I would think, and damned handy into the bargain. But, please, no more details. I would much prefer we remain friendly."

"There's nothing of friendship about it. You sent us notes revealing just enough information to bring us here, and now you want something in return for your silence. Correct?"

Puck picked up the crystal decanter and gracefully went about refilling his guests' wineglasses. "Well spotted, sirs. Yes, that's exactly what I would like. Something in return for forgetting certain events that transpired in Gateshead last spring and your presence there. Nothing earthshaking. A piddling thing, actually. I would like a small—not infinitesimal, yet nothing grand—*entrée* into London Society. A few introductions, taking time to be seen conversing amicably with me in the park, perhaps an invitation to accompany you two grand and socially acceptable personages to a sporting event. I feel confident I can take it from there."

"Do you hear that? Do you hear that! I will not!" Dickie Carstairs exploded angrily. "A bastard, foisted on the *ton?* With *our* blessing? Unheard of!"

The baron waved his companion to silence. "Your brother Beau tried that, years ago. Tried it twice, as I remember."

"Yes, I know, and with varied results." Puck took up his place at the mantelpiece once more.

He had them, he knew he had them. When they looked at him, they had to see enough of Beau to know he wasn't the sort to bow and scrape, and enough of Jack to think twice about doing anything to…upset him.

"I am not my brother Beau, gentlemen. Nor am I my brother Jack. We are all sons of the Marquess of Blackthorn, all born on that same, sadly illegitimate side of the blanket, but we are not all the same person. Beau, bless him, once assumed he needed acceptance. Jack rejects all of Society. Privately, I believe he thinks you're all fools."

"And you?" the baron asked, his eyes narrowed.

"And I?" Puck shrugged, elegantly, in the French manner. "I ask little of life, actually. I simply wish to enjoy myself and my fellow man. I am a rather entertaining sort, you know. Why, you might even find yourselves liking me. Now, would either of you care for more wine—Dickie, I see your glass is empty again—while we discuss our initial foray into the social whirl? I might suggest Lady Fortesque's masked ball, set for this Friday evening. A trifle risqué, I understand, both the ball and Lady Fortesque, and most of the *Haut Ton* will avoid both, but certainly not above my touch, don't you think?"

The baron, clearly a man who had weighed Puck and found him impossible to ignore, put down his wineglass and stood, signaling for Dickie Carstairs to do the same. "Isobel will most probably be delighted with the notion of such a scandal. I'll see that an invitation is delivered later this afternoon."

"Perfect," Puck agreed, clapping an arm over Dickie

Carstairs's shoulders as he escorted his visitors to the door. "I will see you both at the ball then, won't I?"

"But…but it's a masked ball. How will you recognize us?"

"I won't have to," Puck told Dickie, thinking the man was a most strange choice for an assassin, as no one ever would have suspected him of having an adventuresome soul. "You will recognize me, approach me. I am, you see, *pour mes péchés,* rather singular."

"For your sins? I don't know if I like that," the unlikely adventurer said, frowning as he looked Puck up and down. "I've been wondering if you commissioned that waistcoat here or over in Paris. Damned fine. I probably don't have the belly for something like that. Or too much belly for it, at any rate, but if you could give me the direction of your tailor, I'd—"

"Oh, for the love of— Come along, Dickie," the baron said on a sigh and grabbed the man's elbow as Wadsworth personally handed over their hats and gloves and held open the front door for them. Neither man slipped him a copper for his troubles, but that was the quality for you, cheeseparing, when recognizing a servant's assistance in a monetary way had saved many a man from having his hat and gloves mysteriously and permanently misplaced.

Once the door closed behind his departing guests, Puck looked to the butler. "That went rather well," he said, displaying his pleased and pleasing smile. "Do you have anything interesting for me, Wadsworth?"

"Yes, sir," the former soldier said, reaching into his

pocket. "Found some scribbled note in the fat one's hat-band and copied it out here for you. Doesn't seem to mean much of anything."

Puck took the folded scrap when it was offered. He would never understand why so many men thought hatbands such a safe hiding place, but wasn't it nice to know that Mr. Dickie Carstairs was so predictable. "Really? That would be too bad, wouldn't it? In any event, you're a jewel beyond price, Wadsworth. I'll take it from here. Thank you."

He unfolded the scrap and read its brief contents as he returned to the drawing room.

My apologies. Impudent rascal! Humor him, please. He's harmless. Saturday, usual place and time. New assignment. J.B.

Puck smiled as he crumpled the scrap and tossed it into the fireplace. "Ah, Jack, and won't it be lovely to see you again...."

CHAPTER ONE

THE LARGE TOWN HOUSE in prestigious Berkeley Square
had come to Lady Leticia Hackett via her mater-
nal grandmother in lieu of a dowry, and tied up in so
many clever legal strings that her ladyship's high-living,
deep-gambling father could not sell it to settle his debts.

Reginald Hackett, Leticia's loud, crass, uncouth,
shipping-merchant husband, had come to her courtesy
of that to-let-in-the-pocket father, the Earl of Mentmore,
bartering her good name and impeccable lineage to the
highest bidder, a climbing cit who suffered from the
delusion that his deep pockets could buy him entry to
Society.

Her daughter and only child, Regina, was a gift from
the gods and the only reason Leticia didn't imbibe more
wine than the considerable amount she did.

The two women were closeted in Regina's boudoir,
the single room in the place, other than his wife's bedchamber, Reg Hackett dared not enter. The last time
he'd had an itch he wanted scratched without the bother
of leaving hearth and home for the mistress he kept in
Piccadilly, Lady Leticia had unearthed a small silver
pistol from beneath her pillow and taken off his left

earlobe with a remarkably precise shot. If she'd been sober, she probably would have missed him entirely.

He didn't enter his daughter's bedchamber because, although other than using his brain to lie, cheat and steal his way to a fortune, he wasn't what anyone would term a particularly intelligent man, he did know enough to realize that Regina despised him.

And that was all right with Reg. His daughter was a commodity, rather like a full hold of India silks safely pulled up at the London Docks that he would sell at inflated prices to idiots who would otherwise be forced to do without. That's what business was all about. Buy at one price, sell at another, higher price. He'd bought his well-born, titled lady, and now he would sell her whelp to a title.

The girl was pretty enough, if she kept her mouth shut, and Reg had a strong desire to be related by marriage to one of the premier families in England. Thank God she hadn't been born a boy. He wouldn't have known how to shop a boy any higher than he'd shopped himself. Regina should snag him an earl, at the worst, even if a duke was out of the question. When you'd been born in a gutter, being able to point to an earl and say "mine" was as good as ten thousand prime shares in the Exchange.

Reg was right about his daughter's looks. She seemed to have been hatched entirely without his help, for she bore no physical resemblance to the man save a small mole just above the left, outer corner of her upper lip, which looked just fine on her, he supposed.

For the rest of her, she had her mother's dark brown hair with hints of red to it, eyes so blue they were startling and made dramatic by long, curling black lashes and winged brows above a straight nose so aristocratic it made Queen Charlotte's look like a plum pudding in comparison.

Oh, yes, Regina was a beauty, all right. Cold as her mother, but what else was to be expected? As long as she kept her legs crossed until he got her bracketed to a title, that's all Reg would ask of her.

"Turn around for me, darling," Lady Leticia said, waving her wineglass in her daughter's general direction. "It's your first Season. We can't have too daring a neckline."

Regina looked at her reflection in the pier glass and put both hands to her neckline, tugging it higher. Her mama, bless her, had always been a little bit embarrassed about her daughter's fairly ample bosom. She'd gone so far as to say it wasn't ladylike and was a sure sign of the inferior blood passed along to Regina by her paternal grandmother.

Regina had never met the woman, who had died before Regina was born, but if there were anything wrong, lacking or overdone in Regina, blame could always be laid on her father, her grandmother or "inferior blood." When she was five and accidentally broke one of her mama's favorite figurines, she had been quite astonished when her mama had not accepted her declaration that, "I didn't do it, Grandmother Hackett did."

"The neckline is fine, Mama," Regina said as she

turned around, doing her best to "back" her breasts into herself, which she did by rounding her shoulders forward. "I'm very nearly acceptable."

"You are completely acceptable," Leticia declared hotly and then took another large swallow from her wineglass. "They have to accept you, they've no choice. I can trace our family bloodline back to—"

"Back to the fifteenth century, and the family fortune all the way to last Tuesday, when Papa once more had to pay off more of Grandfather Geoffrey's and Uncle Seth's gaming debts before they both could be tossed into debtors' prison. Yes, I know."

"Impertinence is not a trait you inherited from my side of the family," Leticia said sulkily, reaching for the wine decanter. "The blue suits you, by the way. A wonderful match for your eyes—which you will keep lowered, if you please, along with your chin. Debutantes are shy. Gentlemen are piqued by shyness."

"I can't imagine why. I should think they'd be bored spitless. Thank you, Hanks," Regina said as her maid clasped a single string of perfect pearls about her throat. She then crossed the room to her mother and bent down to kiss the woman's thin, papery cheek, holding her breath because her mama thought to cover the smell of spirits with copious amounts of perfume, which in reality only made things worse on both counts. "Aunt Claire and Miranda will be here shortly. I should go downstairs now. Will you be all right?"

With a sidelong glance at the cut-glass decanter, Leticia nodded her head. "I have company."

Regina opened her mouth to remonstrate with her mother but thought better of such a useless exercise. Instead, she looked enquiringly to Hanks, who winked at her. The wine had been watered. Good. After the first decanter, Leticia's palate must turn numb, as Regina's watering of the second (and sometimes third) decanter had yet to be noticed.

"Then I'll be on my way. I believe Miranda said something about our hostess's fine desserts, so I'm taking my largest reticule along with me so I can bring home a sampling for you."

Leticia brightened. "Lemon squares. If it's Lady Montag's soiree, there will be lemon squares. Simple, but her cook is wonderfully talented."

"It's not too late to accompany us," Regina suggested, wishing her mama would go out in Society more than she did. Cousin Miranda was a pleasant enough companion, but prone to recklessness and, more than once, had to be scooted out from behind some potted palm and away from some half-pay officer when it was time to leave.

"I'm certain your aunt Claire will prove sufficient as chaperone. Now go along. Hanks and I will be fine. Won't we, Hanks?"

"Yes, my lady," the maid said, dropping into a curtsy.

With one last, warning look at Hanks, Regina picked up her reticule and shawl and headed for the staircase, arriving in the foyer just as a footman announced that the elaborate Mentmore coach awaited her in the Square. The Mentmores hadn't had a fine crested coach until Reginald Hackett had purchased one for their use during the Season, with the caveat that his Regina was never to be taken about town in anything else.

She hastened outside and was handed up into the dark coach, seating herself on the rear-facing seat, beside Miranda's maid, Doris Ann. "Am I late or are you early?" she asked her cousin and then frowned as she noticed that her cousin was alone on her seat. "Miranda? Where's Aunt Claire?"

Her cousin's laugh tinkled (Regina might have said tittered, but everyone else thought it delightful), and she patted at the golden curls that were Regina's secret envy. Anyone could have dark brown hair, but Miranda's locks were extraordinary and highly in fashion at the moment, as were her fairer-than-fair skin, petite stature and, it would appear, her nearly flat chest.

"Mama is enjoying a rare evening at home as Aunt Leticia is serving as our chaperone this evening," Miranda explained, and then the tinkle-titter was repeated.

Regina's eyes narrowed. "That's not amusing. I told Mama Aunt Claire was accompanying us."

Miranda gave a dismissive wave of her tiny hand. "As if you've never lied to her before. And if you haven't, then it's high time you started. Not that Aunt Leticia probably remembers half of what anyone says to her, what with the— Oh, I'm sorry, Reggie. I talk without thinking, I do it all the time, don't I?"

"You do a variety of things without thinking," Regina told her, squeezing her hands together on her lap. "Now tell me where this coach is heading before I knock on the roof and have it turned back to Berkeley Square."

"No, you can't do that! I can't go alone, and I simply *must* go. You complain that no one wants you save for your papa's money. Well, nobody wants me at all. Papa may be a viscount and Grandfather Geoffrey an earl, but the entire world knows we're all next door to paupers. Oh, Papa will find some rich merchant for me, I suppose, as Grandfather did for Aunt Leticia, if no one more suitable falls madly in love with me before the Season ends—but not as rich as Uncle Reginald and probably twice as crude. Before that happens, I want to have some *fun.* I've been planning all week. Doris Ann, show her." She motioned to her maid, who then reached down to the tapestry bag at her feet. "What do we want with a horrid, boring recital, when we can go to a *ball?*"

"A ball? I'm not dressed for a— What are those?"

"Dominos," Miranda said proudly, grabbing at a mass of emerald-green silk and pulling it onto her lap before Doris Ann passed a similar silk creation, this one in scarlet, to Regina. "And the masks, Doris Ann. Show her the masks!"

One after the other, two half masks were lifted from the tapestry bag and handed to Miranda and Regina.

"Aren't they *glorious!*" Miranda exclaimed, holding hers up to her face. It was cunningly flirtatious, almost catlike, sewn all over with closely set green glass stones that matched the emerald silk, with larger stones topping off the many curving tips, which fanned up and out at the sides and top, rather like emerald flames. "See? These satin ribbons tie behind the head. They're both pretty, but I really like this one best, if you don't mind?"

"You look like a cat," Regina said, looking down at the mask in her hands. "And I mean that in the nicest way. Mine's...white."

"*Ivory*, Regina," Miranda corrected. "It's shaped much like mine, except for that part that covers your nose, and isn't that the most gorgeous lace? And all those tiny seed pearls curling all over? And those tiny little silken rosebuds? And the lovely satin ribbons? Oh, stop frowning, Reggie. It's pretty!"

Regina looked at the mask again. Yes, there were rosebuds, three of them. One at either side of the mask and a third that, once she had it on, would be smack in the middle of her forehead. She plucked them off even as Miranda *eeked* in protest before breaking into a wide grin and clapping in delight.

"Then you'll go?"

Regina looked down at the mask. She fingered the decadent scarlet silk puddle in her lap.

She wavered.

"I'm certain I was told that masquerade balls are not as acceptable as they once were."

"Well, of course they're not, silly, or else I wouldn't have had to steal the invitation from my brother's desk, now, would I? But since Justin is out of town at some boxing mill, in any case, why should the invitation go to waste? Besides, the hostess is Lady Fortesque, and I know Justin has spoken of her more than a few times, so the whole thing is still...*reasonably acceptable.*"

Regina fingered the silk once more. Scarlet. Debutantes did not wear scarlet. They didn't wear masks, either, she felt fairly sure. She knew for certain that they didn't attend balls without a parent or other chaperone present.

"What happens at a masquerade ball?"

Miranda shrugged. "I would suppose that everyone hides behind their masks until such time as they're told to take them off. Not that we'll do that, of course. We'll be long gone by then. But while we're there..." She paused, probably for dramatic effect. "While we're there, we tell no one our true names, and we're free to dance and flirt and— Oh, Reggie, please say yes!"

Being a debutante was boring. It probably was supposed to be boring, so that everyone would quickly find someone suitable, marry and never have to do it again. Being a Hackett, daughter of the poor, martyred Lady Leticia and the totally unacceptable Reginald, Regina had endured her share of impolite stares, snide innuendo and even a few horrified mamas, who had physically escorted their sons in the opposite direction when there was a chance of having to stop and exchange pleasantries with the wealthy but socially inferior Miss Hackett. Except for those titled but poor as church mice peers who might entertain lowering themselves to courting her father's money. Those *she* avoided, much to her papa's chagrin.

To be able to dance—yes, and to flirt—without

anyone knowing her name? To not be the coarse, jumped-up shipping merchant's daughter or even the sad, drunken Lady Leticia's daughter, just for a few stolen hours?

Sensing that her cousin was wavering, Miranda pressed her case. "We'll be wearing these lovely capes to conceal our clothing. Doris Ann and I found them in the attics, and they don't even half smell of camphor, not since we aired them. Can you believe my parents once actually were young enough to have worn them and these masks *aeons* ago? That's why you get the scarlet one, since Papa is so short and you are so horridly tall, like your father. But not everyone is so boring as to just wear dominos and masks. Some of the guests will come in complete costumes. There will be knights and shepherdesses—all sorts of fanciful things. Why, who knows, Reggie. Perhaps by the time midnight strikes, you will have kissed a devil. Isn't that beyond anything *exciting?*"

"Neither of us will be kissing any devils," Regina said, holding the mask to her face as Doris Ann tied the satin ribbons to keep it in place. "We'll stay for an hour, no more than that, and then make a late appearance at the recital, just in case your mother or mine ever chances to speak to the hostess. We will be late because one of the coach horses turned up lame. Also, Miranda, you will not leave my side, nor I yours, for more than the space of a dance. Agreed?"

Miranda was already struggling to push her arms

into the sleeves of the concealing domino. "Oh yes, yes, agreed! Most definitely agreed!"

"And if we're caught out, I'll tell everyone it was all your idea, and that you kidnapped me."

"Reggie! You wouldn't!"

"No, probably not," Regina agreed. "But I was just now remembering the time Mama and I visited at Mentmore and you blamed me for tossing you into the ornamental pond."

"And they believed me and not you," Miranda said, tying the strings of the domino under her pert little chin before pulling the hood up and over her hair. "That's because I look so sweet and innocent and you look… well, never mind."

"Oh no, you don't," Regina said as the horses drew to a halt outside a large building lit with flambeaux that cast strange shadows inside the coach. "I look so *what?*"

Miranda fidgeted on the seat. "Well, Mama says decadent, but Papa says exotic. And Justin…"

"Yes? My idiot cousin Justin says what?"

"He says you always look like you're *ready.* And stop looking at me with your eyes all gone wide that way because I don't know what that means, but Mama said he shouldn't talk like that in front of me. Come on, Reggie. If we only have an hour, let's make the most of it."

"I suppose now I have Grandmother Hackett to blame for something else," Regina grumbled as she tied

the strings of the scarlet domino around her throat and
covered her hair with the hood. "All right, I'm *ready.*"

HE WORE HIS DARK blond hair parted on the side and allowed it to hang loose to his shoulders, covering the
thin, golden strings that secured the mask to his head. It
had been fashioned for him by the premiere costumer in
Paris, following Puck's own design. It fit him perfectly,
as he'd submitted to the molding of what some would
call a death mask so that the costumer could work with
an exact model of his customer's bone structure.

It was a three-quarter rather than a half mask,
smoothly curving down over his nose and cheekbones
and rising to his hairline, all of it hugging his face. The
design was simple: no lace or frills or jewels or feathers for Puck. Instead, the impact from the mask—and
it was considerable—came from the paintwork applied
to its smooth surface.

His inspiration had been a Catherine wheel. Eight
widening, pie-shaped wedges of dramatic color ema-
nated from the center of the wheel, located at the bridge
of his nose, rather in a pinwheel design, yet all sleek
and of a piece. Painted gold gilt wedges cut down the
right side of his nose and across his lower cheek, up and
over his right temple, the left side of his forehead, out
from his left eye and across his upper cheekbone. The
reverse for the other four "blades," all of those painted
in deepest ebony.

All one saw of his face beneath mask and flowing

hair was his wide, full mouth, his leanly sculpted chin and a pair of amused blue-green eyes.

The result was mesmerizing. He'd planned for mesmerizing.

And he hadn't stopped with the mask.

He was dressed all in black, even to his waistcoat and the lace at his throat and cuffs. He wore a full, knee-length, black silk courtier's cloak lined with shimmering gold and carried a long, ebony stick bearing black streamers and a gold serpent-head top. A ruby the size of a pigeon's egg and ringed by diamonds nestled in the spill of black lace that was his cravat. He carried a shallow, wide-brimmed, black musketeer hat adorned with a fat, curled black feather.

Paris had exclaimed over him when he'd first donned the costume; the lovely Lady de Balbec most of all, he recalled with a smile. She'd pleaded with him to leave the mask on, even as she eagerly peeled away his clothing and pulled him down on top of her, coyly begging the "masked stranger" not to ravish her. Women had the strangest notions at times, but that's what made them all so delightful.

Tonight, as in Paris, in a ballroom filled with uninspired dominos and devils, kings and harlequins, milkmaids and fools, he was as startlingly different as night from day. He knew he'd draw attention. Why else had he bothered to come?

As he saw the Baron Henry Sutton (black domino, black mask—how very uninspired) and Mr. Richard Carstairs (court fool, down to the bells on his hat and shoes), Puck swept one side of his cape back and over his shoulder, exposing the shimmering gold silk, flourished his hat and made them both an elegant leg.

"Gentlemen, my honor," he said smoothly.

"Yes, yes, the bastard's honor," the baron groused. "What in blazes do you call that rigout?"

"Sin, gentlemen," Puck drawled smoothly, making a small business out of adjusting the black lace at his cuffs. "I call it Sin."

Dickie Carstairs lifted up his mask and scratched at the side of his nose. "He has a point there, Henry. Doesn't exactly look like a day in May, does he? Can we go now? These bloody bells are giving me a headache. Or do we have to introduce him to anyone?"

"Unfortunately, that is the purpose of the exercise," the baron said, casting his gaze out across the large ballroom.

Puck did the same. It was a rented room, as even Lady Fortesque wouldn't dream of hosting such an affair in her Portland Square mansion. She'd been quite clever in the way she'd employed screens and tall, obscuring plants to cut the boxy dimensions of the place while at the same time providing privacy and secluded couches for those who wished a romantic dalliance.

Servants wearing satyr masks circulated with trays bearing gold-painted glasses filled with heady mead, and they were hard-pressed to keep the trays full, as whatever courage hadn't been obtained by concealing one's face behind a mask could be found in a glass or two of the potent, honeyed brew.

He saw a tall man dressed all in furs paying court to a bewigged and patched Marie Antoinette. There was a scattering of other costumes, but for the most part, the guests had covered themselves only with dominos and plain-to-clever masks.

After all, concealment was the order of the evening.

"All right, over there," the baron said after a moment. "Let's begin with the good king Henry Tudor, shall we? He's actually Viscount Bradley, and no, he didn't have to stuff his doublet with straw, although there may be some sawdust in his stockings, to give him a leg. He's horse mad, if that helps."

"It does. I shall apply to him for advice about setting up my stables. And who is that with him?"

"That's Will Browning," Dickie Carstairs informed him quietly. "Wildly popular. If he were to accept you, you'd at least be able to count the Corinthians as your acquaintance. But he won't. No title but still too high in the instep for you."

"He's forever jumping a fence or shooting pips out of playing cards or milling down a man at Jackson's, but he prides himself most on his fencing," the baron added.

Puck ran his gaze up and down the tall, rather athletic-looking figure. "Does he now?" he said, smiling. "Then I shall have to challenge him to a friendly competition, won't I?"

The baron shrugged. "Why don't you just do that. Once you're stuck in bed recovering from the pinking he gives you, Dickie and I won't have to be bothered introducing you to anyone else. Come along, let's get this over with, shall we?"

Over the course of the succeeding twenty minutes, Puck was introduced to no less than ten gentlemen of the *ton*. He was utterly snubbed by two, shook hands with three, three more had served with Beau on the peninsula and expressed delight in greeting the man's brother. He had arranged a meeting on Sale Day at Tattersalls with Viscount Bradley, who had attended Eton with his father, and a fencing match with Mr. Browning, who had taken Puck's measure, just as Puck had taken his, and declared that he looked forward to cutting such a brash upstart down to size.

Puck had, of course, failed to mention that he had studied with the famed Motet at the *Académie d'Armes de Paris*. Some things should be a surprise.

Now Puck was bored.

"You two fine gentlemen know no women?" he asked as Dickie Carstairs snagged another golden cup of mead from a passing satyr. "I do not ask that you introduce my unacceptable self to your sisters or your wives, who would not be in attendance tonight in any case, but are there no females present who might find it within their sympathy to invite me to their next small party?"

"Lady Fortesque," Dickie offered. "But you probably already met her as you came in. Harriette Wilson and her sisters and a few other courtesans are probably somewhere about and a clutch of canaries from Covent Garden and some low-born actresses, as well. If you're looking for a tumble, nothing beats an actress, I say. The good ones even make you believe they like it. What?" He rubbed at his side, where the baron's elbow had just jabbed him.

"Jack's mother is an actress," Henry Sutton said quietly and then bowed to Puck. "My apologies, Mr. Blackthorn. My friend appears to have left his brains at home this evening. However, to answer your question, no, as far as I can see, Lady Fortesque confined her invitations to the gentlemen and then populated the room with…amenable barques of frailty, if you understand my meaning."

Puck allowed himself to be forgiving. "There are considerably more men in attendance, I did note that, yes."

"And now there will be two less, although I am sure the number of females will swell once, as Mr. Carstairs so rudely pointed out, the theaters close down for the night. I can already see where this evening will go and do not wish to be any part of such public debauchery," the baron said, bowing once more. "Enjoy your first taste of London Society at its most base, Mr. Blackthorn."

Puck returned the bow, offered his thanks and watched as the two men took their leave, Dickie's arms gesturing wildly as he most probably asked the baron what he'd said that was so upsetting. Dickie Carstairs, Puck had decided, most probably drove the wagon and dug the holes after Jack and the baron had dispatched the targets; he seemed qualified for little else.

He should probably go, as well, as the idea of *enjoying* himself in this overheated, painfully obvious setting for anonymous yet public liaisons did not appeal. He'd never been at a loss for female companionship when he'd wished it, and the very last thing he *wished* would be to bed an actress. He'd seen where that sort of folly could lead.

Puck turned rather abruptly, his mind having taken him somewhere he preferred not to go, and all but cannoned into one of the guests.

"I beg your pardon, I was not— Well, hello, beautiful lady."

"How would you know? I'm wearing this ridiculous mask."

Puck was taken aback by this pert answer nearly as much as by the clear disdain in the young woman's voice; he hadn't been dismissed out of hand by a female since he was thirteen. But that reaction faded quickly as his attention was captured by the most amazingly clear blue eyes framed by lashes so long and dark he could scarcely believe them real.

And that mouth. Not only pert, but wide, and lush, and definitely inviting. There was a small brown mole—no, beauty spot—at the upper-left corner of those sensuous lips, which only added to the overall impression of sensuality. Of carnal knowledge and the pleasures of sex. A woman wasn't born with a mouth like that without knowing what it was for or how to use it.

He put his hands on her shoulders, noting that she

was rather tall for a woman, and boldly inspected the rest of her.

She was slimly built, her scarlet silk domino hiding most of the curves he felt certain were there but unable to conceal the fact that the breasts beneath it were wonderfully full and high and, he was equally certain, Heaven to touch, to tease, to taste.

Best of all, she was here. He leaned forward, smoothly insinuating his mouth beside her ear so that she'd be sure to hear him above the hubbub around them.

"We'll dance, you and I," he whispered, sliding his hands down her arms, cupping her slim waist beneath the domino even as he took her right hand and raised it to his lips.

Her fingers were cold, although the room was stuffy and overly warm, but she did not move away from him. Her gaze did slide toward the middle of the floor, where couples were gathering as the musicians struck up a waltz.

"No, not here. You're much too exquisite for this motley crew," he soothed, and then twirled her about, deftly maneuvering them toward the opened French doors and out onto the narrow, moonlit balcony.

Once there, seeing that the rather crude benches to either side of the doorway were occupied by amorous couples who didn't seem to mind an audience, he let go of her waist but not her hand, turning her about to lead them down the wide shallow steps and into the meager, flambeaux-lit gardens.

She didn't protest but just lifted her skirts and followed where he led.

It took some doing, but he finally managed to locate a small clearing devoid of other occupants. There was no bench, but the grass seemed plentiful enough, and there was always that stout tree trunk to lean her against as he got to know her better.

Know her body better. Intimately.

He already felt sure he knew *her* enough.

She was here, wasn't she? She was apparently willing. What more did he need to know?

"What is your name, scarlet lady?" he asked her, looking into her wide, unblinking eyes, feeling himself becoming lost in those clear, swirling depths.

"I'd first know yours. Is it Mr. Black or Mr. Gold?" she said, showing spirit yet again.

Puck laughed. "It's neither. My name is Robin Goodfellow."

The truth was rarely believed, and it wasn't now.

"Oh yes, I'm quite sure that's correct. And I am Titania, Queen of the Fairies."

"Ah, fair Titania," Puck allowed, quietly surprised that she would know the characters from Shakespeare's farce until he realized that she must be an actress. He was about to break his most sacred rule and tumble an actress. "Then you do not believe me?"

"No more than you believe me, no. But does it matter? I don't imagine you've brought me out here for an exchange of names."

"And why have I brought you out here?" he asked,

even as he lifted the silken hood back and off her head, revealing a mass of artfully placed curls nearly black in the dim light.

"I'm not entirely certain. I was rather thinking it was to kiss me."

"To kiss you," Puck repeated, taken aback. She said the words as if they were dangerous in the extreme. "And you came here to be kissed?"

"I didn't think so, no. But now that I am here, I may as well be hanged for a sheep as well as a lamb, don't you think? I'm convinced my—my companion is taking full advantage of this rather exciting bit of freedom. The masks, you know. A stranger's kiss in the moonlight."

Puck's brain was sending out alerts his libido pushed aside as ridiculous. She was an actress, that was all. She was most probably playing the coy maiden in hopes that the novelty would excite him.

And her ploy was working, probably even better than she had hoped. His mind was being seduced by her feigned naiveté, while the rest of him was growing hard with a base passion he hadn't experienced since he'd been a randy youth who could have embarrassed himself at the mere thought of touching a female breast.

"Then, my queen of the fairies, we will begin with a kiss."

Because he thought she would wish him to play along with her small charade, and because the idea of doing so only increased his growing passion, Puck lightly cupped her chin and leaned in to put his mouth to hers.

Oh, and she was good. She did not disappoint. She allowed the kiss, but did nothing to encourage him to deepen it. She did not put her arms around him, did not immediately begin to grind her body against his, the sure signal of a professional who wished the act over and done and several gold pieces slipped into her purse.

But she'd miscalculated, badly. Her supposedly untutored mouth presented not only a challenge, but a frisson of delight that went straight to Puck's manhood, which now strained against his trousers.

A kiss. A single kiss, and he was ready to set her up in her own apartments, give her anything she wanted: diamonds, pearls, her own carriage and stable. One kiss, and he was the fool he laughed at, enslaved by a woman whose cold-blooded profession it was to jumble the wits of idiots like himself.

Idiots like his own father.

He lifted his face away from hers and looked into her magnificent eyes.

He saw no guile. No greed. No reaction at all save what might be termed confusion.

Oh yes, she was good.

But he was better.

This time he didn't approach her gently. He swooped, openmouthed. He took her into his arms, his lips slanted across hers, his tongue probing, his teeth nibbling, his hands traveling down her back and then coming up and around to cup her lush breasts. He insinuated his right thigh between her legs, pressing upward against her sex.

He kissed her mouth, her throat, bent her back over his arm to press his lips against the smooth expanse of skin above the neckline of her gown.

And all the while, he crooned to her in French. How lovely she was. How he was being made mad by her virginal game playing. What he would do to her to reward her, how he would do it, how she would know she had never been made love to before, no matter how many men she'd had.

And she whispered back to him: "I have a hat pin poised to stick in your ear, and I will do it if you do not release me at once."

The words were clear, and they had been pronounced in flawless French.

Puck hauled her upright and put her away from him, staring at her in astonishment. This was no whore for hire. He'd been duped. By God, had he been *duped?* And by some idiot slip of a girl out for a lark?

"*What* did you say?"

"Nothing half so horrible as you did, I'm sure," she answered as she pulled her domino shut and raised the hood back over her hair. Her hands shook, but her voice was firm and clear. "I'm leaving now. Do not follow me."

He held his arms out to his sides to prove himself harmless, once more smiling, surprisingly under control. "I wouldn't think of it, I assure you. Only first a word of warning, you little tease, as next time you may run into a different sort of bastard. One that would be at pains to demonstrate how ineffectual a hat pin can be. And something else. Never threaten before striking, but merely strike, or you may never get the chance. Now run away, little girl. Run until you're safely home and under the covers."

She didn't wait for him to repeat himself but only lifted her skirts and ran back down the path toward the lights of the ballroom.

Puck followed after her at a walk, trying to remember what he'd said to her and what he'd suggested, believing her to be something she was not. He wondered if he'd scarred the girl for life.

She'd certainly made an impression on him, one that would be difficult to shake.

CHAPTER TWO

WHERE IS SHE? WHERE IS SHE? Why did I allow her to join the dance?

Regina whirled about, went up on tiptoe, pushed past goatherds and devils with pointed tails, searching for an emerald-green domino.

Where is she!

She'd have to stop crying, or else she wouldn't be able to see anything. She had to stop thinking about what had just happened...what could have happened. That man! So wickedly handsome, so dangerous in his black and gold.

What had she done?

Had she lost her mind?

The things he'd said! And she'd listened, fascinated by the words, shamelessly intrigued by his touch...and her reaction to both.

Regina clutched at her suddenly queasy stomach, wishing back the sweet, honeyed drink she'd downed earlier almost as if it had been water, for it had been so hot and stuffy and even rather smelly in this horrible ballroom. What had been in that cup? Nothing too terrible, surely. It was only honey....

She fought down the urge to cup her hands to her

mouth and loudly call out Miranda's name, knowing she could not cause a scene, draw attention to either one of them. They would both be ruined if anyone knew they had attended this clearly unsuitable ball.

Why, there were people kissing people everywhere she turned. Giggling and touching each other in lewd ways as they passed by each other in the dance. It hadn't been like this when they'd first arrived, but now it was. As if every tick of the clock served to strip away another fetter of society, leaving only the baseness beneath.

"Here now, my pretty, hold there while I take a look at you." A large man wearing the costume of a highwayman, complete with a brace of pistols tucked in the sash around his waist, had grabbed her arm and showed no signs of letting go. "I've come for all your valuables. Pass them over, starting with a kiss from your fair lips."

Never threaten before striking, but merely strike, or you may never get the chance. Regina plunged the hat pin into the fleshy back of the man's hand and ran off when he yowled in pain and immediately let her go.

She wasn't sure which level of Dante's Inferno she was in, but she needed to get out. Now.

She looked behind her, terrified that the man who called himself Robin Goodfellow might be following her, but he wasn't there. Nobody she knew was there, not that she knew him.

If only she could find Miranda!

At last, she made her way through the maze of screens and plants and couches to the main entrance and the small antechamber where a few maids and such were seated, ready to assist their mistresses if necessary.

"Oh, Miss Regina, you're here! Thank the Lord!" Doris Ann clasped Regina's hands in hers, squeezing them so hard it was painful. "She's gone. My Miss Miranda is gone!"

Regina tugged her hands free, not without effort, and tried to calm the maid. "Nonsense, Doris Ann. She's misplaced, that's all, and most probably on purpose. When did you last see her?"

"But I never did," Doris Ann said, sniffling. "Not since we first got here. It's nearly midnight, and you said one hour, Miss Regina, and it has been nearer to two. And she promised me. She promised she would listen to you, if you'd only come with her. I thought you both were gone, seeing as how you didn't want to come in the first place, but now you're here, and she isn't, and I thought for certain she'd be with you and—"

"All right, all right, let's be calm, Doris Ann," Regina said soothingly. "I'm aware that we have been here well over the agreed upon hour, but if I was... detained, then surely it must be the same with Miss Miranda."

"I popped my head in there when no one was looking, and there's strange and wicked goings-on in there, Miss Regina. I heard two of the other maids talking, you understand. You should neither of you have come here."

"And we'll be leaving the moment we find Miss

Miranda, I assure you. Now, this is what we'll do. We'll go inside the ballroom and look for her. You go to the left, and I will go to the right, and— Doris Ann! Don't you dare shake your head no to me."

"I tain't going in there. There's wicked goings-on in there."

"Yes, you've already said that. But your Miss Miranda is in there somewhere." *Or out in the gardens somewhere.* "You do love her, don't you?"

"Yes, Miss Regina. But there's wicked—"

"Do you wish to tell Miss Miranda's parents you were a part of this? That you helped Miss Miranda find the dominos and masks, that you knew what was going to happen tonight and did nothing to stop it? That you came home without her?"

Doris Ann licked her thin lips. "I am to go to the left, you said?"

Regina breathed a sigh of relief. At least she would have help. "Yes, to the left. And if you find her, bring her right back here. Grab on to her if you have to, and don't let go until she's back here. Do you understand?"

Doris Ann nodded, looking fearfully toward the ballroom. "Oh, laws. They're taking off their masks, Miss Regina. Weren't you and Miss Miranda to be long gone before they took off their masks?"

"Oh, God…"

How could she go back into the ballroom now that people were removing their masks? They would wonder why she kept hers on, and with everyone behaving so badly, it was even possible some forward person would try to remove hers for her.

But she had to find Miranda. Even if it was just so that she could wring her neck.

"Is there a problem?"

Regina recognized the voice and realized that the man who called himself Robin Goodfellow had found her, was even now standing directly behind her.

"No. Thank you." She kept her back to him. Had he taken off his mask? If he had, was he as handsome as she'd thought him? Would he still be laughing at her? Would he expect her to take off her own mask? Had he really meant what he said when he'd been kissing her, speaking to her in French while he thought she didn't understand? Could she ever look at him after she'd heard what he'd said, knowing that she knew that he knew that she'd understood him?

"All right, then. I'll leave you to it, whatever it is."

No! Don't leave!

"Mr. Goodfellow—wait." Regina bit her lip for courage and then turned to face him, ridiculously relieved that he still wore his mask. "I…I seem to have misplaced my companion."

"Ah. So she—or he—disappeared while you were otherwise occupied?"

"Don't be any more obnoxious than you can help, if you please," Regina said irritably. "You know that I'm not who—what—you supposed, and not without reason, because I know I was behaving badly, so I do not fault you for that, and I will apologize for…for leading you on or whatever you think it was I may have been doing— Doris Ann, stop crying! But it is of extreme importance that I find my cous—my companion, and that she and I leave this place at once."

He jerked his head back slightly. "E-gods, you mean there are two of you? And yet not with a whole brain between you. All right, please allow me to offer my assistance. How is she dressed?"

Regina clasped her hands together in front of her, trying to keep them from shaking. This was serious. Miranda could be anywhere, doing anything. Just look at what *she* had done, and she'd never considered herself to be half so stupid as Miranda!

She quickly described her cousin and what she was wearing.

Robin Goodfellow—really, how could she think of him as any sort of help when he'd told her such a ridiculous name—shook his head. "No, sorry. I pride myself on being more than mildly observant, or I did until about a quarter hour ago, but I don't recall any petite blonde dressed in an emerald-green domino. Or wearing such a singular mask. Perhaps we should try the gardens?"

"She wouldn't be so foolhardy as to— Oh, never mind," Regina said as Robin Goodfellow grinned at her in a way that had her palm itching to slap his face. Even wearing that very strange and intriguing mask, she knew that the fellow thought life was one huge lark. Maddening, that's what he was—but her options weren't all that thick on the ground at the moment, and

Doris Ann could hardly be counted as one of them. She had no choice. "Yes, let's try the gardens. Doris Ann, you stay here while I go with Mr. Goodfellow, and if she returns here while we're gone, you have my permission to sit on her!"

Robin Goodfellow took Regina's hand and led her back into the ballroom, where at least half of the candles had been snuffed out and, although the orchestra played on, no one was now dancing along with the tune.

"It will be nearly impossible to locate her in the dark like this," she complained. "Why on earth would they have removed half of the— Oh!"

She quickly squeezed her eyes shut and turned her face against Robin Goodfellow's shoulder, although the memory of what she'd seen had probably already been burned into the back of her eyes for all time. Had the woman no shame? Clearly not. Not if she allowed herself to be leaned forward over the rear of a couch while her full skirts were lifted and the man standing behind her was grunting and pushing himself at her like some barnyard animal, his breeches at his ankles. Three other now unmasked men were standing about, glasses in hand, watching, raucously cheering him on, clearly awaiting their turn.

"What appears to be the— Ah, so you saw that, did you?"

"No. Look away," she whispered, squeezing his hand.

"Well, at least he's dressed as a goat. And they've formed a queue, assuring the strumpet of a profitable evening," he said. "And now, young lady, you know why your mama warned you never to accept an invitation to a masquerade ball. Especially one hosted by the infamous, not to mention lascivious, Lady Fortesque."

Regina raised her head, fighting the bizarre impulse to look behind her once more, because she couldn't possibly have seen what she'd just seen. "I highly doubt she would have thought that was because I would see my own *father* in the queue. Please, I can't stay here."

Robin Goodfellow stood his ground as she tried to drag him away. "Your *father?* Which one is he? No, never mind. Let me at least hazard a guess here. You don't wish for me to totter on over there, tap him on the shoulder and ask him for his assistance. That could be awkward."

Regina's bottom lip trembled, and she knew she was either going to laugh or dissolve into strong hysterics. She was losing her mind, that's what was happening. *"Please."*

"My most profound apologies. But now, at least I don't think you'll faint, will you? I'd take you back to your maid, but I need you to help me identify your cousin, should we find her."

"I know," Regina said, wondering how much good she would be in the search as she refused to raise her gaze above the shoe tops of the other guests. "Just please don't leave me."

He took her hand once more. "I won't," he said, and she believed him.

A half hour later, following a sometimes embarrassing, if oddly educational, search of the gardens, they returned to the anteroom carrying an emerald-green silk domino and the remains of a half mask missing some of its green glass stones.

Regina could barely put one foot in front of the other. They'd found the—dear Lord, Robin Goodfellow had called what they'd found *evidence*—at the very back of the gardens, near a gate that led to an alleyway, and he'd noted that there looked to be signs of a small struggle.

In any event, in any case, Miranda was gone.

Regina plunked herself down in the chair beside a terrified Doris Ann, put her masked face in her hands and at last gave in to despair.

Her cousin was gone. Disappeared. Vanished. Abducted.

"Stay here," Robin Goodfellow told her and then placed his hand on her shoulder and waited until she managed to nod that she'd heard him. "I'll take this domino and mask with me and show them around to the servants. There has to be someone who remembers seeing your cousin earlier in the evening. Maybe that someone remembers who she was with at that time."

"Miss Regina?"

Regina raised her head and carefully eased the mask away from her face enough to wipe at her wet cheeks. "We'll find her, Doris Ann."

"Yes, Miss. But if we don't?"

Regina's entire body sagged at the question.

She would have to tell Mama, who would cry and bring up Grandmother Hackett again. Papa would be

livid that she might have destroyed his dream to marry
her to a nobleman. They'd have to tell Aunt Claire and
Uncle Seth. They'd be aghast, terrified.

And everyone would blame her.

Not that such a minor thing mattered. What mattered
was that Miranda was gone, God only knew where and
to what purpose.

Regina picked up a green glass stone that had fallen
into her lap.

And she hadn't gone voluntarily.

She squeezed her hand around the stone and closed
her eyes, began to pray.

"Regina?"

She looked up at the sound of her name, frowning
before she remembered that Robin Goodfellow must
have heard Doris Ann refer to her as such. She quickly
got to her feet. "You've learned something?"

"A little. We need to go now."

"Go? But I can't leave. What if Miranda comes back?
She'd need me to be here."

"She won't be coming back." He signaled for Doris
Ann to come with them and led them outside to the
street, where a strange coach awaited, a footman holding open the door, the steps down and waiting. "On my
honor, such as it is, after a very brief stop at my residence for a change of shirt and cravat, I am taking you
directly home, wherever that is. I will accompany you
inside and speak with your mother and whomever else
you wish me to speak with, telling them whatever story
the two of us manage to conjure up on the way. I've al-

ready worked out the broad strokes, but I will leave it to you to fill in the details."

"But…but we have to tell them the truth."

"Only as a last resort and only if you make a botch of the lie. Remember, your father was in attendance tonight. I doubt he'd be best pleased to know his daughter had been here, as well," he said, handing her up into the coach. "How trustworthy is the maid?"

"Doris Ann?" Regina's mind was whirling. He had just said he was driving her to his residence? So that he might change out of his shirt? Was *she* being abducted now? "Doris Ann will not be questioned. She's only the maid."

"And lucky for her that she is. Aren't you, Doris Ann?"

The maid bobbed her head in agreement.

"And she won't say a word to anyone, or else she will be escorted out onto the street without a reference, if not tossed into gaol. Will you, Doris Ann?"

The maid shook her head so violently her mobcap flew off.

"Good. I located the coachman and groom without much difficulty, and they have been persuaded to believe they have been beset by a band of cutthroats who dragged your cousin off at pistol point before disabling the coach, which is why it will not return to your cousin's domicile until morning. Damned uncivilized place, London, even in the finest neighborhoods at times. I'm surprised anyone is safe. Related to the Earl of Mentmore, are you?"

Regina's head was spinning. "How…how…"

"The crest on the door. Only an idiot would arrive at Lady Fortesque's ball in such an easily recognizable coach. How do you think I located the correct coach so easily? You're not very proficient at intrigue, are you?"

"But you are?"

"As a matter of fact, yes, I am, luckily for you. And now that we're settled on that head, my coachman has been instructed to drive straight to the mews behind my residence, where you will remain with the coach while I nip inside to rid myself of this betraying costume. You have between now and the time I return to come up with any missing details sufficient to the problem. I suggest you think in terms of where you were, why you were farther afield from wherever you should have been, why you have no chaperone and why you weren't taken, as well."

"I…I stabbed the man who had hold of me. With my hat pin, the one Mama says all chaste young ladies always carry with them. And…and he let me go."

"Very good, for a beginning," Robin Goodfellow complimented as the coach pulled into a narrow alleyway and stopped just outside a stable. "Perhaps even too good. You've the makings of a commendable liar, Regina."

"Yes, I know. It's in my blood," she said forlornly as he opened the door and jumped out, even before the coach had come to a complete halt.

While Doris Ann sat sniffling, Regina did her best to concentrate on the fib—the great, big, whopping lie—she would tell her mother. Except that her mother had been left alone with her "company," and even if the wine had been watered, by this time of night she would be of no help to Regina or to anybody.

And her father? Regina felt her stomach turn over inside her. No, her father wouldn't be at home when she arrived in any case. How she loathed the man. He was as base and as common and as uncouth as…as any man who would sink to attending such a licentious ball.

She reminded herself that Robin Goodfellow had been there.

This did nothing to lighten her mood, which was rapidly descending into the very depths of desolation.

Yet Miranda's brother had received an invitation. There were bound to have been other men, supposed gentlemen of the *ton,* in attendance.

Were all men so *base?*

It really was too bad she had no desire to enter a nunnery.…

"Miss Regina? How can we go home without Miss Miranda? Her mama will be that upset, and his lordship will go spare, he really will."

Regina reached up and at last untied her mask, tossing it out of the dropped-down coach window with some force. "My uncle Seth will have every right to go—that is, to be angry. Terrified. But we must think of Miss Miranda, Doris Ann. We will think of her, and we will be brave. If not entirely honest," she added, squeezing the maid's hand.

"Yes, miss. And how will you explain Mr. Goodfellow?"

Regina opened her mouth to answer and then shut it again before making a decision. "He said he would handle the broad strokes. We'll leave that up to him, shall we? Now quiet, please, I hear footsteps. Yes, here he comes."

Regina sat forward on the cushion seat and squinted into the darkness, waiting for him to step into the moonlight so that she could finally see his face without that extraordinary mask. She probably would one day convince herself that it was the mask that had destroyed her common sense, that its odd design had somehow enthralled her into doing something she would otherwise have never considered. That her compliance had nothing to do with his pleasant, cultured voice or the way he had placed his hands on her shoulders and nearly caused her heart to stop or the mischief she'd seen in his intelligent blue-green eyes.

It was either that or believing that Grandmother Hackett had taken up permanent residence on her shoulder.

"Oh…" Regina blinked, looked again. "Oh, my goodness."

He was the most handsome man she'd ever seen. Now that she could really see him. He was still dressed mostly in black, but his shirt and his faultlessly tied cravat were startlingly white in the moonlight and he had tied back his long, blond hair somehow. He was English, she was certain of that, but he had a nearly foreign look to him: so very neat, sophisticated, compellingly romantic. The gold-lined cloak was gone, as was the beribboned walking stick that had dropped to the ground when he'd been kissing her, to free his hands so that he could— No, she would forget that, too. She would forget all of that!

He stopped, bent down and picked up the discarded mask before opening the door of the coach. "Lesson number two, fair Titania. Never leave incriminating evidence strewn about for all to see. If you'd kindly pass over the two dominos and your cousin's mask? Ah, thank you. Gaston!"

A second figure appeared, seemingly from nowhere, and Mr. Goodfellow tossed the *evidence* at him as the fellow exclaimed in French, scrambling for the green mask, which had eluded him and fallen to the ground.

"My apologies, Gaston. I have no experience in throwing clothing. Only in catching it, *si vous prenez ma signification*. Burn them, and stir the ashes," he instructed the servant, who then hustled back into the shadows.

Inside the coach, Regina had recovered herself sufficiently to roll her eyes at the man's outrageous behavior. But any feelings of superiority vanished immediately when he bounded into the coach and plunked himself down beside her.

He looked good. He smelled delicious. This was no boy; this was a man. Very much a man. And he was gazing at her in open appreciation.

"Stop looking at me that way. My cousin has gone missing," she reminded him.

"And yet I have not been struck blind," he responded just as quickly. "You are as beautiful unmasked as you were mysterious half-concealed. Doris Ann, close your mouth. Your mistress and I are flirting. Aren't we, Regina?"

"We most certainly are not! And you aren't to call me Regina, any more than I will agree to continue addressing you as Mr. Robin Goodfellow. What a ridiculous name."

He put his crossed hands to his breast as if mortally wounded. "You mock my name? My not precisely sainted mother will be devastated, I'm sure, as she so loves it."

Regina didn't know if she could believe the man, even if he'd told her the sky was blue. "Oh, she did not. I mean, she does not. Stop grinning like that! You're an impossible man."

"Yes, I know. Very well, you may call me Mr. Blackthorn. Robin Goodfellow Blackthorn."

Regina felt hot color flooding her cheeks. "Then you weren't lying?"

"Not completely, no. And now if you will return the favor?"

"Return the— Oh. Hackett. I am Regina Hackett. My cousin is Lady Miranda Burnham, daughter of Viscount Ranscome and granddaughter of the Earl of Mentmore."

"E-gods, all of that? And yet we're still missing one

important fact. Two, actually. Where should I be instructing my coachman to drive us, hmm?"

Regina had been giving that some thought. Her mother was less than useless by this time of night, and with luck could be persuaded upon rising tomorrow that she had indeed accompanied Regina and Miranda this evening. She'd feel more confident if she had a few lemon squares tucked up in her reticule, but her mother could be convinced she'd already eaten them. Regina wasn't proud of these facts or of using her mother's problem so shamelessly, but these were desperate times, and desperate measures were in order.

"I reside for the Season in Berkeley Square, but we will be dropping my mother off there and continuing on our way, seeing as how the poor woman is completely overset by the recent terrible events and must take to her bed with a strong dose of laudanum. We will then drive directly to my grandfather's domicile at Number Twenty-three Cavendish Square, where we will explain all to Miranda's parents. My grandfather, I'm relieved to say, remains in the country, suffering from the gout, so we may see either Aunt Claire or Uncle Seth or, if we are to be extremely unlucky, both of them. What is the other important fact?"

"I'm not sure. I'm still attempting to wade through all those names and titles. Oh, I remember now, and you've already answered it. Your mother accompanied you and your cousin this evening? I look forward to hearing how you'll convince her to go along with your lie."

Regina shot a quick look at Doris Ann, who was coughing into her fist. "That is my problem, Mr. Blackthorn, and I will handle it. Now, please instruct your coachman, as I wish to arrive in Cavendish Square to hear what information it is you learned at the ball and have thus far refused to share with me."

"It's a tale that should not have any telling, not even in Cavendish Square, but if you will allow for some small changes and keep your silence except to sniffle sorrowfully a time or two in the correct spots, it is one I wish to tell only once."

"I *am* sorrowful! I'm frantic."

"You hide it well."

"I'm used to— Would you please just give the coachman my uncle's direction!"

He looked at her strangely for a moment before he leaned past Doris Ann, opened a small square hinged door and recited the Cavendish Square address.

Regina thought about her aunt, who adored her only daughter. "It's that terrible? You know who took Miranda?"

"If I knew the *who,* Miss Hackett, I would have handed you over to my coachman and sent you on your way, and damn your problems with your respective parents when they discovered you'd been at the masquerade. But I only learned a possible *why,* I believe, which makes the *where* immaterial."

Thoughts no well-bred young lady should know enough about to even consider went flashing through Regina's head. But her father owned a shipping company, and he had told many stories at the dinner table about mysterious cargos, human cargos, being shipped off to foreign parts, where the men and children were sold into slavery and the most comely women paraded about on stages, for sale to the highest bidder. He seemed to delight in the telling, probably because each only served to make his wife ill and to seek ever more comfort in the contents of a wine decanter.

How she hated her father.

How she feared for Miranda.

Regina put her hand on Mr. Blackthorn's forearm. "We must find her. We *must*."

He covered her hand with his own. "And I will."

"No," she corrected him. "*We* will. This is my fault. I should have said no. Miranda's incurably silly, but she wouldn't have gone if I had refused to accompany her. I should have known better. If you will not assist me, I will investigate on my own. I will. Really."

He looked at her for long moments, saying nothing until the coach drew to a halt outside of Number Twenty-three.

"Very well. Your uncle will call in the Bow Street Runners, I'm sure, but we two can conduct our own investigation if it will make you more comfortable, which it very well may not, not once I've said what I have to say to your uncle. Still, if you're of the same mind tomorrow, I will meet you in Hyde Park at eleven. Come on foot, with only your maid."

"And you'll be there? You're not just saying that now

to fob me off? Because I know I have been something of an annoyance to you."

"Miss Hackett…Regina. It is precisely because you have been, in your words, such an annoyance to me that I can safely promise you that, yes, I will be there. *Pour mes péchés.*"

"For your sins?"

He stroked one long finger along her cheek and over her mouth, stealing her breath.

"Both committed and contemplated, yes," he said softly. And then he did something that took her totally by surprise—he reached behind her neck and unclasped her pearls, sliding them into his pocket. "You've been robbed, remember? I'll return them to you tomorrow, when you come to the park."

"Were you thinking I might not come? That I'll change my mind?"

"The possibility presents itself, yes."

"Well, I won't! I'm going to find Miranda, and since you're the only person who knows we needs must start with what happened at the ball, you're the only person who can help me."

A groom opened the door and put down the steps and Mr. Blackthorn eased past Regina and hopped to the ground before turning to hold out his hand to her. "And we begin.…"

CHAPTER THREE

THE FIRST THING PUCK noticed once they'd been escorted into the drawing room at Number Twenty-three was the general shabbiness of the place. He would do some investigating of the Earl of Mentmore in the morning, but for now, he believed he could safely assume that if a ransom were demanded for Lady Miranda, the family would be hard-pressed to comply.

Strange. The family had the name but not the money. He and his brothers had the funds but not the name. Of the two circumstances, he believed he preferred his own, and yet, Society looked down its nose at him and accepted Mentmore and his offspring everywhere. A day would come, he felt certain, when one side would have to compromise with the other, and if he were to project a winning side, he would wager on money over birth every time. For one thing, it kept you warmer at night.

"His lordship and my lady will be down shortly," the starchy butler pronounced from the doorway as Regina, who had been pacing the carpet in front of the fire these past five minutes, mumbled a brief thank-you to the man she called Kettering, then quickly found herself a chair and collapsed into it.

"Wonderful," Puck pronounced, as if compliment-ing the man on some lofty achievement. He walked over to the butler and put an arm around the man's shoulder confidingly. "Kettering, you look an intelli-gent man. Can I trust you? Your employers are, I fear, about to suffer a great shock. I say this because I am convinced you will know just how to handle the situ-ation. I would suggest wine for the lady, and perhaps some burnt feathers. Brandy for his lordship?"

"He favors gin," the butler whispered, frowning to show his own distaste for such a lowly spirit and, it would seem, his employer, as well. "Does this concern Miss Miranda, sir?"

"Oh yes, it does, it does," Puck said, shaking his head, his sorrowful expression saying more than his words, drawing in Kettering as if he were a fish on the hook. "It will be left to a fine man like you to keep body and soul together under this roof, I'm afraid. But if there is anything, anything at all I can do to assist you, please do not hesitate to contact me. In fact, I all but insist upon it." He then handed the man his card and a small but heavy purse.

Kettering slipped both into his pocket, one eye on Regina, who sat contemplating her shoe tops, blissfully unaware of what Puck was about. "It would be my plea-sure, sir," the butler said. "I will see about refreshments for you and the young lady, as well."

"Again, wonderful. But no gin for me, if you please. Horrid, bitter stuff."

"There's a bottle of wine in the cellars his lordship has been saving. He'll never know."

Puck patted the man's back and then asked his question. "I only met Miss Hackett this evening and, unfortunately, under trying circumstances. Do you know her well?"

Kettering looked about, to make sure no one was listening from the foyer and that his employers weren't on the stairs. "She's fine enough, sir. Not that it means anything. The mother is sister to the viscount, but the father?" He leaned closer. "In trade. Owns ships. Bought himself his bride, and now he's trying to sell the daughter to a title. The family's that embarrassed, sir."

Puck kept his smile with some difficulty. The butler looked down on Regina Hackett? What a strange world they all lived in. "And yet she's welcome here?"

Now Kettering looked positively evil. "It's like I said, sir. The family's that *embarrassed.* If you take my meaning."

"Yes, I think I do. Pays for all of this, does he?"

The butler seemed to realize that he'd been speaking out of turn and to a complete stranger. "Was there anything else you wanted, sir?"

"Thank you, no. You've been extremely helpful." A gold coin appeared in Puck's hand and also quickly disappeared.

Kettering looked about himself once more, wet his lips and confided, "The mother, Lady Leticia? Poor thing is nearly always three parts over the windmill, and the father is a nasty piece of work. I'd steer clear if I was you, sir. There's better pickings out there for a fine, set-up young gentleman, such as yourself."

"I'll be sure to keep that in mind. Again, thank you, Kettering. Ah, and I believe his lordship and his lady wife are about to join us. And you have some refreshments to organize. Remember, I'm counting on you to keep me informed. Most especially, I think, about the actions of your master concerning this entire affair."

"Indeed, sir. He so much as sneezes, sir, you'll know about it," Kettering promised, bowing to him before scurrying off, not bothering to announce his employers or their unexpected guests.

Yes, in the end, perhaps in ten years, perhaps not for another hundred, it would be money that would decide who held all the winning cards. Money, and charm. Puck, with all modesty, believed he possessed both in considerable measure.

It was a pity he was bound to be tossed out of this house on his illegitimate ear in the next ten minutes by one of the eventual losers.

"My lord, my lady," he said, bowing to each of them in turn as they entered the drawing room. "Please pardon the intrusion, but I must tell you that something untoward has occurred. Concerning your daughter, Lady Miranda. Please, I would suggest you both sit."

"Who the bloody blazes are you?" the viscount asked, his clothing looking as if he'd dressed in haste, a betraying crease on his right cheek announcing that he'd just lately had his head on a pillow.

No, no. I would remain anonymous a while longer.

"The bearer of bad news, I'm afraid. Your daughter has been abducted by brigands."

Well, that neatly served to distract the viscount from more personal questions, as he was immediately too busy attempting to prop up his fainting wife to ask them.

Regina rushed to her aunt's side, sparing only a moment to glare at Puck before she assisted her uncle in getting the woman to one of the couches near the fireplace.

The next minutes were spent with the requested burnt feathers being waved beneath her ladyship's nose by her worried niece while his lordship snagged the decanter of gin from the tray Kettering had produced and drank down two full glasses in quick succession.

Puck stood in front of the fireplace, watching everything, missing nothing, and sipped the wine, which was actually quite fine. Good on Kettering. And good on him, knowing the most direct route to any secret lay with making allies of the servant staff.

At last her ladyship seemed recovered enough to sit up, and the viscount demanded that Puck explain himself.

He, in turn, looked to Regina. "Miss Hackett? If you would be so kind as to get us started?"

The look she shot him this time might have had a less courageous fellow ducking behind a chair, but she didn't waste more than a few seconds on him before sitting down beside her aunt and taking the woman's trembling hands in her own.

"We were on our way to the soiree, as you know. Mama was very much looking forward to the lemon squares— Oh, I'm sorry. My nerves are still overset, because that isn't important, is it? We, that is, the coachman seemed to have gotten lost, turned about in his direction somewhere, I suppose, as he looked for a way around the crush of vehicles on every roadway, and we ended up in a fairly isolated street. Somehow, one of the coach wheels found a hole in the cobbles as we tried to turn the coach, and one of the spokes splintered." She could not hold back a small sob. "Everything just seemed to go wrong."

"Incompetent idiot! I'll have the man's position!" the viscount bellowed.

And you'll be within your rights, Puck thought, taking another sip of wine. *Can't blame the coachman for my lies, but he deserves the sack for delivering his master's daughter to that den of iniquity.*

"Yes, uncle, but it would only have been unfortunate save for...for those horrible brigands." Now she looked to Puck, and there was no mistaking what she wanted him to do.

"Mine own coach was passing by the opening to the street, and I heard a commotion, a woman's scream. I leaped down from my coach and went hotfoot in pursuit of the source of that scream, mine own coachman and grooms assisting me. We arrived on the scene not able to do much more than take charge after the fact, move the ladies to my coach and offer any other assistance I could. But I can tell you the events that transpired as they were told to me by your coachman."

"Then tell us, damn it!"

"Yes, my lord, I was about to do just that. It would seem that several creatures of the night saw an opportunity present itself to them and acted upon it, surrounding the coach and demanding all jewelry and money the occupants might have on their persons."

Lady Claire choked back a sob. "But—but there was no money, and those pearls were paste—"

"Claire, that will be enough," her husband warned tightly. "Continue."

Puck bowed, pretending a convenient deafness to her ladyship's admission. "As you can see, Miss Hackett readily gave over her jewelry—pearls you said, didn't you? And her mother's jewels, as well," he added as an afterthought.

Regina obligingly raised a hand to her bare throat. "We took Mama home before coming here. She was overset. Miranda's pearls were paste? I didn't— That is, I don't believe the brigands knew that. They...they seemed much more interested in Miranda. They seemed very taken with...with her looks."

"Her hair," Puck explained, drawing on what he'd learned at the ball and marking, for future consideration, the fact that Regina seemed to have figured out for herself why her cousin had been taken. "Her blond hair, her blue eyes, her fair English complexion, her,

Miss Hackett tells me, petite stature. Young women of similar description have been going missing in and around London for months now, I understand. It took only a few questions to learn what I am attempting to tell you. A sad, sad story."

"But…but what about Regina?" Lady Claire asked, looking to her niece with what could only be termed displeasure that she was there and her daughter was not.

"They did not take Miss Hackett here because she is tall, dark-haired. The others taken have been servants, shop girls, the occasional actress or ballet dancer, which is why there has been no great stir in society. But your daughter? She'd be a real prize, my lord."

The man looked stricken. "I've heard…whispers. At my club, you understand. Young girls disappearing off the streets. Nobodies. But things like this don't happen to people like *us!* Damn this city!"

"My baby," her ladyship whimpered. "A *prize?* Seth! What is this man saying? What has happened to my baby?"

"And yet it is that, dear lady, which we cannot know," Puck said. "We can only hope for the best." *And that beautiful young virgins bring a higher price at whatever market the bastards plan to sell her, so that she'll be relatively safe until we find her.*

Puck hadn't said the words out loud, but he felt certain that the viscount had heard them anyway.

"I'll…I'll hire a Bow Street Runner. I'll hire ten of them! But quietly. No one can know she's gone. We'll put it out that she's taken ill…that her mother has taken ill…. We'll keep this between ourselves."

"Yes, my lord, that also would be my suggestion. Second only to your daughter's safety is her unsullied reputation. And now, if you will excuse us, I should think Miss Hackett desires to return to her home and see to her mother's welfare."

"Yes, yes," the viscount said, looking at Regina angrily, as if he, like his wife, was incensed that she hadn't been the one who had been taken. "Regina, please inform your father that I will call on him first thing tomorrow. The Runners will demand payment before they'll help us and…and my funds are currently all tied up in the Exchange."

"Yes, uncle, of course," Regina said, getting to her feet with more alacrity than might be seemly. "Aunt Claire, I'm so, so sorry. But we must be brave. We'll find her. I promise we will."

The woman nodded and then went back to weeping into her handkerchief.

Puck held his arm out to Regina, but before she could take it, the viscount asked the question Puck had so far avoided.

"I failed to get your name, sir, or to thank you for the assistance you have rendered us this evening."

"There is no need for thanks, my lord. I was simply fortunate to have come along when I did. Miss Hackett was hysterical and in no fit state to take charge of her mother or anything else."

Regina's gasp of outrage was quickly cut off, but

Puck felt certain he'd hear her thoughts on this remark on the way to Berkeley Square. In fact, he was rather counting on it. If she agreed to accompany him after what he now had to say. Their acquaintance was short, but he felt fairly confident that she would, if only so that she might berate him for calling her hysterical.

"In answer to your question, my lord, I am the third and youngest son of Cyril Woodword, Marquess of Blackthorn."

The earl stuck out his right hand, said, "Marquess of—" and then just as quickly drew it back, his expression suddenly so horrible Puck could have thought himself to have just announced that he carried the plague. "You're one of Blackthorn's bastards?"

Puck inclined his head in acknowledgment. "I am. I am Robin Goodfellow Blackthorn, known to my friends as Puck. A bit of nonsense, yes, but many say it suits me. A word in private, my lord?"

"A— No! There are ladies present. You will leave my house at once, sir!"

"Uncle Seth!" Regina stepped between her uncle and Puck, as if to protect at least one of them from the other. "Mr. Blackthorn has been exceedingly kind this evening. The good Lord knows what would have become of me—Mama and me—if he had not come along as he did. Only think how Papa would have seen the thing if any harm had come to us while I was in *your* coach. You should be thanking Mr. Blackthorn, not ordering him out of the house."

God, I must know this woman better. For so many reasons.

"Thanks are not necessary, Miss Hackett," Puck told her. "Although I would appreciate that private word? My lord?"

The viscount seemed to be considering what his life would be like—and what it would be worth—if Regina's father were to become upset with him in any way. "Very well," he said, and then walked toward one side of the large room, motioning rather rudely for Puck to follow after him.

"You'll keep your eyes and hands off that one," the viscount warned. "Reginald Hackett has plans for her, and they don't include marriage to some jumped-up by-blow. I know what happened last year with your brother and Brean's chit, but Brean is an ass. Reg is not. And he's mean. Mean straight through to the bone."

"Yes, thank you, I'll keep that in mind," Puck said smoothly. "But I've had a thought. Being by inclination a rather observant man, it has occurred to me that being beholden to Mr. Hackett for more than you already might be could be said to hold little appeal. Therefore, I would like to gift you with a sum of money you might use to employ the Runners. Oh, shall we say, two hundred pounds? And as a gift only, my lord. With only one small string attached, that I would be allowed to escort Miss Hackett home this evening."

Puck knew, and Viscount Ranscome knew. A Runner, three Runners, could not cost more than ten or twenty pounds. Puck was offering the man a bribe—a ridiculously generous bribe—in exchange for his cooperation tonight and in future, if need be. Not that either man would say so. Puck was too smart…and Ranscome too greedy.

The viscount goggled and gasped at Puck, rather like a fish that had just unexpectedly found himself tossed onto the bank of the stream, only to be offered a helpful lift back into the water. "You…a *gift,* you said? You wouldn't wish repayment?"

"You insult me, sir. Are we agreed?"

"It's the girl. You want the girl. I know what you're doing here. You want my help, or my silence. He'll kill you. With his bare hands."

"I'll keep that in mind, also, but I hardly think so." Having hatched much of this plan whilst Gaston was fussing over him as he tied his cravat, Puck had put more than one small but heavy purse in his pocket. He extracted the second, heavier purse and, with his back to the ladies, briefly flashed it to the viscount. "Take it. Take it now, or the offer is withdrawn. Ah, very good. You show some small spark of intelligence. The rest, tomorrow, sent over by messenger. Now I shall turn slightly so that the ladies can see, and you will smile and shake my hand. If we meet in public in the days and weeks to come, you will behave likewise. I am your friend, my lord. Your new bosom chum. Even if it kills *you.*"

"You are a bastard, aren't you?"

Puck smiled in real delight as the two shook hands. "In every way, my lord, yes, I am."

REGINA KEPT HER eyes facing toward the front of the coach as Puck sat himself beside her on the seat. "You could have told me."

He adjusted the lapels of his black evening jacket and shot his cuffs. "Told you what, Miss Hackett?"

Where could she begin?

"You could have told me your circumstances. That would have gone a long way in explaining why... why..." She was suddenly at a loss for words.

"Why I behaved like such a bastard in the gardens?"

She shifted about on the seat to glare at him in the near darkness. "That is not what I meant! Besides, we are both going to forget about that entirely. Is that clear?"

"Clear and yet, I fear, impossible. You have a glorious mouth, Regina. I live only to taste it again."

She was going to die. She was going to sink straight into these cushions and expire.

"You can't say things like that to me."

"I can't? But I just did."

She couldn't take her eyes off him. She wasn't sure she wanted to. She felt...she felt so *alive.* "You're being purposely obtuse."

"No, I'm being brutally honest. And, yes, perhaps provocative. I enjoy doing things I'm good at, you see."

She drew her hands up into fists in her lap. "My cousin has been abducted!"

"Yes, and I am still amazed that you seemed to grasp the *why* of that abduction so easily. Do a lot of reading of penny dreadfuls, do you? Chaste maidens, snatched from the bosoms of their families for their beauty, carried off to foreign parts, lost forever behind the walls of some harem. Until the hero saves her or she, to preserve her virtue, takes her own life? Only after twenty pages of hand-wringing and virtuous speechifying, of course. Did you ever wonder, Regina—what good is an intact virtue when you're dead?"

She faced forward once more, not without effort, because it was difficult to look away from his face, those fascinating eyes and their mischievous sparkle that, she was realizing more and more, hid a rather terrifying intelligence. "My father owns ships. Trading ships. Quite a few of them. He has been all over the world and seen things most of us wouldn't believe. He…he has told us stories, and I see no reason to believe he was lying. But I didn't think something so terrible could happen here, right in London."

"Bad things happen anywhere, Regina. One of the servants I applied to with your cousin's description informed me that a barmaid in a tavern he frequents disappeared last week. And he knows of another girl, a milliner, who went missing a few days ago. He said there were more. All of them looking much like your cousin, all of them small, all of them blonde. You and I saw the state of her mask, the obvious evidence of a struggle. She may have gone out into the gardens willingly enough, but that's not how she departed them. No, we can't be completely certain that your cousin was abducted by the same persons *collecting* pretty, petite blondes, but I don't think such a conclusion is too far-fetched, do you?"

Regina remembered the ruined mask, the green glass stones in her reticule. "She didn't go willingly. We were only going to watch, perhaps…flirt a little. It was silly, it was *stupid,* but it shouldn't have been dangerous. And Miranda never would have gone off willingly with anyone and left me alone. It…it was only supposed to be a lark. A little…a little fun."

She took the handkerchief he offered and wiped at her eyes.

"Your uncle will be hiring a brace or more of Bow Street Runners in the morning. Those Robin Redbreasts must have heard about the other disappearances by now and have some idea where to look for her. Nobody can vanish completely."

Regina turned her head to face him once more, looking deeply into his eyes. "You don't believe that, do you? She could already be aboard some horrible ship, waiting for the tide so that it can sail to some foreign port. I've been to the docks with my father, you know. There are so many of them and hundreds of ships. Miranda could even now be in any one of them. Oh, God," she said, her voice breaking, "I'm so frightened for her."

The next thing she knew, Puck had pulled her against his chest, his arms around her as he rested his chin on her hair, rocking her slightly as if she were a child he was attempting to comfort. She wrapped one arm about his waist, holding on, hoping for strength.

And felt something else stirring inside her, something she shouldn't have felt. Not now, with her cousin in such dire straits. Not ever.

Regina had never had anyone to cling to like this. Certainly not her mother, whom she loved dearly but who was as useless as a parent as ears would be on a turnip. Certainly not her father, who had made it clear he saw her as a commodity to be, as he'd baldly told her, "bought low and sold high." Why, she'd never even had a pet that she was sure would have loved her unconditionally.

At last, as his coach slowed, she pushed herself away from him. "I have to stop this. I'm feeling sorry for myself, and that's ridiculous because it is Miranda who's in danger. Oh, and you're horrid, Mr. Blackthorn, because you were about to take advantage of my overset state, weren't you?"

"The thought had danced fleetingly across my mind, yes. Are you certain you're totally against it?"

Regina glared at him, but then her bottom lip began to tremble, and she laughed. "You're incorrigible. A true Puck."

He put his bent index finger beneath her chin to hold it steady and then leaned in and placed a short, chaste kiss on her mouth. "For courage," he said when he withdrew just far enough to look into her eyes.

Regina realized that the coach had come to a halt. She was home.

"I think I probably need it. Will you come inside?"

He shook his head. "I believe it would wiser if my name were kept out of any explanations you will offer your parents. I'm convinced the viscount won't be mentioning it, at any rate. But don't worry. Your father will be much too overjoyed to know that his daughter is safe and will not be asking for too many details. As for your mother…?"

Regina winced. "She won't be a problem."

"I'm sorry," Puck said, stroking her cheek.

"Why? You aren't the cause of any of this."

"No. I'm sorry we have to say good-night. By tomorrow, you will have remembered just how unsuitable I am."

She lowered her head. He was right. He was nothing she could think about the way she was thinking about him now. Her father wouldn't allow his *commodity* to be thrown away on a bastard son, no matter that his sire was the Marquess of Blackthorn.

"We…we are only caught up in the moment," she told him, still not raising her chin. "I have suffered a considerable—several considerable shocks this evening. And you…"

"I am a very bad man," he finished for her.

"Sir," a footman said, having opened the door and put down the steps. "We have arrived."

Puck grinned, looking young and silly, so much so that it startled her. He had so many different sides to him, and she knew she was compelled to learn about all of them. "Some people find it necessary to state the obvious, don't they? My footman will escort you to your door and make certain it opens to you."

Regina nodded and then made a decision. She raised

her hand to his cheek, lifted her head and kissed him, squarely on the mouth, and then withdrew before he could react.

"Tomorrow at eleven. In the park," she said, quickly gathering up her reticule and all but stumbling out of the coach, his laughter following her.

She hiked up her skirts rather inelegantly, belatedly remembering that her shawl was still inside her uncle's coach, but hopeful none of the sleepy Hackett footmen or the butler would notice.

And she probably would have made it to her bed-chamber, where she longed to be alone and think back over every moment of the evening, save for the fact that she heard her father's voice calling to her from the drawing room. The last thing she'd expected, consider-ing what he had been about the last time she saw him, was for him to have returned home so early.

Her shoulders sagged; truly, her entire body sagged, suddenly exhausted. But she dutifully turned and headed toward the sound of his voice.

"Good evening, Papa," she said, dropping into a small curtsy, because that always seemed to please him for some unknown reason. Besides, it was either that or kiss him on the cheek. After where he'd been tonight and what he had been doing, she would rather kiss the fireplace grate.

"Where's your mother? No, never mind that non-sense. We've more important things to discuss."

Reginald Hackett was still a relatively young man, and tall, towering over most other men (although not quite so tall as Puck, she realized with a ridiculous spurt of pride). He was thick in his body, most especially in his chest and shoulders, for he had spent many years laboring alongside his crews, climbing rigging, loading cargo. Regina knew this because her father had told her the stories, taken her to the docks, showed her what he had achieved and recounted again and again how hard he'd worked for his success, how grateful she should be for the fine clothes on her back, the food on her plate, the roof over her head.

And then he'd tell her how she would repay him. "Nothing less than an earl, girl, you hear me? Then squirt out a brace of sons for him, make me grandda to the heir, and nobody'll dare remember Hacketts were ever in trade. Two generations from the docks, girl, that's all it takes. And you name the first whelp Reginald somewhere in his string of names. I'll go the blunt for that, as well. I promised m'mother as much, and that's how it's going to be, understand?"

His mother. Grandmother Hackett. To her father, everything that was right and good about the world. To her mother, who had been forced to have the coarse, domineering Alice Hackett live in her house until the woman died, the bad angel who sat on Regina's shoulder. Her mother loved her daughter, but Leticia could never quite hide the fear that Regina had the makings of a lowborn peasant deep inside her, just waiting for some inopportune moment to pop out and sully her and her family escutcheon.

"Papa, I have terrible news," Regina said as her

father had recourse to the gin decanter, the only thing that bonded him to her Uncle Seth. She had hoped to be able to put off the telling until the morning, but that was impossible now. "Our coach took a wrong turn tonight and brigands attacked us. I'm fine," she added quickly, as her father had whirled about to look at her, his face a thundercloud. "But Miranda was…"

"Well? Spit it out, girl. The idiot girl was what? Beaten? Shot? Raped?"

Regina sought out a chair and sat down. "No," she said. "Taken. Miranda was taken."

He raised one inquisitive eyebrow at her. No sign of caring, of compassion. Simply inquisitive. "Is that so? Taken where?"

"She was abducted by the brigands." Regina hated that her voice was shaking, hated that she was afraid of her father. But she was. He was so large, so physically imposing. She reassured herself that anyone with half a brain in his head would be afraid of her father. "Uncle Seth has already begun making inquiries," she lied quickly. "There is a great fear that Miranda has been kidnapped in order to be sold somewhere. I was left alone because I'm not what they wanted. It's just as you told Mama and me. Terrible men, buying and selling people as if they were bolts of cloth."

"I see," Reginald Hackett said slowly. "And you're not lying to me? She hasn't talked you into going along with some farradiddle about slavers to cover that she's run off with some idiot young pup who thinks he loves that penniless twit?"

"No! Papa, this is *real.*"

"And you didn't help her make up the story, thanks to me telling you about such things? Come on, come on—the truth!"

Regina shot to her feet. "I am many things, Papa, but I am not a liar."

His enraged shout shook the chandelier above her head. "Damned if you aren't!"

She sat down once more, hoping to hide her sudden urge to flee the room. She hadn't realized he knew her that well. "Papa, please…"

"You're mine, aren't you? You couldn't help but lie whenever it suited you. Only good thing about you, other than your worth in the marketplace."

Regina felt a spurt of resentment. "I also have tolerably good teeth," she said quietly. But he'd heard her.

He downed the remainder of his gin and deposited the empty glass on a nearby table before spreading his arms wide as if in apology, one he certainly didn't mean. "You need a thicker skin, that's what you need, girl. I'm only stating facts. All right, all right, never mind. We'll put your sad tale of brigands to bed, shall we? You were up to mischief tonight, the pair of you, but you escaped by the skin of those tolerably good teeth while your cousin didn't. Next time, you might not be so lucky. But there's not going to be a next time, is there?"

Her shoulders visibly slumped. He knew. How did he know? "No, sir."

"So your cousin did not involve you in some elopement? She truly was taken. Seth knows?"

Regina nodded. "He's going to hire some Bow Street Runners in the morning."

"Another dip in my purse," Reginald grumbled. "She hardly seems worth it, except to accompany you in the evenings."

Regina grabbed on to that most important fact. "I can't depend on Mama to accompany me all the places you wish me to go, no. And if Miranda isn't recovered, Aunt Claire will be too devastated to chaperone me. No one is to know she's gone, and once she's safely recovered, it will be as if nothing has happened."

"Ha! Believe that, girl, and you'll believe anything." He walked over to the chair she sat in and stood directly in front of her. Hovered over her menacingly. "She's probably on her back in some low tavern even now, being held down, her legs spread wide for her while every last man Jack in the place takes his turn every which way. They're having her in ways even the devil himself never thought of, and the more she screams, the more they'll like it. Don't you go clapping your hands over your ears, girl! You listen to me! I *know.* Better off dead by morning, that's how I see the thing, and even your idiot uncle Seth will know it, too, see if he doesn't. He won't be looking for her all that long. Dead or a twopenny whore, that's all your fine cousin has left to her. And you'll consider twice now before you even think to take another step off the path I've put you on, stupid girl, won't you? *Won't you!*"

The image that had formed in Regina's mind at her father's crude description tore painfully at her heart, even as she unconsciously squeezed her thighs together. If she hadn't been lucky enough to have met Puck at the masquerade when she was feeling so adventuresome, rather than someone like her father, where would she be now?

Her father was right. She was stupid. Stupid, and foolhardy and very, very lucky.

"Yes, Papa," she said quietly.

"Good. Now give me his name."

She looked up at him in surprise that swiftly turned to horror.

"And don't lie to me again. Brigands," he spat. "In Mayfair? I wondered what you'd come up with, and it's pitiful. Only a brains-to-let looby like my brother-in-law would swallow such a clunker. Then again, he didn't see you tonight, did he?"

Regina thought she might faint. This was worse than anything she could have imagined. "You knew? You let me go on and on—and you *knew?*"

"Got yourself a grand eyeful, didn't you? Yes, I saw you. You and that man you were with, but you were already climbing into his coach and driving off by the time I could locate you again. Followed the pair of you all the way to Cavendish Square, though, figuring the least Seth could do was to see you home safely from there. Now, who is he?"

She ignored his questions because she had questions

of her own. "You knew Miranda had gone missing at the ball?"

"You left without her, remember? You two weren't at a tea party, girl. Things happen. And her disappearance could have been of her own planning. But to answer your question, no, I didn't know for certain. Not until I returned to the ball and asked a few questions. Now you answer mine. Give me his name. He saw you safe to your uncle. I want to thank him."

"No," Regina said, knowing she was visibly trembling now and deathly afraid. Her father had never hit her, never laid a hand on her. He'd always found other ways to control her.

"I'll have your mother put away. For her own good."

And that was one of them. But just this one time she'd say to him what she'd always wanted to say, but had never dared. "You won't do that. It's bad enough you want to foist the tradesman's daughter on the *ton,* Papa. It's quite another to sell the daughter of a Bedlamite to a title."

She flinched as he raised his hand, but then he stopped and smiled, which was worse. "Very well, we'll not bother about the Good Samaritan. Go to bed."

"Yes, Papa. I'm sorry, Papa." Regina scrambled to her feet and fled the room, knowing he hadn't meant what he'd said. Puck had been masked, and apparently no one had recognized him. Still, she couldn't see him again, for his own safety.

Except that she'd have to see him again, to warn him. Otherwise, she felt certain he was foolhardy enough to come knocking on her door. Or worse.

CHAPTER FOUR

"M'SIEUR PUCK. IF you were to do me the kindness to lift your chin so that I might button your collar," the valet, Gaston, crooned in that way he had about him, a politeness of expression far from the rough gutter French he'd spoken when Puck first found him, rescuing the slim, slight fellow from a gang of rough men who had been demonstrating their displeasure with what they believed to be his perversion of nature.

Puck liked his servants loyal, and in saving Gaston, he had found a treasure beyond price. He also held an affection for other misfits in this world. With Gaston, he could say what he liked, show what he felt, without fear of being misunderstood, without worrying about possible betrayal.

"She's magnificent, Gaston. You've never seen eyes like that. A mouth so impossible to resist. And spirit! And intelligence!"

"As you've said, *m'sieur.* Repeatedly. I am so happy for you I am beyond words. The chin if you please, *m'sieur.*"

"I should walk away," Puck said, at last doing as his valet asked. "That would be the decent thing to do. There's no reason I can't conduct my search for her cousin without ever seeing Regina again. None. In fact, it would be pure selfishness for me to involve her at all. I'll tell her that."

"When you meet her in the park, having taken such an unconscionable time dressing for this meeting," Gaston said without expression—which was as good as tapping his employer over the head with a strong mallet.

Puck waved Gaston away and took a step toward the mirror to inspect the man's handiwork. As usual, the valet's effort was perfection itself. "Sending a note around to her residence could be risky for her. Anything put to paper can be risky."

"And I am risky, as well, *m'sieur?* You could send me in your place, to repeat your words of farewell to her, without need for a note. I can remain committed to my purpose when exposed to magnificent female eyes and mouths."

Puck eyed Gaston as he was reflected in the mirror. "You make a valid point. I believe I shall ignore it."

At last Gaston allowed himself a small smile. "I have never before seen you like this, *m'sieur.* The beautiful women, yes, you like them all, romance them all. And then like a bee always in search of nectar, you fly on to the next flower, and the next. How is this one so different?"

Puck snatched up his gloves and softly slapped them against his valet's shoulder. "That, Gaston, is what I wonder myself. And what I do believe I have no choice but to find out. Beginning this morning, in the park.

Feel free to pray for me. I very well may be human after all."

His own words still ringing in his ears, Puck then took himself off for the stroll to the park. He headed for the entrance closest to Berkeley Square, careful to arrive well in advance of the appointed time, to look over the lay of the land, as it were. Not that he was overly concerned that Regina had told her father about the scheduled meeting, but one could never be too careful, and Puck wasn't fond of surprises, unless they were of his own making.

He saw the man immediately. Dressed well enough but appearing to be somewhat uncomfortable in his clothes, his eyes shifting left and right, as if looking for something he did not know but hoped to recognize when he saw it. With every second visual sweep of the area, his gaze would hold for some moments on the female form clad in a light green walking gown and pelisse, a red-haired maid standing just behind her.

So much for the notion of a leisurely stroll with Miss Regina Hackett, who had also seen fit to arrive early. Puck deftly turned and left the park, heading via a slightly roundabout way in the direction of Berkeley Square.

London churches had just completed their noon hour competition of bells when his most recent peek out from his hiding place alerted Puck to the fact that Regina was returning to her residence, her swift steps firm on the flagway, a reflection of her anger and forcing her maid to nearly skip to keep up with her longer strides.

Oh, there was going to be the devil to pay if he didn't get his apology in quickly!

She and her maid were the only ones taking advantage of the fine, sunny day, save a few nurses and their charges and a spattering of old women out seeking fresh air for their health. The rest of the inhabitants of this exalted area of London were just now waking up to their hot chocolate and newspapers.

"Psst!" Oh, for the love of Heaven, she hadn't heard him. *"Psssst!"*

Regina's steps faltered slightly, and she turned her head toward the narrow alleyway where Puck was standing. But when he commanded her to pretend there was something in her shoe and to tell her maid to bend down and help her remove it, Regina reacted with the sort of alacrity a drill sergeant would admire in his recruits.

"Where were you? I waited for nearly an hour," she told him quietly as she braced one hand against a nearby railing and stuck her right foot out to the maid, who quickly fell into enacting her role. Clearly, Regina had shared what the trip to the park was about this morning and had enlisted her aid.

"Someone was watching. You weren't alone. Your father suspects something?"

She bent her head, as if talking to the maid. "My father *knows* everything. He saw me at the ball."

"And now you've grown a tail."

She very nearly turned her head to look at him. "I've *what?*"

Puck smiled at her horror. "And it will *wag* after you everywhere you go. He's behind you somewhere now—no, don't turn around. He'll be much happier and become more lax in his surveillance the longer you pretend to not notice him."

"Oh," she said quietly. "But what shall we do? He can't see you with me. I didn't tell my father your name when he asked."

"A determined man won't have much problem finding his own answer. Your uncle will probably be delighted to assist him."

"Miss?" Hanks, speaking with her position much lower to the ground than she obviously liked, sounded slightly oppressed. "My knees are aching *that* much."

"Oh, I'm so sorry, Hanks." Regina put her foot down and let go of the railing. "I have to go. If you've been waiting for me here all of this time, surely you've managed to think of something, some way we can meet?"

"Cheeky. That's what it is. You're cheeky. I never knew I admired that in a woman," Puck said, longing to pull her into the alleyway and kiss her senseless. "Continue back to your residence and go inside. Wait ten minutes, and then come back out, turn to your right and then right again at the end of the building. I'll meet you there."

"But—but my *tail?*"

"He won't expect you to reemerge quite so quickly, and it's likely past his lunchtime. He'll be nipping off to some pub to drink his the moment he feels you're safely inside. If he hasn't gone when you stick your pretty head outside—lovely bonnet, by the way, though I'd like to see more of your face—you'll hear my warning whistle, and I'll have to think of something else."

"And what would that something else be?" Regina asked as she rifled inside her reticule as if searching for something.

First, the required action with the shoe, and now, the inspection of the reticule, both executed flawlessly and all the while carrying on a conversation with him. What a quick mind she had. She could have been born for the stage...or simply born to deceive. And to delight.

"Miss, we really must go."

"I don't know," Puck said, unable to resist. "How wide are your chimneys?"

Regina lifted her chin and marched on down the flagway, clearly unimpressed by his answer, leaving him to sink farther into the shadow of the buildings and compliment himself on his good taste. He'd used the correct word to describe her to Gaston. She really was *magnificent*.

And then he was off, cutting through alleyways until he emerged on the flagway of Berkeley Square, nearly gaining it ahead of the man still following Regina. He watched as the man walked on and determined that the fellow was or at least had been a sailor, forever marked by his rolling gait.

Sailors most often meant knives, not pistols, and they usually kept them tucked into their waistbands. Puck stored the information in his brain and continued walking, following the *tail* until he'd passed the door that had so recently closed behind Regina, and then continued to keep pace with him as he exited the Square and turned to his left. Another three blocks took them both to a small, discreet basement tavern, patronized mostly by the servants from the local neighborhoods. The *tail* stepped inside and was greeted by several people who recognized him before the door could close once more.

Clearly, the man was a frequent visitor to the establishment. How nice. Gaston always enjoyed meeting new people. In his previous life, before his encounter with Puck, he had met many new people, most only briefly, deftly relieving them of their valuables as he'd been one of the premiere pickpockets in the city.

Puck wanted a look at the sort of *sticker* the man preferred, and Gaston would delight in practicing his old skills. It was always the details that lessened the odds.

Puck hastened back to Berkeley Square and the mews behind the Hackett residence, then nipped into the narrow passageway that divided it from the equally impressive mansion directly next door to it. The two residences had been built so closely together that occupants of the houses could have, if they'd so desired, simply opened their windows and indulged in quiet conversations with their neighbor. Or listened *to* conversations. Or gotten a peek at their neighbor in his or her underclothes or caught them out in some compromising position.

Which were several of the many reasons that these

particular windows in both buildings were closed, and the drapes drawn, and both remained that way no matter what the time of day or the weather. The cobbled pathway still wasn't the perfect meeting place, and a tradesman with a delivery to either house could still appear and discover them, but they'd be here only for a few minutes, and, as Puck reasoned the thing, if he couldn't stare down a curious tradesman, then he didn't deserve to live.

And then she was there, and Puck forgot about everything else as he stepped out of the shadows and took her hands in his. "You bring the sun with you," he told her, "chasing away any shadows."

She tugged her hands free. "We don't have time for your nonsense," she warned him, and then added, "but...thank you."

"The pleasure, and the nonsense, remain mine. Tell me what happened after you left me last night," he said, not liking that she looked faintly drawn, even for all her beauty. She could not have passed a quiet night.

"I already told you that he saw me at the ball. I couldn't believe it! He didn't realize that Miranda had been taken. He thought perhaps she'd arranged an elopement or something with someone she'd planned to meet there. I told him what we believe, and all he had to say to that was that Uncle Seth will be applying to him for the money to hire Bow Street."

He took her hands again, and this time she didn't pull away. "Really? If he does, Regina, please tell me."

She tipped her head to one side. "Why?"

"Why? Let's just say that there is no such thing as too much knowledge when you're…getting to know someone. You should have given your father my name when he asked. I'll assume your refusal didn't delight him."

"He gave up asking quickly enough. But no, he wasn't happy. But that doesn't matter. What matters is how to save Miranda before it's too late. My father says it already is, that she's either ruined or dead or both, but I refuse to believe that. Why risk kidnapping the daughter of a viscount, the granddaughter of an earl, if you're only going to…that is, if you only want to—don't make me finish this sentence, Puck, please."

He squeezed her fingers. "I won't. But, informing me of your uncle's actions to one side, your involvement has to end now, Regina. That's the only reason I came here today. To tell you that."

She sighed. "I came here to tell you that you should forget about helping me, because it's too dangerous for you to continue seeing me. My father would definitely disapprove."

"Thanks to my parents' unmarried state," Puck said, nodding. "I understand that. Your father has set his sights considerably higher for his daughter's future."

She seemed relieved that he understood. "Yes. An earl, at the least. He's never made it a secret that I am the ladder he plans to climb to the next level of London Society."

"I'm sure he has your best interests at heart," Puck told her, watching her closely for her reaction to that statement. She simply didn't seem the sort who took orders cheerfully.

"He has his overweening ambition at heart, and I can see it in your eyes that you know that as well as I do. I mean no more to him than a fine cargo that will bring a top price in the marketplace. But it's Miranda who is important right now. My father believes even Uncle Seth will quickly realize that the last thing he wants is to have her back or even to learn what has happened to her. Certainly my aunt will never feel that way, but Uncle Seth is so weak, and if my father refuses to pay for the Runners, there really is little my uncle can do. If Miranda can be saved, I have to continue on my own."

"You actually mean that, don't you?" She was either insane, or the bravest woman he'd ever met. He preferred to believe the latter conclusion. "Would you care to tell me *how* you plan to effect this rescue?"

Once again, she withdrew her hands from his. But not her gaze. Her beautiful eyes looked straight into his, unflinchingly. "I don't know. I keep waiting for you to tell me not to be ridiculous, that we can continue to meet secretly somehow and that you will help me. I know I shouldn't be hoping for that, that I would be taking advantage of both your good nature and your... your interest in me. But I do desperately need help, and you seemed obstinate enough last night to be the sort of man to demand to do anything anyone said you shouldn't do."

Puck's laughter was instant if short-lived, as they were, after all, nearly within earshot of the street.

Reginald Hackett's reaction to learning that his daughter had been in the company of one of Blackthorn's bastards was easy to imagine. Allowing her within fifty yards of that same unsuitable bastard ever again would be out of the question. The man would go to great lengths to assure himself that such a thing would not happen.

At the same time, Puck had no notion of what the kidnapped Miranda looked like, which only complicated what was already a very large problem—finding one woman in the entire metropolis of London, even if he searched only in the area of the massive docks. He couldn't simply keep rescuing and dragging various unfortunate petite, blonde women to Number 23 Cavendish Square and asking, "Is this the right one?"

Not that he knew how to find and rescue *any* women at all.

Neither did Regina, but Puck felt sure she'd persist in her quest in any event. And *that* he could not allow!

Miranda wasn't the first petite, blonde Englishwoman to have turned up missing in the past weeks. How many were enough to set off to sea with and be guaranteed a profitable voyage? Were there still more to be found, carried off? Or had Miranda been the last one, the best one, the coup actually, and had already been hustled out of London on the morning tide?

But no. Like Regina, he would refuse to consider that. If her cousin was not found and rescued, brought safely back to the bosom of her family, Regina would never forgive herself, her own life would never be the same. Even if he couldn't have her, he couldn't live with himself if he didn't help her avoid that fate.

"Puck? Are you ever going to talk to me again?"

He shook himself from his thoughts and lifted her hands to his mouth, pressing a kiss against the fingers of each hand.

"You shouldn't do that," she told him, but without much conviction in her voice, so he ignored her protest.

"I've only one possible solution, and even I know it's preposterous."

"Preposterous. But not impossible?"

"And definitely dangerous. Even if you obey me in everything, which is essential to our hoped-for success but probably not a part of your nature."

"I can be cooperative. If I think you're right, that is."

"Perceive me, please, as now completely reassured. You're a tolerable actress, do you know that?"

She shook her head.

"Well, you are. You very nearly had me convinced that your mother had been in the coach with you last night. I don't know what you meant about the lemon squares, but whatever it was, it seemed quite believable. And your quick reactions earlier, on the street, were impeccable."

"You're being kind. My father called me a liar. And not a very good one at that. Why are we talking about this?"

So he told her his plan, the one he had come up with while waiting for her return from the park. He had been blessed, or at least born with, a devious mind.

The plan was preposterous. But not impossible.

He would go home and tell himself repeatedly that it was the only way. That he was saving Regina from herself and her determination to find her cousin on her own. That he knew there could be nothing between the two of them save a combined determination to rescue Miranda.

He could tell himself that.

But he wouldn't believe it. For while there was life, there was hope—and without hope, why bother living?

"PLEASE, PAPA, IT's the only answer, for any of us. Uncle Seth? You can see that, can't you?"

Reginald Hackett glared at Regina from behind his desk. A large desk, made especially for him and touted to be superior in size even to that of the Prime Minister himself. That sort of thing meant a lot to Reginald Hackett.

He had planned his private study carefully, filled the walls with portraits of nonexistent relatives, furnished the space with bookcases filled with books he'd never read: all those with red leather bindings placed together, those with blue on their own shelves, repeating the neat rows in all green, all brown, all black.

To Reginald, they were neat, orderly, expensive and therefore impressive. The practice was called "buying their books by the yard" by those in Society who knew a climbing cit when they saw one, however, and the purchaser laughed at by those who knew better.

But there was no one so foolish as to say any of

that to Reginald's face, most especially those who so happily pocketed his money. Such as the Viscount Ranscome, who was at that moment nervously sipping Geneva from his seat on one of his benefactor's custom-made leather couches.

It was two o'clock on Saturday afternoon, and Miranda had been missing since sometime before midnight the previous evening.

"Your uncle has three Runners hot on the chit's trail, Regina," Reginald pointed out, tapping a brass letter opener on the desktop. "For all we know, she could be home now. I still say she gulled you into believing she was abducted by—what was that you called them? Oh, yes. *Brigands.*"

"They might have been footpads," Regina conceded quietly.

She didn't know why her father was concealing from her uncle the fact that Miranda disappeared during the ball. Although she felt rather certain that it had at least something to do with keeping anyone else from ever learning that his daughter had attended Lady Fortesque's masquerade, knowledge of which would be a death knell to all his hopes for her advantageous marriage.

He turned to skewer the viscount with his black stare. "I say it was all a trick and Regina only a dupe. You said as much yourself, Seth, by telling me the coachie never returned to Cavendish Square, leaving that to one of the footmen while he disappeared into the night. There's a reason for that. He was in on it, plain and simple. Your precious daughter has run off with some fool, and she's probably been tipping back on her heels and laughing while you're over there looking like a man bedeviled. You're weak, Seth, weak and stupid. My Regina here would never try such a stunt on me. She knows who is in charge. Your family rides rough-shod over you."

Well, that was cleared up; Regina knew for certain now why her father hadn't brought up the subject of ex-actly *where* Miranda had been when she disappeared. No, not to protect her. To hide the fact that he did *not* have such a firm control of his daughter as he'd like his brother-in-law to believe. That made much more sense. Knowing she was about to make any stunt Miranda had ever tried look like an innocent stroll in the park, Regina lowered her head and began an intense inspec-tion of her intertwined fingers.

"I cannot go out into Society in any case," she re-minded both men. "Not without Miranda. Aunt Claire is entirely too overset to accompany me, and Mama…" She let that last bit hang out there for both men to con-sider. Leticia Hackett had heard the news about her niece and immediately taken refuge in her most trusted friend and companion, the fermented grape. She would never be able to withstand the pressures of having to go into Society and utter massive fibs about her niece's whereabouts. Why, by ten this morning she had con-vinced herself that not only had she been in the coach when it was attacked, but that she had attempted to defend her daughter and niece. That she had failed in that effort had driven her straight back into the wine decanter.

Regina felt terrible about this part of the deception, but only consoled herself that her mother's reaction would be that much worse if she knew the truth… that her daughter had been in attendance at what would probably soon be known as the debauch of the Season. Just the fact that Reginald's name had been on the guest list attested to the fact that the place had been opened to all sorts of unsuitable persons.

"What m'daughter is saying here, Seth, is that your sister is sailing three sheets to the wind upstairs and unlikely to return to harbor anytime soon."

"You shouldn't permit her drink," Seth said in defense of his sister but then seemed to think better of his small scold. "Although each soul finds solace in its own way."

"Letty likes the searching for it best," Reginald quipped, following this bit of wit with a laugh. "My wife's a drunk, Seth. Your sister is a sot. And you're a sponge. You and your father bleed me dry settling your gambling debts. Your idiot son has never been more than a total loss, and your daughter's a whore. Fine family I bought into, isn't it? You've been no bargain, the lot of you."

The viscount attempted to rise in protest but must have quickly remembered that sponges have no backbone—and no pockets filled with a brother-in-law's money—and sat down once more. "I think Regina's suggestion is a good one, as long as she's willing to make the sacrifice. You're a good girl, Regina," he said, turning to address the last words to his niece.

"I am only thinking of Miranda, Uncle. And yes, selfishly, about myself, as well. I would not be comfortable going through the remainder of the Season without her."

"Then you'd damn well better get used to it, because she won't be coming back, not from where she's gone."

The viscount lifted his head, which he'd been hanging between his hunched shoulders. "You say that as if you know, Reg. From where she's gone?"

Regina and her father exchanged looks. She thought he believed Miranda had run off of her own volition, even as he'd detailed for his daughter the horrific things that *could* have happened to her cousin. She'd even considered the idea that this was his strange way of cheering her aunt and uncle, trying to assure them that Miranda was a terrible, ungrateful child, yes, but not in any danger.

Now she didn't know what to think.

"Yes, Seth, from where she's gone. I'd be pointing the Runners toward Gretna if I were you, and considering it's my blunt paying for the trip, you'll damn well do what I say if you know what's good for you. Only chance you've got to pull this mess out of the middens before the stink grows too much for any of us. And pray she hasn't spread her legs yet. She won't be coming back into Society else-wise, that's what I'm saying, shaming herself like that. Look at that Brean girl. Sister to the earl, which is a damn spot higher than daughter of a penniless viscount and her just as to-let-in-the-pockets grandfather the earl. You don't see *her* trumpeting about town this year, do you, after running off with that Blackthorn bastard last year. Regina? Look at me. You heard that story, didn't you? *Blackthorn?*"

She nodded her head, unable to speak. She had heard the story last year, but she hadn't known the name of the man Lady Chelsea Mills-Beckman had run off with. *Blackthorn.* So he knew. Her father knew about Puck, had somehow ferreted out his name. That's what he was telling her now.

Regina fought the urge to spring to her feet and run from the room. Because Puck was wrong. She wasn't that much of an actress. Actresses don't feel their feet shaking in their shoes as they say their lines.

"She won't reach Gretna," the viscount said at last, getting to his feet and remaining upright. "I'll do as you said, Reg, and set the Runners north at once. But in the meantime, I can't see the harm in what Regina here is saying. I can put it out at my clubs. That Miranda has taken ill and the ladies are all retiring to Mentmore until she is recovered. That will serve to stop any gossip before it can start. Then, when the Runners find her, Miranda can be taken to Mentmore and everyone can return to town just as if nothing ever happened."

"If you approve, Papa," Regina said, deciding it was time she got back into the conversation. "I cannot enjoy the Season in any case, not now. We could be ready to depart tomorrow morning. And Mama always strives to…to be on her best behavior when in company with Grandfather."

"She doesn't drink as much when I'm not around," Reginald said, snorting. "That's what you mean." He picked up the letter opener and balanced it by its tips between his fingers, as if weighing his options. "Very well," he said at last. "But one week, no more. Then you're back here and I'll buy myself some turbaned besom to haul you around town. I'll have you settled this Season, you hear me?"

"Thank you, Reg," the viscount said fervently, all but bowing and scraping, like some low servant. "I'll be off now. Thank you, thank you."

Regina lifted her cheek for her uncle's kiss and then watched as he scurried out of the room before turning back to face her father. "Yes, thank you, Papa. I know Aunt Claire will be much relieved."

"The devil with your Aunt Claire's relief. The girl is gone, and that's that. You have one week in the country to get your head clear of your cousin and any notions of sneaking about town meeting up with that Blackthorn bastard. Not that he showed up in the park this morning, did he?"

"I don't know what you mean, Papa. In the park? I was there, yes, but merely out taking the—"

The letter opener went winging across the room to imbed itself in the dark oak paneling.

"Lie to your drunk of a mother. Lie to your uncle, to yourself. Lie to your God if you think you can get away with it—but don't ever lie to *me*. Not ever again."

"It…it was only so that I could thank him again for his rescue and to tell him goodbye," Regina said, frightened enough to reveal the truth but not so frightened that she'd own up to all of it. "He wasn't there."

"And don't tell me what I already know. Maybe the bastard's got more brains than I give him credit for, or he's heard about me. He may have come to your rescue last night, girlie, and for that I won't be chasing him down to break his neck for him. Let nobody say that Reg Hackett is not a fair man. But now we're even, him and me. Sees you again, and I'll break every bone in his body and leave his neck bone for last. You understand me, girl?"

"Yes, Papa," she said, nodding to confirm her words. She should leave the room now, delirious with her victory. But she had to ask her question. "You told me Miranda was abducted and ruined, perhaps even killed. Why did you tell Uncle Seth you're sure she's eloped to Gretna Green? Was that to spare him pain?"

Her father looked at her for a long moment before answering. "Yes. To spare him pain. I'm not the uncaring beast you sometimes believe I am, Regina. I've agreed to send you and your mother off with your Aunt Claire, haven't I, and all to protect your cousin's reputation?"

He'd just contradicted himself. He couldn't believe Miranda to have been abducted and killed, or shipped off to some foreign port, and still say that he was agreeing to action meant to preserve her reputation until she could be overtaken on her way to Gretna Green.

Regina thought it best not to point that out to him.

Instead, she steeled herself and walked around the desk to put her arms around his neck and kiss his cheek. "I'm so sorry, Papa. And I'm so ashamed to have been momentarily intrigued by Mr. Blackthorn, perhaps mistaking gratitude at his timely rescue for something more. I'll never lie to you again."

And with that lie, she left the study and climbed the stairs to her bedchamber, where she opened the side window that looked out to the closed drapes of the building not ten feet away. She slid a white handkerchief beneath the sill so that it could be seen from the ground before lowering the window once more.

Now to go tell her mother yet another lie: that they, along with Miranda's distraught mother, would be leaving for Mentmore Sunday morning at first light.

CHAPTER FIVE

PUCK DECIDED TO follow Dickie Carstairs. For one thing, he was the larger of the two men, and therefore easier to see—although that observation, mentioned to Gaston in passing, was mostly for his own amusement. The real reason for the decision was that the man's intelligence seemed to be not half that of his friend, Baron Henry Sutton.

The Honorable Mr. Richard Carstairs began his Saturday evening with a bird and a bottle partaken with three friends at his club, one of the minor clubs located at the bottom of Bond Street.

From there he made a solitary progression to the theater, Covent Garden, actually, where Puck, who would otherwise not have set foot into the place, endured a second-rate farce and the offerings of three warblers, one of whom actually owned a tolerable talent for carrying a tune someplace other than in a strong wooden bucket.

It was during the second intermission that the baron appeared, seemingly nonchalantly making his way across the crowded refreshment area to, entirely by accident, encounter Mr. Carstairs.

They both evinced some surprise upon seeing the

other, balanced their glasses awkwardly so that they
might shake hands, and then drifted apart once more,
Mr. Carstairs then promptly dropping the note the
baron had slipped to him via that handshake and looking about himself frantically in hopes no one else had
noticed, before scooping down to pick it up.

Truly, Puck thought as he stood in the shadows, sipping from his own wineglass, the farce that played out
during second intermission was by itself worth the cost
of admission.

Once more leaving the baron to his own devices
when the gong alerted the audience that the play on
the stage was about to recommence, Puck followed
behind Mr. Carstairs to assure himself that, yes, the
man indeed was reentering his private box.

But, all things considered—and Puck always made
it a point to consider everything—it was doubtful dear
Dickie would remain there for much longer. For that
reason, Puck inclined his head toward the ever-faithful
Gaston, who immediately left his place of concealment
in order to go down to the street and order the elegant
but unmarked black carriage be called to the front of
the building in anticipation of its owner's departure.

Within five minutes, the curtain on the afore-
mentioned private box was pushed back and Dickie
Carstairs emerged. Once again betraying himself by
looking left and right to assure himself he was unob-
served, he headed straight for the stairs that led down
to the foyer and the street beyond.

Digging holes. Yes, and even that is probably rather

above his expertise, Puck thought, pushing himself away from the wall and following after the man.

When he reached the street, the elegant black town coach was pulling up in front of the theater to inhabit the spot just vacated by the departure of another coach. This one, with its blue paint and yellow-accented wheels, was readily recognizable to anyone who had taken the time earlier in the week to make a passing inspection of the baron's stables.

With a wink to the grinning footman holding the door open to him, Puck entered the coach, and his coachman, brother to the footman and the pair of them years earlier rescued from an unhappy employment as rather unsuccessful housebreakers, immediately implemented the unspoken order to follow the first coach.

"Sometimes, Gaston," Puck said as he settled back against the comfortable squabs and shot his shirt cuffs, "it's almost too easy. However, if you were by any chance considering resting on your laurels, let me remind you that my brother Jack is not called Black Jack for nothing. He probably already knows we're on our way."

"How comforting to learn that one's younger sibling is not entirely a blockhead," drawled a familiar voice from the dark that enveloped the facing seat.

"Your pardon, *m'sieur,*" Gaston apologized fervently. "He took me by surprise, as well. If you were now to lower the knife, kind brother of my *m'sieur?*"

Puck slapped his knees and laughed out loud. "Jack!

You're following them, as well? Don't trust your own compatriots, do you?"

Jack slipped the knife back into the top of his boot. "I trust them to realize they're being followed, if that's your question. I'll admit to being mildly surprised to see you on Dickie's tail earlier this evening."

Puck shrugged in his elegant way. "My fault. I was so busy looking out for what was in front of me that I neglected to look behind me. Considering that I'm rather out of favor with a certain somebody at the moment, that could have proved a fatal mistake. Clumsy. Shame on me."

"The *m'sieur* is too kind," Gaston said, and then sighed heavily. "It is I who was to have his back tonight. It is I who has failed."

"Well, isn't this lovely. The two of you, gallantly trying to shift the blame away from each other. That's the problem with both of my brothers, isn't it? Soft hearts. Soft hearts lead to soft heads, you know, and soft heads are more easily crushed."

Puck made a face in the darkness. "You should write for the stage, Jack. Don't hold a candle to Will Shakespeare, but that drivel might do well enough for some provincial theater."

Now it seemed to be Jack's turn to laugh, but it was a short-lived relaxation of tension between the brothers. "I won't ask why you're following Dickie, for that's self-explanatory. But what do you want with me? Oh, and don't fret about our destination. Henry's coachman has been warned that he is to proceed slowly enough that yours doesn't lose him."

"How you ease my mind," Puck said, that mind actually racing at least three leagues beyond the simple matter of their destination. "Our parents are in good health, or were when I last saw them before coming to town. You did mean to inquire about them, I'm sure."

"I did? No, I don't think so."

"Really? Then you don't know that Papa wishes to speak to all three of us together, at the estate?"

"All three of us? At one and the same time? He may be doomed to disappointment."

"Especially if our mother is there?" Puck opined, wishing there was more light inside the coach so he could see his brother's expression, not that the man ever gave anything away. "I never believed you're afraid of her. And yet you were so careful to avoid her last year, when we buried Abigail."

"We buried the Marchioness of Blackthorn, our mother's sister. I paid my respects to Abby, which was all that was necessary."

"Yes, you did. In the dead of night, with none but the servants to know about it before you were off on your way again. Mama nearly suffered an apoplexy when she spied the token you'd left behind." Puck waved a hand in front of him to erase the words. "No, let's not travel there right now, shall we? I originally wanted to find you tonight to tell you about Papa's request. He really does want all three of us at Blackthorn."

"So he only has to say once whatever it is that he seems to think he needs to say?"

Puck nodded. "Yes, whatever that thing is. He was going to tell Beau last year, as Beau tells it, but then changed his mind when Abby...when the Marchioness died. I would like to be able to tell Papa you'll agree to come to the estate, even give him a date for the thing. Sometime other than in the dead of night would probably be preferable. He's not growing younger with each passing year, Jack, and he apparently feels he needs to say what it is he wants to say as soon as may be. Not that Mama approves."

"I'm sure she wouldn't," Jack said tightly. "You may inform the marquess that I'll give his request some consideration. But not at the moment, I'm afraid. I've other business that will keep me occupied for a time."

"One question, Jack. Which of the two do you hate more? Our mother or our father?"

Gaston slowly sank low onto his spine as he sat beside Black Jack.

"The puppy has grown fangs, I see," Jack said, reaching out to hold on to the strap as the coach turned a particularly sharp corner, revealing the shape of one strong, long-fingered hand, a discreet fall of lace extending from his cuff and a large, black onyx stone set in gold adorning his index finger.

"The puppy hasn't been a puppy for a long time, Jack. And I'm only two years your junior. I propose a pact. I won't again underestimate you if you agree not to underestimate me."

"After the way you've turned the tables on Henry and Dickie, neatly maneuvering them into introducing you to Society? Be careful of Will Browning, he's no man's fool. He might even make a good ally, should you ever need one. But all right. Agreed. Now, what was the second reason you wanted to see me tonight? Telling me about the marquess's summons was only the original one."

"Caught that, did you?" Puck was more than happy to leave the subject of their parents behind them and move on to other, actually safer, ground. He did not underestimate himself, either, but he would be a fool and unfair to the missing Miranda if he did not avail himself of all the help he could enlist.

"The cousin of a friend of mine was, just last night, abducted for reasons unknown but not difficult to be guessed at, given the small evidence so far in my possession."

"Really. And the names of these persons?"

"Are known to me," Puck said silkily. "Suffice it to say that the female who has gone missing is petite, blonde and supposedly quite beautiful. Pure, as it were, and of good family. Only cursory inquiry provided me with the unsettling information that hers is not the first disappearance of a petite, blonde and supposedly quite beautiful young woman here in London in the past weeks. I cannot, of course, vouch for the pureness of any of them. Only the one. I have promised my friend that I will do all in my power to find the one and return her safely to her family."

"Did you now," Jack said quietly. "How very deter-mined of you, I'm sure. Even commendable. And have you spent any time cudgeling your brain as to *why* these females have, as you say, disappeared? And, even more to the point, how do you propose to get *the one* back?"

Puck very nearly obliged his brother by opening his mouth and telling him things he hadn't planned to reveal now, if ever. But then he remembered something. A few somethings.

His brother was his own man, yes. Very much so. But he did at times share his talents with the Crown, as he had been doing last year when Beau and Puck encountered him in Gateshead along with the baron, Dickie, and the unfortunate and most likely now-deceased Noah.

The Crown, although understandably unconcerned with the disappearance of a few females from the lower orders, could not possibly look happily on the notion that its citizens could be removed from its shores with impunity, to be sold as so much merchandise in some-one else's country. Especially its women.

Jack was in London. That didn't mean he had been there long or that he was frequently in the city. Again, the evidence of Gateshead, nearly as far away as the Scottish border, proved otherwise.

And he was here because of some *new assignment,* according to the note Wadsworth had found in Dickie Carstairs's hatband.

So instead of revealing his own plans, especially the more bizarre portions of them, Puck took a chance and said instead, "I think, Jack, if you don't mind, that I'd rather first hear *your* plans for recovering the young women and putting a stop to such a heinous practice. If I agree with them, I may allow you and your bumbling friends to join me."

Gaston pushed himself back to his usual erect posture and smiled so widely that, even in the darkness inside the coach, his white teeth were visible. "Puppy? *Bah, m'sieur* Black Jack, I think *not!*"

REGINA HAD LEFT THE DETAILS to Puck, who had then informed her that she would know them when he did, as an hour spent cooling his heels in an alleyway waiting for her had been not sufficient time to do more than come up with the basics of a plan.

He'd asked her to trust him, and because she had no other choice and because he was so confident, she did so.

He'd also told her not to worry, which had been a waste of his breath for she had worried all night long and continued to worry now.

"Mama, please don't concern yourself with that," she said now, watching as her mother looked about her, counting the few pieces of luggage now lined up in the entrance hall, the special pieces that would travel with them inside the coach. "Hanks has seen to everything, for both of us."

Lady Leticia continued her inventory. She moved slowly, carefully, probably in the belief that then everyone would believe her sober, but the servants were well-acquainted with their mistress's ways.

Poor Mama. She'd once been so pretty. Now she looked tired all of the time, and defeated, her blue eyes so sad and empty, the corners of her mouth perpetually turned down. And she still lacked two years before her fortieth birthday. Her youth had left her early along with any spirit she might once have possessed.

"Yes, dear, but I do not see my special traveling case. I cannot depart without my special traveling case. It… it was a gift from my dearest, departed mother."

The case, in point of fact, had been a purchase in Bond Street a dozen years earlier, fitted out inside to hold a half dozen wine bottles and a supply of glasses. Regina inwardly scolded herself for believing, if only for a moment, that her mother wouldn't notice its absence.

"Hanks?" she said, looking at the maid, who curtsied and then immediately turned and headed for the servant stairs, off to retrieve the case. They had earlier agreed to allow the case if Mama seemed about to make a fuss. If she made a fuss, Papa might hear, and the last thing Regina wanted was to have her father come into the entrance hall, asking what the problem was and perhaps changing his mind and disallowing the trip.

"And I don't see why Fellows couldn't accompany us. Sharing your maid like this? It will appear cheeseparing. You know your father does not wish us ever to look cheeseparing. He became out of reason cross with me when I suggested you did not need more than a dozen gowns for a proper Come-out, if we just changed the ribbons and such on them from time to time. He does not want to ever look cheeseparing."

Regina suppressed a sigh. Her mother lived her entire life attempting to avoid doing anything that might upset her husband. He'd never hit her, as far as Regina knew, just as he'd never physically punished Regina herself. Which had left her to think that the threat he used to keep his daughter in line was the same one he employed to keep his wife obedient, terrified and constantly seeking solace in her wine bottles.

Regina knew that hate was a sin, but she at least very much disliked her father—and her grandfather, who had as good as sold his daughter in order to pay his gambling debts. And, of the two of them, she probably despised her grandfather more. *He* was of the upper classes, an earl, and should have been above such things. Reginald Hackett was Grandmother Hackett's son. No better should have been expected of him.

She patted her mother's arm. "We're traveling to Mentmore, Mama. No one will be counting noses there. Fellows has been charged with overseeing a complete refreshing of both your bedchamber and mine in our absence. That's all been settled, remember?"

In truth, Fellows had been put to the daunting task of ferreting out any and all of Lady Leticia's carefully hidden stores of strong spirits and disposing of them. From attics to cellars, this was a task that would occupy Fellows until their return, for her employer had no end of cunning tricks. Even her cut-glass perfume flasks were not immune.

"No," Lady Leticia said sadly. "I don't remember. But if you do, then I suppose I should, as well. It will be good to see Mentmore again. Your father does not often approve of me being there."

"And Aunt Claire will be with us, to bear you company," Regina reminded her as a pair of footmen held open the double doors that led down to the Square, two more servants holding large umbrellas over their heads, as the morning was both gray and very wet. The crested Mentmore coach stood waiting for them. "Look—she is already in the coach, Mama, waving to us."

"Claire has always been kind. She was sold, too, you know. Her grandfather was a haberdasher in Queen Street. Quite wealthy, and they were said to have been very fine hats. I never saw one, but they must have been excellent. Good enough, at least, to buy her papa a viscount. Pity it was Seth. The hats should have bought finer than that."

"Mama, quietly," Regina said, although the servants certainly had heard the woman. "Ah, and here is Hanks, and your traveling case. Now up you go, Mama, and we'll be off."

She handed her mother over to the servant holding the umbrella over the woman's head and took a moment to surreptitiously cast her gaze around the Square. They were about to climb into the family coach and be driven off to Mentmore. Yes, that had been the plan, as Puck had told her it yesterday, but she still had hoped to see him here somewhere, to be certain he had been able to turn his broad strokes into a more detailed plan.

She at last looked up at the luggage strapped to the roof of the coach, covered in canvas tarps, and smiled her first real smile of the day.

From his seat up on the box behind the horses, Robin Goodfellow Blackthorn, his long, blond hair hanging loose beneath his dripping slouch hat, the coachman greatcoat bearing the Mentmore crest on its back protecting him from the rain, inclined his head in her direction and winked.

PUCK, FRESH FROM HIS BATH after the soaking he'd endured during the earlier downpour, and once more dressed in his usual fashionably cut clothes, his hair tied back at his nape, reclined at his ease in the Grosvenor Square drawing room, one ear cocked as he waited to hear footsteps on the black-and-white marble tile in the entrance hall.

The wait seemed interminable, but at last he was rewarded for his patience. He put down his wineglass and got to his feet just in time to turn a welcoming smile toward Regina as she entered the room, looking about her at the understated splendor that was the Blackthorn mansion.

She looked weary, as if the past two hours had not been easy for her, and he hadn't supposed they would be, at least not until she was allowed to explain to two distraught women that no, they had not been kidnapped, like the unfortunate Miranda.

He put a finger to his lips and walked past her to close the double doors, which would give them some privacy, before he held his hands out toward her. She took them, allowed him to lead her over to the sofa he had just vacated.

"They've agreed?" he asked her as they sat down facing each other, searching her face for some hint as to how his plan was progressing thus far.

"I don't think Mama fully understands yet," she told him and sighed. "Hanks brought her the traveling case, much as I wished not to resort to such a thing. She's sleeping now. Aunt Claire both surprised and embarrassed me by throwing herself on my neck in gratitude. She hadn't wanted to leave London at all, in case Miranda somehow found her own way back to Cavendish Square. I still can't believe we've done it. You're brilliant."

"Be sure to have that put on my tombstone, if you please, after I'm hanged for kidnapping and other assorted crimes."

He was immediately sorry he'd teased her, for Regina's eyes went wide and she squeezed his hands with all her might.

"But no one will know," she said quickly. "We departed in the Mentmore coach, and for all anyone knows, we're already well out of the city and on our way to my grandfather's estate." She tipped her head to one side. "How did you manage that, by the way?"

He still couldn't believe she was here, beneath his roof. Well chaperoned, of course, perhaps even *overly* chaperoned. He should probably kiss her now before one or the other of them realized she was no longer upstairs and came searching for her. But he'd made himself that damn promise to be a gentleman.

"Does it matter?"

"Yes, of course it does. You should be exceedingly proud of your genius and be longing to impress me with the retelling of the adventure. It was an adventure, wasn't it?"

He smiled. "Only a small one. If you'll recall, your uncle's precious coachman was turned off the other night. I merely introduced myself and my few companions as new hires of your uncle, instructed to transport the ladyship and her female relatives to someplace called Mentmore. When the order came round to the stables not ten minutes later for the coach to be ready to travel first thing in the morning, there wasn't anyone who thought to question what I'd said."

"I'll say it again. Brilliant! You really are brilliant."

"I'll concede the point, since you insist. The coach is now draped in canvas and locked up tightly in my stables until your return to London a week hence."

"And we are free to begin our pursuit of Miranda without having to worry that my father will know of it." Regina blinked back tears. "My aunt is beyond distraught, and I feel so very guilty. If I had only insisted the coach be turned about…"

"We might never have met," Puck supplied as she seemed close to tears. "We most certainly would not have kissed. And that," he said as he leaned toward her, "would have been a tragedy."

He touched his mouth lightly to hers, their hands still clasped together. He watched as her eyes fluttered close and a small sigh escaped her lips. He touched his tongue to hers, and she moaned low in her throat.

Slowly, Robin Goodfellow, he warned himself. *There are no masks between us now. No moonlight.*

They touched only at mouth and knee, and yet he felt the heat of her burning into his body, setting it aflame. In his mind's eye, she was already upstairs, in his bed, her dark hair flowing across his pillow, her arms reaching up to draw him down to her.

What he would do to her, where they would go, together. She was fire, she had been born to the flame, her body fashioned for pleasure. To give it, to receive it. Even now, still unawakened, she responded to his touch with some innate knowledge whispered into her ear by Eve while still in the womb. She would prove a lusty, greedy lover, she would dare anything, demand everything, and she would give as good as she got. Together, they could ignite the world.

He skillfully bunched up the thin skirt of her muslin gown and slid his hand under the material, walking his fingers along her inner thigh. And then hesitated.

Don't. Not now. Not yet. You promised yourself. In your idiocy, you promised yourself.

She squirmed slightly where she sat and relaxed her muscles. Eased open her knees.

Jesus.

The silk of her lace-edged undergarment was the coarsest wool when compared to the treasure beneath. Here she was liquid fire, dangerous to touch, impossible to defend against as some of that fire transferred itself to him through his seeking fingers, to course through him, ignite small blazes at his every nerve ending.

He continued kissing her, telling her without words what he would do to her if they were anywhere but where they were. And she knew. She had to know, because she returned his heat with more of her own until his expertise combined with her eagerness. She tore her mouth from his, buried her head against his shoulder and gave in to the ecstasy.

So much for resolve.

Puck attempted to conceal his own struggle for breath, the self-control he was drawing on in order to tamp down his still-alert passions.

He lifted her chin with his hand and looked deeply into her wondrous blue eyes. She was calming, but slowly. He could still see the heat of passion in her eyes. And bless her, no hint of regret. *"Million de pardons, mais aucunes excuses."* A million pardons, but no excuses.

"There's no need for either," she told him quietly. "I tried to forget what you told me Friday, at the masquerade. When you believed I was something that you later believed I was not. I think…I think you were correct the first time. Even your words, remembering them, make my body go all warm and strange inside. I haven't been able to stop thinking about what you said to me in the gardens. In French, as you did again now."

Puck remembered. Every last suggestive, lascivious word, directed, he had mistakenly believed, to a woman of the world, impossible to shock. "I never should have said those things."

"I could say that I never should have listened as long as I did or allowed your kisses...your touch. I'd been holding the hat pin ready from the moment we entered the gardens. You didn't know who I was and had no reason to believe I was anything more than you believed. It was I who knew myself or thought I did. You make me feel so good, and I'm not ashamed to tell you that I like how you make me feel. Alive. You make me feel so *alive,* Puck. Of course, I'd also like to blame Grandmother Hackett for the reason I'm being so brazenly forward and unashamed, but that would only be self-serving."

Puck got to his feet, feeling it safer to put some space between them, as his mind might be thinking nominally normally once more, but his body was still busy considering different plans. So much so that he discreetly positioned his lower body behind the back of a chair.

"I think I need to hear about Grandmother Hackett."

She smiled rather ruefully. "Very well. Other children may have been warned about monsters lurking beneath their beds or that the Gypsies would carry them off if they were bad or refused to finish their porridge. I had Grandmother Hackett. And still do," she ended, sighing.

"She was a terror?"

Regina shrugged. "I never met her. However, everything about me that might not be pleasing to my mother is laid at the woman's door. I'm sometimes sorry she died shortly before I was born and that I never met her. Mama said she picked her teeth at the table and had very large bosoms and was forever talking—loudly and no matter what the company—about her many lovers before and since the dear, departed Joseph Hackett. All, of course, completely unforgivable behavior."

"Oh, yes. Completely. Is there more?"

"Much more. I don't know if it's true, but once, when Mama was rather agitated by something, she confided in me that Grandmother Hackett and Grandfather Mentmore had been discovered by Grandmother Mentmore as they *indulged* themselves in the conservatory. Grandmother Mentmore threw a handy pail of water on them, and that's why Grandmother Mentmore owned at least one diamond necklace that wasn't made of paste."

"Ha!"

"Isn't that strange? I also found it all rather funny, although I never shared that with Mama." But then all hint of humor left her eyes. "Puck?"

He instantly sobered. He'd tried to divert her, get past their recent…intentness. "Yes?"

"Aunt Claire is incensed with my Uncle Seth. He's done as my father ordered, and sent the Runners off toward Gretna Green. My aunt pleaded with him to reconsider, but since my father is paying for the Runners, Uncle Seth feels he must do as he says."

Puck tucked that information away, knowing he now had the man even more firmly in his pocket should he need him. "Your aunt doesn't believe Miranda eloped?"

"No," Regina said quietly. "I told her the truth yesterday afternoon when I visited her in order to tell her that we'd be leaving London. All of it, even about the masquerade. I...I showed her the few beads I had from Miranda's mask. My aunt recognized them as Uncle Seth wore that mask years ago, when the two of them had gone to masquerade balls. They were much more proper then, she told me." She looked at him as if begging him to understand. "I knew she'd be devastated, of course, to realize what Miranda and I had done, but I felt she also would be more cooperative when the coach stopped here."

"I only hope I can alleviate her fears entirely by safely returning her daughter to her."

"You've already helped her. She feels that at least she is doing *something,* being here, and she wants you to contact her grandfather in Queen Street if you would, because she is convinced he will give you any assistance you might need, although her father, she told me, is a total loss."

"Mad as a hatter, is he?" Puck asked her, unable to restrain himself. He'd heard one learned man's opinion that the chemicals hatters dealt with in the making of hats had turned more than one man into a raving lunatic.

Regina nodded. "Like so many of them. Isn't that strange? He's quite insane and locked up somewhere. In any event, Aunt Claire has promised to help with my mother should she prove difficult, leaving me even greater freedom to assist you. You didn't lie to me about that, did you? You're really going to let me help?"

"Yes, even as I admit that the most overpowering reason for involving you this way is to keep you from involving yourself without me."

She nodded soberly, agreeing with his reasoning. "What I don't understand is why my father insisted the Runners be sent north. He made it painfully clear to me that first night that Miranda has been taken by strangers, and now he's insisting she has eloped. He says it's to ease my aunt and uncle's fears, but what is that to the point, if everyone is now looking for Miranda in all the wrong places?"

Puck returned to the couch and sat down once more. He really did need to get to know Reginald Hackett better. "He might believe it would be worse for them if she was found. Or worse for you, in terms of the Marriage Mart."

"Dead or ruined or both," Regina said, nodding her head. "What are we going to do?"

For a moment he debated the wisdom of telling her about Jack but then decided against it. Most especially since Jack didn't know about Regina. Jack didn't share information easily, and what was good for the goose worked equally for the gander. They would meet if they had need to, if either of them discovered anything, and that was enough: Jack hunting hard for the head, Puck searching for the tail. Between them, they might just be successful.

"We aren't the only ones searching for Miranda, or at least they're on the hunt for the men who took her and the others who've disappeared. However, we know when and where Miranda was taken, which gives us more information than may be available to the others. Are you amenable to returning to the scene of the abduction, Regina?"

"Really? *Now?*" She hopped to her feet, clearly more than up to the challenge. "How will we go about it? I mean, will I need to disguise my appearance?"

He stood up, as well. "Unfortunately, London isn't Venice, and the accepted practice of wearing masks everywhere has fallen somewhat out of fashion even there. That bonnet you had on yesterday and keeping your head bowed or turned as often as possible will have to suffice until I can make other arrangements."

"Other arrangements? You'll forgive me if I ask what those are?"

"I'm afraid you'll have to ask that of my man, Gaston. He's even now visiting a costumer near Covent Garden."

She flashed one of her gorgeous smiles, but then it quickly vanished. "No! I will *not* enjoy any of this. Will we be sneaking out your back door?"

"That seems reasonable, yes," he told her and extended his arm so that she took it as they headed toward the entrance hall. "Did you remember to bring along the miniature you said you have of your cousin?"

"The locket? Yes, I did. It's upstairs. Wait for me here."

"I'd wait for you anywhere," he drawled smoothly as he bowed to her, earning a quick laugh before he had the pleasure of watching her lift up her skirts and fairly race up the stairs.

Five minutes later, the brim on her bonnet doing an only fair job of concealing her features, they were in an unmarked coach and on their way to the site of Lady Fortesque's masquerade ball.

CHAPTER SIX

REGINA PULLED BACK the curtain, enough to see the large, rather ramshackle building they had just stopped in front of, and frowned. "Oh, goodness. I had no idea it was so…ordinary. It's rather like a warehouse of some sort? And the neighborhood is not quite the best, is it?"

"Many things look better in the dark," Puck told her as the footman opened the door and put down the steps. "Remember, keep your head averted or downcast as much as possible. And a handkerchief to your face probably wouldn't come amiss."

She did as he said and soon was deposited on the wet cobblestones, her heart pounding with excitement and not a little remembered fear. She removed the handkerchief to say something to him and then quickly replaced it when the smell of what could have been rotting fish assailed her nostrils. "Oh, I don't remember *that,* either."

Puck laughed and pointed to a building on the opposite side of the street. There were tables standing on the cobblestones in front of it, piled high with fish. "We were in the gardens, such as they are, on the opposite end of the building. All right," he said, taking her hand in his. "Here we go."

"Yes, here we go," Regina repeated as they headed for the steps leading to the front door of the building. "Where are we going? There won't be anyone still here since Friday night, will there?"

"The fellows working as servants at the ball are, in actuality, employed by the owner of this building, which I've learned serves any number of purposes. Gaming house...other words that end in *house* I won't bore you with, I believe. One of the servants in particular, one Davy Tripp, was most helpful to me the other evening. I've also already taken it upon myself to learn that the employees sleep as well as work within the confines of this lovely establishment. Now tell me again— I'm brilliant, correct?"

"I was thinking you're smug, actually," Regina told him as he rapped on the door with the walking stick she hadn't noticed in his possession until that moment. "Is that a swordstick? I've never seen a swordstick, but I have read about them."

"It is," he said quietly. "But perhaps you'll allow me to postpone a demonstration of its finer qualities. I don't think any of the gentlemen inside would be much amused."

She shrugged. "Are you adept with it? You can at least tell me that."

"Let's just hope we don't have to find out in the next five minutes." Then he stepped rather in front of her as the door opened. "Ah, my good man. I am here to speak with one Davy Tripp, if you please."

Regina peeked around Puck's shoulder to see a

mountain of a man all but filling up the doorway. He had hands the size of hams, wore an enormous leather apron made shiny with fish scales around his middle, and his face appeared to have been used as an anvil, repeatedly. His features were all but *smeared* across his large, round face, and he had no more than three hairs on his shiny, bald head. If she had been the sort to make up imaginary monsters for her children one day, she couldn't do much better than to recount the man standing in front of her and Puck now.

And then the man spoke. His voice was higher than hers and quite thin.

She almost giggled.

"Davy, you say? Went off out back jist now with some other gentry mort what promised 'im a pot o' blunt fer doin' nuthin' but talkin' ta 'im. Davy, what don't know nuthin'. Yer wants ter talk, mate? That there Davy gots all the luck. I kin talk. Say anythin' yer like ter hear, sing yer a ditty or two iffen yer like. If yer show me some silver."

Puck grabbed Regina's hand. "Come on!" he commanded tersely. He'd just thrown a coin down the steps, which was as good as tossing a marrowbone and not having to order the dog to *fetch*. The very large man with the strangely tiny voice bolted past them both in pursuit of the coin, and Puck and Regina were inside the building, running toward the bank of doors she vaguely remembered dancing through with Puck two short nights ago.

"What's wrong?" she managed as she did her best to keep up with him. "Puck?"

"No time. Just keep running. No, not fast enough. Don't stop. Follow me!" He let go of her hand and ran ahead, his long legs quickly eating up the distance, even as suddenly he was holding something shining and thin and deadly-looking in his left hand. The dozen or more men milling about in the empty hall or idly standing over their brooms all turned to watch, none of them paying the least attention to the lone female in their midst.

Then, as if at some secret signal, they all turned as one and ran after Puck.

By the time Regina reached the doorway, a hand held to her side, pressed against the stabbing sensation that had overtaken her, she had to fight her way through the throng to reach the gardens.

"Puck!"

He was down on one knee beside someone who was prone on the path and in the process of returning the swordstick to its place of concealment.

"'Better three hours too soon, than one minute too late,'" he said, rising to his feet as she raced toward him.

She looked down at the young man. He looked up at her, his eyes wide as saucers, his chest rising and falling rapidly, as if he had been the one to have just run the full length of a very large building and not while wearing his most comfortable shoes. "What?" she asked distractedly. "What did you just say?"

"Only some remembered Shakespeare. *The Merry Wives of Windsor,* in point of fact, not that it matters. Forgive me for running ahead of you, Regina. He's all right, only a tad flummoxed by all this attention. Aren't you, Davy? Here, take my hand and stand up now. The bad man is gone."

"There was a bad man?" Regina clapped her hands to her chest. "Oh, God. There was a bad man? *Really?* Did you—did you stick him?"

"Would you have liked it if I had? That may color my answer."

She turned her most heated look on him. He seemed happy. How dare he seem happy? "I don't find any of this to be the slightest bit amusing, Robin Goodfellow."

"And Davy here probably agrees with you, don't you, Davy?"

The boy—he really was little more than a boy— nodded his head up and down several times, with some feeling.

"And now, Davy would very much appreciate coming with us. Wouldn't you, Davy?"

The boy nodded again but then looked at the sword-stick that was simply an innocent walking stick once more. He attempted to turn on his heels and bolt, but Puck was too fast for him.

"Ah-ah, you don't want to do that. Only think, Davy. The bad man. He wasn't quite finished with you, was he?"

Davy lifted a dirty hand and lightly touched his cheek, which, Regina noticed, was beginning to turn a very angry purple. "I'm guessin' I'll be goin' with you, guv."

"He hit you? The bad— I mean, the person hit you? Why?"

"Not here, Regina. I count roughly a dozen interested parties in the vicinity, which is twenty-four ears too many."

"Oh," she said, remembering their audience. "We should go somewhere else, shouldn't we?"

"What a splendid idea," Puck said brightly, and suddenly she longed to box his two ears.

But she took the arm he offered her as, with Davy following closely behind, they made their way back inside the building, taking their time as they traversed the length of it. Puck had whispered to her that he did not wish them to appear as less than confident, which running for the coach would most certainly do. And he nonchalantly twirled his sword cane once or twice, in case anyone had forgotten its existence.

At some point he'd tucked the sword cane beneath his arm, and now he was using his free hand to flick some imaginary dust from his lapel. Anyone would think he wasn't paying the least attention to the men following after them, but Regina felt certain that he knew exactly how far away the closest man was, and that the man knew that, as well.

Puck confirmed her suspicion with his next words. "Don't look back, love. You would make a charming pillar of salt, but I much prefer you the way you are."

"I understand. We'll chat, shall we? As if we're

taking a stroll in the park. I'll start. How did you know?" she asked him.

"How did I know what?"

"Don't be obtuse," she said, but quietly, as the building that had been so overcrowded with palm trees and couches and screens was now home only to echoes of everyone's footsteps. "How did you know that Davy was in trouble?"

Puck tipped his hat to the very large man with the very tiny voice as they regained the street, and he helped her back into the coach. "I didn't. But as there were only two options open to me, one inevitable at some point, the other perhaps much more unpleasant for our new friend here, I decided that thinking the worst might be in Davy's best interest. Oh no. No, no, no, Davy. Delighted as I am to renew our acquaintance of the other evening, I believe you and your unique fragrance might best be served by sitting up on the box with my coachman. There's a good fellow. Anders here will assist you, won't you, Anders."

The young man pulled at his rather greasy forelock and allowed himself to be led away by the footman.

Regina then waited until Puck had settled himself beside her and the coach was once more set in motion before she asked her next question. "You said you had two options open to you. One inevitable, the other much more unpleasant for Davy."

"I did? No, I'm sorry. I think you're mistaken."

She put a hand on his forearm and squeezed her fingers. "Puck, by all that is reasonable, I should be collapsed in strong hysterics right now, and I am still considering *my* options in the matter, so don't try to fob me off as if I didn't hear what I heard."

He looked down at her hand and then straight into her eyes. "I only thought we'd speak with our friend Davy, and that he could take a look at that miniature you brought with you. But I shouldn't have brought you. I should have delivered you to Grosvenor Square to keep you safe from yourself, yes, but then I should have tied you to the bedpost with a stout rope and not let you out of the house until your cousin was recovered."

"Because of what happened back there?"

He sighed, rolling his eyes. "No. Because the weather remains rather damp, and I wouldn't wish for you to take a chill."

She let go of his hand and turned to face forward on the seat once more. "If you don't wish to answer my perfectly reasonable question, then don't. There's no need to be snide."

"Snide? Me? Or are you going to tell me that you enjoyed yourself back there?"

Her bottom lip began to tremble, and she hated herself for such weakness. "I was frightened straight down to my shoe tops. I didn't know what was happening. I still don't!"

He lifted his left arm and placed it around her shoulders, pulling her closer against him. "Very well, then. The truth. It is odd enough for one *gentry cove* to come looking for someone like Davy Tripp and even more odd for the boy to have two visitors in the same day. Agreed?"

"Agreed," Regina said, enjoying the way Puck was idly stroking her upper arm as he spoke. He'd held the swordstick in his left hand. He was left-handed. She wasn't sure if she'd ever met another left-handed person. He touched her as if he'd been touching her forever, as if touching her was the most natural thing in the world for him to be doing. She certainly felt *natural,* being touched by him. And only two days ago she hadn't even met him. Life was so strange.

"Good. Ergo, as we had come looking for information, it would be reasonable to believe that the other visitor had come on the same mission."

"And again, agreed," she said, snuggling a little closer.

"Ah, just the way I like my females. Agreeable. Ouch! Has anyone ever told you that you have very sharp elbows?"

"I also have my hat pin. You could move along a little faster, Puck. I think I can keep up."

"You're probably already leagues ahead of me. All right. About those options of mine. The first could have been that someone not quite as congenial as ourselves had come to speak with Davy, or even to assure himself that friend Davy never spoke again to anyone."

"I saw the bruise on his cheek. Someone hit him."

"*Someone* had been in the act of sticking a knife into our new friend's middle when I joined the party, as it were. My blade diverted his."

"Oh," Regina said, suddenly not quite so comfortable as she'd been a moment earlier.

"Yes, *oh*. Unfortunately, our Mr. Tripp, grateful in the extreme for my timely intervention, immediately clapped his arms about my legs, and the bad man made good his escape. The bruise you noticed on Davy's cheek is a result of me, attempting to kick free of him. It wasn't poetry, none of it, and I'm rather glad you weren't there to witness my supposed heroics."

"You rescued him, and then you *kicked* him?" Regina's bottom lip trembled again, this time not with the effort to keep back tears, but laughter. "Oh, Puck."

"Not my finest hour, I know. Now, before you ask again, my other option as I ran to the rescue was that I would be rescuing Davy from my brother. Jack."

Regina shook her head. "No. I don't understand."

"Don't let it vex you. Nobody understands Jack," Puck said as the coach stopped in the mews behind the mansion. "Handkerchief to your face again, if you please, as we dash in through the kitchens."

She did as he said, running ahead of him as he lingered to give orders to someone concerning Davy Tripp.

He rejoined her in the drawing room within minutes and went immediately to the drinks table to pour himself a glass of wine. "Wadsworth is seeing to lemonade for you. And some cakes or cookies of some sort."

Regina looked longingly at the wineglass now in Puck's hand. She'd had a fright. A most terrible fright. Having survived it, she did not believe lemonade was quite up to soothing her still raw nerves. But then she remembered the sweet, honeyed brew she'd so enjoyed the other evening at the masquerade, and decided that strong drink might be her mother's *companion,* but she did not wish to make it hers. "Thank you."

"And thank you," he said, sitting down beside her and lifting her hand to his mouth, depositing a kiss in her palm. "You were very brave."

"I don't believe I had a choice," she pointed out, and he smiled at her as if she'd just said something wonderful. "Now tell me more about your brother. Jack. I already know about another brother. Beau, I think? He ran off with Lady Chelsea Mills-Beckman last Season."

"Really? To hear Beau tell it, it was she who was in charge of that particular expedition. I was an innocent party to most of it, dragged into the adventure with great reluctance, of course, and if asked, I'd have to say you might wish to put more credence in the latter conclusion."

"She kidnapped him? Is that what you're saying? I don't believe you."

"No, I don't, either. I believe the word I'd use is *coerced.* Yes, that's better. And, just for the record, if you were to *coerce* me into some mischief, I believe I could be persuaded to comply. In fact, I think that's already happened."

"You think you're diverting me, but you're not. Tell me about your other brother. Jack."

"Black Jack," he corrected and then took a sip of wine before setting the glass on the low table in front of them. "I suppose I should tell you the full story, as long as we're waiting for the servants to introduce Davy Tripp to his other new friends, soap and water."

"You've ordered him a *bath?*"

"As we may have need to keep him near us for a time, I've ordered him fumigated. Now. If you've heard about my brother and the great scandal he and Chelsea made last Season, then you know that he and Jack and I are the sons of the Marquess of Blackthorn but, alas, not also the sons of his late wife, the Marchioness, correct?"

"That was very delicate," she told him, watching his face for any trace of anger or embarrassment. She found neither.

"Thank you, I've had considerable practice." He picked up his glass and took another small sip and then waited as Wadsworth entered the drawing room bearing a tray holding the requested refreshments. "Ah, my favorites," he said, reaching for one of the cookies. "Thank you, Wadsworth. How goes the fumigating?"

"He only got away from Anders twice, sir, and he's now in the tub. Cook was not best pleased, however, when the idiot boy went running mother-naked through her kitchen. Your pardon, miss."

Regina quickly bent her head and concentrated on choosing just the perfect cookie, although they all looked exactly the same.

"Mother-naked? Ha! There is nothing so bad that enjoyment can't be found in it somewhere. Do you love

life, Regina?" Puck asked her once Wadsworth had
bowed and taken his leave. "I do. I love life."

Once again, Regina felt something inside her melting. Simply melting. "I'm liking it more and more, yes.
You were telling me about your family?"

"Yes, I was. You know about Beau. He and Chelsea
now live at Blackthorn with our father when they're not
traveling here and there and back again, riding herd on
Papa's many estates. He would have made a stellar marquess. Beau is the oldest of us and likes to be useful.
For all the scandal of his elopement, he's really not at all
the adventurous sort. Which leads me to Black Jack."

"Who is adventurous?" Regina offered, wondering
how Puck would describe himself, if she asked.

"We think so, yes. Mostly, he's an odd duck. Holds
grudges, I think." Puck took another sip of wine, betraying, at least to Regina's mind, that he wasn't so
comfortable talking about his family as he would like
her to believe. "You see, our father never married our
mother, but he did marry our mother's sister."

Regina blinked. "I beg your pardon?"

Puck drained his wineglass and stood up, walking
around the table to begin pacing in the center of the
large room. "As we grew up with all of it, the whole
thing seems logical enough to us until one of us has to
explain the thing. My mother and father met and fell
in love, but my mother longed to be an actress. She *is*
an actress, in point of fact, with my father financing
her troupe of traveling players lo these many years. She
longs for the theaters of London, but the closest she's

gotten in more than three decades is a small theater in Bath and then only for a fortnight a dozen years ago. But she perseveres. There are times I think her best performances are *off* the stage, but then I remember that Jack is cynical and that I don't find that trait particularly becoming."

"So they didn't marry because she became an actress? I suppose I can understand your father's hesitation."

Puck laughed. "Hardly that. She refused him. But in the end, they made a bargain. She would always love him, and he would always love her, they would always be true to each other—so sentimental—but he would marry her sister instead. Abigail was beautiful, but a child in every way. Their father wanted her put somewhere and would have, Mama told us, without her there to protect her. She couldn't leave, couldn't fulfill her dreams, unless she knew Abigail was protected."

"And your father agreed? Well, obviously he did, for he married her. And Abigail didn't object to her sister becoming her husband's mistress?"

"Abigail wouldn't have understood the word." Puck's eyes went rather soft and faraway. "She was an angel, Regina. Sweet and silly and so innocent. But she was never very well. I can remember holding her hand and how cool it always was to the touch, the tips of her fingers always slightly blue. Mama said it was her heart, that it wasn't strong. One morning last year, she simply didn't wake up."

Regina longed to go to him, but for all that they'd

shared in this same room only hours earlier, this time she held back, sensing that Puck wasn't telling her about Abigail because he wanted sympathy but only to explain something about his brothers, and perhaps even about himself.

"That's all very sad but still difficult to believe. If your parents simply had married, then your mother's sister could have come to live with them, been safe with them. Surely being a wife to the man she loved was more important than being an actress."

"You say that because you've never met Adelaide," Puck told her, a slight, one-sided smile not quite softening his words. "I think she's only half-alive when she's with us, even as she's pretending to be— Hell, sometimes I don't think even she knows who she's pretending to be. At any rate, she sticks to her word. She always comes back each time she goes away, but she always leaves again. She's rarely at Blackthorn anymore. She'd stay for months sometimes, when we were all still young. I know I was born on the estate. But then she'd feel the itch and be gone again. We—none of us, not lover nor sons—were enough to make her happy. We tried. We all tried, sometimes desperately. But she'd always leave. We were never enough to hold her. Not then and not now. Sometimes I wonder…"

"What do you wonder about?" Regina asked him as he didn't say more but just stared into the middle distance.

He shook his head. "It's that cynical thing again. I wonder if she loves anyone, if she ever loved anyone.

I wonder if she just needed financing for her troupe. I wonder if…if she hoodwinked my besotted father into marrying Abigail because then he couldn't marry anyone else and Adelaide wouldn't lose her generous protector. And I wonder if we, my brothers and I, weren't simply mistakes."

Now Regina did go to him, and put her hands on his. She knew why she had been born; her father had always been very clear about that. She knew that her mother loved her but was ashamed of the blood that flowed in her own daughter's veins. And she knew how that hurt. "Oh, Puck. I'm sorry. I'm so, so sorry."

He lifted both her hands to his mouth, kissing her knuckles. "Don't be. I have a father, I have a mother, I had Abigail and my brothers. I've been educated, recently given an unentailed estate I'll be happy to call my home and the run of Blackthorn and this not unimpressive mansion here in town. I've lived in Paris, I've traveled the world, I have never lacked for funds. Whether or not I'm happy is not the world's decision, Society's decision. It's mine."

Regina leaned close and pressed a brief, soft kiss to his mouth. "I've never met anyone like you."

"I should hope not," he said, clearly trying to lighten the conversation. "One Puck is more than enough on any stage. Now, back to the mysterious Black Jack. I told you that Beau and I are either resigned to or uncaring of the events of so many years ago, the decisions that made us who we are." He lowered his voice.

"That would be bastards," he said confidingly, as if she needed to be reminded.

She smiled in spite of herself.

"Good, you're smiling. We've gotten rather smoothly over the roughest ground. All that remains is where we began. With Jack. I wish I could tell you what maggots he carries in his brain, but I can't. I only know he hasn't spoken to either of our parents in years. He refuses any allowance from our father and yet seems more than comfortably deep in the pockets. He lives nowhere that we know of, does nothing that we know about and has this uncanny and often annoying way of knowing everything about us while we, not to repeat myself, know nothing of him."

"Except that he's here, in London," Regina said, for she had not forgotten that. "You thought he might have been the man who had come to speak with Davy Tripp."

"Yes, I left that part out, didn't I? While our mother has put forth the notion that her middle son might have taken up the role of a highwayman and our father believes he supports himself gaming for high stakes, Beau and I discovered quite by chance last year that Jack is actually in the employ of the Crown in some clandestine way. Not that Jack admits to it, you understand, but we happened to trip over him while he was going about his business. God only knows what he's done for king and country. I only know that if he were to be sent looking for me as part of his orders, I would be upstairs right now, cravenly cowering under my bed."

"But he's not looking for you. Is he looking for Miranda?"

"No. He's looking for the men who are snatching up pretty young Englishwomen and selling them on the open market, like so much livestock. Your cousin is just one of nearly two dozen blonde, fair females to have gone missing from London the last two months. She's simply the one you and I care about."

"That many?" Regina could barely take that in. "But why isn't all of London up in arms? Where is the hue and cry? Where is the outrage? Why has there been nothing written in the newspapers about this horrible crime?"

"I told you, Regina. A few shop girls go missing, a maid walks out on her afternoon off and never comes back. There are perhaps a dozen fewer prostitutes plying the streets around Covent Garden. A minor actress disappears, or perhaps just joined a traveling troupe and didn't bother to tell anyone she was leaving. To hear Jack tell it, by the time anyone noticed and began making inquires, the number had risen to that two dozen. There could be a dozen more no one will ever know about."

"But now they've taken the granddaughter of an earl. How did your brother know that?"

"He didn't until I told him. The first young lady anyone really knew about was a Miss Edna Featherstone, daughter of one of the premiere vintners here in London. He took his sad tale straight to one of his best customers, who also happens to be Jack's contact with the government. And no, before you ask, Jack didn't share the man's name with me nor the government office involved, and I consider myself much too fond of my intact nose to ask. It was only while investigating Miss Featherstone's disappearance that, one thing leading to another, those doing the investigating fell onto the trail of disappearance after disappearance."

"And Miss Featherstone is petite and fair and has blond hair?"

"She does. Or did. She hasn't been found. But Jack wasn't summoned to London until a few days before I met you, when the Duke of Norfolk's goddaughter, the only child of one of his royal highness's bosom chums, disappeared. And that, Miss Hackett, is a bit of knowledge you and I will take with us to the grave, graves we don't wish to see for many a long year, correct?"

Regina nodded, finding it impossible to talk.

"Like your cousin, she is in the country, suffering some minor ailment and will be returning to London once she is recovered. God help her. God help all of them."

CHAPTER SEVEN

PUCK SAT IN THE study and frowned over the list he'd written while waiting for Davy Tripp to be brought to him.

Regina had gone upstairs to check on her mother and to take a bath, telling him that she could still smell the warehouse on her clothing. Puck thought the same thing about himself, but as one bath probably would not do to erase the stink of friend Davy, he'd postpone his until after their interview.

"But that isn't the only thing that *stinks* in all of this," he muttered to the empty room, still eyeing the list.

He'd told Jack about Miranda, that she'd been abducted. But he hadn't told him *where* the abduction had taken place, planning to share information with his brother as he shared information with him. He'd remembered that even as he'd bounded off down the length of the warehouse like some rabbit being chased by a dozen hounds. Not that Jack wouldn't have put somebody to following his brother—but that meant following, not arriving ahead of him.

In addition—that was number *three* on his list—Jack didn't know about Davy Tripp, the servant Puck had first spoken to Friday evening, so if he'd set someone to following him, the someone wouldn't have known to ask for the boy. "And again, he wouldn't have arrived at our destination before Regina and me. That's two reasons to cross Jack of my list."

Which he did after dipping his pen in the inkwell once more. He also crossed off the unnamed Mentmore coachman and the word *footmen*. He crossed off the name Doris Ann.

So who else knew where the abduction had taken place?

Again, he looked at the list.

Regina. She was there.

Lady Claire. Regina told her.

The Viscount Ranscome. Lady Claire undoubtedly told him.

Reginald Hackett. He was there.

Then he looked at the list again and crossed off the first three names. All three had one thing in common: none had known about Davy Tripp. He hadn't told Regina about the boy until they'd arrived at his place of work. Miranda's parents could not have known.

He underlined the last name. Three times. And dipped his pen once more, for a new list.

He was there.

He could have observed me talking to Davy Tripp when I returned to the masquerade after seeing Regina safely home.

He sent the Runners north.

Behind that last line, Puck wrote one more word: *Why?*

He underlined that four times.

"Sir?" Wadsworth stepped into the room. "He's as decent as we could make him, sir." Then the sergeant-major-turned-butler reached a hand behind him and pulled Davy Tripp into the room.

The boy didn't look much better than he had before his bath and change of clothes, but at least his entrance wasn't preceded by the smell of him. He had a gaunt, hungry look about him, probably because he was hungry. He was short, perhaps older than his frame would suggest. In fact, he needed a shave.

"Coo…" he said as he looked about the room. "Ain't this plum fine."

"Yes, I'm sure that was what the ladies of the house had been striving for over the years with their decorating efforts—to look plum fine. Thank you, Wadsworth. You may go."

"Are you quite sure, sir? He's the sort would pick up bits 'n' pieces when no one's watching. I've seen his like. Only thing he didn't try to pocket since he got here was the soap. Steered a wide berth around that, he did."

Puck smiled at the exasperated expression on the butler's face. "We could always tie him to the chair? Hold a pistol aimed at his head? Are there any thumbscrews about anywhere, Wadsworth?"

The butler's cheeks flushed cherry-red. "You're saying you can handle him, aren't you, sir?"

"I think so, yes. But please feel free to stand just on

the other side of the door should I suddenly begin hysterically screaming for help. Thank you."

"Yes, sir," Wadsworth said, lowering his head as he turned away and then swiftly giving Davy Tripp a cuff on the ear. "Just so you remember me," he said and then closed the door behind him.

The boy rubbed at his head and glared at Puck. "Why does everyone keep on hittin' me, guv'nor? I ain't done nuthin'."

"I apologize for accidentally introducing my boot to your cheek, Mr. Tripp."

"No, guv'nor, not yer. Yer a right'un, saved me and all. *Him* wot jist left. An' the three coves what tried ter drown me."

Puck coughed into his fist. "It's called a bath, Davy."

"Call it wot yer want, guv'nor. I ain't never doin' it agin." He walked over to one of the tables and picked up a figurine of Aphrodite, ran a still dirty fingernail over the bared marble bosom, grinned and then hastily put it back down. "Why'd that bloke try ter stick me? I didn't do nuthin'."

Puck waved the boy…lad…youth to a chair on the other side of the desk. "How old are you, Davy?"

"Me?" He frowned as if considering a complicated problem. "I dunno. M'maw first put me out ter chimneysweep when I was five or six. Ain't seen her since. She'd know. Then I got too big fer that and got turned off inta the streets. Been a couple of years here, a coupla years there. Been workin' where yer found me a coupla more. Cain't go back there now, can I? Back ter the streets fer me, I guess. An' Tiny took wot coins yer gave me the other night, so it's hard times fer me, that's wot it is. Nope, cain't rightly say I wants ter say much o'anythin', guv'nor. If I gets it wrong, yer goin' ter have them drown me agin?"

"Not at the moment, no, but if you're to remain in my employ, I'm afraid I will have to insist that you maintain at least a nodding acquaintance with the tub. You see, Mr. Tripp, I need your help. Are you willing to help me?"

"T'ain't no mister. Jist Davy. Only gots called Tripp causin' I used ter fall down a lot. Mostly when somebody pushed me." Davy scratched his head, lending credence to the notion that certain sorts of vermin can hold their breath for quite a long time underwater. "An' I'm guessin' that depends, guvnor. Wot's a noddin' quain-tance?"

"THANK YOU, HANKS."

The maid had unearthed yet another handkerchief from somewhere and handed it to Leticia Hackett.

"Yes…thank you, Hanks," Lady Leticia said, delicately patting at her damp eyes and lustily blowing her nose. "I cannot believe you agreed to this tawdry intrigue, Claire," she then said to her sister-in-law, not for the first or even the twenty-third time. But this time quickly proved to be the worst. "You are only a haberdasher's granddaughter, so perhaps you can be excused somewhat, I suppose, and you do care for your daughter. But how dare you expose *my* child to this sort of scandal?"

"Mama, please," Regina said, also not for the first time. "I told you, I am as guilty as Miranda in what happened. I could have said no. I *should* have ordered the coach turned back. But I didn't. It all sounded rather exciting. Wearing masks, dancing with all the gentlemen there and with nobody knowing who we were. Did you never go to a masked ball when you were youn— during your Season in London?"

Lady Leticia drew herself up very straight on her chair. "I most certainly did *not*. I heard about them from my mama, but she told me quite plainly that they'd fallen out of favor thanks to the naughty goings-on that seemed to mark such affairs much more frequently. I have heard a few stories, and none of them are fit for your ears, young lady. My daughter, at a *masquerade*. You could have been taken. You're much prettier than Miranda. How could they have chosen her over you? Oh! What am I saying!" She took refuge in her handkerchief once more.

Regina looked to her aunt and sighed. They'd been at it for more than an hour now, ever since Lady Leticia had awakened from her wine-induced slumber. Going back and forth, back and forth. First the masquerade, and then exclaiming over the fact that she was being held captive in the home of a horrible, baseborn scoundrel who had absconded with them in the way of some desperate highwayman. A prisoner! And in the very heart of Mayfair! It was not to be borne!

"Perhaps a glass of wine…" Lady Claire suggested softly after taking Regina aside while Hanks hovered over Lady Leticia, patting her back and offering yet another handkerchief.

"No!" Regina winced at her own vehemence. "That is to say, I don't think we should encourage that sort of refuge. Should we?"

"She's yet to mention your father," Lady Claire pointed out. "When she considers how Reginald would react if he were to learn what we've done, there may not be enough wine in the entirety of London to calm her."

Regina felt tears stinging at the back of her eyes. "I'm not sorry we did it," she said. "We had no other real choice, not if we're going to be able to help Miranda and be here to comfort her when we find her. And we will find her, Aunt, I promise you that. Puck—that is to say, Mr. Blackthorn—feels we are already making huge strides toward locating her and bringing her home safely."

Lady Claire drew in her breath and nodded, clearly holding on to her composure with all of her motherly might. "No matter *how* we find her. She is my daughter, my darling. With God as my judge, the world will never know anything differently than that. Your uncle…" She pressed her fist to her mouth. "Your uncle is already quietly arranging for Miranda to be wed to the squire's son, back at Mentmore. The boy is *simple,* for the love of Heaven, but Seth says that's all for the better, as he won't know he's been handed damaged…damaged goods. I think…I think Seth would rather she were dead. But she can't be dead. She simply cannot!"

Regina held out her arms and her aunt walked into her embrace, putting her head on her niece's shoulder as she gave way to her grief. She guided the near-to-swooning woman to a chair, and then sat beside her and held her hands as she cried.

Clearly, neither woman was in any shape to go downstairs when the dinner gong was rung. Indeed, Regina didn't know how she could leave them here alone, as they were both so fragile, each for their own reasons.

But she had to see Puck, had to speak with him. While she'd been in her bath, she'd thought over all that had happened so far in this quite eventful day. She'd thought about how delighted she'd been to see him up on the box, wearing the Mentmore livery. She thought about how he must have looked whilst brandishing his swordstick, saving Davy Tripp from an assassin's knife.

She thought about how he had kissed her, touched her…and how she'd responded. Even as she'd dragged the soapy sea sponge over her skin, her body had begun to turn liquid, remembering.

They were going to find Miranda. She had put it in front of herself to find her cousin, and she would find her. Rescue her. With Puck's help, as he seemed likewise determined.

They would remain here, hidden in this lovely Grosvenor Square mansion, not a mile from where her father resided in the belief that his wife and daughter were even now halfway to Mentmore.

She would be well chaperoned by her aunt and her mother.

It was all rather bizarre, but it was all still rational, in most ways.

At the end of a week, or sooner if Miranda were located, her mother, her aunt and herself would climb back into the Mentmore coach and return to their London residences.

And that would be that. An adventure, a rescue, a good deed done, a mistake corrected.

She would never be allowed to see Puck again. Talk with him again. Watch his slow smile widen, reach all the way up to his mischievous eyes. She'd never feel his touch again. His kiss.

One week. Seven days or even less to learn what it was like for a woman to be made love to by a man such as Robin Goodfellow Blackthorn. For certainly no man her father chose for her would hold a candle to the glories Puck had hinted at that night in the gardens outside that terrible warehouse.

She hadn't noticed the smell of fish because he had been there. She hadn't seen the squalor behind the palm trees and draperies because he had looked into her eyes, blinding her to everything else. She hadn't shied at the tawdriness of it all because she hadn't felt tawdry or loose or lacking in morals when he'd kissed her, touched her, whispered thrilling, wickedly naughty things against her ear.

She'd felt alive. *Alive.* As she had earlier, in the drawing room. Not wicked, not naughty, not even simply curious. *Alive.*

"Or," she whispered under her breath as Lady Claire returned to sit beside her sister-in-law, "as my idiot cousin said and I now believe I understand...*ready.*"

She squirmed slightly on her chair as that hitherto uninteresting part of her that lay between her thighs began to feel warm, tingly. She squeezed her thighs together tightly and concentrated on the feeling when she squirmed again, rubbing the tops of her thighs together. She could almost feel Puck's fingers there, stroking her, causing all sort of strange, wonderful sensations to take hold of her, course through her veins with every heart-beat, making her want to open even more for him, so that he could touch her any way he liked, do whatever it was he wanted to do and never, never ever stop.

Just as he'd said to her in the gardens, the words made even more dangerously provocative in French.

Come away with me now, sweet tease, and we will pleasure each other all the night long. We will strip off these masks and with them rid ourselves of all inhibi-tion. You do not yet know me, but I will soon know your every delectable inch, taste your nectar, explore your most intimate, womanly secrets. I will take you where you have never been, touch you in ways you have never been touched. Until you weep with the joy of it.

She could marry the man of her father's choosing, live until she was a very old woman and never hear such words. But she had heard them, and she couldn't get them out of her head.

Didn't want them out of her head.

Regina got to her feet, ordered her breathing to return to its normal rhythm. She walked over to the tall cabinet and poured herself a tumbler of water to wet her suddenly dry mouth.

It was wrong to be thinking of herself while Miranda could be in such dire straits. Wrong.

Do you love life? I do. I love life.

Regina knew she couldn't have answered yes to Puck's question. Not last year, not last week. But for this week, she would have an answer. No matter what the future held for her, what her father planned for her, for this week, she would love life.

And the devil with the consequences!

"Regina? *Regina!* Goodness, child, don't you hear your mother calling to you?"

"Oh, I'm sorry, Aunt Claire, I'm so sorry," she said, hoping her face didn't betray her recent lascivious thoughts as she hastened to sit herself down at her mother's feet, take the woman's hands in hers. She blinked, seeing the smile on the woman's thin face. "Mama? You're not crying anymore."

It was true. Her mother's eyes were shining but not with tears. She looked somehow younger. Happy.

"Your father will never know, will he? That's what you said. He'll never know. He doesn't know. For the first time in twenty horrible years, I don't feel the weight of his thumb on my back. I don't have to cringe when I hear his footfalls in the hallway. I don't have to listen to his crudities. I don't have to look upon his ugliness of mind and soul. He won't tell me how stupid I am, how he will have me locked away for my own safekeeping once you are wed." Lady Leticia closed her hands into tight fists and shook them. "Why was I crying? I won't waste another precious moment in tears. For however long it lasts, I am *free!*"

"Oh, Mama," Regina said brokenly as she laid her head on her mother's lap and gave way to tears of her own.

"So, Mr. Blackthorn," Lady Leticia said as two servants competently went about the business of presenting the final course of the meal served in the more intimate of two dining rooms in the Grosvenor Square mansion. "My daughter tells me you've spent some time in Paris since we gallantly freed the country from the rule of that despot Bonaparte. Is it very gay there?"

"My lady, Paris is a beautiful city. I see now that it lacked only your gracious presence and that of Lady Mentmore to make it perfection on earth. But do allow me to tell you about some of its glories."

Regina blinked back tears, not for the first time since her mother had confessed the scope of her terror of her husband and revealed what she saw as her future once her daughter was sold to the highest title Regina's father could afford.

She had continued her high spirits, commanding Hanks to order a bath prepared for her and then fussing over her toilette, complimenting the maid's clever way with the curling stick, choosing and then discarding three gowns before settling on a flattering butter-yellow gown of Regina's in favor of any of her own.

Of course she would be going down to dinner. Of course she would be civil to Mr. Blackthorn; he was, after all, their host. Of course she would enjoy her meal, as she was famished, truly famished.

Good evening, Mr. Blackthorn, how considerate of you to have us as your guests. What an attractive room. Everything is beyond lovely, really. No, oh no, thank you, no wine, Mr. Blackthorn. Have you any lemonade?

Now Lady Leticia was all attention as Puck regaled her with silly stories of the vagaries of the restored ruler of France, smiling as he confided delicious *bon mots,* actually tittering behind her hand as he dared even more delicious gossip when he saw that she enjoyed hearing it.

Why, one could almost think her mama to be flirting with the man!

Once or twice Regina's aunt had caught her eye across the table, at first looking to her quizzically, then shrugging her confusion and finally to mouth silently, *he's very nice.*

He was. Puck was very nice. No, he was beyond such a simple word. He was magnificent. He was dressed impeccably, his blond hair tied back at his nape with a black riband, the lace at his cuffs understated and elegant. But better than that, from the moment the trio of ladies had come downstairs, he'd been attentive, witty, polite and kind.

He had apologize to Lady Leticia for having taken her unawares with his mad scheme, assured Lady Claire that he would do everything within his power to see that her daughter would soon be with her mother once more, frightened, yes, but other than that, unharmed.

Lady Claire believed him. That was obvious by the way she took his reluctant hand in hers and actually raised it to her lips in thanks.

He'd blushed then, like an embarrassed youth, and Regina had longed to hug him.

And somehow, with all that faced them, he had managed to make a party out of this first dinner together in Grosvenor Square. Why, even Lady Claire had smiled a time or two and actually added to the conversation at one point, telling a tale she'd heard from the viscount about a French actress who had nearly managed to snare, it was said, Wellington himself with her charms. Lady Claire so wanted to visit Paris, but her husband evinced no interest in anything French, save their brandy.

Regina had noticed Puck's smile rather freezing on his handsome face for a moment when her aunt had been speaking of the "conniving actress," but he recovered before anyone else could see, she was sure, and had quickly turned the conversation to the awe-inspiring architecture of Notre Dame.

And while he romanced the ladies—surely, there

was no other word for the magic he was dispensing with such ease—she never felt neglected. When he looked at her, which was often, it was always with a smile seemingly reserved just for her. He was a magician, an enchanter, and she was more than willing to enter into his enticing web.

He was a boy. He was a man. He looked at the world and saw good, even when surrounded by the bad. He was all that was charming, but she could sense the danger beneath the surface, his intelligence, his delicious humor, his compassion, his willingness to take risks, his thirst for adventure.

Do you love life? I do. I love life.

I will take you where you have never been, touch you in ways you have never been touched. Until you weep with the joy of it.

"Madam does not care for trifle?"

Regina looked up at the butler, Wadsworth, only then realizing that she hadn't lifted her fork to so much as take a single nibble of the delicious-looking confection of strawberries, cake and cream in front of her.

"No, no, I'm convinced it is delicious. I simply cannot seem to find it in myself to take another bite. Thank you, Wadsworth."

The butler signaled silently with one white-gloved hand, and a footman appeared to remove the plate even while Wadsworth turned his attention to Lady Leticia, assisting her from her chair at the foot of the table. The hostess had risen. It was time for the ladies to retire, leaving Puck to his brandy and cigar.

He was on his feet, holding Lady Claire's chair for her, and promised to join everyone in the drawing room shortly.

But Lady Leticia waved off his statement. "I fear I have overdone, Mr. Blackthorn, and have just the touch of the headache. Lady Claire and I will take our leave of you now, in the hope that tea and cakes might be brought to us in my chamber in good time. Mr. Blackthorn, you are an exemplary host, and I thank you for your consideration."

Puck bowed over her hand, repeated his bow to Lady Claire and then, lastly, lifted Regina's hand to within an inch of his lips. "As soon as you can get away, please," he said quietly. "You'll have need of your cloak."

Regina shot a look to her mother, who was chattering animatedly with the viscountess.

"You've learned something?"

"Possibly. I would not involve you except that—"

"You promised," she finished for him. "What if you were to find her? She would need me there, to calm her. I must be with you when she's found."

He appeared ready to say something else, but her mother called to her, and she only curtsied to Puck and followed her mother and aunt out of the room. Looking back only once to see him, his head tipped slightly to one side, his smile deliciously mischievous, watching her as she walked away.

It was difficult not to skip the rest of the way, but she admonished herself to behave. At least for now.

CHAPTER EIGHT

HE'D BEEN IN A FORGETTABLE port city along the coast of the Mediterranean Sea, his ship driven there to escape a storm. No more than eighteen, set loose on the world just as legitimate heirs had been sent out to complete their educations by dipping their toes into as many corners of the world as were not embroiled in war or otherwise off-limits to them.

He doubted his father's notion of a Grand Tour included this squalid, smelly, hot as Hades scar on the world. Older, wiser, Puck might have remained in the dockside inn while repairs were completed on the ship bound for Jerusalem. But believing himself immortal or invincible or whatever young men believe of themselves, he had already abandoned his tutor on the docks of Dover and set off on his journey, eager to see and enjoy life, and this place seemed to be teeming with it.

With all the bravado and naiveté of the young and wealthy, he'd left his valet to his laundry and headed for the center of the town to a place his inn host had, in execrable English, identified as the bazaar.

The sun grew hotter, the stench thicker, the crowds bumping shoulder to shoulder, the cries from the many booths entreating him to come, see, buy. Chickens molted in their wooden cages, parrots squawked from perches, carcasses of animals Puck was hard-pressed to identify hung from the stalls.

He delighted in the purchase of an unusual gold ring for Abigail, as it was made in the shape of a flower, and happily haggled over the price of a necklace for Adelaide, the thing fashioned of three differently colored metals hammered together rather like delicate chain mail. He looked longingly at a small carpet his father might enjoy but rejected it after considering how heavy it was and the fact that he'd have to carry it back to the inn. He did buy himself a cunningly curved knife with an elaborate hilt and similar weapons for his brothers.

The twists and turns, the buildings so close together they seemed almost to touch by the time they climbed to a third or fourth story, it didn't take long before Puck knew himself to be completely turned around, no longer knowing his way back to the inn through the maze of streets.

Finally coming into a more open square, he'd climbed onto a sandy stone wall and, holding on to a flagpole, squinted into what he could see of the distance. He spotted a visible sliver of the clear blue of the Mediterranean and grinned in relief. All he had to do was to walk downhill until he reached the docks. His inn was there somewhere.

With the bazaar finally at his back, the crowds thinned, the jumble of foreign voices became less raucous, and he made good progress along the docks until once again he was faced with a considerable knot of men who all seemed to have been drawn by something taking place in front of one of the larger, more ornate buildings. Clutching his packages, and with smiles and apologies and bows—and one hand clamped firmly on the purse in his pocket—Puck made his way into the crowd and was finally able to see what all the excitement seemed to be about…and for the first time in his young life felt the bloodlust that lies below the surface of any man, the primeval urge to kill.

Up on a makeshift stage was a fat, bearded monster dressed in colorful robes. He was showing his large, white teeth as one of his enormous hands cupped the bare breast of a sobbing, cowering, completely nude, fair-haired woman.

All around Puck, men were shouting, laughing, holding up small leather purses.

"Bastard! Stop at once! I order you—let her go!" Puck's muscles bunched as he took a step forward, determined to mount the stage and rescue the young woman. A burly man standing next to him laughed and grabbed his arms, holding him in place.

The man's English wasn't good, but it was sufficient. "If you were wise, young pup, you'd walk away. Our friend up there is trying to sell used goods and making a hash of it. If she were still a virgin, we'd never see her out here. He keeps the good ones intact for his best customers. It's the brothel for that one. Shame. Pretty enough but without the maidenhead, she's worth only half. Ah, see, Ahmed has bought her. She won't last long in his small Eden. They do things there, I hear, no good Christian like you or me should see."

Puck watched, feeling impotent, as the girl, still sobbing, was led toward a flight of steps leading down to the ground. He could hear her calling on her God in German, begging anyone to save her.

She was almost immediately replaced on the bare selling stage by four black men of varying ages, their forearms chained as well as their ankles.

"No, got enough bucks as it is. Good day to you, sir," the man said. He let go his grip on Puck's arms and turned to push his way back through the throng.

"Wait!" Puck pushed and shoved his way until he'd caught up with the man. "This place. The brothel owned by this man, Ahmed. Can you take me there? I'll pay you."

The man smiled, showing his yellowed teeth and spit some sort of seed onto the planks at Puck's feet. "You one of those, are you?"

"No! I mean, yes. All right, I'm one of those. Take me there."

But then they heard the scream. And the curses.

Everyone pressed forward, the better to see what had happened. Puck punched and pushed until he was at the very front of the crowd, the packages he'd carried dropped to the ground and trampled, forgotten.

The girl he had seen only moments before lay on the dusty ground, surrounded by the bright red of her own blood. Somehow, she had managed to strip her new owner of the knife he carried in his sash and turned it on herself.

Now, Puck's new acquaintance told him, she was good only for the dung heap.

Puck purchased the body from the astonished Ahmed and arranged for a decent burial in a small Christian cemetery located just outside the town.

And then he asked questions. What had happened? How had the German-speaking woman come to be in this squalid place, up on that platform? He'd heard of slavery; in an abstract way, he understood the practice and even the reasoning behind it, although England had long since put a stop to the importation of slaves and warned English shipowners that it was now a crime punishable by death to carry slaves as cargo.

He'd learned that the practice still flourished in some areas of the world where the law either did not reach or was scoffed at as secondary when compared to the probable profits. He'd learned that slaves, the buying and selling of humans, could flourish in any country and not just Africa, as he had naively supposed. He'd learned that white slaves were not as valued as black slaves. They didn't work as hard, and they tended to die faster, but there was a specialized market for virgins. The fairer the skin, the more in demand they were… and there was always a demand.

The ship had been repaired and a few days later, Puck traveled on to Jerusalem. He saw the Greek Islands. He walked the ancient lands, read the epic poems in the shadow of history. But his education had been completed in a forgettable port in an unremembered town.

Over time, he had put the memory at the back of his brain. He'd been little more than a boy, and he had done all that he could.

Now he was a man, and fate had put Puck where it seemed to need him, both to save Regina's cousin and the others and to at last act on the deeply buried fury and impotence of that long-ago day on the docks. That was the thing about life, as he saw it—there were often second chances. The thing was to learn from them when they happened the first time around.

Puck had been idly spinning the large globe in the study, knowing the port town his ship had been forced to stop at was no more marked on this globe than it probably would be on any map. How many places like it existed? How many poor souls had passed through them, still might pass through them on their way to the hell of slavery and degradation? How long would profit trump morality?

That the practice seemed to be flourishing right now, here in London, was not to be countenanced. England couldn't allow it, not when it preached to the rest of the world. Certainly not when it was their own women being taken. Jack had told Puck that his orders had been to find the illicit traders and eliminate them "by any means possible." And without word of what had happened filtering to the populace. The Crown was not to be embarrassed.

That was fine with Puck. He would give any information he had to his brother, do everything in his power to help stop this bartering of human flesh.

But not until Regina's cousin was safe and safely out of it, her life restored, her reputation intact. Not until he, personally, confronted the perpetrators of that particular crime and dealt with them, as he had been unable to do so many years ago. That's what second chances were all about. But it had already been more than two nights since Miranda disappeared. Would he have time?

"Puck?"

He shook himself out of his thoughts and turned to see Regina standing in the doorway, a dark gray cloak folded over her arm. She had removed her jewelry, and her hair had been taken down from its pins, so that its length was now only tied back loosely at her nape. Her gown was modest in cut, and black, clearly not one of her own.

She looked so beautiful, apprehensive even as she attempted to appear otherwise, and he could feel himself succumbing to her on a whole new level. She was so courageous, even as she was clearly frightened. He coveted her beauty, her lush body and had from the start. Now he adored her mind and determined fearlessness, her willingness to dare anything in order to save her cousin. He'd never met her like and doubted he ever would again.

Puck bowed in her direction. "And to whom do I owe the pleasure?" he asked, causing her to smile, which was what he had hoped. "Ah! A moment! Yes, I recognize that smile. It is she, Miss Hackett. What a delight-ful surprise."

"You make a game of everything," she scolded, al-though he could tell her heart wasn't in the insult. "The gown is Hanks's best and the cloak, as well. And these," she said, putting out her right foot to show the jean boot, "belong to one of the housemaids. If we are called upon to run yet again, they'll be much more service-able. Now, where are we going?"

"Not to Carleton House, surely, adorably lovely as I find you at the moment," he told her, speaking of the Prince Regent's residence. "And you won't be leaving the coach, in any event. You and I and the estimable Davy Tripp will be riding about the area of Covent Garden, on the hunt for someone by the name of La Reina, although I doubt that's the name the man was born with. Shall we go?"

Regina took his offered arm. "That's Spanish, isn't it? It means the queen. What an odd name for a man."

"The man performs an odd job," Puck told her, won-dering how thorough an explanation he could safely render and then deciding on complete truth. Life was also an education. But first he'd attempt the more oblique approach. "According to Davy, La Reina works for one of the men who…manage ladies of the evening."

She shook her head as she walked with him through the kitchens, also taking time to wave at the cook and a few other servants who had been relaxing over cups of tea and had quickly leaped to their feet in surprise. "No, I'm afraid I don't understand."

"Gloves off, then?" Puck asked her.

She turned to him as one of the footmen put down the steps to the coach. "I'm afraid anything less wouldn't help."

Once they were settled inside the coach, Davy up on top beside the coachman, and they were moving off down the alleyway to the street, Puck tried again.

"Ladies of the evening, those who are not so fortunate to have found a single gentleman's protection and are forced to…ply their wares on street corners, take their customers into alleyways to complete their transactions and often share their earnings with men, who in turn…watch out for their best interests."

"Oh," Regina said, shocking Puck to his heels. "You mean they use the services of a pimp. A male procurer."

"You shouldn't know that word. Any of those words."

Regina looked down at her hands, which she had primly folded in her lap. "My father has a copy of Mr. Frances Grose's *Classical Dictionary of the Vulgar Tongue* in his study. He ordered all the books at once, although I doubt he's opened any of them. Mr. Grose was, I understand, an antiquarian of some note at one time, before his fortunes forced him to publish whatever he could, and I thought the volume would be educational." She sneaked a look up at Puck through her eyelashes. "It certainly was."

"You read it all? You didn't realize what it was and quickly put it down? Worse, it would appear you've committed some of it to memory."

"I'm not invited to as many social events as Miranda. I had the time."

"And the inclination," Puck teased, feeling certain that if it were not so dark in the coach, he might see her blush.

"I blame Grandmother Hackett. Kindly do the same, please. And tell me more about this man, this La Reina. I do not shock as easily as I should, Puck."

"It would appear, however, that I do," he said, grinning at her as the coach made its way through the darkened streets. "Very well, I'll tell you everything Davy told me. You already know that there have been other disappearances, other women taken, some of them right off the streets."

"Yes, you told me. Shop girls, maids."

"And prostitutes. La Reina is employed by a pimp in a neighborhood very close to the location of what is now the infamous masquerade ball. He is, according to our new friend Davy, a slightly built fellow, although very good with a knife, if pressed to use it. In order to protect the pimp's entourage, as of late, the man has been fitted out as a woman of negotiable virtue, spending his working hours on those same street corners, should one of his employer's ladies encounter a problem with any of her customers. Where the sight of a burly man might keep customers away, La Reina appears as no threat to them. After all, everyone still has to make money, no matter the potential danger."

"That's...rather ingenious. La Reina must make a tolerable female?"

"If we locate him, you can be the judge of that. His appearance was clearly enticing enough to have a few men attempt to snatch him up off the streets very late Friday evening as he walked alone, as a man would be more prone to do than an unaccompanied female. They let him go when they realized their mistake and once introduced to the man's talented blade."

Regina's eyes grew as round as saucers.

"Friday evening? The same night Miranda was taken? But that's marvelous—I mean, I'm certain Mr. La Reina didn't think so, but it might be extraordinarily lucky for us. You're hoping he can tell us more about Miranda's kidnappers, aren't you?"

"That is the object of our small excursion, yes," Puck said, delighted that Regina had understood their mission so quickly, ecstatic that she had put both her hands on his forearm in her excitement and was looking at him as if he'd just hung out the moon for her. "You may kiss me now," he said, perhaps tumbling into the land of the romantically giddy.

"My, and aren't you full of yourself this evening. I should think I'd want to reserve any reward until we locate Mr. La Reina," she told him, her tone light and teasing. "But if you were to insist…"

He cupped her cheek in his hand. "Ah, and I do."

She was smiling as he touched his mouth to hers, and he quickly took advantage, pulling her fully into his arms as he deepened the kiss.

She wasn't shy, and she was clearly a very apt student. This kiss was a far cry from their first, yet even more exciting because he knew not only the body now but something of the woman, as well. She was so much more than merely a comely physical vessel, an attractive outlet for his carnal desires. She was mind and heart and humor and so much more.

Her father's ambitions be damned. Society be damned. The whole hypocritical world be damned. She was his. He didn't know how he would achieve the impossible, but he would find a way. They were meant to be, fate had stepped in and chosen for them.

He broke the kiss at last, pulling her even closer so that he could whisper into her ear. "I'm mad for you, you know. Quite possibly insane."

"I know," she whispered, rubbing her cheek against his.

Puck very nearly laughed out loud. He put his hands on her shoulders and lightly pushed her away from him. "I beg your pardon? You *know?* Well, aren't you the cheeky thing."

Her light laugh set his heart soaring. "Puck, you've just been kissing me. Rather heatedly, I think. You've taken…certain liberties and have allowed me no end of liberties you should have denied me, and that could very well lead you into troubles no man would take on lightly. My father is a formidable man. He would have your liver on a spit if he was to know the half of what you and I have been doing since we first met, including the fact that you had the audacity to have all but kidnapped his wife, for pity's sake. That all said, I would much prefer that you are mad for me, rather than simply mad. Oh, and if I'm wrong, please don't tell me, as I seem to be quite alone with you inside this coach."

He looked at her for a long moment, his lips firmly pressed together, before his shoulders began to shake and he at last gave way to hilarity. To give her credit, Regina allowed him his amusement for a full minute before she told him to stop.

"I apologize," he said, then chuckled one last time. "Really. I'm being serious now."

"No, you're not," she shot right back at him. "You're never serious, even when you are. You see not only the humor but also the hope in everything. It's one of your most endearing qualities. I'd be terrified, otherwise, so thank you. Now, is that Davy shouting something from the top of the coach?"

Puck immediately leaned across the coach and opened the small door used to converse with the coach-man. "Mr. Tripp! Do you see our man?"

"Aye, guv, I sees 'im. Lookin' mighty fine all trucked out in pink this evenin' he is, guv."

"Stop the coach and hop down."

"Will do, guv," Davy said and then raised his voice. "You there! I sees you, Mr. Queen! I gots a fine gentry mort 'ere wants ter talk with yer. *Hey, stop!*"

Puck retrieved his sword cane from the floor and turned to Regina. "Stay right here. I mean it. I'll bring La Reina to you."

She nodded, biting down on her bottom lip.

He took her face between his hands and planted a quick, firm kiss on her forehead, then was out of the coach and running after Davy Tripp's departing back, a vision in pink loping along ahead of them, skirts raised to reveal hairy legs and bony knees.

Mr. Queen unexpectedly ducked into an alleyway, and Davy skidded by the opening on the wet cobblestones as he belatedly tried to change direction, landing on his backside in a puddle, putting himself out of the running.

"Up you get, Mr. Tripp—no time for lollygagging!" Puck shouted as he, not making Davy's mistake, took the corner more carefully and then put his entire mind to running as fast as he'd ever run, at least since that night in Toulouse, when he'd nearly run afoul of a determined gendarme as he'd climbed down the drainpipe from the mayor's daughter's boudoir.

Thanking his usual good luck for the full moon, he avoided heaps of fetid garbage, a pair of feral cats that were busily mating in the middle of the alley as well as two supposed humans doing the same thing up against a rough, wooden wall, and was able to catch hold of La Reina's skirts just as he was in the act of vaulting over a ramshackle fence.

"Hold there! It's only talk that I want from you, and I'll pay for that pleasure. Handsomely. Or not, if you try kicking me in the head again, young lady."

"I ain't nobody's— Leave off me!"

Puck grabbed at one flailing ankle and, with his fist twisted in the material of the gown, gave a mighty yank. Down came La Reina. Unfortunately, the ramshackle fence immediately became a casualty, thanks to the man's tight grip on it.

Puck lost his footing but not his grip, and was suddenly on his back, covered by both La Reina's flailing body and several ancient, heavy, rain-soaked boards of the fence.

He wrapped one strong leg around both of the small man's and his forearm around the fellow's scrawny neck, effectively cutting off his air while daring splinters and much more as he then rolled the fellow onto his stomach, his arms trapped beneath him.

"Try for your knife," Puck warned him tersely, still recovering his breath, "and you and I will become even more intimate, much to the displeasure of both of us. I am not by nature a violent man, you understand, but you've done my rigout what I'm sure is a mortal injury, and I am not best pleased with you at the moment. Try me again and I may cease being so pleasant."

"I...I can't breathe!"

"Really?" Puck allowed shock to color his voice and loosened his hold fractionally to give the man air. "And must you? I mean, if you were to answer my questions, you would need breath to speak, I suppose. But if you were to continue to refuse, I wonder that you'll need breath." He leaned close to the man's ear, locking his forearm tightly across his windpipe once more. *"Ever again."*

La Reina or Mr. Queen or whoever he was immediately began bucking, trying to get Puck off him, an exercise, the man soon realized, almost laughable in its futility.

"Wot...wot you wants ter know?"

Puck immediately relaxed his grip and leaped lightly to his feet, locating his swordstick on the cobblestones and unsheathing it before La Reina could disengage his snagged skirts from the destroyed fence. When he at last had managed to—dear God!—adjust his bodice to a more discreet position and straightened, it was to find the tip of that same swordstick an inch away from his nose.

"Your sticker, my sweet, soiled dove," Puck crooned as Davy Tripp stepped forward from the shadows. "You will kindly remove it from your person and drop it over there—" he indicated the side of the alley with an inclination of his head "—where my associate here—yes, indeed, that would be you, Mr. Tripp—will then retrieve it."

An efficient-looking knife went skittering into the base of the brick wall.

"Wot did yer go runnin' fer, Mr. Queen? I told yer. The gentry mort only wants ter talk."

"A small lesson, Mr. Tripp. When you wish to speak with someone who might not wish to be spoken with, you do not call to him from a distance. You walk up to him and tap him most congenially on the shoulder and then clamp your hand firmly on said shoulder. Do you think you can remember that?"

Davy nodded furiously. "So's that he don't lope off."

"Ah, teachable. Wonderful. Shall we find our way back to the coach now? You first, madam."

"I ain't no madam, neither," La Reina grumbled. "I'll fix you, Davy Tripp, next time I sees yer. Jist yer wait."

Davy, apparently feeling drunk with power, seeing as how Puck still had the swordstick point at La Reina's spine, responded by dancing in front of the man and making loud, smacking kissing noises.

"I see an extended stay in the country in your future, Mr. Tripp, if not a permanent remove," Puck said, once more enjoying himself, or at least as much as was possible when his entire back was soaked through to the skin with none-too-clean rainwater and other liquids he wouldn't care to identify. "And now, if you'll kindly retrieve my hat, I will make it a gift to you. I rather think I shan't be wearing it again."

Davy ran off down the alley once more, appearing again with the wet, dirty, faintly dented, curly-brimmed beaver on his head, held up from covering his face by means of his marvelously protuberant ears.

The copulating couple had gone, although the feral cats were still seemingly enjoying each other's close company as Puck and his small entourage made their way back to the coach. As he got closer, he could see Regina's face peeking out from behind the concealing leather shade, and waved to her.

The coach door was immediately opened, and the steps kicked down. It would seem she was happy for his return. How nice. However, once she smelled him, she might change her mind.

Still, it had been a productive night's work. And it was far from over.

CHAPTER NINE

REGINA RAISED HER bent legs up onto the seat of the comfortable leather chair and arranged her dressing gown so that it covered her ankles. She was entirely modest, thanks to the cut of the dressing gown rather than her own inclinations, the white dimity buttoning nearly to her chin, the lace-edged sleeves covering half her hands.

Her hair was hanging freely down her back, its waves unleashed to tumble where they might, a casual comfort she hadn't appreciated when she'd been younger and longing to be allowed to finally declare herself grown by putting up her hair.

It was strange, the things one thought one could not live without, and once you held them in your hand, the longing seemed silly when compared to the mundane reality.

In any event, Mr. Queen or La Reina or whatever the odd little man's name was shouldn't be too shocked by her appearance if he were to return with Puck. On the other hand, she doubted her dressing gown would do much to encourage Puck. That was unfortunate but also for the best, especially if he learned anything important in his nocturnal travels.

The mantel clock struck the hour of midnight, and Regina wondered yet again what was happening.

They had returned to Grosvenor Square a rather strange group, with herself riding alone inside the coach and Puck and the others up on top. She would appreciate the arrangement, he'd told her rather gleefully, and even from the distance he kept between himself and the coach when he'd first approached, she had readily agreed with him.

He had lost his grosgrain ribbon, so that his streaked golden hair had fallen forward, making him look young and jaunty and meltingly handsome. His hat had been on Davy Tripp's head—making that poor soul simply look silly—and there was a tear in the knee of Puck's trousers. If he had looked any happier, he would have been giggling like a child. Except, of course, for the swordstick he had pointed at the back of the bedraggled La Reina; that had looked considerably less than silly.

Honestly, be they boys or grown men, there seemed nothing so certain to bring a smile to their faces than having had the opportunity to roll about in the muck. Rather like pigs with clothes, she supposed, although the piggery at Hackett House in Hampshire smelled sweet by comparison.

Bored with the pose she had struck on the chair, especially with no audience to see her, Regina wandered over to the bookshelves to peruse the titles, which clearly were well-read. One book in particular caught her attention, as the spine seemed broken. Either well-read or poorly constructed—or abused by a reader more intent on the words than the appearance of the thing. She had to handle it carefully as she slipped it from its resting place, carried it over to the chair and the lit candles.

The Aeneid. Ah, Virgil's epic poem that told of the supposed Trojan Wars. She knew it well. She'd read Homer's *Iliad,* of course, but that epic poem had covered only three days of the ten-year war that was at times variously aided and abetted by the Greek gods of Olympus.

It was *The Aeneid* that had included the fascinating story of the Trojan Horse. Why anyone would accept a *gift* from a departing, defeated army had made no sense to her then and still did not. But, again, men had made the decision, probably drunk with their victory. Any woman would look at such a gift and wonder *why* it had been given, and then have someone quickly dispose of it.

Regina carried the volume back to the shelf and replaced it, smiling as she heard a sound near the doorway. "At least it is not your *perfume* that first announces you this time," she said as she turned with a welcoming smile that quickly dropped away from her face. "Who are you?"

The man did not move from where he stood, almost as if that courtesy was supposed to comfort her in some way. He bowed rather elegantly for a housebreaker, she supposed, and was dressed nothing like one, unless housebreakers were espousing exquisitely tailored evening wear this Season.

He was dark of hair, his skin tanned as if he spent much of his time outdoors, and he was probably the most frighteningly handsome man she'd ever encountered. Very much the man but with a nearly unreal beauty to him, marred only by the intense expression in his disturbingly compelling eyes. He also seemed to know his way about the room, as after his bow, he headed straight to the drinks table without looking in that direction and poured himself a glass of wine from the decanter.

When she was about to scream in either fear or frustration, he turned to her, saluted her with his glass and then downed the wine in two large gulps before finally answering her question.

"A question I could turn back on you, Miss Hackett, were I not already apprised of your presence in what is, or so I'm told, partially *my* residence. I take it my reprobate brother is currently occupied elsewhere. Making a muddle of things, no doubt. Or should I say, making *more* of a muddle of things? He's already in it past his knees, having deposited you and your relatives here. Kidnappers hang, I believe."

Regina longed to take umbrage at the man's description of Puck but held her tongue. Brothers probably always thought their siblings never grow up. "We have not been kidnapped, Mr. Blackthorn. We are guests. You are Don John Blackthorn, aren't you? *Black Jack?* And, if I must say so, rather painfully obvious in the way you are attempting to live up to your name."

His smile transformed his face from cruel beauty

to something much more appealing. "On the contrary, Miss Hackett, I aim only to live *down* to it. Perhaps I find this all rather amusing because it isn't the first time one of my brothers has hidden a woman here at the mansion. Perhaps that's where Puck got the idea. At any rate, please, be seated, and I apologize for my rude behavior. I will, however, ask again—is my brother about?"

Regina retook her seat and once more pulled her legs up onto the cushion, busying herself arranging her skirts over her slippers in order to give herself time to formulate an answer. "He may have gone out," she said at last. "Shall I tell him you've called and wish to see him?"

"Thank you for that polite invitation to vacate the premises. But, no, I believe I'll wait." He sat himself down in the facing chair, gracefully crossing one long leg over the other. "We will wait together."

"Very well, Mr. Blackthorn," Regina said, wishing she had done what was proper, or as proper as the admittedly peculiar circumstances could make it, and excused herself from the room. "But please do not relax in the erroneous conclusion that we shall now chat about innocuous things, as I have no time for such pleasantries. Have you made any progress in your investigation of the disappearances? Are you here to declare success or in the hope that Puck has seen some success to your failure?"

"You've quite the way with an insult, Miss Hackett. My congratulations. But to answer your question,

I might be further along with my investigation if mine own brother trusted me enough to share information with me. Just small, piddling details, really. Such as the location of the masquerade ball from whence your cousin was taken against her will. As I said, piddling."

"He didn't tell you that?" Regina pretended surprise. "Doesn't he trust you?"

"Oh, I'm certain he does. As much as I trust him." Jack's emerald-green eyes narrowed slightly beneath low, winglike brows. "I have wasted one of my best men all of last night and today, following after my dear Robin Goodfellow, making sure he doesn't tumble into some desperate situation, only to learn that he has now seemed to have taken up chasing hapless females down alleyways. Needless to say, my curiosity was piqued. Would you know anything about that, Miss Hackett?"

The corners of Regina's lips twitched in humor, but she managed to restrain her smile. "The only thing that I would know about that, Mr. Blackthorn, is that one of your best men obviously needs to consider spectacles."

"Ah, and now you've caught me out. Allow me to amend that. *One* of my men, not necessarily one of my best. The fact that Puck waved to the fellow from the top of the coach as it drove off earlier this evening— and that my man was so silly as to reveal that to me— is the reason I'm here."

"Puck saw your man? And *waved* to him?"

"Blew him a kiss, actually. My brother has a strong leaning toward the dramatic gesture, I'm afraid."

"And you, of course, would recognize that. Why,

nearly as much so, I suppose, as if you were looking into a mirror," Regina said slyly.

Jack's smile was beginning to unnerve Regina somewhat, as it was very like Puck's, and she did not want to feel kindly toward this strange man.

"Shall we cry friends, Regina? Puck might be more forthcoming if he sees that we two are rubbing along well together, and that can only be of benefit to your cousin. We are soon to be running out of time. Two more young women were taken since I last spoke to my brother. Someone, I believe, is gearing up for an ocean voyage and is busily and none too selectively rushing to gather the remainder of his cargo, as if on some sort of deadline. We lose to that deadline, and your cousin is gone forever out of reach."

Regina's heart skipped a beat. "How soon? What would constitute a full cargo? Do you know? No, don't bother to answer. How could you? How could anyone? No civilized person could possibly understand anyone so vile as to sell another human being."

"Ah, but Regina, it is only in understanding them that we can hope to capture them. We are looking for someone unscrupulous, naturally. Someone who places no value on anything or anyone, other than monetary, what that person can do for him, how he can profit from them." Jack smiled again. "You wouldn't happen to know anyone like that, would you? It would make our search that much more simple."

"No," Regina said softly, her throat suddenly gone tight. "I wouldn't…I wouldn't know anyone like that."

And then she looked up at the sound of footsteps approaching the study, nearly giddy with relief to see Puck rather affectedly shooting his cuffs as he strolled into the room. What an impossible man. It was clear he already knew that his brother was present.

Still, his feigned surprise was rather convincing. It was as if the two men were playing a game; both knew the rules, and both enjoyed the moves.

"Jack, how good of you to visit, even at this unfashionably late hour," he said and then inclined his head to Regina and winked. "And aren't you lovely. Such charming *dishabille,* yet modest to a fault. He hasn't scared you away? Jack, you're losing your touch. The way I've heard it, women and children run from the sight of you. Strong men cavil at your penetrating stare. Etcetera."

"Insolent puppy," Jack said, but with good humor. But then the game-playing was over. "So, what did you learn from La Reina?"

Puck looked to Regina, one eyebrow raised in inquiry. *What did you tell him?*

She shook her head. "He had you followed tonight."

"True, and not just tonight. Dickie Carstairs has been on my heels so long I've given serious thought to adopting him. But he's learned the young lady's name? That is unexpected, since I find myself amazed that the man can find his own way home. Good on Dickie."

Regina bent her head and bit on her knuckle. She should be embarrassed to be here, dressed as she was—modestly, if inappropriately. She shouldn't be enjoying this verbal fencing between brothers, one light to the other's dark but both of them clearly devoted to each other. But her cousin was missing and in grave danger, and she doubted a full team of horses could drag her from this room. She wouldn't be anywhere else!

"Your brother just told me that two more young women have been taken," she said, bringing the conversation back on point, rather like a governess attempting to keep her charges' attention on their lessons while a bluebird sang on a branch just outside the nursery window. "He also told me that you never mentioned the masquerade. Now you need to tell him, and me, what you learned from La Reina."

Puck looked to his brother. "Two? How many is that? I mean, since you began to keep count. Lord knows there are bound to be more."

"Definitely more than two dozen now, including your cousin, Regina. I would think that enough, if not for the fact that the majority are prostitutes, as is the case with the two most recent disappearances, and don't bring the sort of price possible with—pardon me. I am attempting, badly, to say that were I the father of a lovely, fair-haired young debutante, I should be keeping her very close at the moment."

"The Crown still won't allow a warning to the populace? You've told them what you think, and those idiots won't change their minds?"

"No, Puck, they won't, for obvious reasons. Why else do you think they involved me, a person who occasionally does their dirty work for them, a person who, for all intents and purposes, does not exist? And before you start berating me, remember that you've been less than helpful in my investigation. Truth to tell, this buying and selling of white women has been going on for as long as there have been unscrupulous men with money and…certain appetites. If a certain somebody's goddaughter had not been taken, I'd still be in Scotland, cleaning up another mess."

"And they would never have known about Miranda," Regina said, nodding her agreement with Jack. "How many others do you suppose traveled home during their London Season to nurse a slight illness, only to have the world later learn that they'd *succumbed* to those illnesses?"

"I can think of two in the last three years, and I am hardly the one to ask as I am rarely in London," Jack said, looking at Puck. "Now, what did you learn from your little miss?"

Puck poured a glass of wine for himself and then took up his stance in front of the mantelpiece. "La Reina, or more aptly, Mr. Queen—"

Jack held up one hand. "A moment, please. Clearly Dickie's powers of observation can sometimes be, as you said, limited. Our lady is a man?"

"Yes. Dressed as a woman in order to protect his employer's soiled doves. You and I aren't the only souls in London who are aware that women are disappearing from the streets. There's a very quiet army out there hunting for our kidnappers, one way or another. I don't need to say more, do I? Except to add that, amazingly, our Mr. Queen makes a fairly attractive female. In any case, he had the misfortune of being mistaken for a slight, blonde woman—the curse of walking streets not lit after dark—and was taken up by what we can only assume are the same persons who kidnapped Miranda at the masquerade Friday night. Same night, same neighborhood—probably not coincidental."

"Agreed," Jack said. "Go on."

Puck looked to Regina, who nodded encouragingly. "Tell us everything. Please."

"All right. Mr. Queen was grabbed from behind, stunned by a knock on the head but not completely unconscious—probably thanks to the thickness of his wig—and tossed into a shabby black coach. The shades were nailed in place, and it was pitch-black inside, so he could not identify the other occupant. He knew there was another occupant, because he'd landed on her. She, unlike Mr. Queen, was unconscious, not even protesting when he fell on her. He immediately decided not to call out or pound on the door but simply to await his chance. He knew what had happened to him, you see. The coach smelled of laudanum and, as I said, it was totally dark inside, so that showing him Miranda's miniature meant nothing."

Regina bit her bottom lip, holding back what otherwise would surely have been a sob.

"The coach made its way to the docks before coming to a halt, at which time our Mr. Queen, being in possession of a rather ugly knife, greeted his kidnappers with it when the coach door was opened, bounded to

the ground and, to quote the man, 'Used my dew beat-
ers to lope off fast as I could.'"

"'He who fights and runs away…'" Jack quoted, nodding his head.

"Yes, and before you ask, no, Mr. Queen does not remember the street, except that the coach ride had been
no more than a quarter hour in duration, which would
lead us to the London Docks. Added to that, Mr. Queen
remembers an overpowering smell of tobacco, which
would again indicate the London Docks and the new
tobacco warehouse located there. Mostly, however, he
remembers running for his life, which a man dressed
as a woman, his blond wig a casualty of his brief incar-
ceration, might do when he finds himself in a strange
neighborhood. God knows I'd have trouble explaining
myself, were I caught out in such a position."

"Where is this Mr. Queen now?"

"Along with our friend Dickie, I chose not to adopt
him. I'm sure you'll find him back in his usual haunts
in a week or two, if you wish to apply thumbscrews to
him, but I think he's given us all that he knows." Puck
turned to Regina, his eyes soft with sympathy. "It's
progress, sweetings."

"I know. I…I'm just thinking of how terrified she
must have been. One minute at the masquerade, the
next only the good Lord knows where. And being
forced to drink laudanum? That's what they did, didn't
they? Her kidnappers? They drugged her and then
tossed her into their coach as if she were a bolt of cloth
or a sack of meal and drove off with her. And that man,

that Mr. Queen, he did nothing to help her. He simply left her there."

"Yes. He regrets that. Fervently," Puck told her.

"And you point fingers at *my* methods?" Jack said. "Well done, brother. However, the London Docks? Counting warehouses, storage houses, the ships drawn up there? It could take an army of men a month to find what we're looking for."

"True. But that's still better than hunting all up and down the Thames, searching every dock. Unless they had a small boat tied there and the ship is already anchored in the middle of the river. There's no end to the possibilities."

Jack nodded his agreement. "I'll arrange to have some Runners and a few others positioned on the docks, looking out for any unusual activity. God, that sounds so obvious. And pointless. We need to attack this from another angle."

Regina looked from one man to the other. Were they still holding back, not telling each other everything they knew? As she was holding back herself, it seemed possible.

"There is the Trojan Horse," she ventured at last.

Both brothers turned to look at her, Jack with a rather sardonic smile, Puck in some amusement.

"I'm sorry, Regina," Puck said in some sympathy, she supposed. "You want us to declare defeat by gifting the slavers with a wooden horse? Roll it onto the docks and tie a bow around its neck? Or perhaps a sign on its flanks instead? 'You win, we concede, and to prove it, here's a pretty horsey?'"

"This is an example of the famed Robin Goodfellow charm? I'm amazed you've lived as long as you have," Jack said, looking to Regina as if she might launch a physical attack on Puck at any moment. "Forgive him, Regina. He's played the fool so long and so well, he sometimes misplaces his brains. You don't mean an actual Trojan Horse, correct?"

"Thank you, no. I don't. Puck, you know that, don't you?"

"I do. And the answer is no."

"But Puck—"

"I said, *no*. Jack, you know what she's saying, don't you?"

"I think so, but I wasn't aware you did. Thirty men, left inside the belly of the wooden horse, to be dragged inside the gates and then, once the revelry died down, sneaking out to open the gates to the remainder of the army. Regina, your pardon, but what I think you meant to say was that we need a stalking horse. Not a Trojan Horse."

"I don't care if she calls it Prinney's trick pony. The answer is still no. A loud, resounding *no*."

But Regina had the bit between her teeth now. After all, it seemed such an obvious solution. "Puck, you've got to see the reasoning. You said it yourself. Or Jack said it. The London Docks are immense. I've been there with my father, I've seen them. We'd never find her. But if we give the kidnappers a gift?"

"You're not a gift, Regina." He held up a hand to stop her from interrupting. "Do you think I don't know what you're saying? We put you out on the street, wait for you to be snatched up by these bas—no-goods, follow you to their makeshift prison, and you, God help us all, think that you'll somehow wait until everyone is drunk or sleeping, at which point you will be able to somehow open the doors for us."

"Well, yes." It did sound far-fetched when Puck said it. There were several details that would have to be worked out, certainly.

Puck immediately mentioned one of them.

"One, you're not blond."

At least she had a ready answer. "Neither is Mr. Queen. He isn't even female. And he fooled them. Surely you must be able to find a blond wig for me that's better than his."

Jack retreated to the drinks table and poured another glass of wine. He was probably being discreet. Or he was enjoying Puck's discomfiture too much.

"You're too tall."

"Yes, there is that. But Jack said they seem to be getting desperate. Taking prostitutes, collecting females at an astonishing rate. They're getting ready to leave, Puck, and once their ship sets sail, Miranda is lost forever. Jack already said as much before you arrived. You've made astonishing progress, but it's not enough."

The look Puck threw Jack could have melted icebergs. That Jack merely smiled and shrugged certainly didn't help matters.

Regina hastened to continue. "We know where they are...."

"Ha! You said you've been to London Docks. It's little better than what we did know—that they're in London."

Regina wasn't so easily discouraged. "But just think, Puck. We could use the story we invented to satisfy my aunt and uncle Friday night. The coachman can lose his way, there is an accident of some kind. There I'd be. A lady of some quality, alone in the night, virtually unprotected."

"Ripe pickings," Jack said, seating himself once more and again crossing one long leg over the other. "The idea has merit."

Puck looked ready to strangle his brother.

Jack shook his head. "For God's sake, man, climb down out of the treetops. Not Regina. Good God, no. But someone. You said Mr. Queen is not available?"

"He's rather indisposed," Puck said, shooting a sidelong glance at Regina. "He may have cracked a few ribs somehow. Probably when we fell. Then there's the matter of his blackened eyes."

Regina rolled her own eyes. "The man looked perfectly fine when I saw him. You hit him, didn't you? Well, good for you. I would have liked to hit him a time or two myself. Leaving Miranda like that? And he was armed. He could have helped her."

"I know a woman..." Jack said, getting to his feet. "We...we have a history. For the right price, she may feel the risk worth taking."

Regina shook her head vehemently. "No, we can't ask someone else to take such a risk. It's my fault Miranda is in the fix she's in. I gave in to my own curiosity and agreed to accompany her Friday night. She's a goose, bless her, but I'm supposed to have more sense." She looked beseechingly at Puck. "Please. Maybe nothing will come of it, but we can't know if we don't try. And you'd never be far away. You could merely follow us after I've been...you know. Taken."

Jack clapped a hand on Puck's shoulder. "I'll return tomorrow, at ten. We'll discuss this again. In the meantime, I'm for the London Docks. Maybe we'll get lucky, and the horse can remain in the stables—or the carpentry shop. Regina?" He made her a rather elegant bow. "It was my distinct and humble pleasure. Good night."

"Good night, Jack," she said, watching as he left the room, wishing him back because she could feel Puck seething behind her.

"He didn't tell you anything," she pointed out once Jack had gone. She turned around to face Puck. "We told him things, and he managed to tell us nothing. Do you think he knows nothing?"

"He told us that two more young women have been snatched off the streets. Did he seem surprised when I mentioned the London Docks? It's difficult to tell with Jack, what he knows, what he doesn't know."

"He knows that we don't have much more time. Why didn't you tell him about the masquerade ball?"

"I don't know. Habit?" He smiled. "The fact that he plays his own cards close to his vest? Or perhaps that it seemed silly to have us both going down the same path. Well, at least now I won't have Dickie Carstairs dogging my every step. The fellow is as subtle as a charging boar." He held out his hand to her, and she took it, getting to her feet. "I haven't had time to tell you how fetching you look in that muslin armor. Virginal as a nun, and yet all I can think about is how I would enjoy loosing every one of those innumerable buttons."

Regina felt her body softening inside but fought the sensation. "Don't attempt to distract me, Puck. The Trojan Horse was my idea, and I want to be a part of it. You wouldn't let anything really terrible happen to me."

"Your blind trust bids fair to unman me. But no, it's out of the question. You did hear what I said about La Reina, didn't you? Picked up, conked on the head and tossed? And worse, what they did to Miranda. Laudanum. You expect me to stay in the shadows and *watch* such a thing?"

Regina sighed soulfully. "You're right, of course. It was a half-formed idea, spoken before I could work through it to the flaws. But Jack seemed to think it might be something we could try."

"Jack enjoys other people's discomfort. If he came here tonight to better understand why you're here, he's now had his answer. I've become putty in your hands. But not so much that I'd allow you to put yourself in danger."

"Thank you. I'll admit that the idea terrified me. I just keep thinking about Miranda and what she must be enduring right now. Sometimes I think I'll go mad, imagining she thinks we've deserted her or that we've decided that she ran away on her own. How she feels. What she's thinking. She could be thinking that no one is looking for her or that we believe she's dead. She has to be thinking of her mother, how the woman is grieving for her lost daughter..." Regina dropped her head into her hands. "My mind won't stop, Puck. There has to be something I can do other than sit safely in your coach while you chase horrible little men down alleyways. That we can do."

He opened his arms to her. "Come here," he said and folded his arms around her. It felt like coming home. He pressed a kiss against her hair. "We're going to find her, Regina. These men aren't fools. They'll keep her safe. They'd lose too much profit, otherwise."

"If...if she was violated," Regina said into his shirtfront. "Are you sure of that, or are you just attempting to calm my fears?"

"No, I'm sure of that," he said, and she peeked up at him, surprised by the intensity in his tone.

"How do you know?"

He looked at her, his eyes clear and honest. "When I was taking my Grand Tour, I heard some stories of the slave trade. Virgins are highly prized. If we can find her, get her back, she can be taken to the country to recover from her fright and then return to society as if nothing ever happened."

"Who...who buys these poor young women? What sort of horrible men buy them? Do they place orders with these terrible men? Bring me a blond white woman? As if they might be ordering a new shirt?"

His smile was rueful as he dabbed at her wet cheeks with his handkerchief. "Yes, rather like that, I think. Not being human themselves, they have no compassion for the human race in general. Your cousin, I'm afraid, is a valuable commodity to her abductors, and…and an expensive toy for the purchaser. I'm sorry, sweetings. There's really no delicate way of putting it. Now come along, it's bed for you, and for me, as well. We're going to have another full day tomorrow."

She nodded, avoiding his eyes. "I hate being alone," she told him, unable to hide her feelings. "The minutes drag, as they did tonight as I waited for you to finish with Mr. Queen. And my mind races. It goes places I don't want it to go, drawing pictures I don't want to see, but I'm powerless to stop any of it. Can you imagine how Aunt Claire feels, if I'm so overset?"

Puck took her hand in his and led her toward the stairs. "And how are the ladies since we saw them at dinner? I know it's impossible to make them comfortable."

"Aunt Claire is closeted with her prayer books, alternating between hope and tears. But Mama is quite comfortable," Regina said, summoning a smile from somewhere inside her. "She actually told me tonight that being here is like widowhood without the widow's weeds or any feelings of sorrow. I hadn't realized it, but I can't remember a time Papa didn't keep Mama close to him. He has never left either of us in the country when he had business here in London. And it turns out that we did the right thing in bringing only Hanks with us. Mama's dresser, Fellows, according to Mama, is one of Papa's spies. I don't know if that's true or not, but I am worried. Mama always seemed to be able to supply herself with…with her strong spirits. Do you suppose my father *likes* that she drinks? That he has made certain that she always has a ready supply?"

Puck nodded his head shortly to the two footmen sitting in the foyer, dismissing them for the night, and turned to mount the stairs. "What do you think, Regina? I don't know the man."

"I don't think I do, either." Regina pressed a hand to her mouth for a moment, coming to a decision. "Am I an unnatural daughter to dislike him so much? Am I so desperate for answers that I'd even briefly entertain the idea that— No, it's ridiculous. Impossible."

Puck squeezed her hand. "The only impossible thing in this world right now, Regina," he said as they hesitated in the upstairs hallway, "is the thought of leaving you alone tonight."

She opened her mouth, attempted to speak, to say something, anything. But no words came to her lips.

"I'm sorry," he said, shaking his head. "You're under considerable duress, and I'd be a rotter of the first order to take advantage of that. Your nerves are rubbed raw, with good reason, and your mind is racing every which way. Everything, every moment, seems desperate, either moving too quickly or dragging too slowly. You wouldn't know this, but you are a soldier the night before the battle, caught between fear and anticipation, your every sense heightened. If I look reasonable to you, Regina, it's because you know I understand your anxiety. But people do foolish things at times like this. Believe things they wouldn't give a second thought to at some other time. I'm not the man for you. I'm only the man who's here."

"And I'm only the woman who's here?" she asked him quietly.

He slowly shook his head, still gazing deeply into her eyes. "No. I won't lie and say that. Even though I should."

Her breath caught in her throat. He was so dear. So honest. So much better than he thought he was, than the world thought he was.

"I don't want to be alone tonight, Puck," she said at last. "You're not simply the man who's here. You know that. Tell me you know that. Please."

"This can't work, Regina. All I can do is ruin your future."

"Isn't that my decision? Can't we just talk some more, at least. I won't sleep, in any case. Not thinking what I'm thinking. What…what happens after that isn't something we need to discuss."

"I shouldn't have done what I did this afternoon. You're vulnerable, and I took advantage."

At last Regina felt some stirrings of anger. "Oh yes, I can see that. Such a simple little goose, that Regina. A longing look, a few kisses, and she will allow any liberty. Clearly, Mr. Blackthorn, you have a duty to save her from herself."

Puck smiled. "I've never been much for duty."

He took her hand once more, and, together, they walked down the dim hallway and entered her bedchamber.

CHAPTER TEN

WHAT HE WAS THINKING was criminal, on so many levels.

She was just as he'd told her. Vulnerable. Young, just awakening to what it was to be a woman rather than a girl. Her cousin had gone missing, most probably to a terrible fate impossible to conceive in its brutality. Her mother clearly was not a stable woman, not the sort Regina could turn to for advice.

She was in his house, beneath his roof. The bastard's roof. There could be no future for them; she knew it, he knew it.

All he could bring her was disgrace and her father's wrath.

All she could bring him was a desire unfulfilled or a memory that would never leave him, with the empty years stretching in front of him, his heart forever lost.

God, how his mother would swoon with it, enjoy the drama of it all. She'd think it all delicious. And yes, inevitable. She'd always liked Shakespeare's tragedies best. As Juliet, she must have died on the stage five hundred times. Lovely as she still was, in the past few years an audience couldn't be faulted for thinking her Juliet now succumbed to old age.

Puck smiled at the thought and then mentally

slapped himself. Even when he was serious, deadly serious, there was always that spark of ridiculousness in him, trying hard to get out. It was a curse.

He watched as Regina used a thin taper to light more candles around the room. The full moon shone in the windows, the draperies not yet closed. Did her maid forget to draw the draperies, or did Regina always sleep with the drapes pulled back over the sheer silk curtains? Did she like to watch the stars or wake to greet the morning sun?

He knew so little about her. She'd waved away the beets tonight at dinner. She didn't like beets. She might like the morning sun on her face.

She loathed or feared her father. Or both.

She felt, tasted, like Heaven.

They could flee to Paris. To America. He had the money; she'd want for nothing. He'd take the mother, if she insisted. The mother, the maid, her pet spaniel, if she had one. He'd go anywhere, dare anything, to have her.

And he knew nothing about her.

Was love insanity, or insanity love?

And did either condition explode into a man's life in the space of only a few days?

She walked over to the small fire and sat down on the hearth rug, her virginal dressing gown puddling around her, the firelight catching in her hair, casting warm shadows over her perfect features, her flawless skin. She looked across the room at him and smiled, in embarrassment, in trepidation and with some hidden sorrow.

Yes. The answer to his question was yes. Yes, it could. Full-blown. Without rhyme or reason.

"There are any number of chairs in this pile," he said as he joined her on the floor. "But you're right. We'll be most comfortable here. Naughty children, gathering around the fire when they should be in bed, fast asleep. But you've already said that you won't sleep. Tell me the thoughts you're so certain won't allow sleep."

"Your brother said something tonight, just before you arrived." She looked down at her entwined fingers as she spoke. "He said that the person we're looking for is a man without heart. A man who sees others as devices to pad his pockets. Without morals or scruples. A man uncaring of another person's pain. A man solely interested in profit."

Puck nodded his head. "I agree. It takes a special sort of snake to do what this man, these men, are doing. On both ends of the sale."

"And if that person…if that person owned his own shipping company?" She looked up at him, tears swimming in her eyes.

Puck was shocked that she'd come to his same conclusion, and didn't bother to dissemble. "You'd accuse your own father?"

"Now do you see why I could never sleep tonight? The moment Jack said the words, I could see my father's face as clearly as if he were suddenly in the room with us. Jack had just described my father to me."

"Owning ships doesn't automatically make the man a suspect...."

"He has a business partner," she added quickly, and she could hear a desperate hope in her voice. "Mr. Harley. Benjamin Harley. I've only met him a single time, when Papa took me to London Docks to show me his latest purchase, a huge trading ship he said would make the shareholders in the East India Company swoon in jealousy."

"And your opinion of Mr. Harley?" Puck was doing his best not to react or to overreact.

Her shoulders sagged. "A cipher," she said sadly. "But much better educated than Papa. He speaks to the...the customers, I suppose they're called. Oh, and he keeps the books and ledgers. Nobody but Papa and Mr. Harley may see them. Know the cargo, the destinations. Papa said that's because he trusts no one. Pirates, you understand. He's very leery of pirates."

"He's leery of something," Puck said ruminatively. "When he took you to see his new ship, was it berthed at London Docks?"

She bit her bottom lip. Nodded. "But, no, I don't remember more than that. I was much younger, and the London Docks had just barely opened. There was so much noise, so many people...."

He took her hands in his. They were cold, and trembling. "Regina, listen to me. It's a grand leap from having a father who wants you to marry well to believing he...dabbles in white slavery."

"I know. I want to be convinced I'm wrong, seeing

an easy answer because we need an easy answer. Not that it's easy to think of one's own father as so evil. And it's Miranda, Puck. Surely he wouldn't countenance such a terrible thing. But…"

Puck leaned closer to her. "Yes. But?"

"He sent the Runners north. Remember? He told me he was certain Miranda had been kidnapped, even said she was probably taken by…by white slavers. He was… quite graphic in his description of what would happen to her. Yet he ordered my uncle to send the Runners north, saying she'd eloped. Why would he do that? He told me it was to spare my aunt and uncle pain, but— well, his words didn't ring true to me when he said them, and they don't now."

"I would think, for the sake of his family, if you're right, if your father is somehow involved, he'd have found some way to have Miranda freed once he realized she'd been taken. No, I can't see a man knowingly sending his own niece into such horror."

"She's in her second Season and with signs of needing a third, as she has no dowry. Papa finances everything. The town house, Miranda's gowns, the horses. My uncle's gambling debts while he's in town. My cousin Justin's gambling debts. Everything. He's often told me he wishes us shed of them, and he will be once I'm wed to a title. He plans to cut them off without a bent farthing, or at least that's what he says. Their… their usefulness to him will be over, you see. Even… even my mother. She just told me he's threatened her with a madhouse, once I'm married."

Puck was fast running out of reasons not to think Regina's father could be a suspect in the disappearances. In any number of crimes, the worst of them his treatment of his own family.

"Your father has a warehouse at London Docks?"

"Yes. I do remember the sign. It was fresh and new. Everything was fresh and new. Hackett and Harley Company. The sign was two Hs, rather curled into each other."

"And you'd feel better if I were to take a drive down there tomorrow, to take a look at this building?"

"I feel like a terrible, unnatural daughter. But yes, I would also feel better if you did that. As long as I can come along."

"You're in the country, remember? You and your mother and your aunt? You can't be seen by anyone who might recognize you."

"You took me along tonight," she pointed out, not unreasonably.

"In the dark, and you remained inside the coach. What if your father is on the docks?"

"I'm not the only one he might recognize, if he's there. He knows about you, Puck, remember? He'd have to wonder why you were there."

"He won't recognize me," Puck said before he could think, and immediately regretted his words.

"Oh? And why won't he recognize you? Oh, wait. Didn't you say something about your valet visiting a costumer? You're going to wear a *costume?* Yes, of course you are! Did he get one for me, as well? Look at you! I can see it in your eyes. He did, didn't he?"

"It's the heat from the fire. Temporarily muddled my brains, so that they forgot to put a brake on my tongue," Puck ruminated, sighing. "Yes, yes, Gaston managed to procure a few costumes for you, as well. God, hanging's too good for me. Even Jack wouldn't go so far."

"Then you're going to allow me to accompany you?" She leaned forward and touched his knee. "Say it, Puck. Say, yes, I will take you along."

He took her hand and raised it to her mouth. "I want you to know that I understand how you feel, Regina. I tried to imagine one of my brothers being taken and how I would dare anything to find him, bring him home safely. If someone told me no, I'd simply find my own way. But, damn it, Regina, I'm a man, and you're—"

"And what? I'm helpless? Hopeless? Bound to get in the way?"

He smiled and feigned a slight ducking motion, as if she might strike him. "That last one, yes."

Her shoulders sagged. "At least you're honest. I can't shoot or fence. I've never…punched anyone. But surely there's some way I can be helpful."

Again, Puck smiled. "No, no, sweetings, I'm not laughing at you. I'm remembering something that happened last year, with my brother and his Chelsea. She also wanted to help in a…a certain situation. I finally understand why Beau was so set against it. He was like a bear with a sore tooth the entire time, I swear it. Although, in the end, she performed rather well."

"Did she have to shoot, fence or punch anyone?"

"I know what you're saying, Regina. No, she didn't. But just because Beau was so befuddled by Chelsea's charms that he'd allow such a thing doesn't mean that I— Bloody hell, I just walked straight into that one, didn't I?"

"You did?" Regina asked, but her eyes betrayed her feigned innocence. They were nearly dancing with glee.

"If I say yes, will you agree to obey my every order the instant it's given, not ask questions, not fight me in any way?"

She nodded furiously, a child agreeing to the medicine if the sugarplum reward was included in the promise.

"And you'll be able to sleep now?"

Her eyes were the windows to her soul. He saw the sudden hurt, the confusion. The question. The—God help them both—desire.

He reached out and cupped her cheek in his palm. "Yes, sweetings, I feel it, too. A sadness, deep as any ocean. An emptiness that needs filling, even as we'd never, either of us, felt such an emptiness before. It could be the moment, Regina. That's all it could be, a longing of the moment brought on by the events of these last days. Not even a full handful of too-short days, Regina. Hardly enough to know anything more about each other than that we could make magic together."

"And it's wrong to want that," she whispered. "The magic?"

"Oh yes," he said, moving closer to her. "It's wrong. So very, very wrong..."

His mouth closed over hers as he gathered her to him, his arms going around her as he eased her down onto the hearth rug.

He kissed her, again and again, teasing at her mouth with his tongue and teeth, his hand working at the buttons that ran down the front of her virginal dressing gown.

Virginal. There were ways. Ways he could have her, that she could have him, without physically taking her virginity. Leaving her intact for the man she would one day marry. He'd shown her one way that afternoon.

There were others.

He eased the dressing gown from her shoulders, exposing the thin night rail that was easily shifted to reveal her right breast to his touch. He cupped her fullness in his hand, teased at her nipple with his thumb. Caught her sigh of pleasure with his mouth.

She was perfection. Glory. And instantly responsive.

She flowered beneath his touch, her body soft and inviting, her nipple hardening, inviting further intimacy.

He pulled her up into a sitting position across his lap and kept his mouth on hers as he worked to free her night rail, tug it above her hips, so that he could reach up under its bunched-up hem to touch her bare belly.

Her bare buttocks, the weight of her against his manhood, roused him almost painfully. He wanted to be inside her. Deep, deep inside her. He wanted her heat, her tightness.

But that was not to be.

She held on to him, her arm around his shoulder, her head pressed against him as he took her nipple into his mouth and began stroking it with his tongue, even as he moved his hand down over her belly and between her legs. She was an instrument of delight, and he was playing her. Bringing her pleasure.

She was breathing audibly now, her body wet and warm and welcoming to his every intimacy. He would take her to the brink, and then over…and then take himself off somewhere to figuratively slit his wrists, because he was very close to losing his mind.

Come on. Yes, that's it, my darling, open for me. Feel good. I want you to forget the world, forget everything and just feel.

And then she was pushing at him, rolling off him and scurrying a few feet away to sit facing him, drawing her dressing gown around her, her knees bent, hugging herself, turning into a small ball of passion and… good God, fury.

"Regina? What's wrong?"

"What's wrong?" she repeated, her voice shaking. "Do you think I'm an idiot? No, don't answer that. I know you don't think I'm an idiot. Maybe you simply think I'm selfish. Look at you. Prepared to be the martyr, or whatever it is you think you're doing. Give her what she so blatantly asked for—that's what you're doing, isn't it, Puck? All for me and nothing for you. You'd have me, but you'd protect me." She roughly wiped at her eyes with the backs of her hands. "Do you have any idea how that makes me *feel?*"

He very nearly opened his mouth and said *good?* But although the annals of history are filled with the stupid things men say when they're attempting to be helpful, even he knew that was wrong.

Besides, she was already answering her own question.

"I'll tell you how it makes me feel. Cheap. Tawdry. Selfish. Is that what you wanted me to feel, Puck?"

"Christ, no," he said, getting to his feet and holding his hands down to her, to help her rise. "I'm an idiot. I'm sorry, Regina. I'll go now."

She rolled her eyes. Actually rolled her eyes. "If only I had Grandmother Hackett here to appeal to her for advice. I had no idea it would be so difficult to be rid of my virginity. Are all men so stupid, Robin Goodfellow, or just you? You've made it clear that you want me. Haven't you? Or were you only flirting, being gallant, saying what you thought you should say?"

He was rather wishing for the grandmother, himself. Because he was totally at a loss at the moment. Anything he said, he felt certain, would be wrong. "Regina—"

"'Come away with me now, sweet tease, and we will pleasure each other all the night long. We will strip off these masks, and with them rid ourselves of all inhibition. You do not yet know me, but I will soon know your every delectable inch, taste your nectar, explore your most intimate womanly secrets. I will take you where you have never been, touch you in ways—'"

"Sweet God," Puck interrupted in shock, taking her by the shoulders. "It sounded much more romantic in French, didn't it? You committed that trash to memory?"

"Trash?" She tried to pull free of him again, but this time he held her in place.

"Yes, damn it. Trash. Said to a woman I thought to be something she was not. A woman of the world, not a—damn it, Regina, not a *virgin*."

She stilled, no longer struggling. "Oh? So what do you say to virgins?"

She was going to drive him insane. "I don't know. I've never bedded a virgin. Frankly, you scare the hell out of me. There. Happy now?"

She blinked twice, bit her bottom lip for a moment, and then—damn it—she smiled. "So that would mean that I am asking you—for I am asking you, Puck, make no mistake about that—to debauch your first virgin? That, in a way, you are as new to this as I am?"

Puck looked to his left, to his right.

"What are you doing?" she asked him.

"Searching for my dignity. It's got to be around here somewhere."

"Oh, Puck…" she said and slid her arms up and around his neck. She took hold of one end of his riband and pulled open the bow, then threaded her fingers into his hair. "I'm so sorry. But I'm afraid it's gone off somewhere with mine."

He laughed softly and scooped her up into his arms to carry her over to the bed. "Good. Let's see what sort of trouble we can get into before they both find their way back."

This time, his hands were sure and certain. This time, she was naked in his arms. This time he wasn't choking on either his tied cravat or his good intentions.

They touched. They sighed. They laughed. Her kisses enflamed him, her touch went from tentative to certain in the space of a few heartbeats.

The whole world would wish to be him, if they only knew the glory that was Regina Hackett. All woman, from her head to her toes. Every inch of her kissable... and kissed. Her every curve explored, some with exacting detail, even as she stroked him, learned him, seemed to glory in the feel of him.

She sighed her pleasure, moaned with each new ecstasy, allowed her lush woman's body to dictate to her, give to him, welcome each new intimacy. And all while taking liberties of her own. She was on a journey of discovery, and making the most of every step along the way.

And he was learning, as well. He, who thought he'd experienced everything, known everything there was to know about this business of men and women, knew himself to be on his own voyage of discovery. Because this was more than mere sensation. Simple physical pleasure.

What he felt now was earthshakingly intense. Each touch had meaning. He'd never thought himself to be a selfish lover but never before had giving pleasure been more important than taking it for himself. His heart soared when she sighed, it thrilled to the way she lifted her hips to grant him greater access to her secrets…and it shattered into a million pieces when at last he pushed inside her and broke through the final barrier keeping them two people rather than one.

"I'm sorry, I'm sorry…" he breathed against her ear as she went very still, her fingernails digging into his back. "But now it gets better. I promise."

"Show me," she whispered. "There's more. I know there's more. I still feel so…so— Oh. Oh, Puck, yes. That's…oh."

He moved slowly, withdrawing slightly before sinking into her again, counting silently—in Italian, not his most proficient language—in order to keep himself from exploding now that he was enveloped in the tight heat of her. But soon her small cries of pleasure turned slightly desperate, and she was pulling at him, her fingernails once again digging into his back, her hips rising up each time he withdrew, drawing him back.

He had to see her face. Had to see what was in her eyes. Needed it as he needed air to breathe. He pushed himself up, pressing his palms against the pillows, straightening his elbows, his long legs between her thighs, their lower bodies joined.

"Now?" he asked her, grinding himself against her, looking down into her beautiful face in the candlelight.

She put her hands on his arms, lifting herself to him,

her breasts creamy perfection, her chin tipped up as she strained for every last bit of pleasure he could give her.

This time when he moved, it was with the sight of her pleasure feeding his desire, the heat of her urging him on. He buried himself in her, again and again and again, until her body took her past mere desire and lifted her beyond the confines of the earth for those few fleeting moments of purest physical joy that made the rest of life worthwhile.

And then Puck did something he'd never done before in his life. He withdrew and gave in to his own pleasure only after collapsing on top of her, his release hitting hard against her lower belly in a climax so intense he briefly wondered if he might die with it.

CHAPTER ELEVEN

REGINA LOOKED INTO the mirror at the reflection of her maid. "Nothing?"

Hanks pushed another pin into the mass of hair she'd wrapped tightly around Regina's head, in preparation for the black wig waiting its turn on the top of the dressing table. "Nary a drop, miss, not since we got here. Seems almost unnatural, it does. Only time I see her hands shake is when she talks about having to go back. Poor mite. Breaks my heart, seeing her like that."

Having her own mother referred to as a poor mite, and by a servant who one would think would envy her much loftier position in life, was difficult to hear. But in many ways, it was true that Leticia Hackett was a woman to be pitied.

"I should go see her before I leave, but how would I explain this?" Regina asked, touching her hands to the bodice of her gown.

"She's napping yet again," Hanks told her. "Doing a lot of that. Napping. And the poor countess? I don't think she's slept a wink since she got here."

Regina nodded, then winced as yet another long pin was twisted into her mass of hair. "I spoke with her this morning, and told her we think we're making progress. I hope that wasn't a lie. It's unnerving that she's so grateful, when we haven't really *done* anything."

"Yes, miss. You're not to know, but Mr. Puck spoke with her ladyship this morning, as well, and he all but promised her Lady Miranda would be home safe and dry very soon."

Several hairs came out by their roots, Regina was certain of it, as she abruptly swiveled about on her chair. "He *what?* How could he do that?"

Hanks was a practical woman of small imagination. She merely shrugged and said, "I suppose by opening his mouth and saying the words, miss. He made her that happy."

"He gave her false hope, that's what he did." Regina was incensed.

Again, the maid shrugged. "Crying could be false fears, just as easy. Even if we don't know nothing, ain't it better to be hoping than fearing? Time enough for either one once we know what's true. And her ladyship ate up all her breakfast this morning, and that ain't too terrible, I'm thinking, miss."

Regina relented. "No, I suppose it's not. How many more pins are you going to stab into me, Hanks? I feel now as if there are hundreds of them."

"I think that about does it, miss. Now, to figure out how this thing works," Hanks said, picking up the wig and looking at it critically. "Ah, there's the front, don't you think? Now hold still, miss, and we'll get this done."

A few minutes and several small adjustments later,

Regina was ready to take on her role of widow in mourning.

She was dressed top to bottom in unremitting black, her skirts rather full—the product of a bygone age, bits of black ribbon here and there, the buttons made of jet. Her gloves were really black lace mitts with her fingers left free. Her black boots laced to her knees and were not only cracked with age but two sizes too large. Her now coal-black hair was covered by a long, black veil that also effectively hid her face. She carried a large reticule, also black, with a posie of black roses pinned to it, and Hanks handed her a large black umbrella with a brown wooden handle.

"I wouldn't recognize myself," Regina said as she inspected her reflection in the long mirror in the dressing room. "I think I'd also cut a wide berth around me. Everything stinks of camphor."

"Yes, miss, it does that. That's what comes from people not dying every day, things gets put away. Here's the last thing, sent up by Mr. Puck himself." So saying, she took hold of Regina's left hand and slipped a heavy gold ring on her finger, the center of the ring bearing an emerald nearly as large as her knuckle.

Regina held out her hand to admire the thing but then frowned. "Why on earth would he want me to wear anything like this? Everyone will notice it and remember it. I know I would."

"You'd have to be asking Mr. Puck that, I suppose," Hanks said as she hastened to the doorway that led straight onto the hallway and opened it. "He's waiting on you now."

Regina gave her reflection one last look, accepted the black, lace-edged handkerchief Hanks pressed into her hand, and headed for the doorway, stopping only to ask, "You like him, don't you? Mr. Puck."

Hanks blushed to the roots of her hair. "I'm not so old as to not know pretty when I sees it," she said quietly. "And he says 'thank you, Hanks' when I do something for him, like fetching up that there ring for him. Knows my name. And thanks me."

"And he's pretty," Regina repeated, trying not to smile.

"Prettier than most, yes, miss. Maybe just not this morning."

Her interest piqued, Regina hastened downstairs to the drawing room, where Puck was standing with his back to her, looking down at something in his hand.

He, too, was dressed all in black, the full cut of his coat also out of fashion for at least a decade or more, his pantaloons rather baggy and his white hose yellowed with age. She could see the mourning band pinned to his left arm…and smell the camphor from where she was standing.

"Are you sure we're supposed to be the mourners and not a pair of corpses?" she asked him and then gasped as he turned to face her. "What is *that!*"

Puck raised a hand to the *thing* on the side of his nose. "This? You don't like it? It doesn't make me look distinguished?"

She walked closer—although the *thing* could be seen very well enough from a distance—and inspected him. His hair was hanging loose to nearly his shoulders, and it seemed somehow gray rather than blond. Looking closely, she could see it had been liberally powdered. And his complexion was darker, as if stained with tea or something. But it was the *thing* that caught and held her interest. "It's a wart. Isn't it? Oh, Puck, that's ugly. Truly ugly."

He grinned in what appeared to be extreme pleasure. The wart didn't move. "Yes, you've gotten the better end of it, with that ring. Don't lose it, pet, it cost a good ten shillings."

She looked down at her hand. "It's not real?"

"It's the best glass money can buy," he admitted readily. "And memorable."

At last she thought she understood. "Like that *thing* on your nose."

"Precisely. People will look at us, and if asked to remember something about us, they will remember that we were mourners and that you wore a lovely, whacking great emerald ring and I had a wart on the side of my nose big as a baby's thumb. Oh, and the coffin."

"There's going to be a coffin, as well? And who will be in it?"

"Us, if we don't play our cards exactly right. Are you ready to go? You look wonderful in that wig, by the way. The black suits you. You'd look wonderful without any hair at all, I wager. I'd kiss you, but my wart might fall off."

She shook her head, seeing how clearly Puck was enjoying himself. "You know, I was quite nervous this morning, wondering how I could face you after...after last night. And now I'm wondering why I was so concerned. You make life so *easy* for people, do you know that? We can't help but join in your games."

"Not entirely my game, puss. I must make my bow to my sister-in-law, Chelsea, who first pointed out the brilliance of parading death in front of people, people whose first instinct is to look away from it. I'll tell you the whole story one day."

"I look forward to hearing it. Now tell me exactly what we're going to be doing, please, as I must admit to not having considered a corpse. Just the two of us in mourning."

"On the way," he said, stuffing the note he'd been reading into his pocket and taking her hand. "The hearse is waiting in the mews."

"The— Oh, Puck, you do nothing by half measures, do you?"

He leered at her, still looking young and wonderful, even with the wart, or in spite of it. "In all things, madam. In all things."

"Wretch," she grumbled as he led her to the rear of the house, feeling a blush stealing into her cheeks.

They passed by a few servants, who variously goggled or giggled, the cook dropped her stirring spoon when the two of them entered the kitchens, and the next thing Regina knew, she was sitting up on the wide plank seat alongside Puck and the driver of the hearse, a man with a faint resemblance to Gaston. If Gaston had a belly big as a house, that is, and bright red hair beneath his large black top hat.

She looked about the equipage as they headed out onto the street. "The black ostrich plumes are a lovely touch," she remarked, looking at the enormous feathers sticking up from the heads of the two black horses in the shafts and from each of the four top corners of the hearse. Then she turned about as best she could to peer in through the dusty windows of the hearse. "That's an actual coffin, isn't it? Is…is there an actual *body* in it?"

Puck kept his face free of expression. "Our cousin Yorick, yes."

Regina chuckled softly beneath her dark veil. "Alas, poor Yorick, I knew him well."

"Ah, but that is incorrect, pet. Still, a common error. The correct speech by our good friend Hamlet goes rather differently, with no *well* about it. 'Alas, poor Yorick! I knew him, Horatio: a fellow of infinite jest, of most excellent fancy: he hath borne me on his back a thousand times.' Etcetera. Thanks to my mother, I've got a head full of Shakespeare. And can't seem to *shake* it."

Regina rolled her eyes. "That was rather pathetic," she teased. "Now tell me why we're dragging Yorick with us."

"That's simple enough. We're having him crated up and sent by sea to Minster-In-Sheppey for burial."

"Minster-In-Sheppey? Sounds a lovely place."

"I have no idea. I merely thought the name intriguing. It's located on and named after the Isle of Sheppey, in case you're of a geographical bent of mind. One of England's oldest churches is located there, along with a nunnery founded over one thousand years ago, although it's no longer active."

Regina looked at him, her jaw dropped. "You did more than simply pick out a name, didn't you? Why?"

"One never knows when one will be taken to school and asked questions. A convincing lie is a well-prepared lie." He turned a bright smile on her. "And now you're looking at me as if you might be slightly afraid of me, wondering just what sort of man I am."

"Not really. I think you're a very clever man. I'm only wondering why you've found the need to be so clever."

Beside her, Gaston sniggered.

"That had an ominous sound to it, Gaston," Puck said, looking across at his valet. "Would you care to enlarge on it?"

"*Non, m'sieur,* I think not. I prefer to hold my tongue inside my head rather than in my hand, *oui?*"

Regina looked from valet to employer and back again. "You think you're very amusing, the pair of you. Don't you?"

"Ah, you hear that, Gaston? Miss Hackett is made of stern stuff. Didn't I tell you she is magnificent?"

"Repeatedly, *m'sieur.*"

"You told him that?" Regina asked, feeling rather pleased. Extraordinarily pleased, as a matter of fact.

"Indeed. I also informed him that you are intelligent,

obedient and trustworthy, all of which you will be as we reconnoiter the London Docks."

"Like a faithful hound," Regina muttered, suddenly not so flattered as she'd been a moment earlier. "Thank you so very much."

"You're so very welcome, Miss Claridge—you are Miss Marianna Claridge for the duration, should anyone ask. I don't expect that you'll have to speak to anyone, but it's always, again, best to be prepared. And now for the obedient part, if you don't mind. I will be leaving you in Gaston's capable hands as I make inquiries about the transport of Cousin Yorick, and you will hold your handkerchief to your face—beneath the veil, if you please—while keeping your ears and eyes open for anything or anyone who seems to be even slightly out of the ordinary. Can you do that?"

"I believe I will able to manage, yes," Regina said, losing charity with Puck by the moment. "I seriously doubt, however, that one of my father's captains will be willing to take a coffin onboard or make a stop to *deliver* it to the Isle of Sheppey."

Puck's grin grew annoyingly wide. "You don't think I look impressive enough to sway one of his captains? Don't spare my feelings, madam. It's the wart, isn't it? It puts you off."

"Puck, please be serious. I know you're trying to put me at my ease, but I won't be that until Miranda is home safe and dry, so just tell me what you plan to do."

He reached over and squeezed her hand. "Very well. What I plan to do is reconnoiter the area, hopefully be invited inside one of the buildings, preferably the office, and to see and hear whatever I can. That, and to pocket a key if I can manage it so that I might return later to inspect the building at my leisure. I'm proficient enough, aren't I, Gaston?"

"Not so fine as me, *m'sieur,* but not a bumbler, either," Gaston admitted.

"Oh," Regina said, rather nonplussed. "Am I in the company of thieves?"

"One reformed thief and one very bright pupil, I would say," Puck told her as Gaston threaded the hearse through the ever-increasing traffic of drays and open wagons clogging the streets around the London Docks.

The three fell silent, as the shouts and cries and general noise would have meant that any conversation take place at a near bellow, and merely looked about at the daunting task they'd set themselves.

London Docks was a city in itself, it seemed, just as large and imposing now as it had been when Regina was much smaller and everything had seemed enormous.

They were close enough to see the masts of the trading ships that were tied up at the wharves or anchored in the river, so many of them that it would not have surprised her if a sailor could walk from one deck to the other for a mile without ever getting his feet wet.

"It's impossible," she said to no one in particular, her spirits plummeting all the way to the toes of her too-large boots.

"What?" Puck asked her, putting his mouth near her ear.

"I said, it's impossible. You could hide an entire herd of elephants here, with no one the wiser."

In fact, unless her father was the guilty one, they could spend the next several years searching for the slavers and find nothing. She had to hope that her father was guilty, which was a terrible thought all on its own.

"Finding the elephants would be easy. We'd just follow the dung carts."

Regina snapped out of her unhappy reverie to look at Puck. "What did you say?" And then she smiled, shook her head. "You won't cheer me up, Robin Goodfellow. We've set ourselves an impossible task."

"A journey begins with the first step," he reminded her, pointing to a large brick warehouse that had appeared as Gaston managed to turn yet another corner, most people giving the hearse a wide berth. "The sign blowing in this fairly fetid breeze. A pair of *H*s, intertwined—see it?"

Regina drew in a deep, rather shuddering breath. "I see it."

PUCK ALIGHTED FROM the plank seat of the hearse, his boot heels lightly striking the cobblestones even as his eyes darted left and right beneath the concealing brim of his hat, picking out the most visible members of his small army, already in position.

There was *La Reina's* burly employer, pretending an interest in a wagonload of crates marked in Spanish. George Porter had lost five of his finest earners to the slavers, and once Puck had convinced Mr. Queen

to introduce him to the pimp, Mr. Porter had been eagerness itself in offering his assistance and that of his
entire crew. Save for Mr. Queen, who was…convalesc-
ing.

Puck counted three men besides Mr. Porter, each
of them doing his best to appear uninterested in what
was going on around them yet each wearing the tight,
wary look of those who existed only through their fists
and wits. There were also four women, clearly soiled
doves, rather unambitiously plying their wares as they
moved about the expanse of cobblestones fronting the
H and H Company, each of them looking at least as, if
not more, deadly than the men.

And over there were the hatters. Not nearly as physically impressive and twice as recognizable, as each
had topped off their shabby rigouts with fine-looking
hats well above their ability to purchase them. Miranda's great-grandfather was ninety if he was a day and
deaf as a post, living in a narrow but well-appointed
house in Piccadilly. Puck had been forced to yell his
words into a brass ear trumpet all during his visit, but
the man's mind, when it heard those words, was quick
to pick them up and use them.

And, alas, standing just at the entrance to a narrow
alleyway between two enormous brick buildings was
one Dickie Carstairs, his pudgy frame dressed in the
red-and-white striped shirt of a sailor, a ridiculous, flat-
brimmed straw hat on his head. Jack had an odd sense
of humor.

Jack was there, as well; Puck knew he could count

on that, just as he knew he would never see him unless his brother wished it. But it was comforting to know that Dickie Carstairs wasn't the one who would truly have Puck's back if this small adventure went suddenly sideways.

It warmed the cockles of Puck's heart, it did, and he felt rather prideful of his unconventional troops.

"*Psst!* What are you waiting for?"

Puck looked up at Regina, who dutifully had the handkerchief pressed to her face—*beneath* the thick black veil. "It's called getting the lay of the land, puss. I hear all the best reconnoiters do it. Now behave yourself."

"*Oh!*" she began but then went silent because she was, bless her, an obedient sort, and because he'd walked away from her, just in case she'd decided to make an exception today.

A few enquiries later, he was knocking on the small door cut into the much larger sliding doors of the brick building, stepping back and tipping his hat slightly when he heard a key turn in a lock and a florid-faced man wearing an aggrieved expression finally pushed the door open.

"Oh, I say," Puck began nervously, "it would seem I have disturbed you, sir. My most profound apologies, I'm sure. But you are Silas Lamott, yes? My name is Aloysius Claridge. I was told by any number of the men milling about here that it is you and you alone I must speak to on this…delicate matter. May…may we possibly be more private, Mr. Lamott?"

Silas Lamott's gaze went to Puck's funereal clothing and then beyond him, to the hearse that stood out in the throng of activity the way only a hearse can do. "You got a body in there, or are you come lookin' for one?"

Puck chuckled appreciatively at this small bit of wit. "Oh, very good, Mr. Lamott. Very good, indeed. The former, I'm afraid. Although I am looking to, well, to be *shed* of it." He looked back toward the hearse and raised his hand in a small wave. Regina tentatively returned it. "Not within earshot of my sister, I beg you."

Lamott shrugged his shoulders and turned, motioning for Puck to step over the low threshold cut into the door and follow him into what was at first glance a cavernous tomb of a building, more than five stories in height and packed everywhere with crates and boxes and wrapped, oddly shaped items. The only windows were nearly at the top of that five stories, lined up just below the roof, leaving the walls free to be used for stacking, as well, and the only door to the world Puck could see was the one he'd just entered through.

A second look showed him that the rectangular building was not completely turned over to storage. There were a few bumped-out areas containing their own doors, such as the office he was being led to at the moment, and to his left, a staircase that ran to at least one hundred steps and a large structure neatly suspended forty feet above the brick floor.

Puck stopped dead and pointed. "My goodness, Mr. Lamott, whatever is that? A *house,* all but floating in the air? How unusual. Don't tell me you had to climb down all those stairs to answer my knock. I do apologize!"

What was usual was that Silas Lamott answered Puck. Most people did. He seemed interested in what people had to say, which was always the trick of it. People dearly loved to talk, most especially about themselves and, of course, the trials in their lives.

Even the wart didn't seem to turn Mr. Lamott away. In fact, he seemed fairly fascinated with it. Puck lifted a finger to touch it, make sure it had not begun to slide, as it was warm in the warehouse and the wart was only wax.

"No, no, my office is just here." As if to prove it, Lamott used the same key he'd used for the small door on the lock to his office. "And not a house, Mr. Claridge. That up there is for the owners. Like small gods, they are, standing up there from time to time, peerin' down on us, watchin' to see if we're workin', if we're stealin'. All the money's up there, too, the way I hear it. Ain't never been. Ain't nobody ever been, come to think of it. Besides, the real work is here."

Puck looked inside the small, cluttered office before taking a step inside. "Oh my, yes, I can readily see that," he said appreciatively, watching where Mr. Lamott put the heavy ring of keys after unlocking the door. He'd placed them on his desk, atop a pile of official-looking papers. How convenient. Yet it wouldn't do to take the entire ring, for that disappearance would be noticed almost immediately. Just the office key, longer than the others, and distinctively black in color.

Not an easy task, but certainly not overly daunting to a student of the great Gaston. Why, under his valet's tutelage, Puck had learned how to make things much more substantial than a mere key *disappear;* most notably, the dear *Comtè* Maurice Angoulvant might still be wondering how his private correspondence from his mistress had disappeared from his locked safe, only to turn up in a gaily wrapped gift delivered to his lady wife, who had reason to need forgiveness for her own slight straying from her marriage vows. Clearly a much less potentially problematic solution than the dear lady's possible tearful confession of her liaision with *le beau bâtard Anglais.* That the *Comtè's* treasonous correspondence with an Austrian anarchist had been read and then neatly replaced in the safe before the letters were removed had not crossed the harassed man's mind…at least not until his arrest.

Puck reached toward the keys and then neatly bypassed them, to pick up a small, black, wooden statue of inferior design and execution and turn it about in his hands. "What a truly marvelous piece, Mr. Lamott! African? I pride myself on learning as much as I can, at every opportunity. You've been to the Dark Continent? Yes, of course you have. You must have traveled to many exotic ports. How I, a mere banker, forever stuck in the City, envy you your adventures, Mr. Lamott! You must tell me how you managed such a prize."

Silas Lamott flushed proudly, watching Puck's hands

as he turned the statute once, then again. "That was a long time ago, Mr. Claridge, when I still commanded one of the ships. We don't stop at the African ports anymore. Not since the new laws."

"Ah, yes," Puck said, returning the statue to its original resting place, drawing back his hands rather clumsily, nearly tipping over an earthenware mug containing the dregs of the man's morning chocolate. "Whoops! Nearly came to grief there, didn't I? My apologies, sir."

The key ring was in his pocket now, the office key soon detached from the ring.

Mr. Lamott righted the mug and the statue, which had fallen onto its side, and then with Puck's help, straightened the pile of papers that had begun to slide sideways on the desk.

The key ring was back on the desktop, unearthed from beneath one of the sliding piles of papers.

"It's of no matter, Mr. Claridge. And my fault for the mess. We've got six ships to get ready to sail in the next few days, and five more just docked in the last week and needing unloading. We're at sixes and sevens in the whole shipyard."

"And here I am, taking up your valuable time with my small request. A thousand apologies, Mr. Lamott. Allow me to keep this short and to the point. I have…a problem, Mr. Lamott. One I believe you and I, if we were but to put our heads together, might be able to solve. You saw the hearse? My sister?"

Lamott narrowed his eyelids. "We don't carry

corpses, if that's what you're thinking. They're bad luck aboard ship."

Puck's smile positively beamed. "They aren't a whacking great lot of good luck on land, either. Especially this one. Cousin Yorick was a trial alive, and he seems to be determined to be a trial dead, as well. Hanged himself, you understand, after a plaguey run of luck at the cards. Local church won't bury him among the decent folks. The vicar was most adamant."

Lamott nodded sagely. "That's how it should be. Don't want his sort in with the good folk. Can't you plant him outside the gates?"

"We could, but my sister would have none of it. She insists on a proper burial. You've seen her out there. Doesn't trust me to do it right. I've been at my wit's end, Mr. Lamott. I've spent more on ice these past two days than I care to think about. But I can't tell you how determined my sister can be. Even to go so far as to come with me down here, where she certainly has no business being." He sighed the sort of sigh only bankers can manage, most often as they're denying a loan application. "Women are good for only one thing, I say, Mr. Lamott, and they don't do it sitting up, if you take my meaning." He reached into his pocket and withdrew a small silver flask. "Have you any glasses, Silas? It has truly been a trying morning. Your company is not the first I have applied to today. With luck, it will be the last, as I can see you are not only a fine businessman but a reasonable one, as well."

Lamott's right hand disappeared beneath the top of

the desk only to reappear along with two short glasses, his thumb and forefinger unhappily stuck inside them, even though they were not precisely pristine in any event. "We'll drink to a happy conclusion to your problem, Mr. Claridge."

"Aloysius, please," Puck said as he poured two inches of fine brandy into each glass. "I've got m'damn cousin out there packed up in ice and m'sister not willing to bend an inch. I need a friend, Silas, and I'm willing to pay. Handsomely."

A small but heavy purse was suddenly sitting between them on the desktop.

Lamott reached for it, but then stopped. "It wouldn't be worth my life to order a ship to turn into port other than the one assigned to it. I'm sorry, Mr. Claridge."

"No, no, it's I that am sorry," Puck protested, nudging the small purse closer to Silas. "I have convinced my sister that Yorick can be buried in the church grounds of an ancient church on the Isle of Sheppey, that I have all the arrangements already in train, and she has agreed to allow me to have it shipped there. You know of it?"

Lamott nodded, his eyes still on the purse. "Close enough, but I still can't order it. I'm sorry."

"Your loyalty is to be commended. My story to my sister, alas, is not so laudable. I have no idea if Yorick could be buried on the Isle of Sheppey, I have not so enquired and in truth don't care. It is enough that she believes it. All I need from you, Silas, is for her to see the man's coffin being loaded onto your next ship to leave port. What you instruct your seamen to do with that coffin once the ship reaches open waters? Well, it is of no concern to me, but I understand that burials at sea are not that uncommon?"

"I…I'd have to have the captain's cooperation," Lamott said, still eyeing the purse.

A second, smaller purse appeared beside it.

"Better?" Puck asked.

"Oh yes, much." Both purses disappeared so swiftly it could be wondered if Lamott had studied under a Gaston of his own. "The Gemini sets sail soon as the tide turns. They'll be casting her off soon, but there's still time to load the coffin aboard. Got to get the Gemini out of the way, you see, 'cause Mr. Hackett's own Pride and Prize will be tied right here, to be loaded up over the next two days. Always special, when the Pride and Prize is loaded up, seein' as how it only sails twice a year. Has his own men and all, even doin' some of the loadin' at night." He leaned across the desk even as Puck leaned forward; clearly he was about to be taken in on some confidence. "We think we know why."

"Why?" Puck asked, forcing his eyes to go round as saucers. "Is…is he doing something illegal? Perhaps… perhaps I was being hasty. I don't want to be involved in anything illegal, Silas. It's bad enough I'm deceiving my sister. I am a banker, as I said. I have my reputation to consider." He held out his hand across the desktop. "If you would kindly return the purses?"

"What?" Clearly Mr. Lamott was aghast. Not to

mention already drawing up a mental list of how he would spend his unexpected riches (and half of the ship captain's share). "Oh no, no, Mr. Claridge. You misunderstand me. There is nothing illegal about what it is Mr. Hackett and Mr. Harley are about. The cargo's that *precious,* you see, that's what it is. Nobody can know it's going aboard. Mr. Hackett is a very important man. Married to an earl's daughter he is, and I hear he's got his sights set on a duke for his own daughter. He's probably rich enough to buy her *two* dukes."

"Well, there's nothing wrong with ambition, is there? Very well, Silas, I will take you at your word." Puck stood up, repocketing the flask only after pouring the remainder of its contents in Lamott's glass. With luck, the man would sleep away the afternoon and never realize his key was gone and then spend the remainder of the day looking for it. "Shall we go see about starting poor Cousin Yorick off on his final journey?"

"And his introduction to the fishes?" Lamott joked, already seeming to feel much happier than he had a few short minutes ago.

Puck stopped at the door to the outside and turned to look up at the strange, floating structure one last time. Size was difficult to gauge from this distance, but it seemed large enough. If one wasn't overly concerned with the niceties, it could easily hold two dozen women and their jailers. But it could not hold them without gags, restraints, or else the workers would hear their struggles, their cries for help.

If Miranda was up there in that godawful limbo,

if any young women were up there, shut away in the dark, at the mercy of unscrupulous men, then God have mercy on all of them.

Puck reluctantly turned his back on what could be nothing, or the answer they'd been seeking, and stepped out through the small doorway, blinking against the sunlight.

"Trouble," he heard as he held up a hand to shield his eyes. But, otherwise, he did not react to the beggar holding out his hand for a farthing. "Two buildings south of here, right on the docks. Three women, all dead. Bring Regina."

"Get away from me, you raggedy piece of filth," Puck demanded, waving a fist at Jack, whose bent-over figure was covered in rags, his frizzled gray wig and beard pure works of art. "Silas, can't you keep these beggars clear of your place of business?"

Silas stepped menacingly toward the beggar, but Jack had already melted back into the constant milling crowds that populated the docks and had disappeared.

"Never mind," Puck said pettishly, suddenly eager to get this over with and be on his way. *Three women. All dead. Bring Regina.*

To identify her cousin's body. Why else would Jack want her?

Gaston saw his master approaching, and hopped down from the seat, hastening to open the rear doors of the hearse even as Silas Lamott commandeered several dockworkers to take possession of the casket.

"I will order that a prayer is said over the body before it is—"

"Yes, yes, thank you, Silas. You're a fine Christian man," Puck said, clapping him on the back and turning for the front of the hearse. "Driver, I want my sister out of this place as quickly as you can manage."

He hopped up on the bench seat beside Regina, who was looking rather upset about something. "Mission accomplished, puss. Why the long face?"

"You didn't even introduce me," she told him. "I had a lovely, small speech prepared. I was going to tell him about the summer Yorick and I went sailing, and he saved me when the boat tipped over. I was going to weep a little. I got the ring, but you got the wart. I got to be here, but you got to have all the fun. Do you think that's fair?"

God, he could kiss her. She was splendid! But now was not the time.

"Gaston, turn this damn thing and head south, parallel to the docks. Two warehouses down and then stop. We'll walk to the docks."

"What's happening, Puck? What's going on? What happened back there?"

"Nothing happened back there," he told her, taking her hand in his and squeezing it tightly. "You need to be brave, puss. Jack just got word to me that there's been a discovery."

"Jack? But how? I was watching, and no one approached you aside from that dirty old—oh, my. You're all play actors, aren't you? What sort of discovery?"

Puck chanced a quick glance behind him to see that his small, diverse army was following the hearse. It was a shame a lecture or two on the subject of discretion hadn't been possible in the short time he'd had to muster his troops. Because there they were: ruffians, harlots, hatters and the hapless Dickie Carstairs bringing up the rear in his red-and-white striped shirt. They were having their own parade.

"You have to be brave, Regina. You have to sit here and listen and not react. You have to be strong and prove to Jack that you will be a help and not a hindrance. Do you understand me?"

"What was discovered, Puck?" she said in a small voice. "Did Jack find Miranda? Is that what you're trying to tell me? Did he find her? Is…is she dead?"

"There are three bodies. We don't know if Miranda is among them. We don't know anything. I can take you back to Grosvenor Square, Regina. You don't have to do this."

Her eyes were bright with unshed tears. "But I do have to do this. I have to tell you if Miranda is one of these poor dead women. Oh, God, Puck, can't we move any faster?"

CHAPTER TWELVE

ONCE, REGINA HAD CONSIDERED herself the victim of circumstance. The circumstance of her father's ambition to establish himself in society. The circumstance of her grandfather's greed and his willingness to sell his only daughter. Indeed, her very birth only part of a larger plan. And she had resented it; she had resented all of it.

Miranda had been born through similar circumstances, with her father having sold his title for a price that included a haberdasher's granddaughter, meant to produce children who could be traded for further influxes of funds. And in her own way, Miranda had chafed at her circumstances.

They neither of them had wished to be seen as bargaining chips, to be sold to, in Regina's case, a title in exchange for a fortune, and in Miranda's, a fortune in exchange for a title.

They were, the two of them, little more than pieces of merchandise with a heartbeat.

And powerless.

They both knew that one day, one day soon, the people in charge of their lives would point in some direction and say, "There, this is where we want you, and you have no voice in our decision."

Regina knew she had hidden in her books and her anger, in denying the inevitable. Miranda had struck back more openly, engaging in silly exploits meant to torment her parents.

But certainly, neither of them had ever thought one of them could end up dead.

There was a slight *thump* on the glass behind the plank seat, and Regina turned to see Jack's face behind that glass. He gave a slight nod in her direction even as he was tugging off the wild beard of his costume and picking bits of glue from his cheeks.

"How…?"

Puck opened the small glass door that separated the land of the living from that of the recently deceased (who certainly didn't need a handle on their side of the glass). "Couldn't afford your own hackney, Jack?" he asked his brother.

"Once the coffin was gone, I decided you had the room for another passenger. Did you tell her?"

"What little you told me, yes. Is there more?"

"There is." Now he was stripping off his ragged jacket and shirt. "If you were to face forward, Regina, both our blushes would be spared."

Regina quickly did as he said, as it would appear he was now reaching for the buttons on his trousers.

"You've acquired quite the entourage, brother," Jack said conversationally. "I hesitate to give compliments, but you begin to impress me."

"I shall treasure those words until I am old and gray," Puck said, winking at Regina, who could only feel her frustration, and her fear, growing. "Is it too hopeful for me to think you've brought other clothes with you?"

"I compliment you, and in return, you underestimate me? Very well, brother, if that's how you wish to play it. Tell your man to turn this hulking thing at the next corner. He'll not be able to miss the crowd, I'm afraid."

"Is he going to tell us what he knows, or isn't he?" Regina burst out at last, longing to murder both of them.

"Jack?"

"Yes, all right. I wish I knew more, and that we could spare you, Regina. It would seem that late last evening one of our intrepid Waterguard stumbled over a small craft of some sort being rowed through the darkness and shunning any need, it would seem, for lanterns to help guide them. Suspicious behavior, at the very least, you'll agree.

"The Waterguard approached, called out for the small vessel to halt, submit to a search and whatever else those fellows say when they're being officious. Before they could move closer, there was the sound of a splash as something was tossed overboard. A search of the craft revealed nothing and, again referring to our intrepid Waterguard, the vessel was released."

"Go on," Puck said, his jaw tight.

"I think you know where this is going, Puck, and I apologize in advance, for there is no easy way to say this. No more than two hours ago, something bobbed to the surface and became caught in someone's oars.

Three women, bound together, gagged, weighted with chains. Like barrels of rum strung on a line and dumped by freetraders when there's danger of being discovered by revenue officers. Only, in this case, once the contraband was submerged, there was no recourse to hauling up the booty later."

Regina threw back her veil. She leaned forward as quickly as she could and vomited up her breakfast as Puck held on to her so that she wouldn't fall between the shafts.

"Where are they now?" Puck asked even as he handed Regina his handkerchief. "The bodies."

"Still on the docks. I would say that the advent of a hearse could only be seen as a welcome relief for everyone involved. Let me handle this, Puck, and we can have the bodies loaded and removed somewhere for examination. We don't want Regina to see them as they are now, agreed?"

"No!" Regina forced herself back under control, her concealing veil in place once more. "I can't wait until you think everything is *proper* for me. I need to see those women now. I need to know *now!*"

She looked ahead, straining to see what she'd never wanted to see, as several in the crowd respectfully stepped back at the sight of the hearse, just as Jack had predicted.

Gaston, who had been quiet as the dead himself for all of this time, began shouting for everyone else to move aside, back away, that there was business to be done. But even he couldn't get everyone to clear an area large enough for the hearse and horses to progress more than another few yards. Death would seem to have a devoted audience when it was macabre rather than mundane.

"All right," Jack said behind her. "Follow my lead."

"I don't see that we have any other choice," Puck agreed, looking to Regina, who did her best to appear less terrified than she felt. "We will keep good thoughts, puss. There is no good news here, but that doesn't mean it will be the worst news."

There was another *thump* as the rear doors to the hearse opened and the equipage was lightened by the departure of one live body...which probably came as a bit of a shock to anyone within sight of the hearse.

Puck was already helping Regina down from the plank seat, making sure her veil was in place, when Jack reappeared beside them, this time clad as one of the famous Bow Street Runners, also called Robin Redbreasts because of the bright red waistcoats they favored.

Regina, even in her mental turmoil, was beginning to see a pattern emerging with the brothers. Remember a large emerald ring, remember a hideous wart on the side of a nose, remember a bright red vest. And forget to commit the rest to memory. Where had they learned such methods of deception?

And then Puck answered her unspoken question.

"We are both our mother's children, aren't we?" Puck said in seeming appreciation. "While others played at soldiers and sportsmen, we dressed up and became part of Mama's plays. Do you think, Jack, that we might both enjoy it too much?"

"'The play's the thing,'" Jack quoted shortly and then pulled a thick wooden baton from somewhere and began clearing a path through the throng, Puck and Regina in his wake...along with several of the ragtag parade that was Puck's unconventional army.

Regina grabbed hold of Puck's hand and held on tight. "He quotes Shakespeare at you? But that line was Hamlet's, about his plan to drop hints about his uncle's guilt into a play that he would write, just to see if the man reacted to the words."

"True enough. And, if our admittedly hopeful suspicions prove correct and we're lucky, at some point we will see King Claudius flinch."

"See my father flinch," Regina said quietly, still hating herself for her willingness to believe in her father's guilt. No, more than that. The *hope* that her father was guilty, so that Miranda might yet be saved. "We aren't that far from his warehouse, are we? That far from his ships. Not...not far from where everything happened?"

"Don't think of that right now, Regina. I don't want you to do this, but I can't stop you. What you're about to see will be far from pretty, understand?"

She nodded, biting down hard as another wave of nausea threatened her. "I can do this. I have to do this."

Jack and his baton at last succeeded in peeling back the last remaining layer of interested bystanders, revealing an open circle of wharf. In the center of that circle was a canvas tarp, hastily rolled out to receive the bodies as they'd been hauled up from the boat to be so crudely displayed.

"Oh, dear Christ, have mercy on them," Regina whispered at her first sight of the bodies.

They had not had quiet deaths, these women, and they seemed unquiet even now, their limbs bent here, there, locked into awkward positions. They'd been chained to each other, wrist to wrist; the weight of those chains more than enough to drag them beneath the surface of the water and keep them there.

They looked to be smiling, until it became understood that they had been tightly gagged, forcing their expressions into open-mouthed grimaces.

Their clothes were sodden and unrecognizable as to their quality. Their feet bare.

They were all much of a height. They were all three of them blonde.

Regina knew she needed to get closer, even bend down over the bodies, if she was going to see if any of the dead women was Miranda, but her feet refused to move.

Suddenly she was pushed aside by a large man who strode toward the tarp with a purpose, his hamlike hands drawn up into fists. He was followed by three other men as well as a quartet of women...all of whom Regina recognized as being nearby as she'd sat waiting for Puck outside her father's warehouse.

With the air of a businessman about him, the man

bent over the tragic tableau and then called for one of the women to join him, repeat his action.

The woman bent, looked and then screamed.

"Keep her here, Puck," Jack ordered quietly before joining the man and his entourage. The trio of burly men began folding the tarp over the chained-together bodies and made to lift the awkward burden.

"What's happening, Puck?"

"It would seem that my new friend, Mr. Porter, has identified the bodies and has claimed them as his property. Miranda isn't among them, sweetheart. She's not here."

Regina's knees nearly buckled as she collapsed against Puck, who pulled her away as the men and their burden passed by them, Mr. Porter walking behind, his *ladies* clinging to each other, weeping copiously.

The hatters followed, holding their bowlers against their stomachs by way of paying their respects.

"They'll be making use of the hearse," Jack told them as he rejoined them. "And your valet, I believe, until he's taken them where they wish to go. Are you amenable? If so, I have a closed coach in the next street, which I suggest you retire to with both decorum and some haste. Unless I'm wrong, which I rarely am, and that isn't one Mr. Reginald Hackett just now stepping down from that chaise. As you seem to be showing some interest in the man, I have done so, as well. I'll see you both back in Grosvenor Square."

Regina didn't look; she didn't dare. But from the

way Puck turned her about and insinuated them into the crowd, she felt certain Jack had been right.

Seemingly out of nowhere, a seaman appeared with two nondescript gray cloaks, tossing one to Puck and gently placing the other around Regina's shoulders, lifting the hood up and over her head while asking if she would please consider removing her mourning veil.

"Coach just down that alley, in the next street. Good seeing you again, Mr. Blackthorn, if not that thing on your face. Good day to you, miss."

"Thank you, Dickie," Puck said, "it's good to see you again, as well, and may I say I think those stripes suit you all hollow."

"The devil they do. But it's my job to be noticed, so's that Henry and Jack back there aren't, if you take my meaning."

"Damned if I don't, yes," Puck told him in obvious admiration, and then he guided Regina into the mouth of the alleyway, leaving Mr. Carstairs behind to be *obvious.* "We're almost there, puss. Or do you want me to carry you?"

"No, no, I'll make it. I'll be fine," she promised him. She held true to her promise all the while they were making their way down the length of the narrow alley that ran between two huge, tall, brick warehouses, Puck turning often to check behind them, until they were safely inside the closed coach and on their way back to Grosvenor Square.

Only then did she begin to cry…believing she might never be able to stop.

PUCK HAD BEEN MANY things over the course of his not-all-that-inconsiderable time on this earth. But he had never before felt so powerless, not even in that nameless port, looking down on the body of a desperate woman who had solved her problem the only way she could.

It wasn't a feeling he liked or wished to experience again.

He palmed the long black key, idly turning it over in his hand, wondering if he held the key that would answer all their questions, wondering how those answers would affect Regina.

"Mr. Blackthorn?"

Puck turned about to see that Lady Claire had quietly crept into his study and was now looking at him in some trepidation.

"My lady," he said, bowing to her.

"I...I just spoke with my niece, Mr. Blackthorn. She told me you are making progress. Is that true?"

"We're hopeful, yes," Puck said, motioning with a small sweep of his right arm that her ladyship could be seated, if she so desired.

The lady, it would seem, chose to stand.

"Those poor, unfortunate women. Regina didn't want to tell me about them, but I could see she was troubled, and insisted. I can only imagine their terror as they were forced to the rail...and then the dark water closing over them. I will have nightmares for weeks, if not forever. That anyone could be so cruel..."

"We're not dealing with men of conscience, my lady. But as I've said, your daughter is more valuable to them than most anyone else they've managed to take up as... as part of their cargo. Special care will be taken of her. Still, you must be prepared for her to be rather fragile when you are reunited."

"*When*, Mr. Blackthorn?" Lady Claire smiled wanly. "I want to have hope, but I fear that hope is waning. More and more, I find myself wanting to believe my husband's brother-in-law and that Miranda is halfway to Gretna with some unsuitable young man she believes holds her heart. And...and I know that something terrible—monstrous—is happening here in London, and I commend you for your efforts, I really do. But I do not think my niece should be involved in anything more. She is caught between determination and fear, and not a little guilt, I'm afraid. I cannot be a good aunt and condone her further involvement. Not...not even for my daughter."

Puck closed his hand around the key until it bit into the flesh of his palm. "I cannot begin to tell you how much I regret the events of earlier today, ma'am. But your niece is a headstrong young lady. And braver than you could know."

Lady Claire looked up at Puck for a long moment before nodding her head and looking away. "Regina is convinced her father is somehow involved. Could that be possible?"

He didn't answer at once. Lady Claire was desperate. Her only daughter had gone missing. Her niece had told her about the drowned women, about Reginald Hackett's possible involvement. What sort of maggot could enter the head of a woman who believed the way to her daughter might lie through the man? What would she dare in the name of that daughter?

"Perhaps it is time you and Lady Leticia actually did visit Mentmore, ma'am?" he ventured at last. "I don't know that anyone could convince Regina to do the same, but the comfort of family is always preferable to your current situation here, in my decidedly bachelor household. If you were to suggest it, perhaps Regina would agree?"

She returned her gaze to his face. She wore the haunted look of a person standing over a bottomless pit. "You think I will go to him, don't you? Confront him. I am not that brave, Mr. Blackthorn. Would that I were, would that my husband could find it in himself to face the man down. I want only your opinion. Please."

"Then yes, my lady. I do think he might be involved. But I must add the caveat that in a world filled with suspects, it may be mostly wishful thinking that we are even now heading in the correct direction. Otherwise…"

"Otherwise, we might never find Miranda," Lady Claire ended for him, getting to her feet. "My heart aches for my daughter. My mind worries for my niece. And I am selfish enough to risk her, I suppose, if she can be of assistance to you. But please, protect her, keep her safe. Even if you can't do the same for Miranda. You're a good man."

Puck held out his arm to her ladyship and walked her to the door of the study, where he bent to place a kiss on her cool cheek. "I thank you, my lady, and let us both pray your confidence in me is not misplaced."

He then escorted her down the hallway to the base of the stairs, watching as she slowly mounted them, heading back to the solitude of her assigned bedchamber, before he turned once more for his study.

He needed a drink. Perhaps several drinks. Maybe they'd wash away the thought that he was attempting to play God with other people's lives, with their hopes, their fears. Because, damn it, he was only a man, one man, and far from perfect. If he failed, Miranda and many others would be lost. If he failed, Lady Claire would be destroyed. If he failed, Regina would never again be able to look at him and not remember that failure, or at least he would not be able to forget it.

If he lost, or if he won, Regina would still be lost to him. She had turned to him for help, for comfort, and he had given her passion, a reason to forget, if only temporarily, the ugliness of what was happening in this city, what was happening to her cousin.

Once the cousin was found, dead or alive, he would have no further excuse to salve his conscience. It would be time to walk away.

Puck reentered the study and went straight to the drinks table to pour a glass of wine. If Reginald Hackett was their man, Puck knew he couldn't walk away. But even if he wasn't, the man was still a despicable excuse for a human being. How could he ever walk away, knowing that? How far would he have to go to forget her?

He sensed his brother's presence in the room even before Jack spoke.

"You handled that well. She's really caught between that proverbial rock and a hard place, isn't she? Fear for her daughter, concern for her niece. Praying you'll find the one, all but certain you've deflowered the other. Balancing one against the other and choosing the daughter, as would be reasonable, tacitly condoning the deflowering, if it keeps you interested enough to continue the search for the daughter. She knows she can't trust Hackett, is aware her own husband is a total loss. So she's made her choice, put in with you, dear brother, and has let you know she will turn her head to anything else. Of the two sexes, I've always said the female is shrewder, the more practical."

Puck's hand hesitated as he held the open decanter of his glass for only a single heartbeat before he poured a measure and turned to look at his brother, who was sitting at his ease in one of the armchairs flanking the fireplace, one leg crossed over the other at the knee. "I so look forward to your words of wisdom. Please, your opinion on Regina's mother, while you're in the mood to wax profound."

"The so-fragile Lady Leticia?" Jack shrugged his elegantly clad shoulders. "I should think you'll have a devil of a time rousting her from this snug bolt-hole you've offered her. She, too, has looked at what is happening, assessed her options and is content with trading her daughter's innocence for her own temporary respite from what is, I'm quite sure, an untenable situation. If

Regina told her what we suspect, the woman is probably even now on her knees in her chambers, praying the man is guilty and that he hangs for his crimes, freeing her from her prison—and damn the inevitable scandal. Whether Hackett is our culprit or not, you might want to consider ridding the world of him. He's not a very nice man."

"Albeit a mysterious one. Even his own man of business doesn't seem to know much about him."

"You obviously didn't grease the right palms. But no matter, you've got the lady to woo, as well—and an army to raise, my congratulations on that head— with not as much time to devote to the problem as I do. Used to be a slaver, our Mr. Hackett, you know, back before the Crown outlawed it, made it a hanging offense. Hackett, for a few years, but mostly his father before him. Their fortune? That's pretty much built on the helpless souls they transported. That may be information you'll want to keep from Regina. The trade may have been legal, but that doesn't make it smell any better, does it?"

"It must have been an eye-popping amount of money he paid the Earl of Mentmore, for the man to hand his daughter over to the son of a slaver. Or perhaps the money was the only consideration, and Lady Leticia didn't figure in the decision as anything more than a bargaining chip."

"It's sometimes difficult to love one's fellow man, isn't it, Puck? You know, with the war and all, the various embargos, a man could need to consider another stream of revenue than what he could derive through legal means. Smuggling, for one. And then there's that notion that dogs always return to their vomit."

Puck nodded. "He'd go where he could be assured the highest profit. Interesting irons on those women today, I thought. Not the sort one would see every day—able to bind several people together on a string, rather like a line of pack animals. I saw such irons somewhere, years ago. How do they do it, Jack? How does anyone take hold of a woman, defenseless, terrified, unable to even beg for her life, look her in the eyes—and then toss her over the side to drown? *How?*"

"When we find those men, we'll ask them," Jack said, his eyes going dark. "After that, if you see some need for a court of law and the King's justice, you will kindly oblige me by walking away. Understood?"

"I'll never question your methods again or the reasons behind them," Puck said, once more remembering the previous year and his thoughts on the eventual ending of the man he'd help put in Jack's custody. "So—our friend Dickie isn't the buffoon I took him for?"

"I helped you there by agreeing with you. I'd say he's the bravest of all of us, willing to show his face in order to lead attention away from Henry and myself. And you must admit, he plays his part very well."

"We all play parts, don't we?" Puck asked as he sank into the facing chair, feeling maudlin. "Except maybe Beau. He found what he was looking for, even as he didn't know he'd been looking."

"And you," Jack asked silkily. "Have you found what you've been looking for in that girl upstairs? You certainly worked a miracle to get her there."

"The miracle would be to keep her, and I don't see any way to manage that." He looked at his brother. "Do you?"

"How to keep her? You've applied to entirely the wrong man for advice on that head, little brother. Entirely the wrong man." Jack looked at his wineglass and then drank the remainder of its contents in one long gulp.

Getting Jack to open up was difficult in the best of times, but in this worst of times, Puck felt he may have just found a crack he might be able to wedge wider. "Have I just stepped into territory you'd rather left unexplored?"

"What did you learn once you'd managed to get yourself inside the Hackett warehouse?"

"Question answered," Puck said with a smile and a shake of his head. "Very well, brother Sphinx. I didn't know what I'd learn, frankly. My objective was merely to get inside and then see what I could see. Oh, and to hopefully come out with something like this." He held up the key. "Would you care to return to London Docks with me later tonight for some good-natured skulking?"

Jack didn't smile. Jack rarely smiled. "It would have to be tonight, yes. By tomorrow, the locks will have been changed unless the man is more idiot than we think, and we don't think he's an idiot, do we?"

"We think he's a monster," Regina said from the doorway, her voice low and intense.

Both Puck and Jack got to their feet, Puck looking to his brother and mouthing the words *she does not go with us.*

Puck walked toward her, his arms out, and took her hands in his. "I thought we'd agreed you were going to remain in bed for the remainder of the day. You've had a considerable shock."

"I've had my eyes opened, that's what I've had done today. Do you know that I've dared to feel sorry for myself all these years? I've thought of myself being sold to the highest bidder—when I had no notion of what that really means. I'm ashamed of myself. Because I've never been cold, or hungry or really afraid. Because I do have the power to say no and mean it, and take my chances in the world, if I dare. My shackles were never real, Puck, not in the way of the shackles those women wore, both before they were captured and afterward. I told you I wanted to be there when you find Miranda, and I meant it. Now I want to be there—need to be there—when those other poor, terrified women are found. I've sat and wrung my hands long enough. I need to *help.*"

"Oh, *brava,*" Jack said, clapping his hands softly. "You put me in mind of someone I once knew, Regina. Puck, let me answer your earlier question, at least in part. She is clearly determined. If you want to lose her, refuse her. Women such as Regina are not the frail creatures we men often find the need to make them. And now I'm off. Midnight seems like a fine time for us to meet where we met this morning. Do dress appropriately."

Jack bowed over Regina's hand before taking his leave, although she seemed to have offered that hand out of habit only, for her attention was all on Puck, her expression determined. Puck would have said *mulish,* except that if he wasn't the most brilliant man in creation, he at least had a healthy sense of self-preservation.

Which, alas, didn't keep him from saying what was on his mind.

"What in the devil makes you think you wouldn't be in the way?"

She looked at him in some shock. "In the way? Oh," she said, rolling her eyes. "You will persist in thinking I'll just be one more thing for you to worry about, don't you? Did I *get in the way* earlier today?"

"You threw up all over the horses." *Shut up, Puck. Shut up, shut up, shut up!*

"Was it really necessary for you to remind me of that?" she asked, and this time her expression was definitely mulish. Beautiful. But mulish.

"Regina, be reasonable." *Wrong word. Of all the words in Samuel Johnson's Lexicon, that was exactly the wrong word. Never, never ever ask a woman to be reasonable. Females always think they're reasonable.*

"It's you that isn't being reasonable, Puck. Miranda is *my* cousin. The building you plan to break into belongs to *my* father. I am *not* going to stay here and tend to my knitting while *you* risk your life to save *my* cousin, investigate *my* father. I have a responsibility. I…I can stand watch. I can…I can rifle through drawers, read journals as we search for clues. There has to be something I can do!"

Puck mentally tried to put himself in Regina's shoes, and he could readily understand where they pinched her. She'd seen the bodies. If her father had been involved in those deaths, she had to be torn between wanting to unmask him and proving him innocent. Hate him, despise him, she was still blood of his blood.

And what had Jack told him? *If you want to lose her, refuse her.* Puck couldn't know what had happened in his brother's past, but clearly, whatever it was had cost him the woman he loved.

"All right," he said at last, nearly shouted the words. "All right! But damn you, woman, if you so much as ask me *why* when I give you an order before you react, I'll break your neck myself. Understood?"

She smiled. "Yes, Puck," she said meekly. "Thank you."

A goose didn't exactly run over his grave as he saw her answering smile, but he knew he recognized that smile as being the same sort he'd seen on Chelsea's face last year when she'd gotten Beau to agree to one of her outlandish plans.

Men were doomed, it seemed apparent to Puck now, when it came to knowing how to say *no* to the women who recognized the power they held over them. Except for Jack, of course. Clearly he'd said no. Just as clearly, he still regretted it.

Puck could only pray he would not live to regret saying yes.

"We don't have a lot of time. Come on," he said gruffly, grabbing her hand and half pulling her toward the hallway, on his way upstairs to his chambers and the disguises Gaston had procured for them. He'd find something appropriate for her to wear, even help her manage the unfamiliar buttons and whatever. He wouldn't leave her side for a minute, because he would need every second of that time to bring home to her the dangers she insisted on facing, brave, foolish girl that she was. Idiot that he was....

REGINA BELIEVED SHE should be ashamed of herself for bullying Puck into agreeing to take her along tonight, but she was too determined to take the time to indulge in such womanish emotion. Puck might not be convinced that Reginald Hackett was behind the terrible crimes taking place in London right now, but Regina believed in her father's guilt with her whole heart.

She also didn't have time to investigate exactly why she believed it, knowing some of her reasons were self-serving and others meant that they were nearer now to finding Miranda than they would ever be otherwise.

And if she was wrong, if they all were wrong, well then, didn't they need to know that, as well?

"What are you doing?" she asked Puck once they were in his dressing room and he was looking at her as if trying to decide something. "You're not changing your mind, are you?"

"No. But I don't think any of Gaston's array of costumes will work for you tonight. Widow, streetwalker, matron. Stay here. Don't move. I'll be right back."

"Yes, sir," she said dutifully, and then immediately *moved* once he was gone. She walked over to his dressing table, picking up one of a pair of silver-backed brushes and admiring the flowing script of his initials, as they'd been engraved on each one. With the tip of one finger, she lifted the cover of a small, ivory-inlaid jewelry box and inspected the pieces she found inside, most taken by the large gold ring with the enormous black onyx stone at its center. His brother wore a similar ring on his index finger; she'd noticed it the first time they'd met.

"A gift from my mother," Puck said from behind her, "on the twenty-first anniversary of my birth. We each got one when we reached our majorities. Beau traded his somewhere on the Peninsula for enough chickens to feed his troops."

"Jack wears his," Regina said, replacing the ring. "I wasn't being nosy, you know. I was only…all right, I was being nosy. Why don't you wear yours?"

"Perhaps because I can't help but wonder if the *B* carved into the stone stands for Blackthorn or bastard. Our mother has a perverse sort of humor. The better question might be to ask why Jack wears his. But don't, because I have no answer for that one. I've found you something to wear."

Only then did she notice the clothing folded over his arm and the pair of soft suede boots he carried in his hand. "You expect me to wear breeches?"

"No. I expect you to stay here and wait for me to return. But since you insist on coming along, I don't want to have to deal with skirts and shoes impossible to run in if running becomes necessary. These won't be perfect, but Gaston is nearer to your size than anyone else I can think of. Now, let's get you undressed."

"Now?" she asked, noticing that there were enough candles lit in this small dressing room to make maidenly modesty impossible. Not that she was a maiden anymore, but that didn't mean she had changed overnight from modest to...well, whatever was the opposite of modest. "I'm sure Hanks could help me..."

"Don't deny me the only pleasure I might have this evening, puss," Puck said, tossing the clothing onto a nearby chair and advancing toward her, the devil in his eyes. "I said we don't have much time. But we have enough."

Regina felt that now-familiar tingle between her legs that signaled to her that her body would rather she didn't *doth protest too much,* which she hadn't wanted to do in the first place, although surely she should make at least a show of reluctance.

"Do...are you going to change, as well?"

His answer was to strip off his jacket and begin working on loosening his neck cloth.

"You're impossible. You do know that, Puck, don't you?" she said, backing up a step, her gaze riveted to his chest as he opened the buttons on his waistcoat and then immediately began loosing the buttons of his shirt, even while the neck cloth hung loose around his neck.

"I'm also ahead of you," he pointed out as he tugged the tails of his shirt from his waistband.

She knew what he was doing. He was distracting her. Putting on a bit of foolery to mitigate some of the horribleness of what she had witnessed today, shift her mind from the pathways that led her to more fear for Miranda and away from disturbing thoughts about her father's possible involvement in the most despicable occupation on earth.

And, bless him, it was working. Or maybe she just wanted it to work. Whatever the reasons, his and hers, the world had suddenly narrowed to this small room... and that was fine with Regina.

Each small move he made sent the taut muscles of his chest and stomach to rippling, which for some reason made her mouth go suddenly dry. He'd slipped off the black riband that held his long hair in place so that his hair fell forward around his face, making him look young and yet somehow dangerous. The stark white of his shirt contrasted with the golden tan of his skin. The soft mat of blond hair on his chest glinted dully in the candlelight.

The man was beautiful. The man was a menace.

Regina lifted her hands to her bodice and began unbuttoning the row of small pearl buttons that helped contain the too-lush breasts that had once been the bane of her existence but that, she thought privately, Puck had found no complaint with the previous night.

The buttons undone and the style of the gown simple, it was easy enough to gather up her skirts and tug the whole thing up and over her head and toss it aside, leaving her clad only in her chemise. And her evening slippers. And her strand of pearls. And her blushes.

He smiled, and she felt her nipples growing taut beneath the thin cloth.

He shrugged out of his shirt and waistcoat at the same time and then took hold of one end of his neck cloth and slowly dragged it from his neck. He was bare to the waist now, with only his tight breeches and high-top boots remaining to keep her from having to bury her head in her hands or stare until her eyes popped out of her head. As it was, there was no ignoring the bulge in his breeches.

She backed up another two steps, only to feel the closed door to his bedchamber at her back.

"You…you make everything a game."

"And every day an adventure," he agreed, picking up a small, straight-backed chair and moving toward her. "I want you to prove to me that you'll obey me tonight, Regina. Without hesitation. Without question. We'll call this part of your preparation. Are you willing?"

She was half lost in fascination, in feeling. And yet he'd not even touched her.

"Yes." She felt her stomach flutter, the tightness between her thighs sending out a silent call to be noticed, attended to. If this was the blood of Grandmother Hackett now heating in her veins, some earthiness her patrician mother feared, then *huzzah* for Grandmother Hackett. "Yes."

Puck placed the chair just beside her. "Put your hands on my shoulders, Regina. For balance."

She did as he said, her palms burning when they touched his bare flesh. They were only inches apart now, and she needed him closer, needed his mouth on her, his hands on her.

"Now raise your right leg for me, sweetings. Rest your foot on the seat of the chair."

"But—" At her protest, he raised one eyebrow and smiled at her, as if to question her reluctance.

She did as he said to do, even as she lowered her forehead against his shoulder. Grandmother Hackett's blood could only take her so far. The rest she had to leave up to the hypnotic sounds of Puck's voice, the hungry yet somehow amused and adventurous look in his eyes.

"Give me a moment," he told her, his hands leaving her. "Ah, that should do. The French are good for a few things. Their wine, their language…their clever inventions. This time I won't leave you. I promise."

What followed was all sensation. All surprise and reaction and glory as he lifted the hem of her chemise and put his hand between her legs, finding her, stroking her, calling up feelings that robbed her of all her strength, her will, so that she could only give herself over to him, to whatever he wanted to do, however he wanted to use her.

When she felt him push inside her she nearly wept with the feel of the way he filled her, completed her.

Yet she couldn't get enough, there would never be enough.

He kept his mouth close beside her ear, whispering to her in French, the words bold, explicit, describing what he was doing to her even as he was doing it, telling her how she made him feel, how tight she was, how her heat enflamed him.

His words as much as his body took her beyond rational thought, fueled her hunger with more hunger until he put his hand between them and lightly pinched at her most vulnerable, sensitive center, taking her abruptly from mere delight to euphoria, to a place where there was only physical pleasure, only her core, her white-hot center and what he was doing to her, how he was doing it, how he should never stop, never stop, never stop.

"Venez avec moi, Regina. Meurent la petite mort avec moi et jugent quelle vie est tout environ. Faites-la maintenant...la font maintenant! Ah, cher Dieu, sweetings, *oui! Est-ce qu'il est d'être vivant!"* Come with me, Regina. Die the small death with me and feel what life is all about. Do it now...do it now! Ah, dear God, sweetings, yes! This is what it is to be alive!

Sobbing, Regina clung to him, all the horror of the day gone, forgotten, and life made bearable again....

CHAPTER THIRTEEN

IF PUCK DIED TONIGHT and woke up in Hell, he wouldn't ask why Heaven had been denied him. He'd know why.

Regina would follow him anywhere now, without question, without hesitation. That he had brought her along on this fool's mission was the most damning of the things he had done since he'd first met her, and the most potentially dangerous.

And yet, as he watched her, sitting at the same desk Silas Lamott had occupied only hours earlier, carefully turning the pages in one of the journals they'd found, he couldn't help but admire her courage, her intelligence. Had it been worse of him to bring her along or worse to say her sex somehow made her unqualified to be a part of what was happening all around her?

"Mr. Lamott was right, Puck," she told him, closing the large book and placing her folded hands on top of it. "There are twenty-three ships named here but none of them the *Pride and the Prize.* And yet it's tied up just outside. We just saw it."

"And riding high in the water," Jack said as he rejoined them in the small office, "ready for cargo. This place is nearly as large and sprawling as Buckingham Palace, although not quite as aesthetically pleasing. I had time for only a cursory examination, but none of the crates nearest the front of the warehouse is marked for the *Pride and the Prize*. Whatever is to be loaded onboard isn't here. Doesn't that seem odd to you? You told me your Mr. Lamott said the ship is scheduled to sail in two days."

"That two days might have changed, now that some of the cargo has been lost," Puck said, wincing at his own words. Three women had died. He couldn't think of them as cargo.

"London's streets are never safe, according to my father," Regina said, getting to her feet, smoothing down her breeches. "But tonight, they're probably more dangerous than ever before."

"I put a word in the ear of our friend, Mr. Porter," Puck told them both. "He agreed to alert his— We'll call them fellow entrepreneurs, shall we? In any event, there's bound to be a dearth of prostitutes walking the streets for the next few days. But no longer than that. Mr. Porter made that plain, as well. Losing the occasional female is all a part of his cost of doing business. Blow out that candle, sweetings. We're done here. It's that cunning suspended room I want to see before we leave."

He carefully slid the black key in amongst a pile of papers on the desk, having no more need of it. He'd already bent open the ring that had held it with the other keys on Lamott's key ring, so that it might be supposed the loss had been accidental. The key might be discovered, it might not, but at least it lent some credence to the idea that it had been misplaced, not taken. In fact, they'd already planned to smash in the small doors to both the warehouse and the office as they left, breaking the locks, so that no one would stumble onto the notion that Mr. Lamott's visitor of earlier today had come back tonight to have himself a look-round.

After all, how else could the two currently unconscious guards be explained away?

"How many crates did Dickie and Henry take?" he asked Jack as they made their way toward the long, narrow flight of stairs. The break-in should look like a robbery, but to have simply broken down the door at the outset would mean more chance of discovery, so they'd decided to leave that bit of vandalism until last.

"Four. It seemed a nice round number. Dickie's hoping for tea, but he'll just as easily settle for bolts of cloth. His mother, I understand, is partial to French silks."

"And you really believe my father will swallow the idea that this was nothing more than a robbery?" Regina asked, her strides getting longer and more confident as she seemed to become accustomed to the freedom of breeches. He might have a problem on his hands if she enjoyed that freedom too much. Although he, in turn, could think of little to argue against the sight of her womanly form in Gaston's best buckskins.

"One can't be sure, but one feels obliged to at least make the effort," Jack told her, flashing one of his rare smiles.

"You live for this, don't you?" Puck asked quietly as

they stopped at the base of the stairs, peering up into near ink-dark blackness, for the moon was no longer full and the light coming through the high windows was minimal. There were at least four landings that Puck could see, the stairs cutting back on themselves as they climbed into the dark.

"I confess to some small joy in my work, yes. Hold tight to the railings. I don't wish to end my evening by scraping either one of you up from the floor."

Jack started up the steps first, Regina behind him and Puck bringing up the rear, in case she might stumble.

"You'll remain on the topmost landing, remember?" he reminded her as they climbed, carefully, slowly. "Until we see what's inside."

"I remember," she said, and Puck went back to wishing the moon full once more, as he was sure it would improve the view in front of him. He settled for giving her backside a quick pat and rub, which nearly made her stumble.

"Sorry," he said quietly.

"No, you're not," was her quick answer, and he chuckled softly at her boldness. He'd never met her like and knew he never would again.

"Locked," Jack said once they'd reached the final narrow landing. "This is one door we definitely don't want to force. I bow to your expertise, brother."

"Yes, as well you should." Puck knelt down on one knee even as he extracted a small, flat leather packet from his pocket and selected one of the tools, the use of which had been meticulously taught to him by Gaston.

In a moment, the door was open and Puck stepped inside the inky blackness.

He didn't have to see anything to sense that the room was empty and that it had recently been occupied. He believed he could actually smell the fear that had resided here. The fear, the sweat, the rotted food, the stench of human waste.

"Oh, God," Regina said from beside him, and he could tell that she had her hands pressed over her mouth and nose. "What went on here?"

"Stay still, sweetings," Puck instructed as he took a short, fat candle from his pocket along with a small, cleverly designed tinderbox. Within a few moments, the candle was lit, and he was able to see a rusted ship's lantern sitting on a table. He lit that, as well, the shadows cast by the light putting illumination to the ghastly scene.

There was a small desk and two chairs, giving credence to Lamott's tale of the owners sometimes coming up here to watch the men working below them in the warehouse. A quick check of the single drawer in that desk showed it to be empty.

There were a total of four windows, but heavy leather shades had been not only lowered but bolted to the wood frames, with heavy locks holding those shades in place: not a temporary arrangement but one that could be employed when necessary. There were two large buckets located near the pallets, taking the place of chamber pots and clearly not recently emptied.

The room, no more than twenty feet square, was otherwise bare, save for three rows of thin pallets placed directly on the rough wooden floor. Beside each pallet was a thick stake. Each had been nailed in place, a round hole neatly bored through the top.

"They ran the chains through those stakes," Jack said, going down on his haunches to inspect them more closely. "See the wear on the wood? That's from the sliding of the chain. I imagine there were manacles then attached along the length of the chain, one for each pallet. Can you picture it, Puck? I'm sure that's how it works. Some limited movement allowed, but for the most part, they'd be confined to within a few feet of each pallet. Chained, suspended in the air, cut off from any help, a guard watching them, with them, at all times. Hell on earth, Puck, Hell on earth."

"How many do you count?" Puck asked, watching Regina. Hands still to her mouth and nose, she had begun rocking back and forth on the heels of her borrowed boots. She'd questioned. Now she had answers. Not all the answers, but enough to have shattered her world.

"Two dozen even, if each pallet was occupied. And a tidy but not enormous profit. For all we know, the *Pride and the Prize* makes other stops along the English coast before heading out into the Channel and the open sea. To put up provisions they wouldn't want to take the chance of doing here and to load more cargo. Then there's Calais, Caen, Brest—there's no small number of ports before heading to the Mediterranean market-places, as it seems logical that this would be their final destination. All in all, perhaps one hundred at a time, with the virgins commanding the highest prices. I wonder how often the *Pride and the Prize* goes to sea."

"Twice a year," Puck answered, watching Regina as she slowly walked through the debris, kicking at it with the toe of her boot. Suddenly she squatted down, her hand out, reaching for something. "No, don't touch anything, Regina," he warned her. "It's all filth."

She didn't listen to him, probably hadn't even heard him. She picked up a long strip of material and turned her ashen, wide-eyed face to him. "I recognize this. Miranda's gown that night…it was fashioned of this material."

"Jesus, this isn't right," Puck swore quietly. "I have to get her out of here, Jack. Now. We've seen enough."

Regina threw down the ragged strip of softly pat-terned, ivory silk. "She was here, Puck. Miranda was here. I told you I could be useful. You wouldn't have known that. But I did. I do. Miranda was here, with all the others. Oh, God, Puck. Where is she?"

All three of them turned at the sound of a sailor's whistle, the sound of five short, shrill pips coming to them through the open door to the stairs. It was the signal and the count they'd agreed upon when Dickie Carstairs and Baron Henry Sutton had been put to the job of sentries. Five pips, one for each two men.

"Company times ten," Jack said shortly, blowing out

the lamp even as Puck reached for Regina and pulled her close beside him, afraid of losing her in the dark. "And we're stuck up here with no way out but those stairs. Clever damn prison, I'll give them that, and the last place we want to be right now. We have to get down the stairs while Dickie and Henry keep them busy as long as they can. Are you ready to run?"

"Ready," Puck said, squeezing Regina's hand before abruptly hefting her body up and over his right shoulder, both his arms wrapped tight around her legs. He'd planned that, as well, believing they'd move faster this way. That she didn't protest told him she agreed.

Jack led the way, pistols in either hand, while Puck was fully occupied in holding Regina safely against him. Down they went, negotiating turn after turn, the staircase seemingly endless as it disappeared into the gloom below them, their boots loud and echoing on the bare wood. Everything depended on being able to be free of the steps before anyone else entered the building.

As Puck ran, his mind whirled, and he cursed himself for his stupidity. All but hurling himself down the stairs. Twenty steps. Forty. Two landings already behind them. Halfway there.

All the planned subterfuge was for nothing; Hackett had known they were coming. He'd heard about the lost key and guessed right, that he was under suspicion. He'd quickly moved the women. He'd only put two easily subdued men on guard. He'd hidden another of his men inside the warehouse, watching, waiting and then giving some sort of signal once the quarry was neatly trapped in the suspended room. If Dickie and Henry weren't outside to alert them, they would have been captured without a chance to defend themselves.

That had to be it. Why hadn't Jack thought of this possibility? He was the professional whatever-he-was. Puck could only do the next thing, and then the next, hoping each time that he'd chosen correctly and wasn't about to get them all killed.

And Hackett couldn't know his own daughter made up one of the small party of intruders. Her hair tucked up inside a knitted toque, her height, her long legs encased in Gaston's buckskins, the lack of a moon. He wouldn't know. Unless he caught them. They could not be caught!

Seventy. Eighty. Had he come far enough? Could he chance a jump from this landing? Yes, he'd chance it. He really didn't have a choice. His teeth rattled, and his knees nearly buckled as his boots hit the floor. Regina gave a small *oomph* as all the air in her lungs was jolted out of her.

"Sorry, puss."

Puck started running toward the concealment of the towering crates. Jack waved him to the left, and Puck followed. Now the darkness was their friend.

Dickie and Henry could be counted on to delay things, to take care of as many as three or four of Hackett's men, but then they could either run or stand and die. They'd been instructed to run.

And after that, Puck knew they were on their own.

Jack, damn him, seemed eager for a fight, heavily armed as if planning for one, even hoping for one. And yet he'd also been the one to tell Puck to bring Regina. Why? Because Jack was an arrogant son of a bitch, and never considered losing at anything? Probably. Damn him, damn him, damn him.

But Jack also had been the one to inspect the warehouse while he and Regina had searched Lamott's office. What had he seen? Had he found another way out? Had he known to look for one? How? He'd better have another plan up his sleeve, or Puck might kill him himself.

"Over here," Jack said, running on the balls of his feet now so that his soft-soled boots made no noise. Puck did the same, following Jack between two towering piles of wooden crates and heading, if Puck could trust his sense of direction in the dark, straight for the brick wall.

"It's here somewhere. Every rat has a bolt-hole," Jack whispered, swiftly but quietly lifting aside crates as Puck lowered Regina to the floor, holding her close against his chest. "Dickie found Hackett's earlier while he was reconnoitering outside. Clever boy, our Dickie. All I had to do once we got here was to count off steps from the front wall to the correct distance. It's somewhere right in this area. He and Henry should have made their way here by now, on the outside, but we can't count on that. Prepare to be met. Hackett's no fool."

"A second way out? Nice of you to let me know. A tad tardy, however."

"Now, now, little brother. Don't pout. You know I was never good at sharing."

Puck helped move aside more crates, which were all empty, mere decoys. "It wasn't pouting I was thinking of doing. You're an arrogant ass, Jack, do you know that?"

"Yes, but you trust me, just as I trust you."

"We do? I think we may both have to work on that aspect of our association a bit more. Is that it? I think you found it, Jack." He squeezed Regina's hand. "Ready to go, puss? Time to say our goodbyes to this lovely establishment."

"There's really another way out? Oh, thank God!"

"*Shh,* Regina," Puck warned her. He wasn't going to forget his belief that someone else was already inside the warehouse. "Jack, you take her. I'll bring up the rear. There's a little something I still have to do."

"Puck, no." She grabbed on to his shoulders, her fingertips all but boring through his jacket, and he pressed a kiss against her temple.

"You gave me your word, sweetings," he reminded her as Jack pushed the last of the wooden crates to one side, completely exposing a low wooden door—no more than a hatch, really—cut into the brick. The walls of the warehouse had to be a good three feet thick, which would make the escape hatch a short tunnel.

Damn! They'd have to drop to their hands and knees in order to navigate the low opening, leaving them vulnerable when they came out the other side. Maybe Hackett wasn't as brilliant as he'd thought.

Except for one thing Hackett did not know: Puck did not care for small spaces. Small, dark spaces, most particularly. But Jack knew it because he'd been there when Puck, at the age of six, had gotten accidentally locked into a cupboard in the stables—dark and peopled with many-legged things that bit and crawled over him—and had been forced to remain there for hours until he was found. That probably explained why Jack had withheld the information about this particular small, dark space.

"This leads to a wooden shed, built against the wall. I don't know what it's like inside the shed, just that Dickie found what he was sure was a tunnel but didn't want to risk investigating it, in case he was found where he shouldn't have been. At any rate, be careful as you exit. Can you manage it, Puck?"

Three feet or a little more. He could do this. Any fool could do this. It wasn't even a real tunnel, as tunnels went. And since Jack was going in first, the many-legged creatures would be scattered before it was Puck's turn. Not that he had any fear of insects, because he didn't. At least, not any he'd admit to.

"Of course," Puck said shortly.

"I'll go through on my back," Jack told him quietly, shoving one pistol in his waistband but keeping the other at the ready. "That will help some. Regina, I want you to hold on to my ankle so I know you're with me, understand? When I tell you to let go, you let go and remain inside the tunnel until I say you can come out. Puck, I'll give you the all clear when I can. Let's go."

And then Jack had her, and Puck was on the move, the knife pulled from his boot, his eyes and ears on alert as he took up position between two stacks of crates.

And waited. Everything had happened in the space of a minute, two at the most. Yet it had felt like a year, and would be another year until he was sure Regina was safe.

But the wait wasn't nearly that long before he heard a commotion at the door, the hollow, echoing sound of boots on the plank floor as men began running through the enormous warehouse, the sound of voices raised, shouting instructions. Almost immediately, heavy boots pounded up the stairs not twenty feet away from him, as if the men were sure of their mission. Five pips might have been all Henry'd had time for, because their pursuers clearly numbered more than ten. They were making enough commotion to rouse the dead, noise probably meant to fill the intruders' hearts with fear.

And closer, a small sound which he hadn't been meant to hear. He'd been right; someone else already had been inside the warehouse before they'd arrived.

And at least this one man knew about the bolt-hole, knew where to look for the intruders. One of Hackett's most trusted employees, no doubt.

The man approached cautiously, bent nearly in half but unintelligently holding his knife in front of him, too far ahead of his body, making it mere child's play for Puck to kick it out of his hand. It went noisily skittering across the floor.

Before the man could react, the hilt of Puck's knife came down on the back of his head, and he dropped to the floor.

Puck could have run then, as he'd heard Jack's short whistle giving the all clear for him to make his way through the tunnel. But he hesitated, even as the sound of shouts and heavy boots once again hitting the stairs, this time on the descent, drew closer.

He was rapidly running out of time.

But how did he give up this prize, this man who had been trusted enough to know the location of Hackett's escape hatch?

He couldn't do it. The man was leverage if nothing else. He'd be a fool to leave him behind.

Puck grabbed hold of the back of the unconscious man's collar and dragged him to the wall, then dropped to his knees and, still holding on to the man, began backing his way through the rough, brick-lined tunnel, dragging the not inconsiderable weight of his prize after him.

He immediately broke into a sweat, not because of his burden but because, when he looked, the brick roof of the tunnel was no more than six inches above his head. And closing in. He could feel it rubbing against his back each time he hefted the dead weight to move it forward. It was like being buried alive. Once again, the urge to abandon his prize nearly overtook him.

"Over this way! I heard somethin'!"

"Damn," Puck swore, breathing heavily as he tried to maneuver backward, now with both hands cupped beneath the man's chin, his fingers interlocked. His elbows scraped against the bricks. He'd lost his riband somehow, and his hair fell over his eyes, tangled wetly against his cheeks. His panic intensified, even as he tried to tamp it down. He should let go, but this man might be their only way to Miranda and the other women.

Three feet? He should be well out of the tunnel by now. But he wasn't. How large was this shed? He felt as if he was dragging the man uphill now, and the floor had turned from brick to packed dirt. How much of the tunnel continued into the shed?

His now scraped and bloody knees on fire, nearly out of breath, he tugged, inched, tugged again. He would not give up or give in to his stupid fears. He couldn't, even if that meant capture.

At any moment, Puck expected to feel a sharp tug as somebody on the other end of the tunnel saw this man's feet and grabbed on. Would he let go then? He prayed he didn't have to make that decision.

The man began to rouse, commenced struggling, so that Puck quickly shifted his grip to that of a stranglehold, the man clawing at his hands, his nails digging into Puck's flesh.

Like Grim Death, Puck hung on. Regina needed answers. This man had them.

"Jack! If you're not dead, grab my damn ankles— *pull me the hell out of here!*"

CHAPTER FOURTEEN

THE RETURN TO Grosvenor Square was not everything it could be in terms of dignity, but it was quick, and they moved with purpose.

Within an hour, the older ladies had been roused, their belongings packed, and they, Regina and their luggage hustled into the unmarked coach that would deliver them and the reliable Gaston to a nondescript house in Half Moon Street. The coachman had been warned to take a circuitous route and be certain he wasn't being followed.

Puck and Jack were standing in the drawing room, giving instructions to Wadsworth, whose only reaction was to grin rather wickedly.

"Done this last year, seems to me, sir," he said, scratching at a spot just above his left ear.

"Last year it was that fool Brean who came here looking to break Beau's nose for him," Puck pointed out to the butler. "Reginald Hackett is not in the same league. He'll demand entry. Give it to him. Understand?"

"Let him *in,* sir? In this house? Never say that, sir."

"But I am saying it," Puck told him, looking to Jack, who merely nodded his agreement. They hadn't had much time to talk, to plan, but there had been enough to agree that Hackett would arrive here, and soon. Other than that, all Jack had told him was that he would be content to stand back and watch, as the way his brother's mind worked had begun to interest him greatly. "Bring him directly into this room, and leave him here while you come to fetch me. Offer him refreshments, even with the hour so late. Be kindness itself, Wadsworth, and let it drop that you were told to expect him."

"If you say so, sir. But it's that queer, thinking someone is going to come calling in the middle of the night. I'll go roust a pair of footmen, I suppose. And the cook."

"You do that," Puck told the man's departing back; Wadsworth had been a soldier, and he took orders well, even while able to think for himself. He probably was already thinking that he should tuck a pistol in the back of his waistband, just on the off chance it might be needed. Good man, Wadsworth.

"How far have you and your fellow merry torturers gotten with our new friend?" Puck then asked Jack, who had just poured himself a glass of wine.

"More than halfway there, I'd say. Loyalty wouldn't appear to be his strongest suit. Dickie's almost disappointed we're moving along so quickly."

"He's the same man Hackett sent to the park Saturday morning, you know, to see if Regina was being met. I recognized him once we could see him in the light. So I think I was right—Hackett trusts him."

"He shouldn't. The man's become quite the canary," Jack said, smiling. "Not that I want to interfere with your plan—and it's clear by that unholy gleam in your eyes that you have one—but how are you going to explain those nasty scratches on the backs of your hands?"

"I'm not. Hackett and I have no secrets about what happened tonight. I would imagine he'll be offering me something."

"Yes. Money. His sort always believes it's all about money."

"And it doesn't hurt that I'm a bastard," Puck pointed out, rubbing at the worst of the scratches. "You'd best get back to it, whatever it is you're doing."

"You know what we're doing," Jack said quietly. "You also said you wouldn't question my methods."

"And I'm not. No one who saw those women today or that room tonight would be idiot enough to cavil at whatever methods you use to get the information we need."

"Because we need it quickly. It can't be easy, moving two dozen women a second time in one day, but that's what he's going to have to do now that we have his man. Unless he doesn't have to know that, which would make our job much easier. Let me take care of that part of the problem while you go after Hackett. And you're still certain he's coming here?"

"Oh yes. Definitely. He knows someone is on to him. I'm the obvious choice. Although I wasn't about to trust him to figure that out completely, at least not without some small assistance. I took a moment to leave one of my cards propped up on the table in that damn prison."

"Something you neglected to mention earlier." Jack shook his head, even as he clapped Puck on the back. "Little brother, you're a strange man. Perhaps even stranger than I."

"Don't damn me now, since we seem to be rubbing along together so well," Puck teased. "I merely thought it was time the two of us met, officially."

"But Regina doesn't know. Otherwise, I can't imagine her meekly going along with your plan to relocate to my small hideaway in Half Moon Street. Have Wadsworth send someone to the cellars once your visitor has arrived, if you please. I, too, would like to meet Reginald Hackett."

Puck was genuinely surprised. "You? I thought you were the man who doesn't exist. You'd let him see your face?"

Jack shrugged. "Needs must, I would say. He can't think you're operating alone. Not if you're going to convince him of the danger he's in."

"True enough," Puck agreed, walking with his brother as far as the door to the cellars, making alterations to his prepared speech as he went. "One look at that face of yours would probably prove to turn an entire army on its heels."

"For the sake of brotherly harmony, I'll ignore that. If I've got what we need, I'll give you a signal when I join you. Something subtle, I imagine. You'll recognize it."

"Something less than *I know where they* are shouted

at the top of your lungs, one can hope. All right." And then Puck headed for the study at the back of the house to wait out the time before Reginald Hackett came calling.

He sat behind the desk, pulling at his breeches where the material irritated the scrapes on his knees caused by his half crawled, half dragged progress along the rough floor of the tunnel, which had extended a good six feet into the shed before opening up behind a concealing wall with yet another hidden door. He hadn't had time for more than a quick washup and change of clothing, but before the night was out, he planned to find a tub and soak in it for at least an hour.

It had been a hell of a night, and it wasn't over yet, not by a long chalk. Leaving his card had probably not been necessary, as Hackett, again, wasn't a stupid man. He already knew who Puck was and that he'd been with Regina the night Miranda was taken. He had to know that the highly unsuitable Puck was…interested in the man's daughter.

But couple that with the fact that Puck was a bastard, and bastards were always suspect when it came to their character, Hackett couldn't be surprised to believe that having ferreted out what was going on, he would not ask to be cut into the profits.

It was now Puck's job to convince Hackett that he was not only correct in his assessments but that he was still safe. Otherwise, the *Pride and the Prize* might not sail in order to protect its owner…which meant that the current cargo would have to be dumped, jettisoned.

Two dozen women at the least, Regina's beloved cousin among them, were going to die if Puck made a single misstep, betrayed his hand in any way. If he were ever to be his mother's child, tonight would be the night to show it.

He flinched involuntarily when he heard the loud bang of the knocker, clearly wielded by a hand that would have that knock heard throughout the mansion.

Puck slowly counted to ten and then stood up, quoting softly, "'All the world's a stage, and all the men and women merely players: they have their exits and their entrances; and one man in his time plays many parts'— yes, Wadsworth, thank you, I heard the knock. How many?"

"Two, sir. A Mr. Reginald Hackett and a Mr. Benjamin Harley. Three other havey-cavey-looking ones outside, which is where they'll stay if they don't want their heads knocked together. Sir."

"Very good. May I say how much I applaud your ferocity. And you've sent someone down to—"

"I already told him, yes, sir, with your compliments. And he said to tell you he has what you want, and that his compliments are returned. Rather jaunty, sir, for the circumstances."

Puck's step was immediately lighter. He was beginning to understand, if just in a small way, the thrill Jack gained from his *work*. A man felt most alive when in the most danger. Even giddy, unless Puck was more singular in that particular reaction, which wouldn't surprise him. And was what he was feeling anywhere on a par with what their mother experienced moments before taking the stage? If so, no wonder she clung to the profession so tenaciously. It was heady stuff.

"Now that is good news, Wadsworth. Thank you yet again. Please make sure my belongings are en route to Half Moon Street, and if I don't have time to speak with you again for a bit, I'd like to make certain you'll ask Cook to prepare her special trifle for dessert the evening after next. Oh, and no beets."

Wadsworth clicked his heels together and bowed most smartly. "Good luck to you, sir. As for reconnoitering, the one is nothing but a smidge, but the other looks an ugly piece of business. A big brown bear in a well-cut suit, I'd say, sir."

"I've only seen the fellow briefly and from a distance, but I would have to say I believe your description borders on the brilliant. Again, thank you."

Jack joined Puck halfway down the long hallway. Jack quickly agreed to follow Puck's lead, and together they entered the drawing room to face the adversary, Jack's dark to Puck's light, Jack's scowl to Puck's broad, welcoming smile.

"Mr. Hackett," Puck trilled gaily, assuming the role of genial host as he walked across the expanse of the room, his right hand outstretched as if delighted to meet the man. No sense in trying to pretend he'd never clapped eyes on him before this moment. "How good of you to join us. This happy event has already been too long delayed. May I be so bold as to inquire about the well-being of your daughter? Lovely young woman, if a trifle *outré,* daring masquerade balls."

Reginald Hackett looked to Jack and then back at Puck. He blinked a single time, obviously a deliberate move meant to intimidate, and then seemed to attempt to mill Puck down with only his intense black stare.

Puck winked back at the man, feeling a sudden desire to see if he could goad more reaction than just the stare. "*Combien délicieux, pourtant scandaleux un risqué, oui?* I was happy to rescue the minx, so no need for thanks there. But shorten the leash, Mr. Hackett, that would be my advice. I know you've sent her packing to the country, and I consider that a reasonable first step, although in this case, the barn door had already opened, hadn't it? And a few other doors opened just tonight, didn't they?"

Now Hackett looked down at Puck's hands, at the angry red gouges and scratches that were so very obvious, and then at Puck. "Get on with it, you fool."

Puck, appearing undaunted—or simply oblivious to insult when directed at him by a mere tradesman— turned to bow to the *smidge,* which was an apt description of Mr. Benjamin Harley, and then quickly introduced Jack as his brother and *business partner.*

"H and H, B and B—although Jack and I would never think to lower ourselves to do anything so *déclassé* as to hang out a sign advertising our…ventures. Would we, Jack? No, no, don't answer. Jack rarely speaks, you understand. He's…more of a man of action,

I'd guess you'd say. I like to think of him as the brawn, while I lay claim to the brains."

Puck could sense his brother stiffening beside him and nearly laughed. But after all, if this was to be a play they were enacting, then why not at least open with a farce? Was he not, as his French friends called him, *le beau bâtard Anglais?* More importantly, he had to shift any possible suspicion away from Regina. He'd like to think he'd succeeded on that head.

"Enough of your twaddle! You broke into my warehouse tonight. Three of my men are dead."

"Only three?" Puck shook his head. "Perhaps not as much brawn as I'd supposed. Do you think to deduct their worth from our share of the profits? How much would that be, precisely? They are dead, which proves they couldn't be worth more than, oh, say two-pounds-six apiece? No? Oh, all right. I'll go to three even, but no higher."

"He said profits, Reg," Mr. Harley said quietly, speaking for the first time. "You were right."

"Stubble it, Ben."

"Oh no, no, no. If your partner told you my brother and I are interested in making a profit, then yes, Mr. Harley, your partner is exactly right. Would you believe our father, now that his year of mourning is over, is planning to marry this chit of a girl in hopes she'll prove, well, *fécund.* Ah, a frown. You don't know the word? He's hoping she'll push out sons, Mr. Harley. *Legitimate* sons. He has quite cut us off in anticipation of that happy event, as a matter of fact, and Jack and I have between us decided we would not enjoy a life of penury. What to do, what to do? We were, quite frankly, at our wits' end, living here as squatters only until the last of the quarter."

A little truth, a few small fibs, an outright lie—put together, they made a most plausible story, or at least one that should hold up for the length of time they needed.

Puck turned his attention once more to Regina's father. If he indeed had been performing on a stage, he could imagine those in the farthermost rows now leaning forward on the edges of their seats, intent on his every word. Who here was the villain, they'd be asking themselves—the obvious thug or the seemingly foolish young sprig of fashion who'd suddenly become so interesting?

He began his next monologue.

"And then *you* came along, didn't you, Mr. Hackett, thanks to your daughter's small escapade, not to mention the sudden disappearance of her cousin. You kept the cousin your procurers brought to you, even after learning her identity, even knowing her eventual fate? A fate, some would say, worse than death. That's a cold man, Reginald, a cold man."

Puck paused, almost believing he could hear the booing and hissing from his imagined audience. By rights, Hackett should already be ducking the rotted fruit and empty bottles flung at him by those in the pit.

"Nevertheless," he continued. "Meaning only to satisfy my own idle curiosity, I began to poke about, ask a few questions. But you know that, don't you? You seemed upset, even went so far as to have me followed the morning I was to meet with your lovely daughter, if I'm correct in that assumption, and I think I am. Well, my interest immediately became more concentrated, as you can readily imagine. Picture, if you please, my surprise as I went about attempting to satisfy my curiosity—and my eventual delight when I found what I found. How fortuitous! Others may look at you and see naught but another climbing cit, but not I. No, no, not I. You are to my brother and myself no less than manna dropped from Heaven. A glass of something wet, Reginald? Would you care for some wine? Although you've more the look of a gin man, I think. There must be some geneva somewhere about for the servants, who favor that horrid piss."

"You insolent pup! I could have you dead like *this,*" Hackett said, snapping his fingers in Puck's face.

"Oh, very impressive, Reginald, if predictable," Puck said, some of the amusement finally leaving his voice. "I suppose that means you've brushed aside my inquiry about refreshments? Very well, we'll move on. But as we do so, would it be crass of me to point out that you're making rather empty threats, standing in *my* house, with my brother holding a pistol directed at your midsection? Jack? You are holding a pistol on our friend Reginald, aren't you?"

"I am now," was Jack's answer along with the slight sound of a small, silver pistol being cocked. "You could warn a person, you know."

"You wouldn't shoot me in cold blood," Hackett retorted, not even looking toward Jack. "I've got the cargo, I've got the ship. I know the buyers. You've nothing without me."

And here it was. The moment.

"Oh, *au contraire,* Reginald. You see, we've got the previously elusive Mr. Harley now, thanks to you, delivered straight to our doorstep. Don't we, Mr. Harley? You don't look the sort who couldn't be convinced to cooperate. And then think—only a single *H* on that lovely sign. Oh, the possibilities!"

The slight man staggered where he stood. "I...um... that is..."

"Head or heart?" Jack asked conversationally, raising the pistol a fraction.

Puck wished he could order Reginald Hackett dead. But the man was Regina's father. Still, the temptation was there, within him, he who had believed himself a civilized gentleman.

Reginald Hackett threw his arms out in front of him. "Wait! *Wait!* I can see I underestimated you. The pair of you. I could use men like you in the right places. Let's talk this over. Tell me what you want. There's no reason we can't come to some sort of agreement."

Puck spread his hands as he said, "But why would we need to do that? From where I stand, Reginald, my brother and I, along with our new friend, Benjamin, hold all the cards. Speaking of which, Jack here has several gambling debts, rather large ones. You must know how relatives are—a constant drain on the pocketbook. Oh, that's right, you have the earl, don't you? And your brother-in-law, the viscount, as well, I suppose? We should split a bottle one day, Reginald, commiserate together. No? At any rate, we should probably address my brother's debt now, before anything else."

"All right, all right," Hackett said, his massive head bobbing up and down as if attached to his body by a spring. He was a large man, an imposing man, and at the heart of things, he was a bully. Fortunately, like with most bullies, at the first sign of defeat, he became a coward, albeit not one without plans. He clearly believed that he could talk his way out of his present unexpected predicament, at which time he would collect himself and launch a counterattack on the posturing imbecile now crowing over him. "What do you need? Five hundred pounds? A thousand? Separate, of course, from our other arrangement. We can have an arrangement, can we not?"

"That depends," Puck told him, putting out his left arm as if holding Jack back from his intended elimination of the man. (Hark, what was that? A sigh of frustration from the bloodthirsty crowd in the balconies?) "I admit that yet again, my curiosity all but overwhelms me, along with my interest in our share of the—do you slavers term it booty, or is that left for respectable pirates? Huh, respectable pirates. Is there such a thing? As opposed to those who deal with the white-slave trade, I would put forth that there must be pirates who wouldn't deign to touch you with a very long pole. But never mind, you are not required to answer.

How soon can we expect to see a profit from the sale of these unfortunate women? As you have surely surmised, I was on the docks today and saw some of your handiwork. If you keep tossing the ladies to the fishes, I wonder if there will be any profit at all. Sloppy, Reginald. Damned sloppy. I abhor waste."

"No, no, they were no great loss. They've already been replaced. And there's two that will each bring five times what all the others will fetch put together. And... and a third worth even more. I can personally vouch for her purity. I've special plans for that one, a certain party even Ben here doesn't know about. Yes, a very *particular* client. You need me. And I can use a pair of bright young men like you and your brother. Really! Some of my customers are like you—talk in circles, like they're better than me. I'm too plain-talking for them, and Ben here thinks he can keep his hands clean if he only works with the books. There's more than enough for everyone. I could make the two of you rich! I'm a generous man. Twenty percent. I'll cut you in for twenty percent."

"Dear me, now I'm insulted," Puck said, shaking his head. "Jack? Are you insulted? *I'm* insulted."

Jack made a small noise. Rather a growl. Some of his best acting, really, Puck thought.

"All right. Thirty."

Puck tapped his index finger against his lips, as if considering Hackett's proposal, enjoying the sight of the droplets of sweat running down the man's florid face. "Forty. And pardon my frankness, but I feel I need to say that I dislike haggling with merchants. Even a bastard son of a marquess has some standards."

As Hackett had to know he didn't plan to pay the brothers with anything more than a knife in the ribs the moment he could arrange it, he nodded his agreement. "You drive a hard bargain."

"Currently backed by a large pistol, yes. And I'd sail with the cargo, you say?" Puck asked, pushing for everything he could get. "That sounds rather delicious. I do adore travel. It edifies the mind. Where would I be going?"

Hackett visibly relaxed. "Here, there. And without a bird onboard who wouldn't do anything you asked if you told her you wouldn't sell her. *Anything.* Just not the virgins."

"How extremely disgusting of you, Reginald. As if I would touch a whore," Puck told him, managing a laugh. The monster was talking about his own niece, terming her his most profitable merchandise! "But now, we must return to less pleasant subjects, I'm afraid. I'm also a desperate man, sadly without other prospects. When can we expect to inspect the merchandise? It was difficult to tell the quality of those I saw today."

"No need to see them. They're safe where they are, no thanks to you. Just…just the pair of you be at the *Pride and the Prize* Wednesday night at midnight. We load then, before moving out into the river, and sail with the tide before light. Agreed?"

Knife the one once he leaves the docks, drop the other overboard in chains once free of the river. Prob-

lem solved. Puck imagined he could read every word of the plan in Hackett's obsidian eyes.

"You make it all sound so appealing. All right, agreed," Puck said and then looked to his brother, who had just cleared his throat. "Oh, and the five thousand pounds?"

"*Five* thousand? I thought we'd agreed on one."

"Alas, no, Reginald. *You'd* agreed on one. With no profit until the merchandise is sold, we will need some funds immediately, to tide us over, you could say. Can't leave my own brother here to starve in a gutter until I return, now can I? I'll expect a draft on your bank first thing tomorrow. And now, good night. Thank you so much for stopping by, but I believe we can carry on without you until we meet again. I must see to my wardrobe, for one."

"You want the draft delivered here? You'll be here?"

"Where on earth would we go?" Puck answered somewhat testily, walking toward the foyer, sure Hackett and Harley would follow. "Just see that the draft is here before noon, because I have some need of visiting my own banker by one."

The door had barely closed on their visitors' backs when Jack uttered a scathing string of oaths that would have impressed a Tothill Fields tinker.

"I couldn't have said it better myself," Puck told him in some admiration as they reentered the drawing room. "I mean that, truly. Some of that bizarre playacting was actually enjoyable, which makes me question my own sanity. It's his own niece who he believes is so special.

You know that, don't you? Man's a monster, and I need a drink. Several, in fact. God, that Regina has had to endure him. The man is a pestilence."

"You're very good, you know. Better than I would have imagined. Although I probably could have survived without being termed the brawn to your brains."

Puck smiled, even though his heart wasn't in it. "Would you have shot our new partner Reginald if I'd said to shoot him?"

"The thought crossed my mind. Now, if you're wondering what my answer would be if you'd asked me if I would have raked the barrel of that pistol across his ugly face, loosing several of his teeth, just on general principle?"

"Yes?" Puck prodded. "And what would that result have been?"

"Among other things, Wadsworth summoning the maids to clean up the carpet. But shooting him was out of the question as we couldn't have been sure Harley knows everything we need to know. Hackett knew that, too, not that he isn't even at this moment making plans for our untimely demises."

Puck poured two measures of wine and handed one glass to his brother. "True. But we do know the women are still alive, we do know he plans to sail Wednesday night."

"And that he'll try to have us both killed long before Wednesday night unless he decides to do the deed on the docks, where he clearly feels most safe."

"Yes, that's also a possibility I considered while he

was still here. Was I too heavy-handed about having that meeting with our banker tomorrow at one, and we'll be out and about, making ourselves easy targets?"

"Probably not. For all your bravado, he still clearly believes he's smarter than both of us. I can sympathize with his reasoning. You were very nearly the twit, you know. I was close to wanting to knock you down myself. Now, before we both conveniently disappear into the night, would you like to know where the women are? Not that you'll enjoy the news."

"Why won't I?"

"Because they could be any of three places. Wherever they were an hour ago, they're bound to already be on the march to a second one. Our friend downstairs wasn't included when the women were removed from the warehouse, so he can't be any more definite than that. Another warehouse, this one in Southwark, would be his first choice—he graciously offered to lead us there as well as the two other sites if we aren't first-time lucky. A defunct tavern right on the docks or, the worst of the lot, a warren of ancient prison cells in some sort of tunnels open to the Thames that probably have been there since the Romans held our fair island."

Please, no, not another tunnel.

"Nothing is ever easy, is it?" Puck put down his empty glass. "We should be leaving for Half Moon Street before Hackett has the wit to set up sentries to watch us. I need to see how Regina is holding up, and we all need some rest before we begin searching again.

We don't have that much time, not if Hackett has realized we have his man."

"His man is dead, unable to tell us anything. He's just not been discovered yet, inside the tunnel, his legs neatly sticking out into the warehouse. Poor man was garroted while trying to protect his employers. He'll be seen at first light, if not sooner. Untrusting of the caliber of Hackett's gang of ghouls, I believe Henry plans to set fire to one corner of the shed, sending smoke into the warehouse, just to help things along."

Puck cocked one eyebrow as he looked at his brother. "I thought he was going to lead us to the other three possible sites."

"He's doing that right now, with Dickie and Henry. Then he's dead. Don't look at me in that manner, little brother. It's the only way to trick Hackett, so that the women won't be moved to a new, fourth hiding place, and lost to us. Unconscious or missing, neither will do what we want. Dead, on the other hand, accomplishes what we want."

Puck considered this information for a few moments, and then nodded his agreement. This was a deadly game they were playing, and when weighed against those terrified women, the choice was simple. "Just let me inform Wadsworth that the trifle should be saved for Thursday night...."

CHAPTER FIFTEEN

REGINA SAT IN THE TUB, her knees drawn up against her chest, both the room and the water warm enough, yet she couldn't seem to stop shaking. She would think she was finally fine, and then a sudden tremor would hit her, shuddering throughout her entire body.

Her cousin's prison. The filth, the smell of fear. *Miranda, Miranda. What are you thinking? Have you lost all hope? Do you know we're looking for you?*

Thoughts of what she'd seen on the docks in what seemed like a lifetime ago and what had happened in the warehouse refused to leave her mind. They'd nearly been caught. Puck had stayed behind, long enough for her to have reached a level of silent hysteria that would have had her collapsed to her knees, sobbing with loss, had he not finally appeared up out of that tunnel, looking filthy, exhausted and yet triumphant.

When all she'd been was terrified.

All her life, she'd thought herself a victim of her birth, her future not in her control. But she'd been housed, clothed, fed…and safe. She didn't know what it was to be cold or hungry. She'd felt oppressed, yes, but never abandoned, alone. Desperate.

She'd never *dared* anything. Left to her own devices,

there would have been no masquerade ball, no abduction, no meeting Puck, no desire, no passion…no *life*. She'd existed. She'd never really *lived*.

When this was over—and at some point, with either success or defeat, it would be over—what then? She couldn't go back to simply existing, she just couldn't. She could never face her father again, not without wishing him dead. It wasn't going to be enough, rescuing Miranda. Reginald Hackett had to be stopped, arrested and made to pay for his crimes with his life.

And then what of those he left behind? His wife, his daughter and the entire selfish family he'd bought and paid for? The scandal would rock London and destroy all their worlds.

Would the Crown confiscate his fortune—his ships, his warehouses, his fine country estate, his London mansion? That wasn't outside the realm of possibility.

Regina knew she couldn't be certain that her mother's family would take them in, house and feed and care for them. After all, they could claim ignorance to Reginald's crimes, and their titles would protect them from the worst of the scandal. But not if they took in the wife and daughter, brought them under their roof. Not then.

Puck will take us. Puck will keep us safe.

Another tremor shook Regina's body.

Selfish, selfish, selfish! You saw all you saw today, and all you think about is yourself!

"Regina?"

Regina sighed, closing her eyes for a brief moment, and then looked toward the doorway. "Yes, Mama?"

"I don't understand why we're here," her mother said, advancing into the rather Spartan bedchamber. "Your Aunt Claire said it was necessary that we leave Grosvenor Square, but when I asked her why we should abandon such a lovely hideaway, she simply began crying again, and I felt it unfair to push at her. But now I've come to you. Is your father on to us?"

"On to us, Mama?" Regina very nearly smiled. Her mother had taken to what she called her small *adventure* with surprising alacrity and enthusiasm, even if the full import of what may be happening to her niece had clearly not completely penetrated her mind. To Lady Leticia, a promised week without her husband had been reason enough to turn a blind eye to what might be an unfortunate liaison between her daughter and one of Blackthorn's bastards. Perhaps her mother was selfish, too.

Only then did she notice the wineglass in her mother's hand.

"Please don't look at me like that," Lady Leticia said, cradling the glass against her breast, the vessel clearly a treasured possession. "I was upset, being roused so rudely as I was. It's only the one portion. Or two…" She trailed off, and Regina could see the familiar *softness* of her mother's features, which indicated that she'd been seeking comfort from a familiar friend. "I thought certain we were being taken back to Berkeley Square.

I can't go back there, Regina. I will surely die if I go back there. I've been dying there for a long time."

"Oh, Mama…" Regina reached for the toweling sheet that had been left beside the tub and stood up, not knowing what she would say to her mother, what she *could* say.

She shouldn't have worried.

Lady Leticia shook her head, sighing. "I wanted to have them bound, you know," she said, staring at Regina's bare breasts. "As they did to me after you were born and your father insisted on a more sturdy wet nurse than he said I could have been. Perhaps that would have helped. Milkmaids are known to be overly generous in the region of the bosom. Others of the lower classes. It's not seeming that my own daughter should—well, I blame Grandmother Hackett."

Regina quickly wrapped the toweling sheet around her body before her mother's attention could be drawn to the flare of her daughter's hips, also to be numbered among her failings. She couldn't very well hide her less than ladylike height, another cause of concern for her mother, but she did what she could. "Yes, Mama," she said. "I'm so sorry."

Lady Leticia dismissed this apology with the wave of one hand, the one holding the nearly empty wineglass. Noticing it as if surprised to see it still there, she then drank up the wine in one long gulp. "No, no, it's not your fault. I suppose men are attracted for some reason, although your dressmaker confided in me that she finds it much easier to create for those less well-endowed. Not that a dressmaker should have anything to say in the matter." She frowned, as if searching her mind for something she might have forgotten. "Was there something else you wanted, Regina?"

"No, I don't think so, Mama," Regina answered, unashamedly grateful for the wine that had clearly begun to both mellow and muddle her mother. "It's well after three, isn't it? I suppose you're very tired?"

Lady Leticia pushed at her hair, which had begun to sag, thanks to Hanks's necessarily quick application of pins as she had helped the woman dress for their short journey to Half Moon Street. "Yes, I believe I am." She looked into her empty glass and frowned. "I think I'll return to my chamber now, such as it is. Good night, sweetheart."

"Good night, Mama." Regina managed to hold her smile until her mother had quit the room, but once the door had closed, her composure gave way, and she could barely stagger to the bed and throw herself down on it before bursting into tears.

She cried for Miranda. For all the women who had ever been in her father's clutches…taken from all they knew and loved, bound in chains, sold to the highest bidder. Or drowned like unwanted kittens. She cried for her mother, who had lived her entire married life in fear, for all the wasted years, her wasted youth. She cried for herself, knowing that was wrong, selfish. She cried for Puck, who had put himself in such danger. She cried until she didn't know why she was crying. She simply couldn't stop.

She felt the touch of a hand against her temple, gently stroking the hair back from her wet cheeks, and nearly jumped out of her skin, then settled as she heard Puck's voice close to her ear. "It's all right, sweetings," he crooned softly. "It's all right. I promise. Everything is going to be all right."

He eased himself against her in the bed, his long form pressed to her back, gathering her close, taking her pain, holding her against his strength.

"It's not, you know," she whispered quietly. "Even if we get Miranda back. She'll never be the same, Puck. None of us will ever be the same. How could we?"

He slipped an arm around her waist, his mouth still close to her ear. "But we can be strong for her. We can right a wrong."

Regina's bottom lip trembled. She tried not to say the words but couldn't hold them back. "I want him dead," she said, her voice catching on a sob. "I'm as bad as he is, Puck, because with all of my heart, I want him dead. For…for what he's done to Miranda and to my mother… and to all of those poor women. He's a monster, and his blood flows in my veins. How…how am I supposed to live, knowing that? How can you even look at me?"

She wanted comfort. Perhaps even forgiveness. She didn't know what she wanted.

But, whatever it was, it wasn't what she got.

"I thought you were crying for your cousin, your mother and, as you said, all of those poor women," Puck said almost coldly. "But you're too busy feeling sorry for yourself to think about anyone else. My mistake."

Regina struggled to sit up, forgetting about the toweling sheet, which quickly dropped open to her waist. "How dare you! It's not your father who did this."

"True," Puck said, pushing himself up against the headboard, crossing his long legs in front of him. "All my father did—or shall I say all he did *not* do—was to marry my mother, thereby branding his sons bastards in the eyes of the world. It was left to my brothers and me, however, to decide who we are, to take the measure of our worth, to build our own lives. Who decides for you, sweetings, hmm?"

She didn't know whether to hit him or hug him. "I do," she admitted quietly. "I decide."

He put a hand to his ear. "I'm sorry, I didn't quite hear that."

"I said, *I* decide. *Me.* I'm not my father. I'm not Grandmother Hackett or even my mother. I'm me. Who I am and *what* I am are up to *me.* That's what you want me to say, isn't it?"

"That's what I want you to *believe,*" he corrected. "Because, from where I'm sitting, I think Regina Hackett is fairly wonderful. And brave, tremendously brave. Not to mention…fetching." He said this last as he lowered his gaze to her bare breasts.

"Oh!" Regina exclaimed, at last realizing she was all but naked. She quickly pulled the sheeting up and over her lower-class breasts. "You could have said something, you know."

"And spoil the view? Hardly. Especially now that

you've done it for me, just as I was about to avail myself of what I hoped was an invitation."

Regina felt her nipples hardening beneath the toweling, even as her very center tightened pleasurably in response to his words. "Of all the things I should be doing tonight, this is probably the very last…." she said, unable to avoid looking down at his trousers and the bulge that told her he was becoming similarly aroused.

He took hold of one end of the toweling and slowly, so slowly, drew it from her body, leaving her naked to his gaze.

"There's comfort in the oblivion of physical pleasure, Regina. It's why we mortals seek it. No thought, no regrets, no room for anything but the journey…and the destination. No need to think but just to feel. To escape, to fly free. Let me take you there, sweetings. Let me fill you with the delight that leaves no room for anything else."

She sat there, transfixed, her legs tucked up beneath her, watching him look at her, feeling his hands on her even though he'd yet to touch her. He was seducing her with his words, filling her mind with wild imaginings. Ridding her mind of all she wanted gone.

He was so clever. She was so willing to clear her mind of everything but him.

She needed him to touch her. She needed his touch more than she needed air to breathe. He left the bed to stand beside it, stripping off his clothing, his eyes never leaving her, his soft words spoken in French now, intoxicating her senses, telling her how much he wanted her, how her pleasure would be his delight. He stood before her now, naked, glorious, displaying his need. The small, hard bud between her thighs contracted almost painfully.

But he stayed at the side of the bed, not joining her as she thought he would. Instead, he smiled almost impishly—even at his most intense, he remained Puck, seeing humor in all things.

"Puck...you can't just stand there," she said nervously.

"True enough. But I've just had a thought. Come here, sweetings," he said as he reached over and took hold of her ankle and pulled her toward him, splitting her legs around his hips, swiftly filling her completely. The move was so sudden and so neatly done...so blatantly sexual in nature. He was here, she was here; they would use each other to rid themselves of the ugliness of the day.

She tried to reach up her hands to him, and only then did he lift her, find her mouth, kiss her almost fiercely, his hands kneading at her breasts.

In little more than an instant it was as if they had become one person, the heat of their passion fusing them together. She held fast to his shoulders, tightened her legs around his waist, longing to be even closer, knowing that was impossible.

She ceased to think. She could only feel.

When he broke the kiss, it was to whisper hoarsely against her hair. "Nothing else exists now, sweetings, nothing else is real. The world begins and ends here, with us."

Slowly, he began to move inside her. Deep, deeper… impossibly intimate. She clung to him like a limpet, arms and legs wrapped around him as he tumbled their joined bodies onto the bed, holding on for dear life… because he was her life. He gave her life.

But it wasn't her life that he wanted right now. It wasn't life either of them sought, but oblivion.

"*La petite mort,* Regina. Remember? Find it with me. The little death. Don't be afraid, let me take you there. We die together, just for the moment…."

And then she let go, let everything else in the world go, and allowed the impossible to take over, take control, until they collapsed onto the bed together, totally satisfied, totally spent.

"I take it all back. You're no innocent. You're a witch," he said, breathing heavily against her hair.

"I know. And you're a bastard. We're well suited, I think," she responded, nipping at the side of his neck. The world would come crashing back soon, but for now? For now, she was free. Puck had made her free. He knew her better than she knew herself, knew what she needed even as she floundered about, hopelessly lost. "Thank you."

"You're welcome," he said, pulling her close, all gentleness now, all protective and comforting. "Idiot."

"Oh? In that case, I'm quite fond of you, too."

"That's good," he told her. "Otherwise, at least for a few moments there, I would have thought you were trying to kill me." He drew her closer. "This may or may not reassure you, but for the moment, we're in Black Jack's capable hands. He's making arrangements of some sort but warned me to be ready by five o'clock. I say we, because I'm not fool enough to ask you to remain here. You have an hour, sweetings, no more. Try to sleep."

"If you'd said that to me when you first came into the room, I would have told you sleep was impossible. I also would be badgering you for anything you might know about your brother's plans."

"And now?"

Regina yawned into her hand, which was answer enough. She curled against him, her head on his chest, and closed her eyes. For just this one hour, she would leave her fate in the hands of the gods.

THEY STEPPED OUTSIDE and into a fierce storm. Wind-lashed rain wet them to the skin before they could make the dash from the mansion to the mews. Lightning lit the dark like brief bolts of sunlight, and thunder boomed close behind each new white-hot streak. Puck supposed it could have been worse, but he wasn't sure quite how. Unless there were fire-breathing dragons in the cave.

An unsmiling Baron Henry Sutton held back the flap of the covered dray wagon, and Puck was quick to lift Regina up and into it without ceremony.

As Puck made to follow, Jack grabbed his arm and took him to one side. Together they inspected the

sturdy, closed wagon Henry had unearthed from somewhere and driven into the mews behind the mansion,
four stout horses in the shafts. "It's not much for speed
but hopefully we'll be returning here with a full cargo.
You've probably already guessed our destination."

"The cells, yes. Anything else would have been too
easy," Puck answered, suppressing a shudder. "Dark,
cold, undoubtedly damp. Rats big enough to have eaten
all the bats, or at least we can hope. Am I correct?"

Jack only nodded. "I had no idea such things existed
anymore. I've been in Blackheath Caverns, but I don't
think this is a part of them, not this far into the city.
Henry believes the Romans must have housed galley
slaves there at one time. The caves open right onto the
river, but they're isolated, mostly hidden by green-
ery. From the water, you'd never suspect the openings
were there. Five of them, total, spaced out over about
fifty yards of shoreline, possibly even man-made. Two
guards patrolling up and down out in front, another
two on the—well, let's call it a cliff, but it's not all that
high. We can only hope the caves haven't sunk to near
tunnels over the centuries. With this storm and the tide
about to turn, the damn things could flood. Hackett
isn't making this easy."

"So you've already seen all of this for yourself?"

"No, just Henry and Dickie. Dickie's still there, in
case the women are moved yet again. Five caves. A true
warren of hidey-holes and cells inside each, I'm sure,
with the women possibly scattered, not all in the same
cave. The man doesn't take the best care of his mer-

chandise. It will take some time to find them all, but we'll work quickly. I'd suggest you and Regina remain with the wagon until we bring the women out and she's reunited with her cousin. She shouldn't see what she might see. Plus, frankly, she'd only be in the way."

"As would I?"

Jack rubbed at his forehead, probably forgetting that he'd smeared lamp black all over his face as had Henry…and a third figure, standing very much at his ease some distance away, a gloved hand resting on the hilt of a sword strapped to his waist. "This is what we do, Puck, and we're tolerably adept at it. We clean up messes for the Crown. We kill when necessary and without hesitation. You were surprisingly brilliant with Hackett earlier, but you're too good for what's needed now. You've the soul of a poet, brother mine. You've got a heart…and something to lose. You're no killer. Besides, someone has to stay with Regina and the horses."

Something to lose. And you don't, Jack? Is that it? You have no heart? Are you so good at what you do because you don't care if you live or die?

"I managed the tunnel in the warehouse, Jack. I'm fine. We're fine, Regina and I both. With five caves, you'll need all of us to do the searching. We didn't come this far not to get to the finish line."

"This isn't a damned horse race, Puck. Nor is it a play, where you control the lines. If you were to end up face-to-face with Hackett, with Regina standing beside you to witness what happens next—could you do it? Could you shoot her father while she watched? No, don't say anything, because we both know the answer. You'd try to spare Regina, try to apply reason to an unreasonable position, and with a man like Hackett, that could be a fatal mistake. I meant what I said, Puck. You were brilliant with Hackett, I couldn't have done better." Jack clapped a hand on Puck's shoulder and finished, not unkindly, "But now the brawn is in charge."

So you do have something to lose, Jack. Your younger brother, whom you've been avoiding these past years, just as you've avoided Beau and our parents. What are you afraid of, Jack? What did you lose that you'd choose to stay away, isolated, rather than allow yourself to admit to any emotion at all?

"I'll say it again. You always were an arrogant horse's ass, weren't you?" Puck said without heat. "Let me know when you're done posturing, and we can get on with this. Rain's running down my back."

Jack's smile was quick and brilliant in his dark face. "I really do like you, brother mine. I begin to think I missed a lot, not getting to know you and Beau better these past years."

Puck was quick to take advantage of this slight opening his brother had given him. "It wasn't Beau and me who avoided you, Jack, and the past isn't the future. Once this is over, we'll all go to Blackthorn. It has been dog years since we were all together."

"Puck, this isn't the time to be discussing family reunions."

Jack was right. This wasn't the time, and with the wind and rain nearly drowning them, neither was it the place. But Puck knew he had a duty; perhaps it was the poet in him, as Jack had said. "He gave Beau an estate, you know. Unentailed. And me, as well, last year. You know that's what he wants, to be sure we're all taken care of. Let him, Jack. Let him do this. Let him make amends for not marrying our mother or whatever the hell it is he wants to do. You might have a lot of years ahead of you to regret it if you don't."

Jack was silent for some moments. "I'll think about it," he said at last. "You're worse than a wife, do you know that?"

"There's the insulting Jack I don't really know but definitely would like to become better acquainted with someday. All right, I'm done now. But first, who's our swordsman, or is that something I really don't need to know?"

Jack glanced back over his shoulder and then smiled at Puck. "You already do know him. And as long as we're tossing the word *arrogant* around so lightly, I believe you were planning to pink him one day this week, showing off your froggie-learned swordplay. Something I would warn against attempting, most strenuously, by the way."

"Will Browning?" Puck asked, peering into the dimness. "Henry and Dickie introduced me at the masquerade. Don't tell me Viscount Bradley is skulking somewhere in the shadows, as well."

"Hardly. I think he's afraid of his own valet. Now, unless you'd like to stay here and discuss Wellington's strategy in his last campaign or the cunning cut of your best waistcoat, I'd suggest we be on our way. With this storm, dawn isn't going to be one of our problems, but the tide might be troublesome."

"I'm in your hands, I suppose," Puck said. Giving Will Browning a rather mocking salute, he then turned and climbed into the back of the wagon. Not a play? Didn't Jack realize that he was the biggest actor of them all?

Once inside, Puck squinted, trying to pierce the nearly nonexistent light inside the dray wagon that smelled strongly of ale, which was probably its usual cargo, but Regina's face remained too deep in shadow for him to see her clearly. He found her hand and squeezed it, and she returned the pressure, but neither of them spoke as the wagon lurched forward.

They were on their way. This was it, their last chance, and they both knew it. What if they didn't find Miranda? What if the girl was somehow already dead? Or gone mad—and that was a distinct possibility. What if Hackett was at the caves and put up a fight? Regina could say she wanted her father dead, but to be there when the man died?

It must be hell inside her head right now. Hope, fear, anticipation, dread. And yet she simply sat there, holding his hand, determined to be there when Miranda needed most to see someone she knew and trusted.

God, how he loved this woman. He should have told her.

But it was too soon.

Yet too late.

He'd known her for a only few days. He couldn't seem to remember his life without her in it. Probably because he hadn't really been alive until the night he first saw her.

He was a poet? The hell he was. A poet would have found the words....

The wagon rumbled over the cobblestones, unsprung and tossing them about inside so that they had to grab on to any handholds they could find.

"Where are going?" Regina asked at last. "Is it far?"

"Now there's the question I should have asked," Puck told her, pressing a kiss against her temple. "From the sound of it, we're heading for some ancient Roman caves located somewhere along the banks of the Thames."

"*Caves?* Why on earth—?"

"It would seem there are some sort of cells there, probably built to hold slaves. Galley slaves or something like that. Your father may have thought he could then move them from there in the dead of night, straight out to the *Pride and the Prize,* bypassing having to return them to the docks. In any event, we know where they are, and we'll soon have them safe if not necessarily dry. What did you tell your aunt?"

"Nothing," Regina said, resting her head against his shoulder. "All she did was look at me when we returned from the warehouse, and then she burst into tears and ran for her chamber. She wants to tell me to stop, I know that, but she can't bring herself to say the words. Miranda's her daughter, and she'd sacrifice me in a moment to have her back. We'll none of us ever be the same when this is over, will we? Not if we fail and not if we succeed."

There was no answer he could give her that could possibly mean anything, so he merely hugged her closer, and the wagon moved forward through the night.

Puck could now make out shapes in the darkness inside the wagon. There were blankets, at least two dozen of them, piled high in one corner. Lanterns ready to be lit for the search. Two large baskets probably filled with food and even wine. Jack had prepared for success and probably never doubted it. In fact, this same wagon had likely been hidden in an alleyway when they'd gone to the warehouse. His men might be good at what they did, as Jack said, but there hadn't been much time to prepare for this trip to the caves.

Barely enough time, in fact, to have Hackett's man lead them to the three possible hiding places and then garrote him and put the body where Hackett couldn't help but find it.

Ruthless men dealing with ruthless men. How many more would die tonight?

"I want you to remain here, in the wagon," he told Regina and then put a finger to her lips before she could mount a protest. "There's nothing you can do to help, sweetings, not until we have the women free, at which point I promise to bring Miranda straight to you."

Regina put her hand on top of his and moved it away so she could answer him. "I agree, Puck. Completely. I'm glad I went with you to the warehouse, that I found that scrap of Miranda's gown. But now I'd only be in the way."

Puck peered at her through the darkness. "You were eavesdropping on my conversation with Jack, weren't you?"

She cupped his cheek with her hand. "The soul of a poet. I think that's lovely and even somewhat true. But you'd also like to knock a few people down, wouldn't you? I think you should. No matter who that person is. I would, if I could, if I were strong enough. But I'm not. So perhaps you could knock down two of them?"

"Come here," he said, drawing her fully into his arms as they sat huddled on the floor. "I think I love you, Regina Hackett. No, that's wrong. I know I love you. I probably should have waited until this is over and then told you. But some things shouldn't wait. I love you. But if you say thank-you now, I may change my mind. I might, in fact, grab Will Browning's sword from him and fall on it."

"Who's— No, never mind. I love you, too, Puck. It's all so complicated, though, isn't it? All so wrapped in everything else. Papa would never give his blessing. But if he's put into prison, if he's sentenced to death, then you would be saddled with the daughter of an acknowledged monster. Even in Paris, would society do more than turn its back on me, as well it should? And what of your parents? A bastard is one thing, Puck, but the daughter of a— You *are* going to ask me to marry you, aren't you?"

"Well, yes, I was, or at least I was until you pointed

out the possible pitfalls," he said, hiding his amusement at her sudden, almost panicked, question. "I mean, I do have my reputation as a bastard to uphold, you know. Having lived my life as the lowest of the low, the thought of marrying beneath me had never occurred. Are you proposing to me, Miss Hackett?"

Oh, how he wished he could see the expression on her beautiful face.

"I don't know. I'm caught between the proposal and longing to box your ears."

"In that case, I say yes to the former but no thank you to the latter. I could give a damn about my so-called reputation, but I am rather fond of my ears. You may kiss me now."

It would seem that Regina settled on a compromise, for she grabbed hold of his ears and pulled him forward to capture his mouth with her own.

But the kiss, as was the moment, was to be short-lived, for the wagon came to a halt. Almost immediately, Jack pulled back the canvas tarp to peek inside.

"It's a rare man," he said conversationally, "who can find something to amuse him while on his way to danger and possible death."

"We're betrothed," Puck informed him, stupid with happiness, quickly removing his hand from beneath the cloak covering Gaston's breeches and shirt...the buttons of which had somehow come open.

"My felicitations, I'm sure, and my condolences to the lady. We go on foot from here. I've rethought the thing now that I can see the area for myself, and

Dickie has just informed me that Hackett's added another three guards since Henry left to report to me. I believe Regina will have to accompany us. I've not enough men to have you or anyone remain here with her, and I'm not sufficiently enamored of the neighborhood to allow her to stay here on her own."

Regina immediately put her hand in Puck's. "It's all right. I really did want to go. I just said I didn't because it seemed the right thing to say."

Puck kissed her again, a hard, swift kiss, and then helped her out into the cold, slashing sheets of rain, the whipping wind. He could just barely make out their surroundings, but it would be difficult to miss the Thames rushing along a good twenty yards ahead of the horses. The wind-whipped water seemed black and deadly, whitecaps visible in the dim light.

He shot a look up at Jack, still on horseback. "The tide's in. Will we be able to even reach these damn caves? What's the approach look like? How close can we get before we're spotted?"

"It's comforting to know you can concentrate your mind on other things, Romeo," his brother answered, wiping his face with an already filthy cloth, the rain having made a smeared and streaming mess of the lamp black. "And the answer to that is around this convenient outcropping we're hiding behind for the moment. Clearly the caves flood at times like these. They're bringing them out and rather quickly. They're heading straight for us."

Regina grabbed on to Puck's forearm. "We actually

found them? They're actually here? Can you see them? Is Miranda with them?"

"It's all right, sweetings. We'll have her soon enough." By now, Puck had visually inspected as much of their surroundings as possible in the storm. They weren't that far from the city, and London was slowly reaching out to claim the land; there were a few buildings here and there amid the long grasses and trees. He hadn't asked, but from the length of the journey and the scenery around him, he assumed they were not far from Cremorne Road. He'd also noted that theirs was not the only wagon in the small clearing. "Hackett's?" he asked Jack, indicating the wagon with a tilt of his head.

"And a driver, who is no longer of any concern to us, thanks to Dickie. It's rather anticlimactic, actually. We just have to wait here for the women to be brought to us along the path that runs along the riverbank. Now, if you wouldn't mind taking the high ground along with the others, where Dickie will count noses and assign quarry, hopefully we'll be done with this and somewhere warm and dry within the hour. Regina? Hold on to Puck, please, but I might also suggest you close your eyes. Brother? May your aim be as true and steady as your heart. Henry and I are for the highest point of the bluff."

And with that, Black Jack tipped his hat, rainwater cascading off its brim, and turned his mount toward the high, rocky outcropping that presumably separated them from the caves. He dismounted at the base of it, tied his mount's leads to a bush, dropped his hat and rain cloak to the ground and began climbing up the craggy rock face with an ease that told Puck this wasn't the first time he'd attempted such a feat. The man certainly did have talents and a flair for the dramatic.

Will Browning was waving one arm commandingly, silently urging them to hurry to him. Puck grabbed Regina's hand, the two of them running toward the outcropping, which, once the two men had helped Regina on her climb, was really not much more than a reasonably flat-topped pile of large rocks covered in brush and slippery moss.

Puck decided the caves had been man-made and the outcropping they were availing themselves of now was no more than the excavated rock and ground, arranged as a sort of wall or barrier. Sentries must have once stood here, keeping watch on the cells below. The romantic in him would like to come back another day to investigate the area at his leisure. The rest of him was just cold and wet and anxious to have this over.

Dickie was already there, lying on his stomach, motioning for them to advance at a crawl so that their forms would not be outlined against the slowly lightening sky. He appeared to be munching on a soggy meat pie.

Regina did as she was instructed, Puck lying down just beside her, his arm protectively across her back. Together, they looked in the direction indicated by Dickie's pointed finger.

"Where, Puck? I can't see any— *Oh, my God...*"

They half walked, half staggered along the winding path that rose up from near blackness at the water's edge, the long line of females, each wearing a set of ankle chains. Arms around each other, supporting each other, the near rags of their clothing whipping in the wind.

There was a single large man in the lead, and then more were positioned along the line, between the women. Two...three...five. Five men.

Behind them, the path ended just beyond the caves, this time with an outcropping that went all the way to the shoreline. There was only this one way in, this one way out of the area. The Romans had planned well if keeping their slaves where they were easily guarded was their aim, but the same couldn't be said of the location as far as Hackett was concerned, which the man would find out soon enough.

Hackett had probably meant to move the women to the *Pride and the Prize* by longboat, but the storm had put paid to that idea. One way or another, Puck knew he and Jack between them had made enough mischief for Hackett that the man was now acting hastily and making mistakes. Puck actually smiled; he'd always known he'd find some sort of talent inside him. He should tell Regina.

Then he looked at her, saw the fear on her face and decided to let it wait for another time. He turned his attention back to the moment.

Jack and his friend Henry would take care of the two on the cliff; Puck had no thought that his brother might fail. That still left only three against five. But add the element of surprise and their elevated position, and the odds were nearly even.

Will Browning nudged Puck with his elbow and pointed to the cliff, and Puck looked up just in time to see the lone sentry suddenly disappear as if plucked from his position by an invisible hand.

"That's both of them now," Will whispered, although he could have shouted for the noise of the wind howling around them. "Once they're trussed up, Henry will make his way back here to us, and Jack will go after the last man in the line, leaving us only four to play with. Hardly even sporting, wouldn't you say? But that's Jack, always the show-off."

"Yes, in fact, I've just now decided it's a family trait. When do we go?" Puck asked, reaching into his boot for his knife. He had his pistols, but would the powder be dry? Could he hope to hit his target from this distance? No, the knife would be better. Quick and silent. *God, I'm thinking like Jack now. Perhaps I shouldn't have pressed him to come to Blackthorn. We may be in company too much as it is. There's no telling where further association could lead.*

"Puck." Regina was tugging at his arm again. "Puck, look. It's Papa. Oh, God. He's got Miranda. See him? Huddled just there, in the middle of the line. He has a lantern. That's her, Puck. That's Miranda."

"I see her," Puck assured her. What was Hackett doing here in the first place? Had he known the caves might flood, or had he seen through the ruse of planting his dead henchman back at the warehouse? And why wasn't Miranda wearing ankle chains like the others? Had he come to personally claim his most valuable property? "When do we go?" he asked the others.

"Easy…easy," Will Browning warned. "Dickie, old friend. Perhaps you'd care to squash the fellow in the lead?"

"You promised me you wouldn't say things like that again," Dickie Carstairs grumbled, tossing away the last of the ruined meat pie. But he was already getting to his feet, as the first of the line of bodies below the outcropping had nearly reached them. There was a quick flash of blade as he gracefully inched his bulk toward the edge of the ledge. He looked over his shoulder at Will Browning. "Damned insulting, that's what it is. Besides, I was hungry. Missed my dinner, drowning here. Ready?"

Puck planted a quick kiss on Regina's mouth. "Can you make your way back down to the wagon? Help the women climb into it and keep them calm, all right? I'll bring Miranda. I promise." Then he turned to Will Browning. "Ready. Pick which of the others you want. The one with the lantern's mine."

There was a sudden commotion at the end of the line, a short, abruptly cut-off scream, quickly carried away by the wind. The women stopped, turned on the path in order to see what had happened behind them.

"And there's Jack, starting it off for us. One down. Pray for panic, Miss Hackett. It's always our best ally. For king and country, Puck, and for the joy of it," Will

Browning said, his sword drawn as they all watched Dickie Carstairs seem to wind himself up by flailing his arms and then launch himself feetfirst at the man leading the way.

There was an audible *"Ooof!"* as he landed on the man's back.

What followed was pandemonium; there was no other word for it. Women screamed, cried, tripped over each other in their desire to make good their escape. The two remaining guards dropped their weapons and scrambled up the side of the low cliff, intent only on their own escape.

"Henry will be so pleased, seeing them heading directly for him," Will Browning said, grinning. "I think I'll join him."

All of which left Reginald Hackett and his niece nearly isolated on the path, standing stock-still, as in Puck's mind's eye, everything and everyone else faded away. All that was left was the sound of the wind and the rain and his own heart beating madly in his ears. Jack was wrong. He could kill Reginald Hackett if he had to. In the space of one of those loud heartbeats. And he'd feel no more remorse than if he'd stepped on a particularly ugly water bug.

Thanks to the rain, Puck's descent to the narrow path was more slide than leap, but he landed on his feet, his knife in his left hand, blinking against the rain.

"Out of the way! Move!" he shouted to the women. "Keep moving forward! You're safe now! Keep to the path! Head for the wagons!"

One of the young captives flung herself against him, hanging on tightly as he tried to shake himself free. "Please, sir. Take me home. My father will pay you well, I swear it! Please! Oh, God, please, *please!*"

"I've got her," Dickie said, pulling the girl away. "But your man appears to be taking a flit."

Puck turned his attention back to the path to see Hackett dragging Miranda with him as he headed back toward the caves. Why? Was there another way out? Rats always have another bolt-hole. How had they forgotten that? "Damn it!"

He started after them, pushing his way through the panicked women, slipping on the muddy path, just able to see Hackett abruptly stop, glance back over his shoulder and then look to the now-visible, dark mouths of the caves, as if measuring his chances of reaching one of the entrances before Puck was on him.

"Give it up, Hackett! It's over! Let her go!"

Hackett hesitated and then must have weighed his options and decided the odds of making good his escape weren't all that favorable.

So he increased them.

He dragged the screaming Miranda to the edge of the path and then roughly flung her away from him. She toppled backward, tumbling into the dark, fast-moving water of the Thames.

Puck didn't spare so much as a look toward Hackett as that man then raced into one of the cave entrances. There was no time to launch his knife at the man's back. No time to do more than drop that knife, throw off his rain-soaked cloak and hat, run to the spot where Miranda had quickly disappeared beneath the surface and follow in after her.

CHAPTER SIXTEEN

REGINA HAD DONE as Puck asked her to do, although she'd wanted more than anything to remain where she'd been, able to watch what was happening. She'd seen Miranda. She'd seen her cousin, alive. To then turn away, even knowing that Puck and his brother and the others wouldn't let anything happen to her, had been the most difficult thing she'd ever done.

But those poor, terrified women also needed her. They needed to be told they were safe now, and to believe it. She'd barely made it to the bottom of the outcropping when the first of them appeared at the end of the path. Quickly, she wrapped her rain cloak around her, to hide her breeches. Her attire was one thing that could wait to be explained.

"You're safe! Stop running! You're safe! We're here to help you!" she cried out as she ran to them, waving to indicate the wagon. "Over there, in the wagon—there's blankets and food! Nobody is going to hurt you anymore!"

"An' how does we know that?" the woman in the lead turned to ask her companions. "Heard that clunker afore, ain't we, ladies? I say we keep movin' on our own, I do."

"Oh, give over, Madge," another said, pushing past her, walking remarkably well considering her ankle chains. "The way I sees it, anythin's better than them caves. Come on, everybody! Can't move us about mor'an they already have, I say. Mayhap this time's the charm!"

"Now there's a smart young lady, and *charming,* as well. You're all safe, and that's a fact, although not dry, eh? But we'll soon fix that," Dickie Carstairs said as he strode forward, holding up what looked to be a large key. He had been holding a young girl's hand but left her to approach the others. "And see what I've got. Who wants to be first?"

He was immediately surrounded by a wet, bedraggled throng, all loudly demanding to be first to have her ankle irons removed. All but the one Dickie had ushered into the group, a girl Regina believed to be younger than her. Small, slight and seemingly unable to do anything more but stand where she was, her hands to her mouth, and sob.

Regina hastened to the wagon to retrieve one of the blankets before going to the girl and draping it around her shoulders. "You're safe now. I swear it. I'm Regina. What's your name? Where do you live? Are you all right?"

"I want to go home," was all that the girl could manage as she rocked back and forth on her heels. "Please. I want to go home. I want to go home."

"I've got her, miss," Will Browning said, appearing seemingly out of nowhere. "I think I know where this one belongs. Her and one other. Jack commissioned me to return them both. Discreetly, of course. Better that no names are mentioned, if you take my meaning. All the way around."

Jack and his friends were like ghosts, appearing and disappearing, and they probably wished she had never seen their faces or heard their names. "Yes. I do understand. Thank you." She looked around the clearing, the sky having at last brightened somewhat, the rain falling away to little more than a drizzle. "Where's Puck?"

Will Browning didn't answer her at once, and Regina's heart did a quick, painful leap in her chest.

"Mr. Browning? I asked you a question. Where is Puck? And where is my cousin?"

"Jack's on the path. Jack and Henry both," he told her even as Dickie knelt in the mud, unlocking the young girl's ankle chains. "It's safe to go there now."

Regina opened her mouth to ask another question but feared the answer too much to hear it, so she just took to her heels, running toward the path and the caves. The path was more than muddy now; it was rapidly being overtaken by the rising tide, water now entering the caves. It was all she could do to keep her footing.

She saw Jack and the baron standing just outside those cave entrances, but neither of them saw her. They were intent on looking at the river.

"Jack! Jack, where's Puck? Where's my cousin? Where...where's my father?"

"Will and Dickie have everything in hand here, Jack. I'll retrieve my horse, go on ahead," Henry Sutton said, avoiding her eyes. "The current's fairly swift. We'll get to the other side of this outcrop and begin checking downstream. He could have gotten her out somewhere, Jack. Anything's possible." He looked at Regina and lightly tipped his hat. "Miss."

And then he was gone, running back down the length of the muddy path.

"No," Regina said, slowly shaking her head. "No."

Jack reached out his hand to her. "Regina…"

She clapped her hands to her ears, slowly backing away from Puck's brother, unwilling to listen to whatever he had to tell her. *"No!"*

"He went in after her, Regina. It was either go after your father or save Miranda. It was his choice, the only one someone like Puck could have made. It's ours not to give up hope." He grabbed her hand. "Now, do you stand here or come with me?"

Her lips were numb. Her entire body had lost feeling. "I…I'm coming with you."

Now she did take his hand when he held it out to her and, together, they made their way back along the overrun path. Twice, she nearly fell, but both times Jack's strong arms pulled her upright, until at last they reached the outcrop and the wagons.

Dickie, who had been in the process of handing out food from one of the baskets at his feet, looked toward them, a half-eaten chicken leg in his hand.

"Know all about it. Will's on about his business. I'm good here, got all these lovely ladybirds set to be returned to their nests. Going to be a while, though. Where do we meet up?"

"Grosvenor Square!" Jack shouted, still holding on tight to Regina's hand.

"And the bodies? Got a couple, you know."

"Leave them. Time we were gone. We're here too long as it is."

"Fine by me. You'll find him, Jack," Dickie assured him. "If he's anything like you, he's too stubborn to drown. Where's Hackett?"

"In the caves or gone," Jack said as he lightly vaulted into the saddle and then had Regina take his hands so that he could lift her up, place her sideways in front of him. "Don't wait around for him. We know how to find him."

And then they were off, Regina holding tight to Jack's waist. His mount's iron shoes clanged against the wet cobblestones as he turned onto one of the streets running parallel to the river, taking them downstream for what seemed like forever but could only have been a few minutes.

"There's some small docks where the river begins its turn ahead of Battersea Bridge," he told her. "With luck, he's managed to stay afloat that far."

Regina only nodded. Jack was interrupting her prayers. Her most fervent prayers. She didn't ask how Miranda had come to be in the river. She didn't ask about her father. There was no time for questions. If Puck was lost to her, there would be the rest of her life to ask questions, but by then she wouldn't care about the answers.

There was little traffic on the streets save for wagons loaded with fresh produce coming in from the countryside and a few complaining cows being led toward Mayfair, where their owners would hawk "fresh milk, fresh milk," and the servants of the wealthy would come outside with their pails. The city was coming alive, as it did every morning, and if Jack and Regina made an odd sight, nobody seemed to have time to take notice.

Jack at last reined in his horse and lifted Regina down to the ground. "Henry's checking along the shoreline, but I doubt Puck could have reached the shore, not in this current and not with your cousin with him. If he's got her."

"He wouldn't leave her. He wouldn't let her go. Not Puck." Regina was trembling so hard her teeth were chattering. "So what do we do now?"

"Now we search those piers ahead of us. And we pray the current didn't push Puck too far out into the river. Do you see those trees, Regina? That higher ground? That's where we were. If he was going to be able to save himself, the piles holding up these piers are the logical place."

She looked around at the tumbledown buildings that lined the river here, the several long, wooden piers jutting out into the water. The docks seemed to have mostly fallen into disuse, probably when the London Docks had opened. Still, there were enough rough-looking men about that Jack drew his pistol from his waistband as they half walked, half ran toward the pier closest to the caves, and they were left alone.

Their boots struck the boards of the narrow pier, and the structure seemed to shake on its moorings. Regina squinted upstream, praying to see two heads above the rapidly flowing water even as Jack dropped to his belly on the boards and leaned over the edge, shouting, "Puck! Damn you, Puck—where are you?"

Nothing. Only the sound of gulls wheeling overhead.

Regina cupped her hand around her mouth. "Puck! Miranda! We're here! Where are you?"

"There!" Jack leaped to his feet, pointing to the shoreline just ahead of the docks. "See them? Down there! How did he manage to— How the devil is he holding on? Sweet Jesus!"

And then they both were running back along the length of the pier and then scrambling down the muddy bank, to the ancient stone wall that lined the shore.

Puck was smiling up at them. *Smiling!* His blond hair plastered to his face, his skin nearly blue with cold. And he was *smiling*.

"Took…took you long enough," he managed. He was holding on to the top of the wall with one hand, his arm wrapped around Miranda's still form. "I was going to let go, hope to snag one of the moorings, but I wasn't sure I should chance it. Not…not the best morning for a swim, I think. Probably should have left the boots behind."

"Oh, *Puck*," Regina said as Jack hauled Miranda's

limp body up and over the wall and laid her in the weeds. She knelt down beside her cousin and spread her sodden cloak over her, if only to protect her modesty; it certainly wasn't going to do much else. "Is she all right? Oh, God, she isn't moving!"

Puck was out of the water now and on his hands and knees beside her, breathing heavily. "She kept struggling," he told her. "I'm afraid she's going to have a very sore jaw when she wakes up."

Regina's eyes went wide as she touched her hand to Miranda's frigid cheek. Only the fact that she had seen her cousin's chest rising with each breath had kept her from strong hysterics. Still, she knew she was mere moments away from collapsing to the ground, sobbing in relief. "You *hit* her?"

Jack hauled his brother to his feet. He held on to Puck's shoulders for a long moment and then roughly pulled him into a quick, tight embrace. "I thought you were gone." Then, just as quickly, he almost roughly pushed him away. "You look like hell and smell like the river. I'll go scare up a hackney before the three of you freeze to death. Damn heroics. It's the poet in you. I did warn you."

"Brotherly love," Puck said with a chuckle as he sank to his knees once more, clearly exhausted. "That took a lot out of poor old Black Jack. Is she all right? She was fighting me, pulling me under, and my boots didn't help. I may have hit her fairly hard. I never struck a woman before, Regina… I didn't enjoy it."

"But she's alive. You saved her life." She wrapped

her arms around him, squeezing almost fiercely, because she'd thought she'd never see him again. "When I...when I realized what had happened..."

"Shh," he told her, rocking her against his strength. "I'm the proverbial bad penny, sweetings. I always turn up again. Ah, and it would seem your cousin is waking up. Not that she'll probably be happy about that...."

Regina looked to her cousin, who had begun making faces, squeezing her eyes shut. She moaned once, and then her eyes shot open wide, and she turned on her side, retching, bringing up half the river, it seemed, before her stomach was empty.

Regina held on to Miranda's shoulders, trying to soothe her, telling her she was all right, she was safe... and for that sympathetic gesture was rewarded by her cousin suddenly turning toward her, arms flailing wildly, her hands drawn up into fists. "Let me go! Let me go! You *bastard!*"

"My recent blow to her face to one side, I don't think she's referring to me," Puck said, grabbing Miranda's wrists before she could hit Regina again. "Lady Miranda!" he said sharply. "You're safe. Look—look who's here. It's Regina."

Miranda slowly calmed, her panicked expression changing into one of dawning knowledge, and she finally looked at her cousin. "Reggie? *Reggie!*" And then her eyes rolled up in her head, and she fainted.

PUCK WARMED THE SNIFTER of brandy between his hands as he sat in the study in Grosvenor Square, the fire in the grate more suited for a winter's night but welcome all the same. Enough brandy, and he might succeed in getting the taste of the Thames out of his mouth.

Madness. These past few days had all been madness, with the worst of it saved for the moment he'd plunged into the dark water and somehow come up with a handful of Lady Miranda's hair, dragging her back to the surface with him.

She'd fought him. His boots, filled with water, tried to drag them both down again. He'd been instantly freezing, instantly weak, the cold sapping his strength, the current pushing the two of them along like corks bobbing in the ocean.

He didn't know how long they'd been in the water, but he'd known he couldn't last much longer. His chances would have improved if he'd just let go of the girl. But that was out of the question. He'd never be able to face Regina if he did that. He'd never be able to face his own reflection in a mirror. So he'd save her, or he'd drown. Those had been his only two options: triumph or tragedy, with no middle ground. It was the damned poet in him.

The current had pushed him toward that wall, and he'd managed to fling himself high enough up out of the water to grab a tenuous handhold on the rocks. But Miranda was dead weight, and he was fast losing his grip. He'd been just about to let go, try for one of the pilings of the pier, when he'd heard Jack's shout.

And then he'd seen Regina's face, and suddenly he was strong again. He held on. For her. For the two of them.

It was nearly noon now, and the ladies had all been reunited, Gaston having personally driven Lady Claire and Lady Leticia back to the mansion, although he'd not been best pleased to have left the bathing of his employer up to lesser mortals. Puck had eaten something—he really couldn't recall just what it had been—and now he was waiting impatiently for his brother to show up and fill in any details he might have about the rescued women, and one Reginald Hackett.

Before anything else could happen, Regina had to know her father's fate; they all did.

If the gods were kind, the man was even now floating facedown inside one of the flooded caves.

Dickie Carstairs had been and gone, having succeeded in delivering the ladies of the evening to Mr. Porter, who would then *distribute* them to their employers. He'd blushed as he'd told Puck he'd been given carte blanche to the pick of Mr. Porter's own clutch of soiled doves for the space of one year, an invitation he had declined with deepest regret. And then a strangely solemn Will Browning had arrived, said little, and the two had departed again almost immediately, presumably to their own domiciles, hot tubs and dry clothing but most probably heading back to the river. In any event, they hadn't lingered, nor had they accepted Puck's offer to join them.

A singular bunch, Jack and his friends. They'd accepted him on sufferance, had even complimented him on his *derring-do,* leaping into the Thames to rescue Miranda, but it was clear that he wasn't one of them, he wasn't cut from their same strange cloth. And Puck couldn't help but agree. He would fight when he had to, kill if if it came to that, but he wasn't the sort of man who would ever actively seek out situations where he might be forced to do both. He'd even admit as much to Jack when he saw him.

But Jack had yet to show his face. He'd piled Puck and the two women into a hackney and then ridden off to find the baron and continue the search for Reginald Hackett.

Another hour passed before a slight noise at the door had Puck looking up from his contemplation of the swirling brandy in time to see Jack entering the room, once more looking his dark, handsome and totally inscrutable self.

"Anything?" he asked as Jack made straight for the drinks table and poured himself a glass of wine.

Jack didn't sit down in the facing chair in front of the fireplace but only stood at the mantel, his scowl the sort that would scare small children, and most everybody else, for that matter. "Hackett's alive. And nowhere to be found."

"Damn. You're sure?"

"I'm sure. I found Henry's body along the riverbank. But not his horse."

Puck felt his body grow cold. "How?"

Jack downed the rest of his wine. "I asked myself the same question as I checked out the caves. One of them contains a clearly more recently dug passage that winds around and opens up at the other side of the cliff. Hack-

ett's bolt-hole. I can imagine how it happened. Henry…
Henry was intent on searching the surface of the water,
looking for you and the girl. He wasn't watching his
own back. There were signs of a struggle, but Hackett's a big man. He managed to break Henry's neck. It's
not your fault, Puck, remember that. You only get one
mistake, doing what we do, and Henry made his today.
Two years fighting Bonaparte and never a scratch. Just
to end like this. Will and Dickie took him home, tucked
him up in bed. He'll have died somehow in his sleep.
No one will ever know the truth."

The wineglass shattered in the fireplace.

Puck's mind seemed to be moving in six directions
at once. Hackett's hands, large, strong. Deadly. Hackett's face, probably the last thing the baron had seen
before he died. Hackett. Alive. The only men who
could expose him for who and what he was, send him
to the gallows, here, in Grosvenor Square. His wife and
daughter, Lady Miranda and Lady Claire, also once
again here, in Grosvenor Square. Not that the man
knew that. *Yet*.

"You think he'll cut his losses and run?" Puck asked
his brother, hoping Jack would agree with that possibility. "See what's happened as the end of him here in
England? He's got an easy escape route. All those ships.
The *Pride and the Prize* at London Docks, for one, and
nearly ready to sail. He had to know a day like this
might come. He'd have placed funds in foreign banks,
have a bolt-hole. The man's always had a bolt-hole."

Jack seemed distracted. "I don't know. A man like

Hackett plots to survive. That's not the same as planning for defeat. Right now he's probably kicking himself for allowing two raw amateurs like the pair of us to best him, rob him of his cargo. That's how he'd see it, Puck. That we've robbed him of valuable goods. Not that we've rescued the women, that we had any higher purpose, as it were. He thinks we're as bad as he is, only not quite as intelligent."

Puck nodded his agreement. "All right, that makes sense. We'd decided to take his *cargo* and sell it ourselves. He's probably smart enough to know we're aware he never planned to take us on as his partners."

Jack actually managed a smile. "I don't think I'd like to be Mr. Benjamin Harley right now. Would you?"

"God, I hadn't thought of that. I set the man up for destruction with my attempt at playacting, didn't I? We've got the cargo now, but we don't know the ports of call. Only Hackett and Harley know that. Plus, we'd need the ship. Hackett has to think his partner betrayed him. Benjamin Harley might even be the one who tipped us to the location of the caves." Puck shook his head in some amazement at how all the wrongly assumed puzzle pieces Regina's father may have assembled still managed to very neatly fall into place. "Damn. Should we be dashing off to save the fellow from Hackett's wrath or something?"

"Are you feeling heroic again, brother mine?"

Puck considered this for a moment. "Not particularly. A good man is dead. I care about that, very much.

I don't think I can bring myself to care about Benjamin Harley, no."

"Be careful, brother. You're beginning to think like me. So we're agreed. We leave Mr. Harley to live out the remainder of his life, which can probably now be counted in hours. As to the rest of us? You're the poet, Puck, the storyteller. What would you do now, were you Reginald Hackett, believing what you believe? Play his role for me for a moment."

Puck looked at the snifter in his hand and carefully set it down on the table beside his chair. He closed his eyes, attempted to put himself inside the head of a cold-blooded monster, knowing only what that man knew. "If he means to salvage what he can, remain in England? He'd want the two of us dead, obviously, just as dead as his traitorous partner. If I were Reginald Hackett, Harley would be my first order of business, just out of pure hate and because he'd be easier to dispatch. You and I would be second on that list."

He opened his eyes and looked at his brother. "We have to get the women out of here, Jack. Now."

"Ah, then the brains and the brawn are in agreement. The hunters have just been made the hunted. But what to do with the women? Are we back to Half Moon Street? Every time we move them, there's more chance that someone will see them."

"I know," Puck said, getting to his feet, his mind whirling with possibilities. "They can't stay here any longer, that's clear enough. But no more hiding. I think it's time Regina and her cousin returned to town. I don't know about you, Jack, but I much prefer the role of hunter, and I can't think of a better way to flush out our quarry. Besides, I've yet to formally apply for his daughter's hand in marriage. I don't expect his blessing, but I would want him to know about the betrothal before you take him away, to do whatever it is the Crown thinks best to do with him."

For the first time since entering the study with news of Hackett's escape and the baron's death, Jack smiled. "You know what the Crown thinks best."

Puck walked over to the drinks table and poured out two measures of wine, handing one glass to his brother while lifting his own. "To a true and brave friend. To Baron Henry Sutton, and may the blackguard who took him from us be in Hell before the sun rises tomorrow. *Henri, soldat courageux, nous vous saluons!*"

CHAPTER SEVENTEEN

"PAPA!"

Regina watched as Miranda raced into the drawing room in Cavendish Square to throw herself into her father's arms.

The viscount looked startled, as well he should, but then slowly wrapped his arms around his daughter as she sobbed against his shoulder.

"Look at him," Regina whispered to Puck as they remained in the black-and-white-tiled hallway and watched the awkward reunion. "He doesn't know if he should be happy or horrified. This may have been a mistake."

"One I believe her ladyship will rectify in short order. She's made of fairly stern stuff, I've discovered," he answered, and Regina watched as her aunt, spine stiff and shoulders straight, marched into the room to join husband and daughter. "Kettering, my good man?" he then said, without turning around.

"Yes, sir, Mr. Blackthorn. I am, of course, at your service." The Mentmore butler spoke from mere inches behind Regina, or so it seemed, startling her.

Puck squeezed Regina's hand and whispered in her ear. "Hear that? He's at my service." He turned, still holding her hand, and motioned for Kettering to head for the relative privacy of the hallway. "Yes, Kettering, my very good man. You've sent away the other servants?"

"I did, sir, the moment I received your note. I informed them, as requested, that the viscount had declared a day of prayer for his sick father, the earl, and they were all to take themselves off to church." The butler leaned forward confidingly. "Most are headed for Bartholomew Fair, I believe, thanks to the purse you sent round with the note. They won't none of them be back too quickly. And my congratulations, sir, for having found Lady Miranda."

"Found her?" Puck put a hand to his chest as if astonished at the man's words. "Why, was she misplaced? The ladies have been at Mentmore, remember? Visiting the earl, painting watercolors of some local ruins and whatever else it is that ladies do to amuse themselves in the country."

Kettering flushed to the roots of his hair. "Yes, sir. I forgot…that is, I remember now. But why, sir, may I ask, would the ladies have come back from the country, what with the earl about ready to cock up his toes?"

"Can you even ask, Kettering?" Puck said in further astonishment. "Lady Sefton's ball is this evening, man. If the young ladies are perhaps soon to be forced into mourning and miss the remainder of the Season, well, then they'd best get their husband hunting in while they can. Now, dinner for—let me think—ah, yes, is Lady Miranda's dear brother yet back from his journey? No?

In that case, nothing too elaborate for dinner. I would suggest you have trays sent to the ladies' chambers. And they'll need the coach brought round at nine and not a moment later. Until then, the family is not receiving. Is that all clear to you now?"

Kettering bowed to Puck, even as he pocketed the gold coin he'd just been handed. "I won't forget again, sir. My deepest apologies."

"Of course you won't. You're a good man, Kettering. I knew where your loyalties lay the first moment I clapped eyes on you. Wadsworth?"

The Blackthorn butler stepped forward. "Sir!"

"Mr. Kettering, you may now say hello to Mr. Wadsworth, a man above price and whose loyalties lie with me, in case you may be wondering. And cooling their heels in your kitchens at the moment is the remainder of my equally loyal staff. You will put yourself in Mr. Wadsworth's capable hands, Mr. Kettering. Agreed?"

Regina thought Kettering looked mulish for a moment, but then he nodded his agreement. "As you say, sir."

"Splendid! Wadsworth? I would imagine you'd like some tea now, yes?"

"And a little something to go in it, yes, sir," Wadsworth said, winking at Kettering. "Come along, my new friend," he went on, clapping one muscular arm around Kettering's shoulders in a way that warned he'd be friendly if the butler agreed but was prepared to be less than that if necessary. "We've lots to talk about, we do, the pair of us."

Regina watched in amazement as the high-nosed Mentmore butler went off, meek as a lamb, and then turned on Puck. "Are you mad? Miranda's in no fit state to go to a *ball*. I know I promised not to ask any questions when you were loading us all into the coach and sending us all here, but can you seriously believe you can hold me to that now?"

He grinned at her, but she refused to be mollified, especially when he answered, "I admit to some hope, dazzled by your love for me that you are. But, in truth, I seriously doubted I could hold you to it once you realized you and the other ladies were driving through the heart of Mayfair in the Mentmore coach with the shades down, for all to see you as you return from your recent sojourn in the country."

"Yes. *All*. Including my father. You may have sent the servants away, but word will get to him soon enough, you know it will. And he knows Miranda will tell everyone what happened."

"No, actually, she won't. She can't. We know, her family will know. But the rest of the world will remain in ignorance." Puck squeezed her hands in his. "Think on it a moment, sweetings, for I have. I worried for her at first but not now. You see, and as I'm sure your father has already figured out for himself, she can't tell anyone, not without damning herself. Lady Claire agrees."

"You spoke to my aunt about this? But what if you're wrong? What if my father comes here today? I can't face him, Puck. I can't."

"And you won't. You'll be at Lady Sefton's ball, re-member?"

Regina thought her head might explode. "*What?* You expect me to go with her?"

"You and your mother both, yes." Puck looked into the drawing room, where the reunited family was now seated close together on one of the couches. "Come with me. I'd rather say this only once, and then you and I can find some secluded room somewhere in this shabby pile, and I can make untoward advances on your virtue."

"I'd have an answer for that, Robin Goodfellow," she whispered furiously as he all but dragged her back into the drawing room, "but even Grandmother Hackett wouldn't dare be so frank."

"Mad about you," he whispered back. "I'm simply mad about you. When this is over, I doubt I'll allow you out of my bed for a week. We'll have the luxury to go slow, to take our time. An entire afternoon, just to kiss you. From your head to your toes. *J'apprendrai tous vos secrets, mon amour, et vous saurez le mien.*"

She felt her face grow hot. "Puck! You won't distract me. And I'm not going anywhere, no matter how you convinced my aunt or may convince my uncle."

But then Puck laid out his plan for the remainder of the day and evening, and she was proved wrong…and an hour later, behind a locked door in the small conservatory that had fallen into disuse years ago, Puck was proved right.

He began kissing her the moment the key was safely in his pocket.

They hadn't had a moment alone together since that morning. There had been Miranda and her understandable hysteria once she'd roused from her faint, clinging to Regina, sobbing and laughing and then suddenly still, until a shudder overtook her, and she cried again.

The reunion had followed, once Lady Claire and Regina's mother had been brought from Half Moon Street. It had been heart wrenching to witness, glorious, a mad mix of emotions, which had left them all spent, exhausted.

Reginald Hackett's name had been raised and roundly cursed. Regina and her mother had retired from the room then, her mother to seek out a bottle, Regina felt sure, and herself to sit alone, wondering when it might occur to Miranda to hate her because of who her father was.

And then, just when Regina, having dressed hurriedly after her bath, had hoped to slip downstairs and find Puck, they'd all suddenly been hustled into the Mentmore coach and driven here, to Cavendish Square, only to be greeted by Puck, who had arrived before them via the servant's entrance, all smiles and plans and teases, just as if he hadn't very nearly died.

So now, when they were finally alone, she held on tightly, never wanting to let him go. She could have lost him to the river this morning. She'd thought she had. If she'd lost him, she would have lost herself, because she was a part of him now, as he was a part of her, always and forever.

Five days ago, she hadn't known him. Now there was no life without him.

It wasn't passion she needed from him right now, nor he from her, she felt sure. It was the closeness, the touching, the holding on to what they'd found, the promise of a future, the reminder that they were alive, and life was to be lived.

He kissed her hair, her eyelids. "When I thought I'd never see you again…that's what kept me going, Regina. Life is never fair and often even cruel, but sometimes it can be kind. Because here we are. And we'll never be separated again, I promise."

She pressed her cheek against his chest, glorying in the steady beating of his heart. "You were so very brave. Not just any man would have dared that water to save a woman he didn't even know."

"I agree. It was very cold water, and filthy into the bargain. And then there was the matter of my boots. I'd hoped to perhaps find a fish in one of them when Gaston finally was able to wrench them off me, but no such luck. And the boots, of course, are ruined. As a consequence, if it eases your mind, I've decided to never do anything quite so foolhardy again."

She raised her head to look up into his smiling face. He wanted her to smile, as well, so she did. For a moment, they would pretend to be lighthearted. "You think a similar occasion could occur? Or are you speaking of heroics in general?"

He pushed an errant curl away from her forehead. "Devout cowardice does have its merits, you know. Or would you rather I was more like Jack?"

Her arms tightened around him. "I think your brother is very brave and extremely dedicated to whatever it is he and his friends do…and if you ever dared to join him in any of his exploits I would probably have to lock you in the cellars until you came to your senses. Will we have cellars?"

"I don't know," he said, looking at her with the smile still in his eyes, looking so young and handsome her heart nearly broke. "I do have an estate, by the way. There are sheep on it, I believe, and some cows and a multitude of fields and trees. Oh, and a house. Perhaps with cellars. You may be marrying a bastard, Miss Hackett, but he's a rather well-heeled bastard."

"Married," she said on a sigh. "Is it wrong to think about a future, when everything is still so uncertain? I suppose I know your plan for Miranda is necessary. But my father isn't a stupid man, and quite desperate, no thanks to you. What if he doesn't do what you expect him to do?"

Puck put a finger to her lips. "Shh. Not now. If we only have these few moments, let's not waste them talking about your father. Not when I'd much rather be kissing you."

"Yes, but how do you know he won't follow us to the ball and try to hurt Miranda? I know you said he won't, and your reasoning seems sensible. But how do you *know*?"

He took her hand and led her over to a dusty stone bench, spreading his handkerchief for her before she sat down. "You heard my reasons as I laid them out to the viscount and Lady Claire."

"Yes," Regina said slowly. "And to me. You laid them out to me, as well. We've returned from the country, we may have been seen alighting from the coach earlier. We're attending Lady Sefton's ball this evening, safely out of the way and at the same time very visible to those who need to see us out and about and… happy, as if without a care in the world. Oh, Lord, how will Miranda manage that? How will any of us manage that?"

He squeezed her hand. "You will because you have no other choice. Miranda's future depends on it. I'd go with you, you know that, but it would seem Lady Sefton forgot to send along an invitation to the marquess's bastard son. At any rate, your father will know by now where you are, as I'm certain he's had someone watching the mansion in Grosvenor Square day and night. Until an hour ago, there was someone watching this house, along with Dickie Carstairs, who was making himself quite obvious out there while someone better hidden watched the watcher. But even the watcher is gone now."

"I'd ask you to explain all of that, but as the thought seems to make you happy, I'll let it go. Go on."

"Thank you. Your father will by now have assumed, correctly, that Miranda is no longer a threat to him, as it would be a disaster if it were ever learned what happened to her these last days. Your father will also know that you and your mother were with Miranda. And Lady Claire. He'll have realized by now that he'd been tricked, that you'd never left London, that his daughter and his wife have betrayed him, that you know him for what he really is…and that his new worst enemy has been protecting you."

"More than protecting us. He'll think the worst, and he'll be right. All his plans to marry me to a title are gone now. His entire world, the one he built so carefully, it's all gone now. All because Miranda and I attended that masquerade a lifetime ago." She put her hand to Puck's cheek. "He has so many reasons to want you dead."

"Yes, but I'm also the least of his worries. At first, yes, Jack and I both thought he'd come hunting us and possibly even Miranda. But then we realized Miranda's greater danger—the other captives. No secret is ever a secret for long, Regina. There were too many women, and at least one of them will know your cousin's name, at least one of them will tell someone about Reginald Hackett. Your father's crimes surely will come out, which is the reason Miranda has to be seen tonight— happy, laughing, putting the lie to any rumor that she'd been one of the captives."

"And all with half the rice powder in London on her bruised cheek. I don't know how she'll manage, but if Aunt Claire thinks this is necessary, Miranda will listen to her. But my father…"

"Gone, sweetings. I meant what I told the viscount.

He's gone. He may have thought at first that he could eliminate his partner, eliminate Jack and me and go back to being Reginald Hackett, wealthy shipowner and father to the daughter who would marry a title. But now he's got no other choice but to do the unthinkable. He has to cut his losses and escape England before he's caught and hanged. He's already gone for one last bolt-hole, Regina. There will be a scandal eventually, I won't deny that, but with your father already gone, it will be short-lived, and you and your mother won't be here to listen to it. He's out of your life."

She looked at Puck for a long, long time. He was so handsome, very nearly beautiful. His face was so open, so honest. His eyes so clear.

"You're lying to me, aren't you? You're sitting here holding my hands and looking soulfully into my eyes, and you're lying to me. I believe you about Miranda, I really do. I understand that we have to protect her. I even agree that Miranda would have told at least one of the other captives her name and Papa's, as well. But I don't believe the rest of it. He's not gone. Not yet. He's hiding, perhaps preparing to flee, but he's not gone yet. And somehow you know where he is, don't you? You want me at Lady Sefton's ball tonight so that you and Jack and the others will be free to go after him. You want us all there, to be seen there, pretending to be happy and all unaware, while you and Jack hunt him down and…and do what you're going to do."

"Regina—"

"No, Puck, no more lies. He killed Jack's friend. You

already told me that much. Jack's not simply going to let him sail off to repeat his crimes somewhere else. Is he?"

He lifted her hands and kissed them in turn. "No. No, he's not."

She wet her lips, closed her eyes. Nodded. "And… and you'll be there?"

"I'll be there."

This was her father they were speaking of so calmly, almost coldly. The man who had given her life. The monster whose crimes were numberless, the man who'd allowed Miranda to be taken, the man who'd thrown his own niece into the Thames in order to save himself. An evil man, a creature without heart or conscience. And now, exposed for what he was, on the run. He needed to be stopped, put down, as a rabid animal would be destroyed. But he was still her father.

"Don't. Don't be there, Puck. Please."

THERE WAS A SLIGHT *click,* and one of the bookcases—the one showcasing the blue covers and the green—swung open. A large man carrying a single candle stepped into the room and went straight to the ornately carved desk. He put down the candle and extracted a key from his waistcoat but then hesitated. He moved the candle closer, to see that the lock of the desk drawer had been broken, the wood around it splintered.

Suddenly alert, he looked up, squinted into the darkness.

"Good evening, Reginald," Jack said from his seat

in the shadows. He slowly uncrossed his long legs and stood up, stepping into the candlelight, holding up a thick sheaf of papers in one hand, a thick, leather-bound journal in the other: all the records of all of the man's crimes, as well as the locations of the other ports the *Pride and the Prize* would visit to load more human cargo. Names, locations, profits. "Looking for these?"

Hackett turned at once for the secret passageway, only to come face-to-face with Dickie Carstairs and Will Browning, the latter casually holding an uninspiringly workmanlike yet deadly looking sword, its tip mere inches from the man's chest.

"How—how did you get in here?"

"That's it?" Jack asked him, seemingly shocked. "That's your only concern? How we managed to be here? Really?"

Puck, who had been waiting in the hallway, entered the room now, carrying a large strongbox, its straps cut, its lock smashed. He nodded to the enraged Hackett as he placed it on the desk and pushed back the lid.

"This," he said, lifting out the first of many thick bundles of bank notes, "will be given in your late mother's name to establish a sanctuary for soiled doves. Fitting, yes? And this, Mr. Hackett," he continued, placing several more neat bundles on the desktop, "will serve rather nicely for Lady Miranda's previously nonexistent dowry. Twenty thousand pounds should more than serve to silence any whispers if the scandal can't be entirely contained. And this," he ended, hefting and then pocketing a small, leather pouch, "should cover the cost of my new boots. I imagine there's more. Never doubt it will all be found."

Hackett stumbled into speech. "And there is. There is more. *Much* more! And all of it in coin, gold coin. And it's yours. All of it. But kill me, and it will never be found."

"*Au contraire,* Reginald," Jack said, tossing yet another leather-bound journal onto the desktop. "Ah, you recognize it. You couldn't find it in your late partner's house, could you? That's because we paid him a small visit before you arrived to dispatch him. Mr. Browning here is quite the accomplished housebreaker. The man never even turned over in his sleep. Still, there's a lesson here, Reginald. First, get what you want, *then* use your knife. At any rate, the recently deceased Mr. Harley appears to have been quite the conscientious bookkeeper. So, don't you worry your head about all those lovely gold coins. We know where they are."

Hackett seemed to shrink even as Puck watched. "But you didn't answer Reginald's question, Jack. Allow me. You see, Reginald, rats always have a bolt-hole. You've reminded us of that time and again, in fact, which is why we felt sure you'd use yet another one to come back for your belongings tonight, even as the *Pride and the Prize* is being readied to sail—or it was. The bookcase, Reginald? So painfully obvious. It was rather disappointing how easy it was to find. And, as my brother here has had two men watching this house for days on end now, we knew you had yet to come back here, just as we were certain you would. Because there's another saying, Reginald, one my brother pointed out to me. Dogs always return to their vomit."

"You! You're the dog. *Bastard!* You kidnapped my daughter! I did what I did for her. All for her! And you took her. You *ruined* her!"

He'd blame his own daughter for his sins? Every muscle in Puck's body tensed as he forced himself not to give in to the urge to fly across the desk and strangle the man with his bare hands.

Willing his fists to relax, Puck replaced the banknotes, closed the lid with a definite slam of finality, and then tucked the box under his arm before turning to his brother.

"You were wrong, Jack," he said quietly. "I could do what you do. But I wouldn't be doing it for the reasons you do it, and that would only destroy what Regina and I have found. She knew that even before I did." He took one last look at Reginald Hackett. "I'm done here. For king and Crown, he's all yours."

"King and Crown? Then you're not what you said you were? You're— Wait! Wait! Come back here! What's happening here? What do you think you're going to do with that? Blackthorn, get back here! I demand that you arrest me! You can't let them— Get that away from me! Take your bloody hands off me! Put me down! *Put me down! Please, no—*"

Puck kept walking, not looking back. At the door, he handed the strongbox to an expressionless Wadsworth, who then held open the door for him.

He then walked the entire way back to Cavendish

Square, reciting lines from Shakespeare's *Measure for Measure* inside his head, until his heartbeat slowed and his mind cleared, and the future was all that concerned him.

REGINA WAS SITTING on the topmost stair, her dressing gown wrapped tightly around her knees, when Kettering personally opened the door to admit Puck. They'd returned to Cavendish Square after only an hour spent at the ball, with Aunt Claire pleading a dreadful headache, which probably hadn't been a lie in and of itself, although it was an acceptable excuse meant to get Miranda home now that she'd been seen.

Poor Miranda. She'd flinched visibly when the Mentmore groom had put his hand on her elbow to help her up into the carriage, and her lovely eyes looked bruised and sad, even when Lady Sefton had been so gracious as to compliment her on her gown. A week ago, Miranda would have gone into ecstasy and gaily chattered about the honor all night.

Now she was tucked up in her mother's bed, Lady Claire holding her close to keep the nightmares away, and the viscount had gone off to one of his clubs, clearly intent on drinking himself stupid, maybe even more stupid than he was a week ago. If such a thing were possible. Oh, dear, maybe Regina had changed in this past week, as well. She didn't used to think such things, or at least not quite so often.

Only Regina's mother had been sorry to leave the ball, after telling anyone who would listen that she and her daughter were having a "small holiday" in Cavendish Square as there were painters and other of the "working classes" busily redecorating the mansion in Berkeley Square.

When Regina had asked her why she was saying such a thing, Lady Leticia had merely waved her wineglass languidly, saying, "Dearest Puck asked me to say it, and just that way—the working classes." She'd then lowered her voice to a conspiratorial whisper. "You know, like Grandmother Hackett? And your *father*. Should I have asked him why?"

So Regina knew. Puck and Jack expected Reginald Hackett would return to Berkeley Square, probably to gather his ill-gotten booty or whatever...and whatever was going to happen would happen there.

Had happened there, because now Puck was here. She realized she felt calm, curiously calm. She'd accepted the inevitable.

Puck said something to Kettering, and the butler indicated the curving, two-story staircase with a slight tip of his head. Puck headed for the stairs, his shoulders straight, his expression unreadable.

He looked up as he was halfway up the stairs and seemed startled as he saw her sitting there. "Waiting for someone, Miss Hackett?" he asked her, sitting down beside her.

He leaned forward and rested his elbows on his knees, folding his hands together, clasping and unclasping his fingers as she watched. Waited.

"It went well for you and the ladies tonight?" he asked at last.

"I think so, yes. We did as you said," she answered, resting her head against his shoulder. Together, they looked at the chandelier blazing below them, as if it was the most interesting thing either of them had ever seen. There was a large cobweb laced amid the dusty crystals. Strange, the things you noticed when your mind didn't want to know what it had to be told. "You know, if there's a heroine in all of this, it's Miranda. She was magnificent tonight. She's even forgiven me for being my father's daughter."

Puck slid an arm around her shoulders, and Regina could at last lower her guard, for she was where she belonged. "And have you forgiven yourself for being Reginald Hackett's daughter?"

"I've tried to forgive *him*. I don't know that I ever will, if that's even possible. But I decide who I am. You told me that, and I believe you."

They fell into silence again, just sitting there, content to sit there. The spider danced on its web, large and black, busily housekeeping. The spider probably thought it was safe: weaving its web so carefully, congratulating itself that it had chosen the most unassailable location where it was free to prey on the unwary. King of its silken castle. But even the most carefully constructed web is no match for a determined housekeeper, and sooner or later, the spider would learn that lesson.

"He's dead, isn't he?"

Puck remained quiet for some moments. "Yes, sweetings. He's dead."

Regina inhaled rather shakily. "And were you there when he…when he died?"

"No. No, I wasn't there. Although we were right in assuming that he'd return to Berkeley Square one last time. His servants found him hanged in his study, with all his journals and records laid out on his desk. Jack gathered them up, so that they don't fall into the wrong hands. We know everything now—we know the name of each port the *Pride and the Prize* would have visited after it set sail from London. Jack and others will be visiting those ports to rescue other young women like those we saw. It's all but over, Regina."

"All but over," she repeated dully. "I…I never thought he'd do the honorable thing. That was almost an honorable thing, wasn't it?'

"It was the only logical solution for him, sweetings. Tonight, your father knew he was finished, that there'd be no escape for him. Yes, his death has made everything easier. There may be some scandal, some gossip, but it will be short-lived and impossible to prove. The Crown will see to that. Jack will see to that. And nothing will touch your mother, your cousin or you. In fact, your mother is now a very wealthy widow. She can retire to the country for a year and return to London in the spring. I'm sure her brother will be more than happy to be of every assistance to her."

"With his hand held out, I'm sure. It all sounds so

neat and tidy." She pressed her hands to her cheeks, wiping away tears. "And you're telling me the truth?"

He tipped up her chin so that she could look deeply into his eyes. "As I love you, every word I've said is true."

And, because she loved him, she chose to believe him.

EPILOGUE

REGINA, LAUGHING AND chancing looks behind her, lifted her skirts as she broke from the trees and ran out into the long grass of a Blackthorn meadow. She'd escaped him, or at least she would pretend that she thought so. She ran until she was nearly out of breath and then gratefully collapsed on her back into the fragrant grass and wildflowers.

She put her hands to her mouth to cover her giggles, only to emit a small scream as the horribly grinning ass's head appeared above her.

"Fair Titania!" her pursuer sang out, his voice rather muffled by the wire ribbing and fur and such that made up the contraption, which resembled the ears, head and even shoulders of an ass. "Oberon has placed the magic juice on thine eyes so that he whom you first see will forever hold your heart. Now you will love me."

"Oh no, Sir Bottom, I fear I cannot," she replied. "My heart belongs to another. It is that rascally Puck whom I love, with all of my heart."

"Well then, madam, today is your lucky day. For here is your rascally Puck, always and forever," Puck said, tugging the ungainly contraption up and over his head. He'd somehow lost the riband that held his hair back, and it fell around his face, making him look young and endearingly handsome. "Well, now that we've fatally fractured the Bard's words, I suppose I can be rid of this." He tossed it on the grass before subsiding beside her. "Damn, that thing is heavy. And hot, into the bargain."

"Still, you should probably take more care of it. When your mother showed me the costumes yesterday afternoon, she seemed particularly proud of that dreadful thing. I tried to be kind, but I think she was disappointed in my reaction."

Puck was lying on his side now, propping up his head with his bent arm. "She likes you, you know. She won't admit it, but she does. In her way," he added.

As Adelaide Claridge's *way* was to mix insult with praise, smile with false enthusiasm, Regina only nodded her agreement. "Chelsea said she and her new troupe will probably be leaving soon to perform in the Lake District." Regina grimaced. "Oh, dear, that didn't sound right. I mean, not that either of us will be happy to see her go or any— Stop that!" Regina rolled onto her side and slapped at Puck, who had fallen onto his back, laughing. "She's your mother. You're worse than I am."

He put his arms around her and dragged her on top of him. "Well then, wife, at least we'll go to Hell together, and Beau and Chelsea with us. We can meet in the evenings, close to one of the fires and play a few hands of whist." Then he shook his head. "She didn't used to be quite this bad, you know. Every year she ages, and every year it would seem one of her sons brings home a young and beautiful wife. By next year, if Jack finds someone who can tolerate him and finally deigns to show up here, our mother may go into a sad decline."

Regina didn't argue the point, although she believed there was something other than the fact that her sons had brought home wives that was upsetting Adelaide. The marquess, a very nice if somewhat *weak* man, in Regina's opinion, had been following after his long-time mistress for the past week, ever since she'd come to Blackthorn, clearly trying to appease her for having done something that had upset her.

"Your father loves her very much, you know," she told Puck as he busied himself opening the front buttons of her gown. It was his favorite gown, and she wore it often, not because of the color but because of those buttons.

"If you say so, madam wife. As a good husband, I, as always, bow to your superior understanding of such things."

"You think he doesn't? Really?"

"I think he did, many years ago. Or if nothing else, he was young and marvelously besotted. But now he looks at us, knowing someday this estate and so much else will go to some distant cousin who resides in Virginia or Pennsylvania or one of those places. He has regrets, and I think my mother realizes at last that she would have been better off as the marchioness than the mistress. Only imagine, Regina, an American is to be the next Marquess of Blackthorn. Rather boggles the mind, don't you think?"

"I think it's dreadful, that's what I think, and I think you and your brothers are more charitable than I could ever be were I in your position."

He slid his hand inside her bodice, and Regina knew she probably hadn't sounded as outraged as she could have…as her mind was suddenly becoming more concentrated on other things. Like the way Puck had begun lightly nibbling on her earlobe.

"Oh, I don't know," Puck said, running his hands down her sides and then cupping her buttocks, pulling her against his obvious arousal. "I rather like the position I'm in. Although we're both wearing entirely too many clothes."

"Will you be serious?"

"All right, but just for you and just this once." He rolled her over onto her back, raising himself above her, looking deeply into her eyes. "I'm the luckiest man in the world, sweetings. My love loves me. Not my title, not my deep pockets, not my estate with its sheep and possibly cows—not even my handsome face, although you are allowed to admire it when the mood strikes you. My love loves me, and I love her. What else of real value is there in this world?"

"My poet," Regina said, touching a hand to his cheek. "I imagine you believe in happy endings, as well."

His smile warmed her to her toes. "Don't you, Mrs. Blackthorn?"

She put her hands on his shoulders and pulled him down for her kiss. "Why, Mr. Blackthorn, yes, I believe I do...."

* * * * *

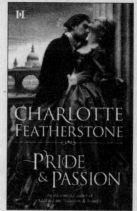

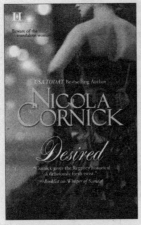

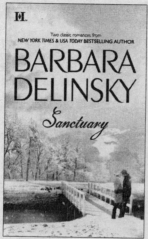

REQUEST YOUR FREE BOOKS!

2 FREE NOVELS
FROM THE ROMANCE COLLECTION
PLUS 2 FREE GIFTS!

YES! Please send me 2 FREE novels from the Romance Collection and my 2 FREE gifts (gifts are worth about $10). After receiving them, if I don't wish to receive any more books, I can return the shipping statement marked "cancel." If I don't cancel, I will receive 4 brand-new novels every month and be billed just $5.99 per book in the U.S. or $6.49 per book in Canada. That's a saving of at least 25% off the cover price. It's quite a bargain! Shipping and handling is just 50¢ per book in the U.S. and 75¢ per book in Canada.* I understand that accepting the 2 free books and gifts places me under no obligation to buy anything. I can always return a shipment and cancel at any time. Even if I never buy another book, the two free books and gifts are mine to keep forever.

194/394 MDN FELQ

Name		
	(PLEASE PRINT)	

Address		Apt. #

City	State/Prov.	Zip/Postal Code

Signature (if under 18, a parent or guardian must sign)

Mail to the **Reader Service:**
IN U.S.A.: P.O. Box 1867, Buffalo, NY 14240-1867
IN CANADA: P.O. Box 609, Fort Erie, Ontario L2A 5X3

Not valid for current subscribers to the Romance Collection
or the Romance/Suspense Collection.

Want to try two free books from another line?
Call 1-800-873-8635 or visit www.ReaderService.com.

* Terms and prices subject to change without notice. Prices do not include applicable taxes. Sales tax applicable in N.Y. Canadian residents will be charged applicable taxes. Offer not valid in Quebec. This offer is limited to one order per household. All orders subject to credit approval. Credit or debit balances in a customer's account(s) may be offset by any other outstanding balance owed by or to the customer. Please allow 4 to 6 weeks for delivery. Offer available while quantities last.

Your Privacy—The Reader Service is committed to protecting your privacy. Our Privacy Policy is available online at www.ReaderService.com or upon request from the Reader Service.

We make a portion of our mailing list available to reputable third parties that offer products we believe may interest you. If you prefer that we not exchange your name with third parties, or if you wish to clarify or modify your communication preferences, please visit us at www.ReaderService.com/consumerschoice or write to us at Reader Service Preference Service, P.O. Box 9062, Buffalo, NY 14269. Include your complete name and address.

KASEY MICHAELS

77591 THE TAMING OF THE RAKE	___	$7.99 U.S.	___ $9.99 CAN.
77463 HOW TO WED A BARON	___	$7.99 U.S.	___ $9.99 CAN.
77433 HOW TO BEGUILE A BEAUTY	___	$7.99 U.S.	___ $9.99 CAN.
77376 HOW TO TAME A LADY	___	$7.99 U.S.	___ $8.99 CAN.
77371 HOW TO TEMPT A DUKE	___	$7.99 U.S.	___ $8.99 CAN.
77191 A MOST UNSUITABLE GROOM	___	$6.99 U.S.	___ $8.50 CAN.

(limited quantities available)

TOTAL AMOUNT	$ _____
POSTAGE & HANDLING	$ _____
($1.00 FOR 1 BOOK, 50¢ for each additional)	
APPLICABLE TAXES*	$ _____
TOTAL PAYABLE	$ _____

(check or money order—please do not send cash)

To order, complete this form and send it, along with a check or money order for the total above, payable to HQN Books, to: **In the U.S.:** 3010 Walden Avenue, P.O. Box 9077, Buffalo, NY 14269-9077; **In Canada:** P.O. Box 636, Fort Erie, Ontario, L2A 5X3.

Name: _____
Address: _____ City: _____
State/Prov.: _____ Zip/Postal Code: _____
Account Number (if applicable): _____

075 CSAS

*New York residents remit applicable sales taxes.
*Canadian residents remit applicable GST and provincial taxes.

HQN™ | HARLEQUIN®
www.Harlequin.com

PHKM1111BL

KASEY MICHAELS

USA TODAY bestselling author Kasey Michaels is the author of more than one hundred books. She has earned four starred reviews from *Publishers Weekly,* and has won a RITA® Award from Romance Writers of America, an *RT Book Reviews* Career Achievement Award, Waldenbooks and Bookrak awards, and several other commendations for her writing excellence in both contemporary and historical novels. Kasey resides in Pennsylvania with her family, where she is always at work on her next book. Readers may contact Kasey via her website at www.KaseyMichaels.com and find her on Facebook at http://www.facebook.com/AuthorKaseyMichaels?ref=ts.

www.Harlequin.com

PHKMBIO11IBCR

ISBN-13:978-0-373-77610-8

MEET THE BLACKTHORN BROTHERS—
THREE UNREPENTANT SCOUNDRELS INFAMOUS
FOR BEING MAD, BAD AND PERILOUS TO LOVE.

Handsome as the devil and twice as tempting, Robin "Puck" Blackthorn lives for the pleasures of the moment. His only rule—never dally with an innocent woman. But when an encounter at a masquerade ball leaves him coveting the one woman who refuses to succumb to his charms, Puck realizes that some rules were made to be broken….

Scandalized to discover that the masked man with whom she'd shared a dance—and a forbidden embrace—is in fact the *ton*'s most celebrated rake, Regina Hackett vows to keep her distance. Yet when her cousin vanishes, it is to Puck that Regina must turn. A on a dangerous journey through London's da will discover that beneath Puck's rogu n who will stop at nothing to protect her to take a chance or an unrepentant sinn

454-BAB-870

"Michaels delectable."
—*Publishers Weekly* (starred review) on *The Butler Did It*

www.KaseyMichaels.com

an HQN book from
HARLEQUIN
www.Harlequin.con